MAD AS BELL

A Samantha Bell Mystery Thriller

JEREMY WALDRON

jeremy@jeremywaldron.com

ALSO BY JEREMY WALDRON

Dead and Gone to Bell

Bell Hath No Fury

Bloody Bell

Bell to Pay

Burn in Bell

Mad as Bell

CHAPTER ONE

Eighteen-year-old Eva Martin shivered on the cold concrete floor. She'd been here twice before, hidden away inside this tiny room. But this third time was by far the worst. If she didn't act now, He'd surely be back for more.

Eva curled her fingers and clawed at the hard floor, trying to push herself up. The fear of Him coming back pushed the teenager past her pain tolerance in an attempt to avoid death.

Gritting her teeth, she pushed her body up with all her might. Her arms had nothing left to give and gave out each time, sending her falling back to the floor. With her cheek flattened against the concrete, she stared ahead, knowing giving up meant dying.

Next to her, the wooden chair she was once bound to lay in pieces. Moments ago, she'd slammed her body against the foundation wall until the chair splintered and snapped. Now her heart pounded with extreme paranoia. She was sure the thundering sounds of breaking herself free would lure in the same monster she was trying to escape.

She didn't have time to ask herself how she got here, or if she knew the man who had taken her. Fleeing her continued torture—and surviving—were the only things that mattered. But if her plan was to work, she had to act fast and certainly couldn't second-guess her decision to run.

Rolling onto her back, Eva kicked off the rope bound around her thighs. Moving as quickly as her body allowed, she ignored the sharp pain that shot down her neck each time her jaw stretched a certain way, and pushed aside the throbbing aches that reminded her she was still alive. Once unbound, she flipped back onto all fours and paused to stare at the door.

Time stalled as she listened.

Silence fooled her into believing someone was there, coming for her, but perhaps it was only the persistent ringing in her left ear leftover from slamming her body hard against the wall.

Everything was pitch-black, but her eyes were sharp. There was a faint glow around the doorframe that Eva couldn't peel her eyes away from. Alone, with only the sounds of her breath echoing off the walls, Eva quietly stood.

As soon as her feet rooted into the floor, her head floated and spun. She was hungry and dehydrated—broken and bruised—but quick to regain her balance. Beneath her tattered clothes, loosely hanging on her thin frame, was a determined spirit needing to be set free.

Eva waited without making a sound. The house above her head creaked with a sudden gust of wind. Feeling the soles of her feet buzz, Eva cast her gaze down and listened as the thick vibrations of footsteps drew closer.

Her eyes widened with realization. He was back.

Gripped by fear and with nowhere to hide, Eva backpedaled away from the door, mistakenly tripping over the same broken chair she'd just escaped. Crashing to the floor, she fell hard on her bottom. A quick yelp passed over her lips before she realized what she had done. Silencing her instinct to scream with a hand over her mouth, her pulse swelled and threatened to burst.

The footsteps grew louder.

Keeping her eyes locked on the door, the thin strip of light beneath it brightened. Eva swiped her hand across the floor, patting between the broken pieces of chair before closing her fingers around the round baton of the chair's leg.

Armed and ready to defend herself, Eva scurried on all fours and positioned herself to the side of the door. Gripping the wooden chair leg like a baseball bat, she sat in a crouched position and braced herself to strike the moment the door opened.

Adrenaline spiked her heartrate, and time slowed. Seconds felt like minutes. When nothing happened, Eva questioned if maybe she'd made the threat up.

Pellets of sweat gathered on her hairline and the moment she closed her eyes, the door pushed opened.

Eva gripped the bat with both hands and pounced. Screaming at the top of her lungs, she swatted the wooden baton against the man's arm, then the backs of his legs. The flashlight he was holding flew from his fingertips and hit the concrete floor, spinning in circles. A dizzying array of light filled the room as Eva continued hitting the man again and again. Her rage boiled over, remembering everything he'd done to hurt her. With each strike, the skull-cracking sound exploded louder until she managed to knock the man off balance. Seeing her chance, she wound her arms back and swung a mighty uppercut, striking the man beneath his jaw. As soon as the bat made contact, the man twisted around before falling face-first to the floor like an anchor dropping to the sea bottom. Not willing to chance it, Eva hit him one last time before turning on a heel and sprinting out of the room.

Skidding over sawdust, she bounded up the framed unfinished flight of stairs and wove through the maze of walls before kicking open the front door. Everything was a blur as she pumped her arms. She kept looking over her shoulder as she ran, thinking she was being chased.

Despite the sharp pebbles of rock digging into each pounding step, shadows were what kept her moving. Soon, she exited the neighborhood and traveled further into the next. Inside the urban sprawl that had become Denver, Colorado, it all looked the same at night.

After an hour of weaving and running, and what felt like miles of jogging, Eva stopped to catch her breath. She had no idea where she was or if she was running in circles. But with the moon up and the stars out, Eva had no choice but to keep going when suddenly a pair of headlights crested around the bend, stopping her dead in her tracks.

The candy red pickup truck slowed its tires and pulled up next to Eva. An arm and head popped out the window. "My God. Are you okay?"

Eva stared at the man—could see the look of shock on his face—and was glad to be alive. In a split-second, Eva knew she had nothing to lose by asking him for help.

CHAPTER TWO

"SHIT," I GASPED AS THE EARRING CLASP SLIPPED FROM MY fingers and fell to the floor.

Chasing after it, I pushed my hand beneath the dresser, patting the floor in search of what I'd just lost. The clasp was just out of reach and, not having time to fish it out, I decided to go without.

Makeup, dresses, jewelry, and perfume weren't really my thing. I preferred sneakers and blue jeans and having my hair knotted up on top of my head with a pencil spiked through it to the costume I was putting on for tonight's journalism award ceremony.

Back on my feet, I checked the time. I was already running late, which wasn't a huge surprise. I'd been chasing one story to the next while managing to keep my job at the *Colorado Times* as well as continuing to create content for my blog, *Real Crime News.* Everything was holding together, but I felt I was one loose thread from completely unraveling.

Moving to the front of the house, I found my teenage son Mason lost in his world of video games. "Mason? Pause it please."

A couple more explosions rocked the flat-screen before he paused and removed his headphones. He said, “Sorry, Mom. I’m in the middle of something.”

Staring at the microphone piece attached to his headgear, I always wondered who he was talking to on the other end of the game, or if he even knew himself. I’d asked a couple of times before and he always referred to his ‘friends’ by their user-handle, which meant nothing to me.

“I’ll be leaving here shortly,” I said reminding him there were freezer dinners waiting and our dog Cooper had already been walked and fed.

“Got it,” he said, sliding his headphones back over his ears. “Oh, there’s a permission slip in the kitchen I need signed.”

I asked what for and he explained. It was the beginning of a new school year and it was an endless request of school supplies, clothes, new shoes, and permission slips for this and that. The list went on and added to the perpetual stress of my personal bank account, but we managed.

“It will be on the fridge when it’s signed,” I said, heading back into the kitchen with Cooper following me close on my heel.

I found the slip on the counter next to the small TV. I flipped on the six o’clock evening news and watched anchor Heidi Mitchell talk about a former president’s recovery from surgery before reading the fine print on Mason’s school slip.

“Since when did schools start monitoring student emails and documents?” I asked myself.

Reading on, the school claimed they were looking for signs of suicidal thoughts, bullying, or any kind of plans for a possible school shooting. But the idea of mass school surveillance had me hesitating to sign off on something I wasn’t sure I agreed with.

Setting the pen down, I flicked to the next local news

station, and the next, feeling my story of missing teenager Megan Hines begin to slip away when my cellphone rang.

"Sam, where are you?" Susan Young, one of my very best friends, said as soon as I answered. "You're not having cold feet, are you?"

"I'm on my way," I assured her. "But it's not like I'll be receiving an award tonight, anyway."

Susan sensed my low mood had something to do with Megan Hines. And she was right. Megan Hines had been missing for three weeks now and still hadn't been found. Our leads dried up and, with them, the public's interest to hear about it anymore than they already had.

"Don't give up on her, Sam."

"I'm not."

There was a quick pause before Susan said, "I left you something in your mailbox."

"When did you do that?"

"When you weren't looking."

I glanced to the front door and imagined Susan's eyes beaming with her gorgeous smile as she dropped something into the box. A car pulled up in front of the house but it wasn't my business partner Erin Tate whom I was expecting to show up at any second. Instead, two young individuals exited the vehicle and headed to my house.

"I'll see you soon." I ended my call with Susan and answered the front door. "Hey Nolan. I didn't know you were coming over." I gave my son an arched look.

Mason shrugged. "I thought you'd be gone by now."

"Sorry, Mrs. Bell," Nolan said, introducing me to his friend Chad.

"Nice to meet you," Chad said.

"You guys behave yourself," I said, gathering my purse and heading out the door. "I don't want to come home to any kind of party."

I shut the door to the sounds of the kids laughing. It was a joyous sound and as warm as the outside temperature. The skies lit up a brilliant orange melon as the sun tucked itself behind the Rockies for the night. Trusting Mason would be responsible during my absence, I opened the mailbox when a drone buzzed overhead and stalled directly above my car.

Tipping my head back, I stared at the machine hovering a hundred feet above the ground for a second before it whizzed off. Not thinking too much into it, I rifled through the mail and tossed the junk back into the box. I kept the small package from Susan and a second envelope. Inside Susan's package were a lucky rabbit's foot and a note that said, 'Good luck tonight.' It was a sweet gesture.

But it was the unmarked white envelope that stole my complete attention. Inside, there was nothing but a few printed words taped together that had me once again thinking about Megan Hines.

You'll disappear with them if you're not careful.

Was this some kind of hoax or something to take seriously? I couldn't tell. When I looked up, Erin arrived in her red Bronco and we had an entire car ride to discuss its meaning.

CHAPTER THREE

ERIN HELD THE MESSAGE BETWEEN HER FINGERS AND I watched her lips flutter as she read what it said for a second time. Then she turned and looked at me and asked, "And a drone flew overhead just before you retrieved this?"

I nodded. "Like someone wanted to make sure I got it."

"Are you sure it wasn't just a coincidence?" Erin held my gaze. "I hear drones buzzing by every time I'm in the park."

"Maybe," I agreed. It was just the timing of picking up the suspicious envelope and seeing the drone that gave me pause.

Erin rubbed her brow. "What is it they're referring to, anyway? Megan Hines?"

That was my initial reaction, but then I remembered what Mayor Noah Goldberg's spokesperson said to me recently. I reminded Erin. "Stay in your lane, Mrs. Bell. Death is closer than you think."

Erin's brows pulled together. "You think this is a threat?"

I shrugged a shoulder. "Or just a bad prank before tonight's award ceremony."

Erin looked at the message again. "Like, disappear with the other out of work journalists?"

I nodded, taking the note back into my possession.

"Who would do that?" Erin's face soured when a car horn honked behind us. She waved her hand to the driver impatiently waiting for us to move and eased her foot off the brake.

I could think of plenty of people wanting to ruin my day, especially since we began reporting on the inaccuracies about the current crime statistics coming out of the mayor's office. Our inboxes were flooded daily with hundreds of tips. Tips of petty crimes, domestic assault, theft, and even murder. Everyone wanted to tally up the crimes—both witnessed and experienced—and have them acknowledged by those in power. What started as a snowflake had snowballed into something larger than either of us could have imagined. It had quickly become impossible for just the two of us to keep up with, and even more impossible to not have the credible tips—which I knew were buried somewhere in the pile—get drowned out by the fictitious stories made up by people not wanting to be left out. Either way, this message—threat—was the first of its kind. Which was why it got my attention.

A couple minutes later Erin stopped at a light and said, "Does it concern you someone you might not know could know where you live?"

"I live in the city." I rolled my eyes in her direction. "It's not like I'm hiding out in a cave."

"It worries me sometimes," Erin admitted.

My routine was predictable. I came and went. The same as anybody else—including Erin. Anybody with enough sense could track me down. It wasn't that hard. Besides, Erin and I were quickly taking on a form of celebrity, which had its benefits, but also its downsides. This being one of them.

"We signed up to have targets on our backs," I said.

With one hand on the wheel, Erin flashed a wide, toothy grin. "Damn right we did."

"Then let's not forget about Megan Hines like it seems the rest of the world is doing."

Erin frowned and dropped her voice to a whisper. "Tell me, honestly, do you think she's still alive?"

I kept silent, not wanting the truth of that question to somehow jinx Megan's life. Erin didn't press for an answer, and we drove the rest of the way in silence. By the time we arrived to the Marriott in Cherry Creek, I tucked the clipping into the glove box, promising myself to let it rest until morning. But as soon as my heel hit the pavement, I found myself being greeted by Mayor Goldberg. He waved his pompous hand at me and pretended to be happy about seeing his two favorite reporters who knew his lies.

CHAPTER FOUR

THREE HOURS AND ONE PERCY GOODWIN STATE Journalism Award ceremony later, Erin and I stepped into the ballroom where the after party was already in full swing. Despite walking away from tonight's ceremony empty handed, we held our heads high as we moved through the knots of murmurs and jovial laughter.

Neither of us was surprised to not receive a single award for our work on *Real Crime News*. It wasn't viewed as a legit news source by the Association, plus we were two women striking out on our own in a male-dominated industry. The mountain we were climbing was steep. We had to work twice as hard as our male colleagues—fighting daily to earn the recognition we achieved. One slip for us and it would be back to the bottom of the hill. But my competitive side had me gritting my teeth at the entire charade, knowing what a simple award could do for our careers.

"There you two are." Susan approached in her flowing red gown. "There are not two more deserving people who should be recognized for their hard work than the two of you."

Susan looked beautiful and had done a tremendous job of

putting together tonight's party. I told her as much before dangling the rabbit's foot she'd given me.

"Hang on to it, Sam." We hugged. "You never know when it will bring its luck."

Susan knew the fight Erin and I were up against. She'd started her own event planning business, *Extraordinary Events*, several years back and had since grown it into one of Denver's leading event planning businesses.

"There is food being passed and champagne flowing." Susan smiled. "And don't forget the beer on tap at the bar." She winked at me, knowing I preferred a craft beer over anything else before excusing herself to mingle with the guests.

We watched Susan glide across the wood floor and settle up against executive producer Owen Daniels. Neither of us was surprised to see him chatting up the mayor. Everyone wanted to win over Owen's influence, and I was certain he also had some pull in TV news anchor Heidi Mitchell's career.

I heard my name being called when I spotted my editor at the *Times*, Ryan Dawson, at the bar. "Want to get a beer?" I asked Erin.

"I'm going to work the room for a bit."

Erin had her eye set on something, or someone, I couldn't see and I turned to congratulate Dawson on our paper's success. The *Times* swept all the column categories and won top breaking news award for coverage of the damaging hail-storm that ripped across the city in early June of this year. It was a nice achievement, and great to know I was part of that winning team.

"Sam," he said, "you deserved to be recognized tonight."

"I'll take front page above the fold over one of those silly awards any day of the week."

"That's why you're still my favorite." Dawson smiled and

raised his glass. "Find Megan Hines and everyone in this room will want your celebrity."

Megan Hines had haunted my dreams since her disappearance and I wanted to find her more than anything, but I wasn't after celebrity.

Dawson asked, "Nothing from King?"

"You know I can't reveal my sources."

"Touché."

Detective Alex King wasn't only a great resource into the Denver Police Department's activities, but he was also my boyfriend who I wished was here with me tonight. Events like these were so much better with him to hold my hand, but instead he'd been called to work.

Dawson raised his glass at a colleague across the room. He turned to me and said, "Don't give up, Sam. Megan's out there somewhere. The police will find her."

I stood with drink in hand, taking in the many faces swirling around me as Dawson left me with my thoughts. Erin was sharing a laugh with someone from a small-town newspaper while Owen was working his charm on Susan.

"Someone should tell them to get a room."

I rolled my neck and found Archie Smith, a reporter from the Bay Area, fill the empty void next to me. Susan now had one hand on Owen's arm as he continued to make her laugh. I knew it was trouble the moment I saw them together. Susan had a weakness for handsome men like Owen Daniels.

"That's my friend you're talking about," I said, giving Archie a sideways glance.

"Between you and me," Archie grinned, "I heard rumors that he sexually assaulted a coworker."

"We can't report on rumors," I said, turning on a heel to direct my focus elsewhere.

Instead of Archie giving me my space, he took more of it. Archie had made a name for himself by reporting on the elusive murders of what he called the Prom Queen Killer. PQK was a serial killer who terrorized the west coast for nearly a decade before finally getting caught. Archie wrote a book about it and I assumed he was now looking for ways to extend his brief moment of fame. Young reporters like him were so predictable, especially on nights like tonight.

"But we can investigate them to see if they're true," Archie said as Heidi Mitchell took Susan's place next to Daniels. It didn't take long for Daniels's hand to travel a little too far south on Heidi's body. Archie laughed. "Want to bet she was the victim?"

Heidi quickly pushed Daniels's hand away and begin searching the room for eyes that might have seen what he had done. Archie's rumor may have been true with the way Heidi was reacting, but I wasn't about to tell him that.

"Talk to me when you have actual evidence to back your accusation." I turned to the bar and asked for another beer.

Archie followed. "Wait, this isn't about my Prom Queen Killer story, is it?"

I rolled my eyes to Archie's browns and sipped my beer. This was exactly about his reporting. I didn't particularly like his tactics, or how he often embellished a story to make it sound bigger than it actually was. I questioned whether or not he was just trying to get a rise out of me. The imbalance of power between Daniels and Heidi was as clear as his insinuation—and anyone with eyes could read the writing on the wall—but what was the real reason Archie sought me out tonight?

"Everyone has to have a career, Samantha." He laughed. "And some of us would prefer not to wait around for it to arrive."

What Archie achieved by age twenty-four was more than I had by thirty. "I don't mean to discredit your success," I said, "but what you did was wrong."

"Wrong?" Archie nearly spit out his drink.

"You sensationalized a serial killer."

"And look where it landed me? I'm here. Alongside the likes of you."

"It was irresponsible," I said. "And dangerous, too. You glorified PQK's work and turned a villain into a hero." I couldn't believe I was wasting my breath.

"If you're worried about copycats, then should we also stop covering mass shootings as well?"

I rolled my eyes and turned to face him. The murmurs circling us grew louder and I saw people begin filing toward the exit. It wasn't a panic luring them outside, but definitely attention-grabbing. I asked Archie, "Why are you here?"

With a glimmer in his eye, he said, "I'm writing a book."

I knew it. "Did your first one stop selling already?"

Archie's eyes glimmered. "A true crime novel about active serial killers who are able to avoid getting caught."

His brief moment of celebrity must have been good to him. "And you expect to find one here, actively working the city of Denver?"

Archie's smirk deepened as he nodded. "Tell me about that missing girl no one but you gives a shit about."

"Oh brother." I set my beer glass down on the counter and prepared to follow the crowd outside to see what was happening. Looking Archie in the eye, I said, "Megan disappeared. There's no proof she's been murdered."

Archie grinned from behind his glass. "Not yet there isn't."

CHAPTER FIVE

HOMICIDE DETECTIVE ALEX KING DUCKED UNDER THE crime scene tape in the Park Hill neighborhood. His partner John Alvarez followed close behind. A call had come in about a body found, possibly murdered, and now a group of onlookers made up of mostly young men barked their hatred of the police from behind the two squad cars blocking the entrance to the alleyway where the victim lay.

Alvarez glanced at the hecklers and said in a low voice, "Why are the people who assume to have all the answers the same people who have nothing to offer?"

"What, John? Afraid of a little critique?"

Night was on the horizon and their shift was just beginning. The community distress was growing, thanks to the ongoing war between the press and mayor's office with no end in sight. Unlike his partner, King ignored his mostly male audience and approached the uniformed officer who'd been tasked with guarding the victim. King introduced himself by name and rank and asked, "What do we have?"

The officer stepped into the soft glow of the overhead

street lamp and showed his face. He appeared shaken up. "It's the worst I've ever seen."

"Who called it in?"

The uniform shrugged. "Called in anonymously."

King shared a look with his partner and let his gaze bounce between the rows of faces staring, watching the police work as if hoping they'd see their declared enemy make a mistake. King wasn't surprised by the anonymous call in this neighborhood. The last thing these people wanted was to be seen cooperating with cops.

Pushing his fingers into latex gloves, King said, "Show me what we got."

The uniform put a hand over his mouth and nodded his head. Stepping into the shadows, King caught his first glimpse of the body. The uniform couldn't go any further, and even King had to look away before he could stomach the gruesome sight himself. It was as bad as the young officer made it out to be—perhaps one of King's worst sightings in all his years on the job.

"Christ," Alvarez muttered. "This kind of shit is what convinces me the devil is real."

King took a deep breath and kneeled next to the victim. It was a girl of about fourteen and she was badly beaten. Her face was swollen like an eggplant—her thin naked body contorted like origami. King tilted his head and met her dull gaze, staring up into the sky—dried blood squeezed out from the corners of her eyes. Pieces of King's heart slowly chipped away as he wondered who she was and why she'd been murdered, left to rot in a desolate city alley.

Alvarez kneeled beside King, titled his head back and forth as he inspected the scene. "Pavement is dry. There's no blood anywhere besides on the victim."

King lifted his head and glanced in the direction of the squad cars. Where was everyone, and why hadn't anyone from the medical examiner's office arrived yet? Something wasn't right.

"She wasn't murdered here." King turned back to face his Jane Doe. "She was dumped."

Alvarez sighed and pointed between her legs. A broken bottle penetrated the girl—more blood oozed out. "She pissed off somebody."

King flitted his gaze over the surrounding alleyway pavement until it backed up against the grimy wall not more than ten feet away. Looking for clues to who might have left her here, there was little information to go on except for the contusions around each of her wrists.

"Perhaps we can pull some fibers from her skin," King said, still waiting on forensics to arrive.

"I'm going to go see if one of our fans nearby saw anything." Alvarez stood and walked off.

King remained kneeling next to Jane Doe, making mental notes when finally an EMS caravan arrived. A team of paramedics pushed a gurney as close to the body as they were allowed before King stood and told them to stop. He wanted this done right—couldn't afford any mistakes. The victim deserved their best police work, even if King believed he was the only one to give a shit about what happened.

"The body isn't ready to be released." King held up his hand and widened his stance. *Not until someone from the coroner's office gave a damn.* Then he looked to the uniformed officer. "Where the hell is the ME?"

"Tonight, you'll have to settle for me." A sergeant from CSI stepped up with his work bag slung over his shoulder.

King sized the sergeant up. *You've got to be kidding? Just one person?*

"Alex," Alvarez called to King. "Let's go. A call just came in. We might have a connection to our Jane Doe."

"Document everything. Pictures. Videos. I mean everything." King rushed past the sergeant making himself clear, even if a bit redundant when telling him how to do his job. "I don't want anything lost. The press is already on our asses for failure to properly report our work. We can't afford to mess this up."

CHAPTER SIX

ALLISON DOYLE PERCHED ON A STOOL IN A HIGH SCHOOL classroom, tucked behind her laptop computer helping Coach Nicholas Bennett organize his girls' volleyball team inventory.

There were jerseys, pads, and shorts piled high on desks as Coach Bennett handed them out to each of his players. Allison recorded what was checked out and smiled at the excited buzz filling the room. The girls were enthusiastic for a new season, returning with hopes of a repeat of last year's State Championship. They'd been at it for the last half-hour and, when the last of the uniforms was issued, Coach Bennett turned to Allison and smiled.

Allison returned his smile and tapped 'Enter' on her keyboard. "Recorded and saved."

Coach Bennett came around the desk and took a look. "Thanks again for doing this."

"Not a problem," Allison said, explaining her Excel spreadsheet. "Anything to help you take your team back to State."

"I prefer to be with the girls instead of having to keep up with the latest software update."

"We do what we do best."

Their eyes met and they shared a smile when one of the girls, Jenny Booth, came rushing to the door.

"Coach," she said. "These shorts are too big." The girl looked down. Her thin legs were swimming in the elastic. "I'm going to need something smaller."

Coach Bennett looked to Allison and they laughed. Bennett said, "Take what you need from the pile and make sure to return the ones you're wearing."

As Jenny did what she was told, Allison kept stealing glances at Bennett. A warm feeling spread across her chest, hoping her attraction wasn't as obvious as it felt.

They'd met two weeks ago at a local coffee shop when she embarrassingly forgot her wallet and couldn't pay for the drink she ordered. Bennett stepped in and paid for her, which led to them sharing the same table. It was that chance meeting where they learned they had a lot more in common than liking their coffee black, and was the reason Allison was here now.

Allison swept her gaze off Bennett's shoulders as he exited the room and was surprised to see seventeen-year-old Naomi Moss staring from the back wall. Her earbuds were jammed into her ears as Naomi gave Allison a deliberate smirk. It was clear the teen could read Allison's feelings for Bennett. Without making a scene, Naomi went back to playing on her phone as Allison placed her fingers back to the keyboard.

Several minutes passed and Bennett was still gone when Naomi surprised Allison. "You like him, don't you?"

Allison swept her gaze up and locked eyes with Naomi. Allison stared at Naomi's heart-shaped face perfectly framed by her jet-black hair, deciding how best to respond. Naomi might have only been seventeen, but she looked much older. A fully formed body with the confidence to match. Which was what worried Allison. These high school girls appeared —*and* acted—much older than they actually were.

"What's not to like?" Allison responded. "He's smart. Cares an awful lot about you kids. Of course I like him."

"No, I mean," Naomi's smile stretched, "you *really* like him."

Allison forgot how intuitive and bold teenagers were, but also how naïve they were, too.

Naomi flipped her shiny hair and glanced to the door to see if Bennett was coming back. Then she turned back to Allison and said, "I see how you're looking at him."

Allison glanced to the clock. It was nearly eight p.m. and time to close up shop. She dropped her feet to the floor and closed the lid on her laptop.

"That's okay," Naomi said. "You don't have to admit it. I like him, too. Mr. Bennett's a hell of a lot cooler than some of the other teachers at this school."

"Is that why you're here?" Allison asked.

Naomi arched an eyebrow and held up her cellphone. "I'm here for the free internet." Her device dinged with a message. "Speaking of which, that's my ride." Naomi skipped out the door. "Adios."

"That's one girl you have to watch," Bennett said as he entered the classroom, holding a pair of athletic shorts. "She's as clever as a meat cleaver."

Allison laughed as she packed up her things, readying to leave for the night. "She's got guts, all right."

With their work finished, Bennett turned off the lights and grabbed his own things. He'd promised he'd drive Allison home. "Naomi is one of those kids who will either make it big or die trying. She thinks she's ready for what the world has to offer."

Allison stepped into the hall. "And you don't?"

Bennett gave her an arched look—the same as any educator would give. “I think she has a lot to learn.”

CHAPTER SEVEN

I DIDN'T BITE AT ARCHIE'S ATTEMPT TO PULL ME INTO believing Megan Hines was dead. Like Dawson said, I couldn't give up on her. But Archie's statement—however erroneous it may have been—did get me thinking.

Leaving Archie at the bar, I followed the crowd to the exit to see what had stolen everyone's attention. As I moved through the halls, I thought how the Prom Queen Killer hadn't been in prison for more than year, yet his known work dated back nearly ten. His victims were girls Megan's age. Bright young women who had an incredible future ahead.

It occurred to me that Archie could be the one to have sent me the strange message tonight. Archie would do something like that if it meant giving him an edge over his rival, which just so happened to be me.

Stiff-arming my way through the glass double doors, I was immediately hit by a wall of obscenities. I stopped and gaped at the scene playing out in front of me.

There was a mob of angry protestors gathered to descend upon us journalists—or as they called us, Public Enemy to the State. It was a far-fetched claim, but they made their point.

I spun around and looked behind me. Keeping my eye out for Erin, I knew she would be in here somewhere, not one to live through secondhand stories. Instead, I found myself staring at Owen Daniels having a clear disagreement with Heidi Mitchell.

Heidi's expression was pinched; his arrogant. *Could it be a qualm between lovers?*

A wave of roars erupted behind me. Turning my attention back to the protestors, I wedged my way to the front lines. My colleagues had their phones out recording the scene, posting it live to their various social media channels. A few of them were stupid enough to taunt the protestors, stooping to their level of insults.

Where were the police? Why would the mayor, who I knew attended tonight's event, want to be affiliated with this behavior? The anger grew between parties and I feared it would quickly escalate out of control if it weren't stopped.

Fake News! Propagandists! Liars! Communists! We were called it all.

Somehow Erin found me in the maddening crowd. She said, "Can you believe this?"

I palmed my own cellphone, recording a quick video of the faces yelling at me. "If they wanted to get their mug on evening news, I think they got it."

That's when I got a call from my friend Allison who said I needed to come quick. There was a possible murder in Park Hill, and something told her the police didn't want anyone to know about it.

CHAPTER EIGHT

When a friend called, I answered. Besides, I didn't need to stay and report on the protests. I'd received enough daily harassment to last several lifetimes. Instead, Erin and I hit the road to see what Allison was witnessing.

"Convenient night to sweep another crime statistic under the rug," Erin said as she drove.

I was thinking the same thing myself when I asked, "When was the last time you saw the mayor?"

"Huh." Erin pursed her lips as she thought about it. "Come to think of it, not since we first arrived to the party. Why?" She turned her head and looked at me. "You don't think he orchestrated the protests, do you?"

"I hope he's more professional than that," I said, but my suspicions were high.

Erin gave me a skeptical look.

We parked on the corner E. 26th Ave and Dahlia Street and met up with Allison who was wrapped up in a big man's arms whom I didn't recognize. She saw us and waved us over. Unwrapping herself, she introduced us to Nicholas Bennett.

He was a tall, handsome man with a strong gaze and I remembered Allison saying she'd recently met someone. After our introductions, I asked to speak with her alone.

"What happened?" I asked, listening to the crime scene tape flutter in the breeze.

"Nicholas was taking me home when we caught sight of the crowd. We stopped to see what was happening and that's when we started to hear rumors that it was a young girl's body that was found."

"Megan?" Erin asked.

Allison's expression was blank. She didn't know.

I shifted my gaze between the far alleyway walls, looking for King. He wasn't anywhere to be found. Nearby, there was talk of gang violence, a prostitute whacked, but my mind never drifted too far from thinking it *could* be Megan Hines who had been found.

I locked eyes with Allison. This was her neighborhood, and chances were good she knew who the victim was. I asked, "But what did you see?"

"That's just it, Sam. I didn't see much of anything." Erin asked what she meant. "Exactly that," Allison said.

A warm breeze kicked up and I swiped my hair out of my face and looked in the direction of the neighborhood crowd, made up of mostly young men, staring behind white eyes and eavesdropping on our conversation. We were the first reporters on scene, working in a neighborhood that often got neglected by both police and the world. It was the exact recipe that made it easy to let a crime go without officially being documented, and was just what the mayor ordered.

Allison continued, "EMS stood around looking agitated for a while before a single officer finally told them to load the body up on a gurney."

"Did you see the police collect any evidence?" Erin asked.

Allison shook her head no and I felt my breathing shallow. I couldn't believe it. First the protests, and now this? We were too late. There wasn't even a body to report.

CHAPTER NINE

"NO WONDER THE MAYOR IS STRUGGLING TO CONVINCE THE public his tough on crime policy is working." King was the first to crack after driving most of the way to the hospital in silence.

By the time they left the sergeant from CSI to document their Jane Doe's crime scene, both men were heated over the lack of resources made available—even more frustrated when they were met by the same resistance from the upper brass who basically told them to do their best with what they had.

"Apparently we don't even have the budget to police." Alvarez shook his head in frustration as King parked near the ER entrance at Denver Health Medical Center.

They both knew the impossible task they were up against. King was a white cop who seemed to care about a historically black neighborhood plagued by high crime rates, and that was just half the battle he was waging. The other half was with his own department. But it was the way the girl was left to rot in the alleyway that haunted King most. Was she alive when she was dumped? He hoped not, but how long had she been there? And what kind of monster were they looking for?

The detectives exited the vehicle and headed toward the entrance. The double doors automatically opened as they approached. They badged their way past the front desk and were quickly met by Detective Holly Gray who worked in the Major Crimes Division.

"I'm a bit surprised LT granted my request," she said. "But the moment I heard about the homicide in Park Hill I knew that I needed to speak with the lead detectives."

"This better be good." King lifted his chin. "We were pulled off our Jane Doe before we were finished working the scene."

"What did you need to tell us?" Alvarez asked.

"Follow me," Detective Gray said. "Another girl has been found. And this one is alive."

CHAPTER TEN

DETECTIVE HOLLY GRAY LED THE MEN DOWN THE hospital corridor and into the Adult Emergency Department. King was already two steps ahead in knowing where she was leading them and why—the victim had been raped and forensics was collecting what evidence they could before it was too late.

Gray said, "Currently, there are hundreds of missing persons cases that we know about." She turned and met King's leery gaze. "That number drops significantly when the victims are black or brown. Your Jane Doe, she was Latina, right?"

"From what I could gather, I'd agree with that assessment."

"Same with mine." Gray stared. "It's the ones that go unreported that keep me up at night. Lucky for us, this one was found alive." She handed the detectives a case file. "Her name is Eva Martin."

King took the report into his own hands and read the file Gray had put together. "Her birthday was today?"

"That's right," Gray acknowledged.

"Some birthday party," Alvarez said.

"So, what happened?"

"Tough to say." Gray shifted her gaze to Alvarez. "She was in pretty rough shape when she was found, but we believe she was kidnaped and held against her will."

"How long?"

"Unsure at this time." Gray gave a solemn look. "She's being evaluated now. We're not sure what happened because she's not talking, but we do know she was picked up on the side of the road late last night."

"Have you contacted family?"

"Like I said, she's not talking. And even if we get her talking, it could be difficult getting answers about her family depending on their legal status." Gray paused. "Tonight's Jane Doe, was she a prostitute?"

King wanted to say yes, but he didn't know for sure. "Victim had bind marks, like she'd been tied up."

Gray exhaled. "Same with mine."

"Sorry to be blunt," Alvarez said, "but if she's not talking, what are we doing here?"

Gray raised both her eyebrows and said, "Eva's not talking, but the driver who picked her up is."

CHAPTER ELEVEN

THE DRIVER'S NAME WAS CHRISTOPHER BOWERS, AND HE looked tired but alert. People were being paged over the intercom as the whooshing sounds of automatic doors opening between hospital wings kept King alert to his surroundings.

Detective Holly Gray had King's full attention, and he wanted nothing more than to link this survivor to tonight's Jane Doe. Getting ahead of this homicide before it slipped through the cracks and the leads went cold was his top priority.

King lifted his cuff and glanced at his digital wristwatch. "What's he still doing here?"

Gripping the files in her hands, Gray quirked a brow and said, "If you saw what he did, you would have stayed, too."

The gruesome pictures of Jane Doe played out behind King's eyelids as he stared at Bowers, hunched over in the hospital chair. Alvarez took the first step toward the witness and King followed, Gray saying she'd stay behind.

"We'll holler if we need anything," King said.

Gray nodded and turned back to the closed door behind which Eva was being evaluated.

"Christopher Bowers?" Alvarez said as he stepped into the waiting room. Bowers stood from his chair. "I'm Detective Alvarez, this is my partner, Detective King. We'd like to ask you a few questions about the woman you picked up last night."

Bowers's head bobbed on his shoulders. "Sure. Though I don't have anything new to say."

"We understand," King said. "But we'd like you to tell us if you don't mind?"

As the next ten minutes played out, King asked Bowers if he had a family of his own. When he said he did, King thanked him for staying to talk.

"I have two daughters myself," Bowers said. "I would hope someone would do the same for me if ever—" Bowers choked on the words he couldn't get out. He couldn't say what he thought had happened to Eva, but they all assumed the same. "I'm sorry," Bowers sat, "I just need a moment."

"Take your time." King shared a look with Alvarez. After a minute of quiet, King said, "Tell us where you found her."

"I was coming home from work—"

"About what time?"

Bowers shook his head as if not knowing for certain what time. "It was after midnight."

Alvarez jotted down notes. "Then what happened?"

"I'm remodeling a house in the Arapahoe Acres neighborhood. It had been a long day, my eyes and body were tired when I saw her just standing in the middle of the road like a deer in headlights." Bowers whispered as he talked and kept glancing in the direction of where Eva was being held.

"Do you often work that late?" King asked.

Bowers sighed. "The market is crazy right now—the amount of money up for grabs is, too. I'm thankful for the work as my oldest is off to college next year, but it's draining trying to keep up."

"I'd like to check the house out sometime." Bowers didn't have any problem with King requesting to visit. King made note of his response. "Did Eva hesitate when you offered to give her a ride?"

"Momentarily, but then she climbed in all on her own." Bowers swiped a hand over his face. "I suppose she knew the chances of getting any kind of help that late was slim."

Alvarez asked, "Did you see anyone else with her?"

"No one. It was just her and me."

"And she asked to come here?"

Bowers shook his head. "It was my decision."

Alvarez lowered his brow. "Based on what?"

"If you had seen the condition she was in, you would have brought her here, too."

King asked, "Did she say anything to you? Did you try to make conversation?"

"Of course I did." Bowers volleyed his gaze back and forth between the detectives. "But the only word out of her mouth was *thirsty*. She kept whispering *thirsty, thirsty, thirsty.* But she wouldn't drink anything I offered. Hell, I don't even know if she can speak English."

CHAPTER TWELVE

DETECTIVE KING HANDED CHRISTOPHER BOWERS HIS business card after telling him he could go home and said, "If you remember anything else, give me a call."

Bowers took the card into his hand and said he would. Then his eyes locked with King's. "Is she going to be all right?"

King couldn't say. He stared for a quick pause before pointing to the center of his card. "My number is there."

Bowers lowered his eyes to King's business card and took one step toward the door when Alvarez said, "I forgot to ask. Were you working alone last night?"

Bowers swallowed and tucked King's card away in his back pocket. "I was. I can't afford to pay overtime."

The detectives watched Bowers leave and Detective Gray strolled up behind them. "I ran his name through the system. Pleaded guilty four years ago to soliciting for prostitution. Class 3 Misdemeanor. Paid the fine and moved on."

King faced Gray. "You think Bowers is guilty?"

Gray's head wagged back and forth like a seesaw as if

unable to decide herself. Gray said, "It certainly crossed my mind."

Alvarez jutted his jaw and eyed Gray. "Why would he bring his own victim here? Wouldn't Eva know who he was?"

Gray rolled her gaze to Alvarez and gave him a stern look. "Eva's not talking. We don't know what she knows."

King was lost in his thoughts, thinking over tonight's Jane Doe as he stared in the direction of where he'd last seen Christopher Bowers. He'd thought about the two neighborhoods; the one where Eva was picked up, and the other where they found Jane Doe. Could Jane Doe have been transported from Arapahoe Acres with hopes of having the cops think she was murdered in Park Hill?

"Let's talk to his employees, see what they have to say about their boss," King said.

Gray opened her case file folder and tore a piece of paper off and handed it to King. It was the address to the house Bowers said he was remodeling. "This will get you started."

King folded up the address and tucked it away in his front pocket when asking, "Was Eva dehydrated when she came in?"

"She was," Gray concurred.

"Thirsty," Alvarez said. "It's also slang for 'desperate for attention.'"

They had two young women with similar bind marks on their wrists. Was their case as simple as linking them to a street hustler pimping these girls out? King wasn't sure, at least not until Eva started talking, but Alvarez might be onto something with figuring out what Eva meant by repeatedly saying *thirsty*.

A doctor exited Eva's room and called over to Detective Gray. Gray handed King a thick dossier of missing persons and said, "Look through there. It's possible your Jane Doe could be one our missing girls."

CHAPTER THIRTEEN

Cooper jumped on me and nearly knocked me over as soon as I opened the front door to my house. His tail was wagging, his long tongue dangling out the side of his mouth.

"Down boy," I said, pushing him to all fours.

After canvasing the Park Hill neighborhood and getting nowhere, Erin and I decided to call it a night. Mason and Nolan were still glued to the TV screen playing video games. Their eyes were bloodshot from hours of gaming; Chad had gone home.

"Mom, can Nolan sleep over?" Mason asked.

"It's a school night," I reminded him. "I think it's time to shut off the games."

Mason and Nolan finished their game as Erin headed into the kitchen and filled two glasses with red wine from my Black Box. I said goodbye to Nolan, told him to drive carefully, and as soon as I turned back around Erin was handing me a glass and turning on the ten o'clock news.

Heidi Mitchell was reporting. Nothing was being said about the Jane Doe in Park Hill, or about Megan Hines. It was just here and now, more gloating about a victory in infrastructure the mayor managed to win.

"Can you believe she took home so many awards tonight?" Erin turned to look at me with a furrowed brow. "There is nothing special about Heidi Mitchell."

I was at the bookshelf fingering the spines when I heard the coverage of tonight's protests come on. Turning to look over my shoulder, I listened to the story we saw with our own eyes. It was your classic me-against-you news coverage and did little to actually provide the public with any real information.

Staring at the screen, Erin asked, "Are we that easily manipulated?"

"I'm afraid we are," I said.

There was more to it than that, and even though I had no evidence to suggest the mayor was behind the distraction, I still thought my theory made sense. Besides, just like the conspiracy I had rolling around my brain, we had no proof a murder in Park Hill even occurred.

I found the title I was looking for and dropped into the sofa chair, ready to read with my glass of wine. Stretching my legs out in front of me, I thought about how a murder was swept under the rug before a single journalist had a chance to report on it. Where had King been, let alone any other detective? The crime scene was noticeably bare and didn't leave me with a good feeling.

Erin rolled her eyes to me. "What book is that?"

I showed her the cover. "Archie Smith's."

"You think he's right? Could there really be a serial killer working our city?"

"Anything is possible," I said, leafing through the pages. "But how would he know if there was? He's not even from here."

"Information travels. People talk." Erin shrugged.

I found myself reading a chapter detailing PQK's victims. Apparently, he had a thing for a certain type of girl. Each victim was popular and beautiful. They had many friends, and secretly a bit of a wild side. And all were between the ages of 16 to 19 years old. It was how Archie came up with the name Prom Queen Killer, but it was the next chapter that really got my attention.

"Listen to this," I said to Erin. "According to this, the Prom Queen Killer communicated to the media through cut-out messages—each word taken from a passage written by his favorite journalists."

"Sick bastard. But we know it's not PQK who left that message for you to find."

"No, but after speaking with Archie tonight, it did cross my mind that maybe he was the one who left it."

"Okay, let's say he did. What's he mean by *you'll disappear with them if you're not careful?*"

I cast my gaze back to the book and thought about Archie suddenly finding himself here in Colorado. The coincidence scared me, but I wasn't quite convinced that was what was happening here. There were obvious differences, and I told Erin as much.

The messages PQK wrote to the press were his way of controlling the narrative. He didn't like how the media described his crimes as being sexual in nature, even though that was exactly what they were. To him, it was about control, wanting to take on a paternal role by giving himself the image he always thought himself as having instead of letting strangers decide who he was. The message given to me was clearly to make me hesitate, and I was still convinced it had everything to do with my desire to find Megan Hines. But who left it for me to find? And was it to intimidate or help? I wasn't sure.

"We'll keep this in mind," I said, holding up Archie's

book, “but I would like to get to the morgue early tomorrow morning and learn the identity of tonight’s Jane Doe.”

Erin stood and gave me a hug. She said, “It’s up to us to give these women a voice.”

I walked Erin to her car and waited on the sidewalk until her taillights disappeared around the corner before heading back into the house. The streets were dark, the house quiet. But I couldn’t get the thought of tonight’s Jane Doe out of my head, so I did what I did best. I sat down and began to write.

CHAPTER FOURTEEN

THIRSTY WAS PARKED ACROSS THE STREET FROM A POPULAR bar near the Denver University campus on the south side of the city when his cellphone buzzed with a message. There were young women everywhere tonight, coming and going, without any clue to the threat that lurked nearby.

He glanced to his phone, opened his dating app, and swiped through the girl's profile pictures who'd just messaged him until he decided she didn't have what he was looking for. Closing out his phone, he pulled the mirror on his face and tipped forward in his seat. Surprised his chin hadn't swollen after receiving the tremendous blow from the wooden chair leg Eva had swung at him nearly twenty-four hours ago, Thirsty was grateful for the small piece of luck. He tilted his head to the side and worked the tension out of his neck with his hand. Thanks to his beard, there wasn't even a noticeable mark.

Thirsty went back to staring at the bar's entrance. Patrons were huddled in circles, smoking and laughing, drunk on youth.

He sat there for over an hour, letting the parking meter

tick away the minutes, spinning the prescription bottle inside his hand. Waiting for the right girl to come along, he was beginning to relax. The drugs were finally taking effect. High on valium and dependent on Vicodin, Thirsty washed his mixture of pills down with a half-pint of vodka when he finally spotted the flowing jet-black hair that gave him reason to pause.

Her angelic white shirt was tightly wrapped around her filled breasts and exposing her mid-drift. The girl's jeans were equally tight fitting, and her boots traveled all the way to her knees. She shared similar features to Eva. Long legs, thick thighs, square shoulders, and head held high. Thirsty admired her confidence. Raising his cellphone to the window sill of his truck, he waited for her to show her face. When she did, he snapped a couple photo unknowingly.

The girl paused and stared.

He swore she looked him directly in his eye.

His heart skipped a beat. Tonight she was with girlfriends, and though they were just as beautiful as she was, they didn't share the same secret as the girl Thirsty had his eye set on.

Unable to take his eyes off his prize, Thirsty wanted to wave and blow a kiss but knew he'd soon get his chance. Turning over the engine, he put the truck in gear and pointed the hood toward her. As the tires rolled right in front of her, he said, "Now that I'm learning your routine, you can't escape me."

CHAPTER FIFTEEN

A HALF-HOUR LATER, THIRSTY CIRCLED THE neighborhood a couple of times before feeling confident enough to turn the wheel into the driveway leading up to the house where he had kept Eva. There was no telling who might be waiting for him—who might be watching—or what had happened to the house after he'd left.

Approaching the front of the building, he pulled down the visor, punched the opener button with his finger and watched the garage door lift. He parked inside and closed the door behind him—tucking himself in for the night.

He still couldn't believe she'd escaped. What a foolish mistake he had made, he thought as he twisted off the cap to the new half-pint of vodka he's purchased on his way here.

With the truck's engine off, he pulled a mighty swig from the bottle. The clear liquid gurgled in the bottle as it slid down his throat, warming his insides instantly.

Breathing out fire, Thirsty wondered if his depression had really gotten this bad. Apparently so, because he was here, cleaning up a mess he thought he'd never have to face.

Another couple of swigs and he screwed the cap back on, exited his vehicle, and entered the house.

Turning on the lights, the house was empty. He ducked under thick plastic hanging from the ceiling and stepped over buckets of paint and mortar. His boots echoed off the sheetrock as he passed through each room before descending downstairs to the basement.

A cool, dry breeze swirled around him as he flicked on a flashlight, illuminating the path before him.

It was here he had once dreamed of creating his Play Pen. A place he could bring his girls and do what he wanted to them without fear of his neighbors hearing their screams. He'd planned it all, down to the last soundproof detail. Though it was still a work in progress, his only mistake had been taking Eva before his Play Pen was complete.

He continued walking. The door to the Pen was still open. He entered the room and shined his light over the floor. The story of what happened was everywhere, masked only by Eva's heady scent still lingering in the air.

Thirsty closed his eyes, filled his lungs with a deep breath of air, and tipped his head back on his shoulders. Memories of Eva played out on the movie screen of his mind. Soon, he exhaled his doubts and remembered how empowering it felt to have Eva in his possession.

Slowly, he opened his eyes and his muscles tensed. He wanted to feel those same emotions again, be the man he knew he could be. Powerful. In control. At his complete mercy.

In a burst of rage, he stomped on the broken chair, further shattering it beneath the sharp heel of his boot. Then he swung his body around and sent his fist flying into the sheetrock, punching a hole in the wall. A loud scream ripped from his lungs as he roared into the ceiling.

He felt trapped—stuck in a life he didn't want to live any

longer. How did he get here? Where did it go so wrong? This wasn't how he saw his future. He expected more—and now needed to escape his past in order to be the man he'd always envisioned.

After calming himself down, he rationalized his situation and worked to gather the broken pieces of chair, along with any other evidence of his kidnapping. He tossed everything into a dumpster out front and added it to the pile of discarded construction material when suddenly he spotted the unmistakable blue and red lights on top of a squad car approaching at a crawl from the north.

Paranoid from the drugs, Thirsty reacted quickly and dove into the shadows before being seen. Pressing his shoulders against the vinyl siding of the house, he watched with intense bug eyes as the police drove by. His heart hammered against his ribs, but they never stopped.

The cops were on to him.

Thirsty grinned as a new surge lit up his spine like a fuse.

He liked the game he'd created—liked the idea of playing hide and seek even better. He was just like the Prom Queen Killer.

CHAPTER SIXTEEN

Now he couldn't be stopped. He was manic and on a binge—perhaps a little out of control.

Thirsty leaned across the center console and opened the glove box. It was dark in the cab of his truck, but a nearby street lamp provided enough light to see. Diving his hand inside, he rummaged around before closing his fingers around an eyeglass case. Bringing it into his lap, he flipped the lid and fingered through the expensive jewelry stored inside, glittering in the light.

"If you want to get noticed, you must peacock for attention." He laughed.

The wolf came out at night, he thought as he clasped the gold necklace around his neck and slid the matching band over his wrist. Next came the rings, followed up by the diamond-studded earring he poked through his left lobe. He'd trimmed his beard down to a goatee at the house and a spray of cologne topped off his appearance. He was ready for the hunt.

After seeing the cops pass in front of the house, something inside of him snapped. Not entirely convinced they were looking for him, he pretended they were. It made his game fun—emboldened him to try his hand at taking another girl.

Thirsty stared into his wild eyes, liking what he saw, then put the truck in gear and eased his foot off the brake. Around the corner were two girls working the streets looking for tonight's customers. He'd driven by them and liked what he saw. As soon as he curbed the truck next to them, he powered down the window and called them over.

"Hey, honey, whatcha you looking for tonight?" a teenage girl revealing cleavage said.

He stroked his chin, letting his gaze fall to her neck. "I'm kind of thirsty," he said.

The girl giggled and commented on his jewelry.

"Get inside," Thirsty responded. "I'll show it to you, maybe even let you wear it."

The girl smiled but didn't make a move. "One hundred for anything you want."

Thirsty eyed the other girl. "I want both of you...together."

The girls looked at each other. Thirsty watched them consider his proposition, hashing out the private details with only their eyes. A second later, the girl leaning on his window sill said, "Okay. We'll do it, but double the price."

Thirsty bit his lower lip and squinted his eyes. His gaze drifted to the valleys of their breasts and their thin necks that he wanted to wrap his fingers around until they could no longer breathe. They were so young, but surely soaked like a dirty oil rag from working these streets far too many nights of the week.

"So, what do you say, mister? You in or not?"

"Step into the light." Thirsty beckoned them closer with his finger. "I want to see your face."

The girl leaned into the light.

Thirsty knew he could do better. As tempting as they both were, they weren't perfect. Besides, this wasn't a challenge. Everybody had a price and they'd set theirs. Unfortunately for them, it was the wrong offer. Then an idea struck.

"Forget it," he said, powering up the window with the girl's thin arm still resting on the sill. She jumped back and squealed as he drove away to find his perfect companion.

CHAPTER SEVENTEEN

NAOMI MOSS FINISHED SCROLLING THROUGH HER WhatsApp account and put her phone down. The man she'd seen staring was still eyeing her from across the Burger King. She whispered to her friend, "Do you know him?"

Jenny Booth swept her eyes off her phone's screen and frowned when casting her gaze across the room. "Never seen him before."

Naomi felt a cool breeze on her neck. "He keeps staring at us."

Jenny ignored the stares and went back to texting. "He's just thirsty for attention."

"It's creeping me out," Naomi murmured. "Maybe we should go."

Jenny dropped her phone down and gave Naomi an arched look. Then she turned to the man, made a V with her fingers and pressed them to her lips, sticking her tongue through them as she wiggled the tip of it.

"Jenny!" Naomi leaned into her friend's shoulder, giggling. "You're crazy, you know that? What's gotten into you?"

The stranger stood and left the building. Jenny said, "There. Better?"

"Yes. Much better." Naomi stuck out her tongue and made a face.

"They just want sex." Jenny's thumbs tapped at her phone's screen. "It's what all men want. Speaking of which," she swept her gaze to Naomi, "have you decided how to respond to Dylan's request?"

"I can't do it," Naomi said.

Jenny furrowed her brow. "He promised he wouldn't tell anyone."

Naomi sighed, unsure what to do. She liked Dylan—a lot. But what he was asking her to do was something she'd never considered before—even if it was what everyone in school did for attention.

"You've been waiting for him to notice you and now that he has, you're going to turn your back and run?" Jenny pursed her lips and gave Naomi a look. "C'mon," she waved for Naomi's phone, "I'll do it for you."

Naomi reeled her phone into her side. "I don't know."

"Fine. If you're not going to give him what he asked for, why not ask for his first?"

Naomi's jaw dropped.

"Guys do it too." Jenny shrugged.

Naomi's cheeks bloomed as Jenny's phone buzzed. She knew guys were doing it too. That wasn't the problem. Naomi just couldn't see herself actually asking Dylan to do it first.

"Who are you talking to?" Naomi asked, casting her gaze to Jenny's phone.

"Mom's late on her bills again." Jenny's shoulders sagged. Then she jumped with excitement. "So, are we doing this for Dylan or not?"

Naomi gave a skeptical look. "We?"

"Yeah. As in, you and me." Jenny's eyes widened a fraction. "I take the photo and you..."

Naomi's gaze drifted to the order counter. "Oh my god, is that Mr. Helton?"

Jenny's hair flung around her neck as she quickly turned to look. "Damn. It is him."

Everything went quiet as they stared. Then Naomi asked, "Do you think he knows how good looking he is?"

Jenny snapped her neck and gave Naomi a look. "Shit. Of course he knows. He probably gets tons of ass."

Naomi giggled, feeling a bit weirded out when she thought of her teacher having sex.

Jenny's eyes lit up. "We should talk to him."

Naomi raised both her eyebrows and shook her head. "No we shouldn't."

Jenny's expression pinched. "There is nothing to be scared of." Naomi watched Jenny open up more of her shirt, fix her hair. Her eyes glimmered as she wet her lips with her tongue. "We talk to him all the time. Now's not any different."

"Now is totally different," Naomi argued. "We talk to him at school. Ask him questions about homework problems—"

"And now we're going to ask him about his night." Jenny leaned closer and lowered her voice. "He's just a teacher who happens to be extremely hot. Relax. Let's just go talk to him."

"Jenny, no." Naomi pleaded. "C'mon. It's late. Let's just pretend we didn't see him and go."

Jenny bit her bottom lip and had a look in her eye that suggested she had something else up her sleeve. "And miss an opportunity like this? I don't think so."

Naomi thought Jenny really was losing her mind as she watched her friend prance across the restaurant, calling out to Mr. Helton. Feeling embarrassed, and slightly regretting her decision not to say hi herself, Naomi turned her attention out the window, hoping Mr. Helton wouldn't see her too. She watched Jenny through the reflection in the window when suddenly Naomi locked eyes with the stranger who had been staring at her before.

CHAPTER EIGHTEEN

NAOMI'S HEART RACED AS SHE PRETENDED NOT TO NOTICE him. The stranger's face was stone-like, his beady little snake eyes penetrating through the glass. Behind the cold stare was a handsome face. Naomi hated herself for thinking it, but it was true. Once again, he was intently watching her as if she was the only person inside the restaurant. *Could it be he thought she was attractive?*

She looked away, pretending she hadn't noticed, and turned to see Jenny still talking to Mr. Helton. Gathering her things off the table, she met up with her friend, finding safety in numbers.

Mr. Helton greeted Naomi with a friendly smile. He asked, "Is something wrong?"

Naomi knew her face was pale, but she turned to Jenny and put on face. "I'm fine."

"Mr. Helton," Jenny looped her arm through the crook of Naomi's, "don't you think Dylan and Naomi would make a great couple?"

Everyone knew Dylan Sanders. He was the star athlete

and one of the most popular boys in the high school. Mr. Helton said, "Depends if Naomi likes him, too."

Naomi opened her mouth but Jenny beat her to the punch and answered for her. "He's messaging her but she won't message him back. Don't you think she should message him back?"

Mr. Helton looked Naomi in the eye and said, "I think you should play hardball."

The corners of Naomi's eyes crinkled. "I like that idea better."

The lady at the counter called out an order number. Mr. Helton turned and retrieved his tray of food. Naomi took her chance to whisper her secret to Jenny. "I asked him to send his first," Naomi said.

Jenny's eyes opened with excitement—her jaw dropping with forced exaggeration. "You naughty girl."

"I don't know what you two are referring to, and I don't want to know," Mr. Helton filled his cup at the soda machine, "but just remember, you have more say than you realize."

"Thanks, Mr. H." Naomi smiled.

Mr. Helton turned toward a table. "I'll see you two tomorrow."

"Dream about you," Jenny whispered to Mr. Helton as she led Naomi by the arm out of the restaurant. Naomi couldn't believe Jenny's courage. Once outside, Jenny asked Naomi, "Did Dylan respond?"

Naomi stopped and glanced to where she'd last seen the stranger sitting in his truck. The tips of her fingers went cold. She didn't like the feeling of being watched by a stranger. Jenny snapped her fingers in front of Naomi's eyes. "Hello."

Naomi's vision focused and her attention was back on her friend. "Huh?"

Jenny licked her lips and cocked her head. "I said, did Dylan respond?"

Naomi found herself once again staring at the empty parking spot. "I saw him again."

Jenny's eyebrows squished. "What are you talking about?"

Naomi told her—the queasy feeling in her stomach spreading. Jenny looked around. "I don't see him anymore."

Naomi brushed a hand over her head. "No. I guess he moved on."

"There is nothing to worry about." Jenny tugged on Naomi's arm and they headed toward Naomi's car. Once buckled in their seats, Jenny said, "Brian is having a party tomorrow night."

"The college boy Brian?"

Jenny's eyes sparkled as she nodded. "I was thinking we should go."

Naomi put the car in reverse, backed out, and turned right at the street. "I'm in."

"Of course you are. If I'm going, you're going. But we should try to score some liquor ourselves, have a pregame party before we arrive." Jenny received another text.

Naomi glanced to Jenny's phone. "Are you going to tell me who you're texting with or not?"

"It's complicated," Jenny said, telling Naomi to pull into a gas station. She needed to refill her vape pod, or at least that was the excuse she gave Naomi.

"And my situation with Dylan isn't?" Naomi clucked her tongue as she turned off the road. "It doesn't matter. I'm sure I know who it is, anyway."

Their eyes met, Jenny looked to see if what Naomi said could actually be true. Naomi's phone chirped with a message and Jenny picked it up and read the text before Naomi could get to it first. "It's Dylan."

Naomi's chest bloomed with heat. She reached for her phone. "Give me it."

Jenny said, "I don't think so."

"Then at least tell me what he said."

Jenny held up the phone and read the message. "Holy shit. This dude wants you so freakin' bad."

"What did he say?" Naomi parked out front—the music still playing through Bluetooth.

"Don't be ashamed of your body." Jenny put on her best Dylan imitation. "You're so beautiful. I just want this to be between us. Show me yours and I'll show you mine." Jenny snapped her neck and locked eyes with Naomi. "You have to do this. If you won't, I will."

Naomi stole her phone from Jenny's grip and read Dylan's text. Her thoughts scrambled. The idea sounded fun and spontaneous, but did she have what it took to follow through? She didn't think so. Her body was already jolted by the idea of sending him a picture of herself. When she looked to Jenny, Jenny nodded. Then Naomi said, "Okay. I'll do it."

Opening their car doors with a squeal, they ran inside the convenience store, giggling their way to the back bathroom door. Once there, Jenny asked, "Want me to take it?"

Naomi shook her head. "Sorry, no threesome allowed tonight."

Jenny laughed. "Okay, but if you chicken shit your way out of this, I really will send him a picture of my boobs and tell him they're yours."

"Don't worry. I'm doing this." Naomi swallowed her nerves and entered the bathroom alone, locking the door behind her.

She stood in front of the mirror for a long pause and let her hair cascade down around her shoulders before adding a new layer of makeup and lip gloss. Then, with her heart hammering, she removed her shirt and bra.

She didn't particularly like what she saw, but her thoughts didn't matter with Jenny standing on the other side of the locked bathroom door. After thinking how much she wanted Dylan to notice her, Naomi lifted her phone, pointed it into the mirror, and began snapping pictures of herself to send to Dylan Sanders.

CHAPTER NINETEEN

Five minutes later, Naomi exited the bathroom with her favorite three pictures saved to her phone. She was light on her feet, full of excitement. She couldn't believe she'd actually done it. Pulling her hair back into a ponytail, she was expecting to have Jenny jump into her arms as soon as she opened the door, insist she see the pictures herself. Instead, Jenny wasn't there and Naomi wondered where her friend had gone.

Naomi cast her gaze to the front of the store. Nothing.

"Where did you go?" Naomi whispered as she looked around, expecting to see Jenny pop out from behind an aisle any second.

Glancing at her cellphone, Naomi went looking for her friend, calling out to her as she weaved through the aisles. "Jenny. Where are you?"

Naomi stopped on the next aisle and knitted her eyebrows. A woman browsing the chips barely looked up and Naomi kept searching. She circled back to the bathrooms, stuck her head inside the women's room again. It was empty —left with only memories of standing in front of the mirror with her shirt off, feelings of insecurity filling her head with doubt.

She checked her phone again. There still was nothing from Jenny.

Thinking she'd missed Jenny say she would meet her at the car, Naomi made her way to the front. Passing the clerk at checkout, she asked him if he'd seen her friend leave.

"Yes," the man said. "She paid for her purchase and left."

Naomi rushed outside, hoping to find her friend vaping near the car. Still, Naomi didn't find Jenny. Beginning to worry, she pressed her phone to her ear and called. When Jenny's voicemail answered, Naomi said, "Jenny, I'm at the car. Where the hell are you? I took the photos, now let's get the hell out of here."

CHAPTER TWENTY

I WAS IN THE SHOWER WHEN I HEARD COOPER BARKING like mad.

"Mason," I yelled around the curtain, "what the heck is going on?"

There was no response. It wasn't like Cooper to act crazy unless something was wrong. I turned off the faucet, wrapped the bathrobe around my body, and stepped out to hear someone banging on my front door.

Who the heck is this?

Padding down the hall, I glanced to Mason's room. His door was shut, his school bag gone from its hook. I assumed he left for school early without saying goodbye. A Post-it on the unsigned permission slip confirmed it. I promised myself to talk to him about leaving without saying goodbye, but first I had to answer the door.

Another quick rap and I picked up my pace.

I told Cooper to cool it. It was too early for visitors, but it sounded like an emergency. When I peeked through the curtains, I saw King impatiently rocking on his heels as the soft morning light warmed his back. As soon as I opened the door, King said, "I was beginning to think you weren't home."

I folded my arms and held my robe closed. I waited for him to hug me, press his lips against mine. When he didn't, I masked my annoyance and asked, "What is it?"

His brow wrinkled. "I need a favor."

I raked my eyes over his clothes. He had the five o'clock shadow and glossy-eyed look of having pulled an all-nighter. It was a familiar appearance, and I suspected I might know what this was about.

"Does this have something to do with last night's Jane Doe?" I asked.

"You heard about it?"

King acted genuinely surprised. "I was at the scene," I said. "Where were you?"

"It's a long story." King's lungs deflated and the look he gave me said it was something he preferred not to share. "But it's why I'm here now."

I wondered what had happened, why it seemed the department dropped the ball on their Jane Doe. Was it done purposely in an effort to cover up another crime statistic by the mayor, or something else I missed entirely? I said, "Care to elaborate?"

King scrubbed a hand over his face and pointed to his unmarked sedan. There was a girl with beautiful long black hair sitting in the back seat, his partner Alvarez in the front. "Her name is Eva Martin."

"Did she know the victim?"

King gave me an unsure glance. I flicked my gaze back to the girl. She looked away every time our eyes met. King continued, "Something tells me she might know what happened to Megan Hines."

My attention snapped back to King. "What makes you say that?"

"She was abducted." King filled me in on the details, and though the information was limited, it was enough to paint a clear picture of what we were dealing with. "She's not saying much. I don't think she trusts men—"

"So you want me to build rapport with her, is that it?"

King gave me a knowing look. "Anything you can get her to say that might help us solve not only her crime, but others, too, would be great."

I understood the opportunity that had suddenly fallen on my doorstep, but what I didn't completely understand was why King was bringing a witness to me. "Shouldn't you be the one to do that?"

King said, "We tried. We don't have the resources to hold her. And she asked me to bring her to you."

Now I was the one rubbing a hand over my face. "Let's say I get her to talk, then what? And doesn't she want to go home?"

King's voice fell to a low rasp. "She doesn't want to go home because she's afraid her kidnapper will see her with cops and kill her."

My thoughts were on Megan as I stared in Eva's direction. "Any idea who took her?"

King shook his head no.

I wasn't ready for this, but couldn't turn it away either. Telling Cooper to sit, I paused to think. Then I asked, "Was her case officially recorded?"

"Sam," King sighed, "you know I follow the book."

"But does the mayor?"

King's head floated up on his shoulders. "Will you help or not?"

Our eyes locked, and I said, "She can stay here for as long as she needs."

CHAPTER TWENTY-ONE

NAOMI TOOK HER TIME GETTING READY FOR SCHOOL, making sure her hair and makeup were flawless. She kept her phone close by, hoping Jenny would message and let her know she was okay. Naomi's last text to Jenny was over an hour ago, and each minute that passed without hearing back, Naomi's worries rose. She pulled clothes from her bedroom closet, wanting to look her best for Dylan.

Jenny was a free spirit, and a small part of Naomi was convinced that maybe her friend had plans of her own. Plans she failed to communicate to Naomi.

All night, Naomi asked herself if it was possible Jenny said she was meeting the mystery person Naomi saw her texting with. The more she thought that might have been the case, the more convincing it sounded.

But Jenny wouldn't go far from her phone, and certainly would respond when Naomi messaged. That was the one fact Naomi couldn't deny and was what kept her stomach tangled in knots. Something wasn't right.

A knock on the door.

Naomi spun around and found her mom, Cindy Moss, at the door. "You got home late last night," Cindy said.

"The assignment took longer than we anticipated." Naomi turned back to her phone and locked her screen in case her mother wanted to snoop.

Thirteen-year-old Laura Moss ran past Naomi's room. "Who's taking me to school?"

Cindy folded her arms and leaned against the frame. Looking Naomi in the eye, she said, "I need you to do it today."

Naomi snapped her head around. "Mom."

"I have that meeting across town this morning. Remember?"

Naomi sighed and turned her back, making sure to tuck away her secret before her mother asked what was wrong. Trudging to her dresser, she sifted through her sock drawer and anxiously waited to hear from Jenny.

"Is everything all right?" Cindy asked.

Naomi closed her eyes, her chin falling to her chest. She wanted to talk, but how could she? If something did happen to Jenny, everyone would blame her. "I can take Laura," Naomi said softly.

An awkward pause followed as Cindy continued to stare. "Don't forget to give yourself enough time to drop Laura off before school. I don't want you to be late again."

Naomi snapped, "I got it, Mom."

Cindy wished Naomi well on her day, and Naomi listened to her mom leave for work before she even thought about leaving her room. She felt bad for snapping, but her concern for Jenny was squeezing every ounce of compassion out of her.

As if on cue, Laura came barreling into Naomi's room. "Mom knows you're hanging out with Jenny."

"So? It's no secret."

"She thinks she's a bad influence on you."

Naomi brushed past her and headed downstairs and into the kitchen.

Laura followed. "What were you really up to last night?"

The image of her standing topless in front of the mirror flashed to the forefront of her mind. Naomi stared at her sister and shifted the conversation. "Are you ready or not?"

"Not."

Laura hurried for her school bag and when she forgot her cellphone charging on the counter next to the fridge, Naomi said, "Don't forget your phone."

"I don't want it." Laura moved to the door and gave Naomi a look that said she was ready.

Naomi arched a single eyebrow.

"What?"

Naomi walked through the kitchen and took her sister's phone into her hand. "What if there's an emergency?"

"There won't be."

"Just take it."

When Laura refused again, Naomi knew something wasn't right. Hacking into her sister's phone, Naomi accessed her messages and began reading.

"Hey." Laura jumped forward in protest. Swiping her hand through the air, she attempted to snatch her cellphone out of Naomi's hands. "Naomi! Stop. Those messages are private."

"I thought you didn't want it?" Naomi held the device high above Laura's head and couldn't believe what she was reading. "Who are these girls? And why are they saying these things about you?"

Laura's face reddened. "Naomi, stop."

Naomi held the phone behind her back and faced her sister. "Is this about your stuff getting stolen?"

"They're just stupid girls who don't have the guts to tell me these things to my face."

Naomi glanced back to Laura's phone. "These are insanely mean things to say to anybody."

"They're just trying to impress the popular boys."

"Who will never read them because they're sent to only you," Naomi reminded her sister. "Regardless, we need to do something about this or they won't stop."

Laura folded her arms, cocked out her hip. "Can I have my phone back now?"

Naomi's own phone started ringing. Hoping it was Jenny, she told Laura she'd meet her at the car. Once her sister was gone, Naomi looked to see who was calling.

"Shit," she said. The person calling was the last person Naomi wanted to talk to, but she had no choice but to answer. It was Jenny's mother, Ruth.

Naomi answered, "Hey Ruth, everything all right?"

Ruth said, "Have you seen Jenny?"

Naomi thought about lying, tell Ruth that Jenny stayed the night and was in the shower. Instead, she said, "I haven't seen her since Mr. Bennett's practice yesterday."

There was a long pause, then Ruth said, "Jenny never came home last night and she's not answering my calls. I'm worried something might have happened to her."

CHAPTER TWENTY-TWO

JENNY BOOTH'S SHIVERS WERE NOW UNCONTROLLABLE AS she lay with her knees tucked to her chest in the corner of an empty room. Her clothes had been stripped from her body and she was left with only the thin covering of her skimpy underwear. No matter what she did, she couldn't get warm. The chill had settled into her bones. It was all she could think about; the need to get warm, the need to survive.

With her teeth chattering, Jenny's thoughts were as choppy as the memory of what happened to her. She couldn't recall the details, couldn't decide if she'd said goodbye to Naomi or if she'd only dreamed that she had.

The room was pitch dark. She didn't know what time it was, nor could she decide how long she'd been here, hidden away from the rest of the world. Was it only a few hours, or had she been here for days?

Rolling like an egg to her opposite side, the pressure inside her skull pounded like a hangover. Jenny instinctively reached for her cellphone as if she was in her own bed at home instead of on a cold concrete floor. Her phone wasn't there, it had been taken along with her clothes. It felt like a part of her body was missing.

She drifted in and out of sleep.

A memory flashed behind her eyes.

She remembered talking to Mr. Helton and having Naomi worried about a stranger staring. She couldn't remember the stranger's face no matter how hard she tried. After that, she drew a blank. Now she was here—wherever *here* was.

"Let me out of here." Her whispers crawled up the walls like spiders. No one answered her pleas for help, but she kept asking to be let free until her throat croaked.

Soon her eyes fluttered closed and she vividly dreamed of being elsewhere.

A door hinge squeaked and Jenny lifted her eyelids. Squinting into the intense flood of bright light filling the tiny room, she pushed herself upright and let her eyes adjust. Someone was at the door but she couldn't see who. Once her vision focused, her gaze flitted around the room, sending her heartrate spiking.

"How did you get these? Where am I?" she said to the imposing silhouette standing in the doorway.

When the man didn't answer, Jenny swept her gaze back to the dozens of photographs stapled to the plywood wall. She was in every photo. They came from all over her life, some being manipulated to be sexual in nature.

"Who the hell are you?" Jenny ground her teeth.

The man stepped forward and Jenny realized he was naked. She scurried back on all fours until her back was up against the wall. The man followed and kneeled next to Jenny. He stared into her eyes from behind a clear mask. Terrified, Jenny trembled. Her pulse throbbed in her neck and she flinched at his touch.

"My name is not important, Jenny," he whispered in a

raspy breath as he stroked her cold cheek. "But I do promise to take good care of you."

CHAPTER TWENTY-THREE

"I PROMISE HE'S NOT AS MEAN AS HE LOOKS," I SAID, referring to Cooper.

Eva Martin didn't react, though it was meant to be a joke. Cooper had a fierce bark, but a soft core. I'd seen him get chased by squirrels who'd had enough of his antics, sending him running with his tail tucked between his legs. But I also knew that some people felt intimidated by him. He was a big dog with a boxed head and was extremely protective of me.

Eva hesitated before entering my house despite her request to be brought here. I assumed she knew who I was because of my column at the paper, or perhaps even my blog. It made sense. Erin and I were crusaders for women like Eva and weren't afraid to use our platform to make a scene. But when I shut the front door a little too hard, I immediately regretted it.

Eva startled and wrapped her arms around her torso tighter. She looked fragile—broken like glass—but something told me that she hadn't always been like this.

I apologized and made sure Cooper didn't get off his bed and do anything else to spook her. The last thing I needed was to send this girl back to the horrors she'd just experienced before I had time to first let her know she could trust me with her story.

Cooper whimpered a soft protest as he shifted his unsettle gaze between Eva and me.

"Detective King said you asked to come here?" I said.

Eva gave me a guilty look and I was afraid one wrong word, one wrong move, would cause her trauma to resurface.

"It's okay. You're welcome to stay as long as you like."

I cast my gaze to her feet, nodding. The soles of her sandals were rooted into the wood floor as she surfed my walls with her eyes. I wondered what it was she was thinking, if it was about me, her being here, or if she was preparing herself to answer the questions she knew I would eventually ask.

"Have you found that girl you've been writing about?" she asked in a soft murmur.

"Megan Hines," I said. "No. She hasn't been found. But I'm hopeful."

Eva inhaled a deep breath and continued taking in my place. There was so much I wanted—needed—to ask her but knew it had to come out slow.

"Is there anything I can get you; are you hungry?"

Cooper sprang to his feet and I heard Eva's breath hitch. I snapped my finger at my dog and told him to lie down. "I'm sorry. He thinks anytime I mention food it's for him."

Eva's beautiful brown eyes met mine and I saw the corner of her mouth threaten to curl upward into a smile. She was gorgeous, a natural beauty about her that was worthy of a model's salary. Did she know how beautiful she was? How could she not? I relaxed a bit, believing we might be able to break the ice sooner than I originally thought.

"This might sound stupid since we don't know each

other," Eva flashed a coy look, "but can I borrow some of your clothes and maybe take a shower?"

"It doesn't sound stupid," I said, knowing enough of what she'd been through to want to do the same if I was in her position. "C'mon. I'll show you what I have."

Eva followed me into my bedroom and I turned to size her up. She was an inch taller than me, but we were similar enough to make it work for the time being. I pulled a t-shirt and gray sweatpants off the closet hangar and said, "Is this all right?"

Eva kept her gaze low and whispered her appreciation. I set her up with a towel and led her into the bathroom where I told her the hot water takes a minute to warm up. Then I mentioned my friend Erin was on her way over and might be here by the time she was finished. Eva knew who Erin was, didn't mind her coming over. But I didn't want any surprises.

I left her in the bathroom with hopes of her being able to wash away everything that happened to her. Then I called Erin on my landline. As soon as she picked up, I said, "You're not going to believe this, but a source to our Jane Doe story might have just walked through my door."

CHAPTER TWENTY-FOUR

WITH ONE HAND ON THE STEERING WHEEL AND HIS VISOR down, Detective Alex King's tires slowly rolled through the Arapahoe Acres neighborhood. He needed to visit the house Christopher Bowers said he was remodeling, see the streets Eva ran through on her mission to escape her kidnapper's grip.

Looking out the passenger side window, Alvarez said, "What was she doing out here in the burbs?"

They knew enough about Eva to know that something wasn't adding up. King didn't like what he saw. "These houses might have great curb appeal," King said, "but who the hell knows what is happening behind closed doors."

Alvarez pointed across the dash. "That's the house there."

King curbed the vehicle and killed the engine. There were a couple pickup trucks parked in the driveway and a dumpster full of construction scraps near the curb. King read the house address and matched it to the one Detective Gray gave them. But was Bowers here? A quick search of the license plates said that he was.

King opened his door and stepped one foot out when

Alvarez mumbled, "I still think we're wasting our time with him."

"Let's just walk around. Make sure his story checks out. Then we'll be on our way."

King shut his door and made his way to the front of the house. The garage door was open, and inside a man was working the table saw. Above the noise, King managed to get his attention. "Christopher Bowers here?"

"Upstairs." The man pointed his index finger in the air.

Alvarez stayed behind to speak with Bowers's employee as King began his journey up the short flight of stairs. He entered the house undergoing an entire remodel, peeking around to inspect the work being done.

Two men were busy hanging sheetrock, and King asked if they were working two nights ago. They said they weren't and King continued up the next flight of stairs following the sounds of air compressors, nail guns firing, and the pounding of hammers. No one seemed to care two cops were here, asking around, and that comforted King.

He found Bowers doing tile work in the master bath, and as soon as Bowers saw him coming, Bowers pushed himself off his knees and stood.

"How is she doing?" Bowers asked about Eva.

King assessed Bowers's work, was impressed, and heard Alvarez catch up behind him. Then he met Bowers's eye, and said, "She's in recovery and has provided a clear ID on her kidnapper."

Bowers didn't flinch at King's test. It was the reaction he was hoping for; Alvarez, too. But instead of backing down, King turned his inquiry up a notch.

"That's great," Bowers said.

King's gaze narrowed. "Was Eva an escort?"

"Excuse me?" Bowers's eyebrows pinched, clearly offended by what King was insinuating.

"We know about your prostitution charge." King paused and stared. "So, did you pick her up, hoping to score?"

Bowers removed his safety goggles and wiped the beads of sweat from his brow. "Like I said last night, I left here after midnight two nights ago and was driving home when I found her standing in the middle of the road. I asked her if she needed a ride, and after seeing the condition she was in, I took her to the hospital. That's it." Bowers shifted his gaze between King and Alvarez, visibly tensing. "I don't know anything more about her than that."

"Does your wife know about your taste for prostitutes?"

Bowers shifted his weight to his opposite foot and narrowed his gaze. "Am I a suspect?"

King locked eyes and allowed an awkward pause to answer for him.

"I'm married." Bowers's tone was clipped. "And no, my wife doesn't know about that."

Alvarez's cell buzzed and he stepped into the next room to take the call in private.

Bowers stepped forward and squared his shoulders with King. "I'd prefer she didn't find out, either. If that woman I picked up was an escort, all I did was help a person in need."

King heard Alvarez return, and a moment later he felt his partner's hand clamp on his shoulder. Pulling him away from Bowers, Alvarez whispered in King's ear, "That was Gray. Another girl was reported missing."

Staring into Bowers's worried expression, King was satisfied in knowing Bowers was at the hospital when this new victim went missing. It cleared him for now, but a hunch kept Bowers on King's list of possible suspects until further notice.

"I'll keep your secret private, but don't go too far," King said. "We might be back for more questions later."

CHAPTER TWENTY-FIVE

JENNY KEPT HER HAND PRESSED TO HER CHEEK. THE kidnapper's touch was forever imprinted on her skin. She wondered if she'd feel it forever—what would happen the next time he touched her? Would he dare put it somewhere she didn't want it to go? Several hours had passed since he left her alone, and she was left with only his parting words.

Talk and be killed.

Deaf to the world on the other side of these walls, Jenny stared at her own image, reliving each moment in time of when the pictures were taken. Each stolen memory was framed inside a glossy sheet that looked freshly printed. The fear it first elicited had long since evaporated into the perfect distraction to the pass the time.

Was that the reason he hung these photographs for her to see? No. They were here to tell her he'd been watching—stalking her for a long while.

Bouncing her gaze between images, she could feel the winter's chill in one, the summer's intense dry heat in another. Whoever had kidnapped her had been watching her since last spring. But there was one particular photograph she kept coming back to, one she couldn't escape.

It was of her and Naomi after school. Jenny could still hear the laughter ring out as they giggled about something a boy said earlier that day. In another photograph, she could still feel the same frustrations ripple across her mind at the memories it brought to light. Soon, tears welled in the corners of her eyes and she wondered if she'd ever go home—ever feel anything other than the misery and desperation she felt now.

Curling up in the fetal position, Jenny stared at the point where the floor met the wall. There was no trim, just a gap in the wall waiting to be sealed. A recessed light had been left on and Jenny wanted nothing more than to turn it off and escape the torture of having to look at her stalker's photographs—especially those that had been manipulated to portray her as something she didn't want to be. A slut.

Her body had warmed considerably since a few hours ago. It was partly because of fear, but more likely due to the fact the air conditioning had been turned off.

Jenny felt the urge to pee for the first time since being taken. She flicked her eyes to the bucket perched in the corner meant to act as a toilet. Next to it, a blanket on which to sleep. It was humiliating and she felt ashamed, like somehow she deserved to be here. There was no toilet paper, no food or water, and she was certain her kidnapper was gone and not coming back any time soon. But was he watching? She didn't know.

A soft drumming through the wall stole her attention.

Jenny listened, trying to decide what caused it. Then the drumming went into a pattern. Jenny pushed herself up and sat, hugging her knees to her chest. Staring at the wall, she thought about tapping back when suddenly she heard whispers.

"Hey. Are you there?"

Jenny froze. She rolled her eyes between the walls and up to the ceiling. It was impossible to tell where the whispers were coming from, but they were definitely human. When she heard them again, she rolled her neck and stared at the door. Her kidnapper's threat to come back kept her quiet.

"I know you're in there," the whisper said. "I heard you come in. What's your name?"

Jenny's heart pounded. When the whispers started again, Jenny snapped. "Quiet. You're going to get us killed."

"My name is Megan. What's yours?"

Jenny opened her mouth and quickly closed it. A part of her thought maybe this was a test to see how well she obeyed her kidnapper's single instruction. Failure was not an option. Her life depended on it.

"It doesn't matter," Megan said. "He's going to kill us anyway."

When Jenny closed her eyes, an image of her kidnapper flashed across her mind. She thought about the clear plastic mask he wore over his face, his dark eyes searching from behind. She didn't know what he looked like, or what color hair he had, and certainly couldn't pick him out from a crowd. But Jenny did notice he had no hair on his body.

"We can get out of this," Megan continued, "but only if we work together."

Jenny listened, thought about her chances. Fear kept her silent.

"So, are you with me or not?"

Jenny's breath labored as she looked to the far wall and said, "What did you say your name was?"

"Megan Hines."

Jenny's eyes rounded. She recognized the name, had seen Megan's face plastered on every news channel the week she went missing. There had been talk at school, too.

"Are they looking for me?" This time Megan's voice was a quiet desperation.

Jenny swallowed and opened her mouth, about to tell her she knew who she was. Megan probably knew Jenny, too. The sudden slamming of a door somewhere inside the house shut them both up.

Jenny's heart raced as she listened to the heavy footsteps draw closer. Darting across the floor, she cowered in a corner and curled her body into a ball, attempting to hide, knowing He was back and coming straight for her.

CHAPTER TWENTY-SIX

Erin was just about to leave her house when she heard a familiar chime ring out from her computer's speakers. She glanced over her shoulder and debated whether or not to march back into her home office and read the message that had just come in or get on her way. Torn, Erin was also anxious to learn what was waiting for her at Sam's after hearing about Eva Martin.

"Screw it," Erin said, deciding to stay. She marched into her office, murmuring, "It will only take a minute."

Dropping her tote at her feet, Erin leaned over her desk, pushed her podcast microphone off to the side, and draped a hand over the computer mouse, waking up the screen. She opened her *Real Crime News* website message board and clicked the notification link.

Today marks Megan's twentieth day gone, she read.

Erin sighed, closed her eyes, and said a quick prayer for Megan Hines. A day hadn't gone by that she hadn't thought about Megan. Megan was her first—*and* last—thought of the day, and twenty days missing felt like an eternity.

"We're still looking for you, Megan," Erin said as she continued to read.

Bringing one hand to her belly, she felt her stomach roll. There were enough people giving up on Megan to make Erin suddenly not feel so well. With her thoughts on the general victimization of women, she lowered herself into her desk chair thinking about yesterday's Jane Doe. Erin hoped she wasn't Megan Hines, but that chance was very real. And despite others giving up on finding her, Erin wanted nothing more than to help bring Megan home.

Tipping forward, she continued to scroll through more comments.

The message board was lighting up with remarks rolling in from around the country. Everyone had an opinion to what might have happened to Megan, but more interesting was how Megan's disappearance encouraged women to share their own stories of abuse and violence.

"Why does it always seem to be women these things happen to?" one commenter asked.

Another post said, *"Men don't understand how scary it can be for us women to walk to work, school, or take our children to the park. Worse, it's usually the men we trust that turn around and hurt us—or, God forbid, kill us."*

Erin glanced to a photo of her mother framed on her wall. She'd thought about her father and what had happened to them both when the queasy feeling in her stomach fluttered up into her chest.

Another chime and the latest comment began working its way to the top of the list. A participant admitted to being a victim of domestic violence, then a few more women followed up with their own stories until the snowball effect grew into something much larger than Erin could have ever predicted. Then, without warning, women began calling out their assailants by name.

Erin felt her heartrate turn up a notch. It was exciting to see, but also dangerous. None of these accusations could be verified, and Erin could only hope it was true. The last thing she wanted was to provide the platform for a smear campaign. Not sure if she should shut it down or not, she let it go. Five minutes later, Erin was walking to her car where she found another message waiting.

Pinched between the wiper and windshield was an envelope, and inside were more individual words cut out from newspaper. Erin didn't know what to make of it, or what was meant by it, but as she held the envelope in her hand, she couldn't help but feel like she was being watched.

CHAPTER TWENTY-SEVEN

"I DON'T KNOW WHO SHE WAS," I SAID, TELLING DAWSON about last night's Jane Doe. "But it's possible the victim could have been Megan Hines."

I'd been on the phone with him since my call to Erin. I could hear Dawson thinking and I diverted my attention back to the TV.

The local news report still hadn't said anything about Jane Doe or Eva Martin. It didn't make sense. How could I have the exclusive on this? The longer these crimes went unreported, the more I believed the mayor was trying to hide something.

"Stay ahead of this, Sam," Dawson said. "Even if everyone else's interests have waned, there is still a story out there waiting for you somewhere."

I glanced to the calendar and thought about how many days Megan Hines had been missing. My red X's were adding up and it had quickly become my least favorite time of day—the time I marked off another day without having found her.

"I'll be heading to the morgue to try to ID our Jane Doe,"

I said, thinking how lucky I was to have Dawson's unwavering support.

"Let me know as soon as you find out," he said before pulling my feet back down to Earth. "And, Sam, I suggest you keep your opinions private—it might be *your* blog but it's your byline in *my* paper."

He was referring the opinion piece I wrote last night about the mayor. There was no way in hell he'd approve it for print, but it needed to be said. I'd put it out to the audience I had full control of to see what might come of it without fears of repercussion. Apparently, I'd managed to get at least one person's attention.

"What I do on my blog is my own business," I said, hearing my front door open. I waved for Erin to come inside. She hurried to the couch and emptied a plastic bag of clippings on the coffee table. I'd wondered what she had, but Dawson was barking in my ear, distracting my focus.

"I'm not ready to go to battle with the mayor's office," he said. "Not until you can deliver more concrete proof that Goldberg is actually hiding crimes in order to make his administration look good."

"Is that a challenge?" I asked.

"Talk to me after you figure out who Jane Doe is."

Once off the phone, I turned to Erin. She was hunched over and focused, busy rearranging the clippings she'd dumped out. I moved to the living room and saw that they were words, just like the cryptic message I'd received.

Erin paused and gave me a look before telling me where she'd found it.

I immediately thought about Archie Smith and what I read about PQK. "Did you see anyone who may have left it?"

Erin hadn't.

I didn't like this one bit. Someone was playing games with us. I joined in, kept moving words around, trying to make sense of them. It was clear we'd gotten someone's attention, but was it Archie or the person behind Megan's suspected kidnapping? I didn't know.

Then I got it.

We both stared at the sentence I'd formed before locking eyes.

"Where is Eva?" Erin asked.

I pointed to the bathroom in the back.

Erin craned her neck and whispered, "Sam, I think I'm being followed."

"Like, followed here?"

Erin nodded.

I pushed my fingers through my hair. I didn't like what I was hearing. Eva was already afraid to go home, and now I feared Erin might have led whoever did this to her straight to my front door. I cast my gaze back to the words and heard the thick bubble of confusion close over my ears.

Eva stepped out of the shower just then, and we both turned to look at her. Our eyes met and I looked once again to the sentence I created from the clippings. The connection seemed obvious, but could this message really be about Eva? I read it again, wanting it to say something other than what I'd come up with. Deep down, I knew this was the message we were meant to receive—*He'll kill the girl if you don't help.*

CHAPTER TWENTY-EIGHT

Eva stared to the front of the house like she knew what we'd just discovered. I looked back, feeling my vision tunnel. There were many times I wished I had more square footage than what I did, but nothing like what I wished for now.

"Everything all right?" she asked.

I erased the sentence we'd just formed with a quick swipe of my hand as I stood and introduced Eva to Erin. "Eva, I'd like you to meet Erin."

Erin ironed her hands down her thighs and stood with a bright smile. "Hi, Eva. It's wonderful to meet you."

Eva flicked her gaze between us before padding forward on tender feet. She traveled through the kitchen, past the dining room table, and into the living room. She looked beautiful even in my tee and sweats. Her long jet-black hair—now washed and combed—cascaded down the center of her back and was absolutely gorgeous. She looked like a college kid taking it easy on vacation break.

As Erin made small talk with Eva, I kept glancing to the coffee table to make sure the clippings didn't resemble anything other than a pile of random words. Eva didn't seem to notice—or at least she didn't say anything—and I never saw her gaze settle on the words.

After a minute with Erin, Eva took a seat on the sofa chair and pulled her knees to her chest. She said, "The shower was wonderful. Thank you."

My smile hit my eyes. "You must be hungry. Can I make you something to eat?"

"I'm sorry for barging in like this, but I really didn't know where else to go."

Eva was holding my gaze longer than when she first arrived to my house. It was another small sign that she was letting her walls down. Though we were complete strangers, there was something about her that made me feel like I'd known her from some time before. Perhaps it was the possible connection to Megan? Or maybe it was that she seemed completely genuine in character—a trait I was attracted to? Whatever it was, I knew she felt right at home.

"Do you have roommates? Family? Anyone we can call to let them know you're here and safe?" I was leaning forward with my elbows on my knees and fingers weaved together. "They must be wondering where you are."

Eva looked down and shook her head no. "I live alone and don't have any family."

I felt my stomach harden at the thought of having no one to call. I couldn't imagine a life without Mason, King, or my sister in it—let alone the girls. I wondered what her story was, what happened to her family, and why she didn't have any friends. But I saved my breath for the questions I wanted to ask about her kidnapping.

An awkward silence settled between us, and I could see Erin getting antsy to ask more questions. But I didn't want to push too hard, too fast. This was the slow road to recovery—maybe even a slower road to learning who took her and why.

"What is today?" Eva asked.

I met her eye and said, "Wednesday, August 26th."

Eva sighed. "I should be in class today."

Erin asked where she attended school and we learned Eva was a sophomore at Denver University studying business information and analytics. "Don't worry about school," Erin said. "It will be waiting for you when you're ready."

"Can you tell me why you requested Detective King to bring you here?" I asked, already having an idea thanks to King's report. But I wanted to have Eva tell me, get her more comfortable talking, and trusting us with the information she was willing to share.

Eva said, "I saw your coverage of Megan Hines's disappearance at some point." Eva's eyebrows knitted when she locked eyes with me. "Is she still missing?"

"She is," I said.

"Do you know how long you were gone?" Erin asked.

Eva thought about her week. "I think I was taken Sunday night."

"Were you taken from your house?"

"A block away from my apartment while I was out for an evening run." Eva wet her lips with a single swipe of her tongue. "At least, that's what I think happened."

"But you don't know who took you?"

Eva shook her head.

Erin met my eye and I quickly shifted my focus back to Eva. I thought back to what King said about how Eva feared her kidnapper would be waiting for her to return. I hated knowing Erin thought she'd been followed here. *Could it have been Eva's kidnapper who had followed Erin?* I hoped Erin was only being unusually paranoid—but the envelope she found on her car told me otherwise.

"You're safe here," I said, glancing to the clippings, hoping I wouldn't regret my words. "But we need to know what happened to you after you were taken. It's not only Megan Hines we're looking for, there might be others, and we think that you were the lucky one who got away."

Eva's face paled. "There are others?"

"We think so."

Erin asked, "Did you see his face?"

Eva shook her head no. "He wore a mask. And he didn't rape me, but I knew he eventually would."

"Did he tell you that?"

"Yes." Eva's words caught in her throat. "He talked in whispers, saying how much he cared."

"Is that all he said?"

"No. He also said he was thirsty, always thirsty." Eva's watery eyes lifted. "I thought I was going to die."

"But you didn't."

"Because I escaped." Eva raised her gaze and speculated why she wasn't blindfolded. "He wanted me to see him hiding behind his mask—wanted me to know what was coming." Eva told us how she got away, how she was picked up in the middle of the night by Christopher Bowers. She'd gotten lucky.

When we thought we had the whole story, a knock on the front door made us all freeze.

Eva's breath hitched as she looked to me. Cooper was in the window barking. Erin gave me a look, too, one that didn't inspire confidence. We were thinking the same thing, asking if this could be the person she thought was following her. I hoped it wasn't.

I stood and said, "I'm sure it's nothing, but maybe you two should go to the kitchen."

CHAPTER TWENTY-NINE

"Is it *Him*?"

This was Eva's fear—that her kidnapper would come back for her. The only difference was that we weren't at her place.

As I stood, I gave Erin a look. Without speaking, she followed my suggestion and took Eva into the kitchen for added precaution.

Another quick rap on the door and I knew Erin would blame herself if this turned into something dangerous for us all. I remained optimistic. Once they were out of sight, I dried my palms on my pants and reached for the doorknob. Taking a look through the peephole, I couldn't believe whose face I saw.

Archie Smith was dancing on his toes, his eyes hopeful he was at the right place.

Anger welled in my chest as I flung the door open. I said, "What are you doing here and how the hell do you know where I live?"

The corners of Archie's mouth curled into a sharp grin. His eyes glimmered as he cast his gaze over my shoulder. "Hey, is that my book I see?"

My hands fell to my sides as my eyebrows gathered with regret. There were many reasons I shouldn't have left his book out in plain view, and this was one of them. But how could I have predicted Archie Smith would come knocking?

The corners of his eyes crinkled. He was looking at me differently now. "You didn't say you were a fan."

Archie stepped forward like he wanted to enter my house, and I blocked his pursuit. "That's because I'm not." He cocked his head to the side and gave me an arched look, as if surprised I didn't want to invite him inside. "This is my private residence and I don't like surprise visits."

Archie smiled. "I'm sorry, I really should have called, but I didn't have your number, I had to follow Detective King."

I silently cursed King for not noticing he was being tailed. He was a better cop than that. I cast my focus to Archie's hand and saw what he was holding, then asked, "What do you want?"

"I want to know who she is."

"Who *who* is?"

Archie chuckled. "The girl the police brought you." When I didn't answer, Archie continued, "Was it Megan Hines? And don't deny that there's a girl inside because I saw her enter with my own eyes."

I dropped my focus back to his hand. "What are you doing with one of my articles?"

"Oh, this?" Archie raised the newspaper above his waist and, as he did, I looked for holes, possible places where words had been cut out. I didn't see any, but that didn't mean I didn't miss something. Archie continued, "You reported on Megan Hines's disappearance more than anybody else. Why is that?"

I knew his angle, knew Archie was hoping Megan would be found dead so he could work his active serial killer theory.

There was no way I was going to tell him about Eva. "And your point is?"

"You'd be the first to know girls like Megan aren't chosen at random."

I repeated myself. "She's not here."

"If not Megan, who is the girl?"

I thought about why Archie was here, what he was doing in Colorado at all. He should be looking into cold cases, murders, not kidnappings or missing persons. And he should be talking to the cops, not me. "I'm sorry, Archie, but that's none of your business. Now, if you'll please excuse me, I really must be getting back to work."

When I turned to face the door, Archie caught me by the arm. I turned and raised my lip with a snarl that got him to back off. He immediately uncurled his fingers and released me.

He said, "Do you know why last night's Jane Doe went unreported?"

My eyes squinted. "How do you know about that?"

Archie tipped his head back. "The same way you do."

Allison told me about the scene, but did she also tell Archie? Impossible. "I'm still looking for answers," I said after Archie asked me again why the Jane Doe scene played out the way it had.

"Then let me save you some time." Archie backpedaled his way down my short flight of stairs. "Perhaps it's because there is an active serial rapist-killer currently working the Denver area that the mayor doesn't want the public to know about. Don't believe me? Ask the girl inside what she thinks about my theory."

CHAPTER THIRTY

"THANK YOU FOR COMING." RUTH BOOTH STEPPED ASIDE and invited Detective King and Detective Gray into her two-bedroom, single-story house in the University neighborhood. Gray entered the apartment first, followed by King. Ruth latched the door behind them both and said, "Please, have a seat on the couch."

After receiving the call from Gray about another girl reported missing, King dropped Alvarez off at the station to work their Jane Doe case while he headed out with Gray.

It was an old house that had been beautifully remodeled in a well-off neighborhood. King perused the home with his eyes, making note of the fashion magazines and cosmetics left out on side tables alongside other knickknacks. The kitchen, to his right, was filled with stainless steel appliances and granite countertops. The counters were clear and clean; the same went for the rest of the house. Gray took a seat on the far side of the couch and King peered out the window into the vegetable garden in the back, preferring to stand.

Ruth was visibly distraught. Her shoulders sagged, along

with her head, and it was clear that Ruth hadn't showered today. It looked like she'd been up all night, tugging out her hair, making phone calls late into the night with hopes of her daughter coming home. Her purple silk robe drifted loose above pink slippers and Ruth couldn't stop coughing.

When their eyes met, Ruth said, "When I phoned the station, I was told to keep my faith, that a crime hadn't been committed. Has something changed? Has my Jenny been found?"

King saw a small glint of hope flash across Ruth's eyes. It had been less than twenty-four hours since seventeen-year-old Jenny Booth was last seen, and protocol generally called for forty-eight hours to pass before officially filing a missing person's report.

But Ruth was right, something had changed. Her daughter happened to share a similar experience as Eva Martin, perhaps even King's Jane Doe, and certainly what the police believed happened to Megan Hines.

"No, ma'am," Gray said. "We haven't located your daughter."

Ruth frowned as she cast her gaze to her fingertips. No longer fidgeting with anxiety, Ruth's movements went still. After the pause in conversation, she lifted her eyes to King. "But you do believe that she's missing?"

With his hands in his pockets, King said, "When was the last time you saw your daughter, Mrs. Booth?"

"Yesterday morning. I went to work and she was off to school shortly after."

King confirmed Jenny made it to school—it was the same school Megan Hines attended, South High—then asked, "Did you talk to her at any time during the day?"

Ruth shook her head no. "I have a demanding schedule. There's no time to call."

"What do you do for work?" Gray asked.

"I clean houses." Ruth stated a few of her clients' locations and King made mental notes of the neighborhoods mentioned. None were in Arapahoe Acres, but one was nearby.

King turned his head and studied the house once again. He knew the rental market in this area—could safely assume what Ruth was paying for rent. Either she was charging more than other cleaners he knew, or she had other income coming in to be able to afford this place.

"What about your husband?" King lowered his eyes to Ruth, speculating Ruth was married. "Does he work?"

"My husband passed." Ruth shifted her eyes to Gray. "A year ago. He left me with nothing and it's been a struggle since."

"I'm sorry."

"I've been following the news," Ruth steered the conversation back to her concerns about Jenny, "and I'm well aware that Megan Hines is no longer being reported on. It's why I called the police about Jenny. It's been three weeks that poor girl has been gone and I don't think it's a coincidence Jenny went missing the moment everyone seemed to forget some sicko was taking girls her age."

Gray said, "Your daughter is seventeen, correct?"

"That's right," Ruth said, confirming also that Jenny and Megan were students at the same school.

King looked for any family photos but didn't see any photographs anywhere. In fact, besides the little trinkets and magazines left out, all the furniture seemed staged, like it came with the apartment. Thinking it was odd, King asked Ruth, "This apartment, do you rent or own?"

Ruth cocked her jaw as if offended by the question. "I don't see how that matters, but I rent."

Gray said she'd need the landlord's name and number and asked, "Is it possible Jenny ran away?"

Ruth snapped her neck to Gray, her expression pinching. It was clear she was beginning to regret her request to have the police come speak to her about Jenny.

Ruth stood and moved to the kitchen, where King watched her dig out a picture of Jenny from her purse. Once back in the living room, Ruth handed it to Gray. "My daughter is smart, popular, and beautiful. So, to answer your question, no. Jenny wouldn't run away. I might work long hours to stay, afloat but I have a good relationship with my daughter."

King asked, "How did she take your husband's death?"

"Like you'd expect. She was devastated."

Gray handed King the picture of Jenny. He studied her face—took in her wavy brunette hair and her rose petal cheeks. Her black eyes pierced King with confidence. There were physical similarities to Megan Hines, but not to King's Jane Doe or even Eva. Now he was asking himself if Gray's cases were even related. "Did Jenny have boyfriends? A job?"

"Nobody serious." Ruth flicked her eyes to Gray. "And no, she didn't work. She wanted to after my husband passed, but I wanted her to focus on her education."

Gray asked, "She wanted to work to help with the bills?"

"That's right." Ruth nodded.

King thought about the ligature marks on Eva's wrists when he asked, "Mrs. Booth, was your daughter sexually active?"

Ruth picked her head up and rolled her shoulders back. "She's human, Detective, but Jenny wouldn't tell me everything. Boys liked her and she liked them, but those details she saved for her friend, Naomi Moss."

"Was Jenny with Naomi last night?"

Ruth shook her head. According to Naomi, they had parted ways after volleyball practice.

"Do you know where we can find her?"

Ruth told them where, pleaded for them to find her daughter, then said, "If anyone knows what happened to Jenny, it would be her."

CHAPTER THIRTY-ONE

I STAYED ON THE LANDING WITH MY ARMS FOLDED ACROSS my chest and watched Archie drive away, making note of the make and model of his car. I couldn't afford more surprises, and neither could Eva. She trusted me to keep her safe, keep her hidden away from whoever had kidnapped her, and I felt like we'd already failed her.

Archie's taillights disappeared around the next bend and, once out of sight, I thought about what he said about the city wanting to hide something as big as a serial rapist-killer case. I didn't know what got him going down that road, but he wasn't that far off in thinking it was possible. If petty crime bothered the mayor, a working serial killer would give him a heart attack.

Was that why Archie was so obsessed with wanting to know more about Megan Hines and last night's Jane Doe? It made sense. He was working leads for his book, but he had a long way to go to win over my trust before I started working with him, even if I held the same suspicions of the mayor, myself.

I stayed out on the steps for a few more minutes to make

sure Archie didn't circle back. My thoughts were still churning as I thought about what to do about Eva. She couldn't stay here, that much I knew. And I wasn't convinced Erin's house would be any safer, but what other choice did we have?

A squirrel ran up the tree and I heard Cooper barking in the window. Even that distraction wasn't enough to get Archie out of my head. Did he come up with this theory all on his own? Or did he read my blog? If so, was that the reason he had an old article of mine in his hand? It was possible, but then there were the messages being left for both Erin and me to find.

I took Archie as someone who liked to play those kinds of games, a person who worked extremely hard to control the narrative in an effort to produce the story he saw unfolding inside his head. A true crime written with the suspense and thrill of fiction would certainly mean a large advance by a hungry publisher looking to cash in, exactly what Archie was after. So why not just come out and say it?

When I heard a car approach from behind, I turned to look. It wasn't Archie, only a neighbor passing through. I waved, they honked, and I kept piecing together today's timeline. If what Archie said was true, he wasn't the one who followed Erin. If not him, then who?

The door opened behind me and Erin joined me on the porch. Closing the door behind her, she asked, "Everything okay?"

I told her about Archie and said, "I don't like how he's showing up unannounced." Erin asked if he was the one to follow her here, and I said I didn't think so. Then I added, "He said he followed King."

"Then he knows about Eva." We locked eyes and I nodded. "I kept her hidden in the back bedroom, but she's spooked, Sam."

"I know," I said, imagining how Eva must be feeling.

"But what really worries me is what else Archie knows that he isn't sharing."

We both feared Archie would reveal Eva's location sooner or later. That wasn't even the worst of it, though. He'd probably taken a photo of her. What he planned to do with it was anybody's guess.

"We should take her to your house," I said, "and do it as discreetly as possible. At least until we better understand what it is we're up against. Then we can decide what to do with her after that."

Erin agreed and said, "I'm afraid she won't feel safe anywhere. Not until her kidnapper is caught."

The thought put chills up my spine. I didn't want to think of her kidnapper wanting to take her again. I checked the time and prepared to call King to give him a heads up about Archie when I said, "Then we better get to work to make sure that won't happen."

CHAPTER THIRTY-TWO

"THE COPS CALLED ME ASKING FOR NAOMI," SUSAN'S friend said.

Susan was on the phone with Cindy Moss. They'd been friends since college, and Susan had even been a bridesmaid in Cindy's wedding. After Naomi was born, Cindy asked Susan to be Naomi's godmother, which Susan gratefully accepted.

Susan paused mid-step and asked, "Is Naomi okay?"

Cindy said, "They assured me she was, and I confirmed it with the school. Naomi is exactly where she should be, but it was Naomi's friend Jenny Booth they were really looking for."

Susan knew how Cindy felt about Naomi's friend Jenny. Cindy thought she was a bad influence. Susan was on her way to have lunch with executive producer Owen Daniels, but she was beginning to have second thoughts.

"Did they mention what it was about?"

"It sounds like Jenny is missing."

Susan tucked her free hand under her elbow and kept the phone pressed to her ear. She thought about Megan Hines.

She knew Naomi went to the same school. "And what, did they think Naomi knew where she was?"

Cindy said that was her assumption as well, then added, "Naomi is hiding something. Her grades have been slipping since she started hanging out with Jenny, and I know they were out late last night claiming to be doing school work."

The crease between Susan's eyebrows deepened. "You don't think they were?"

"My gut tells me otherwise."

"Did Naomi say anything about it?"

"Nothing," Cindy said. "But I could tell she was distracted this morning about something."

"Is there anything I can do to help?"

There was a brief pause before Cindy asked, "Has Samantha mentioned anything about that other girl, Megan Hines? The reason I ask is that if Jenny is missing, I'd like to get a realistic picture of what may have happened. I've tried calling Jenny's mom, Ruth, but she isn't picking up. She knows I don't like Naomi hanging out with Jenny, and of course I won't hear from Naomi until after school."

Susan didn't know anything that hadn't been published, but promised to call Samantha ASAP. She also knew Cindy couldn't get away from work, and Susan wasn't sure she could either, but asked if she could stop by the school and talk to Naomi herself.

Cindy liked that idea very much, then said, "I don't know how to protect Naomi from the world. If Jenny was kidnapped, who's saying Naomi won't be next?"

"Honey, don't go there," Susan said. "Naomi is a smart girl. I'm sure this is just a big misunderstanding."

CHAPTER THIRTY-THREE

SUSAN KEPT HER CELLPHONE PRESSED TO HER EAR AS SHE stepped off to the side and allowed a couple to pass. "You don't sound surprised."

"Trust me," Samantha said through the phone, "if what you're saying is true, I'm surprised."

As soon as Susan got off the phone with Cindy, she got in the back seat of an Uber, unable to take her mind off Naomi's friend Jenny. Once at the restaurant downtown, she called Samantha. Now Susan was wondering what more Samantha knew and if there was anything else that could help calm Cindy's worries.

Samantha asked, "How did you learn about this?"

"Cindy Moss called saying the police were looking to speak with Naomi." Susan paused. "I don't know too much other than that, and neither does Cindy. You haven't heard anything, have you?"

"Not about Jenny Booth. But I had a package arrive this morning from King." Samantha briefed Susan on Eva and how she might be a lead into Megan's disappearance. "I'm still working out the details but I don't like what I'm hearing."

"No. Neither do I." Susan mentioned how she planned to meet with Naomi after school and said, "I'll call you later once I get a better idea of what's happening here."

"Perfect," Samantha said. "And I'll contact King to see what he knows."

Susan told Samantha she loved her before ending the call and tucked her phone away inside her purse, entering the restaurant with a heavy heart. One girl missing was difficult enough, but three? Something was happening and Susan was thankful it wasn't Naomi missing.

The hostess led her to a back table perched against a window with a view where Owen Daniels was already seated. He stood and smoothed down his Caribbean blue tie as Susan approached. The color of his tie brought a smile to her face, and he greeted her with a gentle kiss to the cheek.

Susan smiled, surprised by his warm greeting. She wanted nothing more than to be seen by the handsome man who promised her access to his incredible network of people and happily welcomed his charm.

"I hope you don't mind, but I have a bottle of Merlot on its way," Daniels said as he pushed in Susan's chair.

"That sounds lovely," Susan murmured, concentrating on what was in front of her, trying to push her distractions aside.

When Daniels sat, he locked eyes with her and made her feel like she was the only person who existed. Soon, wine was poured and lunch was served. They discussed business—how great it would be for her career to say she worked with Owen Daniels—but mostly they had fun laughing at each other's stories. And when their conversation eventually died down, Daniels could see something was on Susan's mind.

"I'm sorry, did I say something wrong?" he asked.

Susan brushed her bangs out of her eyes with the tip of her finger and said, "No. Of course not." Susan paused before elaborating. "I received a call from a friend before I arrived and she said her daughter's friend is missing."

"Jesus." Daniels asked about the details, and Susan knew he had the power to bring the story to air. After telling him everything she knew about Jenny, he asked, "Why haven't I heard about this?"

"I don't know." Susan fingered her wine glass. "Maybe because the police are still investigating."

Daniels reached his hand inside his jacket pocket, stood, and pulled out his phone.

"What are you doing?"

Daniels tapped the screen and pressed the phone to his ear. "Putting my best people on this story. If there really is another girl missing, I'd like to be the first to report it."

CHAPTER THIRTY-FOUR

THIRSTY WALKED AWAY FROM THE BAR WITH A SMILE ON HIS face. It was the pretty barmaid who put it there it. She was the one, the young beauty he'd been following, the one he planned to bring into his inner circle when the time was right.

When he was with her, the conversation was easy, the laughs deep. She made him feel worthy of companionship and that meant the world to a manic depressant like himself.

Thirsty edged the partition and passed in front of the flaming grill and the chef working behind the glass. The scent of steak curled the corners of his lips upward as a deep sense of satisfaction bloomed inside of him.

After last night's charades, he'd fallen into a deep, drunken sleep and had nearly forgotten about Eva's escape. According to the news she still hadn't been located, and he was determined not to let the unknown bother him. Instead, he kept his focus on what he could control. Like the barmaid and her sparkling eyes.

Swerving his way through the lunch tables, he was feeling light on his feet when he caught the eye of a tall woman enjoying the companionship of a man. Her hair was beautifully woven into a single braid. He smiled and said under his breath, "If only you were twenty years younger."

He'd started today feeling particularly good about himself. His best attire only improved his mood, and something told him that today would be his day.

He stopped at the hallway leading to the restrooms and turned to see if his bright-eyed young barmaid was watching him. He could feel her eyes on his back, telling him he had her hooked.

Testing his luck, he slowly turned his head. He lifted his eyes and held his breath, his hopeful brow raised above the partition only to be struck with disappointment. He'd lost her attention; she'd already moved on.

"Son of a bitch," he said, imagining how he'd like to wrap her long black hair around his wrist and twist her into submission.

With a jealous pang in his gut, he watched her work. She was smooth and charming as she served her guests. A minute passed before she finally glanced in his direction and caught his gaze. Thirsty immediately perked up when their eyes locked. He smiled and she smiled back.

"That's it, honey, I'm still thinking about you," he said as he turned his back and disappeared down the hall.

He knew her name was Isabel, but only because of her nametag. He liked her name but wanted to know more, starting with her last name. Without it, it would make learning where she lived that much harder. Though Isabel didn't know how much she meant to him, she'd soon find out. He'd make sure of it.

Almost to the men's room, Thirsty thumbed his cellphone's screen to open his image gallery and find the picture he'd taken of Isabel last night with her friends. It brought him great confidence to know he had this image of her and hoped it was the start of a collection.

Thirsty leaned into the men's room door with his shoulder and tucked the device away inside his coat pocket. Isabel hadn't put it together that it was him watching her and her friends last night, and he preferred to keep it that way.

He stepped up to the urinal and unzipped the front of his pants. Tipping his head back, he paused to read the newspaper headline prominently displayed on the wall in front of him.

Teen Goes Missing Without a Trace

Thirsty glanced to the date. It was an old article about Megan Hines, and Thirsty found the temptation to stare into Megan's lively eyes too great to pass up. She was a sexy young woman with a beautifully round face with high cheekbones and piercing brown eyes.

As he shook the last of his urine out of his system, Thirsty looked to his crotch and thought about his Play Pen. He wanted Isabel to join in on the fun.

"Can you believe it? No one is even talking about her anymore," a stranger said in the urinal next to Thirsty. "Like they just completely forgot about her."

"Maybe they found her," Thirsty suggested without looking.

"Nah. It's been too long. No one is ever going to find her."

Thirsty stole one last glance at Megan's picture before turning to the sink. Maybe the man was right, perhaps Megan would never be found. He turned on the faucet and washed his hands, mulling over the thought.

Thirsty stared at the stranger's back. He was still reading the article, and Thirsty wondered what he was thinking. It wasn't much fun when no one seemed to care about what happened to Megan.

Tipping forward on his toes, Thirsty angled his head sideways and raked the tips of his fingers over his face. He'd since shaved off his goatee, confident no mark from Eva had been left. He attributed his strong jawline to his father's good genes. He let a single thought in that Eva would always be the one that got away.

Soon the stranger joined him at the sink. He said, "You come here often?"

Thirsty stared at his own reflection, thinking how he should have worn more jewelry to better hold Isabel's attention. Then he flicked his gaze toward the stranger. "I'm sorry?"

"I get it." The stranger cast his gaze to Thirsty's ring finger. His wedding band was missing, but there was a bold white line giving away his secret. "I come here to escape my wife, too. Especially when that sweetheart Isabel is tending bar."

Thirsty locked eyes and the stranger winked. He didn't like jockeying for position, but apparently Isabel had caught more than one man's eye. He should have assumed. The best ones were always being chased.

"I'll see you out there, cowboy."

The stranger slapped Thirsty's arm and Thirsty watched the stranger exit the room. He turned his gaze back on himself and cracked the tension in his neck—light exploding behind his eyes—before leaving himself.

Making his way back to the bar, he thought about what the stranger said—how they were both here because of Isabel. He'd picked lunch over dinner because it was easy enough to blend in, but not chaotic enough to not be able to steal her attention. Now he wondered if he'd missed his chance. He wasn't expecting competition at this hour of the day, but he'd certainly found it.

Scents of lobster and grilled meat drifted into his head as he meandered through the restaurant, devising his Plan B.

At each table he passed, he kept score of the women he locked eyes with. He judged them on different categories, from dress to make-up, natural beauty, hair, and neckline. Most were much too old for his preferences, but he still liked to play his game.

He kept walking, and once Isabel was within sight, he shortened his gait and felt the cords in his neck tense. Just as he suspected, the stranger from the men's room was holding her hand. Thirsty watched her toss her head back and laugh. He bit down harder.

"Hey, partner," the stranger said to Thirsty. "Come join us. Your next drink is on me."

A man bumped into Thirsty from behind and knocked him off balance. Gritting his teeth, he snapped his neck to see who it was. The man wearing a Caribbean blue tie didn't stop to apologize and Thirsty couldn't believe what he heard the man saying.

"I'm telling you, get on this story." The man wearing a three-piece suit kept walking and talking. "Her name is Jenny Booth, but who you're really going to want to talk to is a woman who escaped her kidnapper's grip. Her name is Eva Martin, and that's the breaking story we want."

CHAPTER THIRTY-FIVE

NAOMI SIGHED. SHE COULDN'T CONCENTRATE ON HER calculus test. It wasn't only Jenny on her mind, but Dylan too. She thought about how her sister was getting bullied and now regretted sending Dylan the photo of herself. Neither of Dylan nor Jenny had messaged back, and self-doubt took root at the base of her curling spine.

Naomi got through first and second periods just fine, but it all started unraveling at lunch. She was missing her best friend and there were the undeniable whispers she heard building behind her back. Naomi didn't know what was being said, but she assumed it was about Jenny. Now Naomi was beginning to think she had done something wrong.

Why did it seem like everyone was blaming her? What if something really bad did happen to Jenny? How would she ever forgive herself? She wouldn't be able to.

Naomi opened her eyes and let her vision focus on her exam. She looked at the equation, but her head only spun. It was too complicated and she was too distracted. Then came a text from her friend, Charlene, who went by the nickname, Charlie, that said, *Dylan got your pic.*

Naomi's heart stopped.

A bloom of heat spread across her chest.

She looked to the front of the class from beneath her brow and saw the substitute teacher with her head down, reading her book. The moment Naomi closed her eyes she was back in the grimy bathroom staring at her topless self, standing in front of a smudged mirror that needed to be cleaned. Snickering behind her had her opening her eyes.

Naomi turned to find the same two boys harassing her. Having had enough, she sprang out of her seat and snapped. "What the fuck is so funny?"

The taller of the two boys leaned forward and asked, "When you get bored...do you ever just play with them?" He lowered his gaze to Naomi's chest.

"Excuse me?" Naomi scowled.

"You heard what I said."

"Hey!" the substitute teacher barked from the front of the classroom. "I warned you two before. The next time you talk, I'll be taking both your tests away and telling Mr. Helton you were cheating."

Naomi turned around, faced the front, and glared at the substitute teacher. Slumping in her seat, she folded her arms across her chest. She hated her boobs for being so big. Ever since middle school they'd been the source of unwanted attention, and now she was afraid that her little sister might also be going through the same thing.

Beneath the desk, Naomi messaged Charlie back. *Did he tell you that?*

A couple seconds later Charlie responded, *I can't believe you actually did it. Dylan can't stop talking about it.*

Naomi sank down further and wanted nothing more than to disappear. Her insides were in knots and she wished Jenny was here to tell her she did the right thing by sending Dylan the picture.

The room settled into silence and Naomi shifted her eyes to the empty seat next to her. If she tried really hard, she could see Jenny sitting there playing on her phone like she normally did when the numbers got hard.

Then she messaged Jenny, knowing she wouldn't respond.

I miss you.

After sending the text, she glanced to the clock. There was one hour left in the day before she could go home, slip into her PJs and curl up in bed. The thought of hiding was comforting, but the finger she felt sliding down the back of her pants wasn't.

"Are you out of your fucking mind?" Naomi jumped out of her seat and stared at the two boys who were laughing.

"What?" the taller boy said. "I know you like it."

"You," the substitute teacher pointed at Naomi, "come sit up here, and bring your things with you."

Happy to escape the boys' harassment, Naomi grabbed her bag off the back of her chair and scooped the test papers into her arms. With her head held high, she marched to the front of the class and slammed her unfinished test on the teacher's desk. "You can tell Mr. Helton I quit."

"Naomi, what's going on?" Mr. Helton said, entering the classroom.

Naomi spun around, her eyes meeting Mr. Helton's gaze and making her throat close up. She felt like crying, but wouldn't dare do it in front of the entire class who was watching.

Mr. Helton looked to the substitute teacher for clarification, and when nothing was said, he turned to look at the class. Their faces said everything he needed to know. He hurried to Naomi and whispered in her ear, "You can finish your test in my office and we can talk about what happened after class."

Naomi didn't protest. She wanted nothing more than to

hide herself away. Once inside Mr. Helton's office, she shut the door and began to cry. She was losing control of everything and didn't know how to make it stop. Then Charlie sent her a message that turned her inside out—*The police are in the principal's office looking for you. What the hell happened?*

CHAPTER THIRTY-SIX

NAOMI FELT NUMB AS SHE WIGGLED THE TINGLING OUT OF the tips of her fingers. If Charlie was right, Naomi knew the police were here to talk to her about Jenny. *Was she dead? Did they find her? What would she say if they asked why she didn't call to report her missing?* Her head swelled and an aching throb moved behind both her eyes.

Naomi didn't want to leave Mr. Helton's office. She felt safe here—felt like if she stayed hidden, her problems would just pass without ever having to confront them. She hadn't picked up her pencil since she sat down to finish her test. She didn't care. It didn't matter. Not with Jenny gone and the cops apparently wanting to speak with her.

Naomi's entire body was weighted down by grief. Feeling annoyed, she stared at the pictures of her math teacher on the wall, imagining her own getaway.

Mr. Helton was an active adventurer, traveling across the world scuba-diving, hiking, snowboarding, and playing sport. It was easy to get lost inside his travels, and Naomi welcomed the distraction. But there was something she couldn't escape. Mr. Helton was one of the last people who spoke to Jenny before she just disappeared, and Naomi wasn't even sure she could tell him why Jenny never showed up to school today. If he discovered she left Jenny behind, he'd hate her.

The final bell of the day rang and Naomi didn't budge. A minute later, the office door opened and Mr. Helton stepped inside. Naomi watched him clear a spot on the desk before he sat on its edge. She tried not to look into his eyes, but when she did, the flood gates released and the tears came.

Mr. Helton glanced at Naomi's closed test book, then flicked his gaze back to her. "Want to tell me what's going on?"

Naomi dabbed her eyes and exhaled a shaky breath. She liked Mr. Helton and knew she could trust him with her secret, but she still hesitated. He was always her and Jenny's favorite. She wanted to tell him about Jenny, but knew he would be devastated by the news. Instead, she said, "It's those boys. The entire class was harassing me."

"Do you know why, Naomi?"

Naomi lowered her gaze to the tips of her shoes. "I don't know."

Mr. Helton unfolded his arms and lifted a cellphone. "I took it from Tommy. You want to know what I found on it?" When Naomi didn't respond, he said, "It's a picture of you."

Naomi's head hung with embarrassment. Suspecting she knew which picture Helton was referring to, she wondered if this was Dylan's plan all along. Now she knew how Charlie had found out about her topless photo. Dylan was spreading it to the entire school.

"You're better than this Naomi," Mr. Helton said.

"It wasn't meant to be shared."

Mr. Helton said, "But it was."

"What can I do?"

Helton was quiet for a long pause. Then he said, "Nothing. I'm afraid it's too late."

CHAPTER THIRTY-SEVEN

EVA LEANED FORWARD IN THE BACKSEAT OF MY CAR AND said, "Park there."

I checked my mirrors and turned the wheel, pointing the hood to where Eva directed me.

After my call with Susan and learning about Jenny Booth's supposed disappearance, I felt as anxious as Eva. Though I hadn't told her about Jenny, she couldn't settle after Archie's visit.

I curbed the vehicle, turned off the engine, and once again checked my mirrors. Erin did the same. It was important we remained vigilant. We couldn't afford to take any chances. It was already after two o'clock and our day was quickly slipping away. There was a lot we still didn't know—even more we had to piece together. I needed to figure out who last night's Jane Doe was.

Eva was quiet, constantly looking over her shoulder, bouncing her knee, and her paranoia was rubbing off on me. As far as I knew, we still had the exclusive on Eva's story, and we wanted to keep it that way to ensure her safety.

Erin twisted around and asked Eva, "Which is your building?"

Eva couldn't keep her hands out of her hair. "That one there."

We swept our gaze to the building across the street. It was an eleven-story luxurious apartment building not far from the DU campus. I watched as a young male dressed in preppy clothes exited the building and turned up the block with his shoulder sling bag.

Erin responded, "You live *there?*"

When I flicked my gaze to the rearview mirror, I caught Eva staring at the young male I had noticed. I wondered if she knew him, and if her kidnapper really would have the tenacity to stake out and wait for her to return. I wanted her to feel safe, but without knowing who took her, it was impossible to know who to look out for. At this point, it was safest to treat every unknown male as a possible suspect.

Eva said, "My apartment is on the seventh floor."

I swept my gaze to the top of the building. I wondered if rent was as expensive as it looked and, if so, how did Eva afford to live here? How did any college kid afford to live here?

Twisting around in my seat, I said, "Okay. Once we're inside, only grab the essentials. We shouldn't stay long." Eva's face was blank, and I wondered if she'd heard what I said. "Eva, did you—"

"No."

"No?"

"I can't go inside." Our eyes met. "What if he's there?"

"That's why we'll go together."

Erin extended her arm and touched my knee. "I'll stay in the car with her."

I turned my head and allowed my eyes to hash out the details with Erin. I gave it further thought and soon understood. It was better for me to go alone. Not because it was safer, because it certainly wasn't, but doing it alone allowed me to see how Eva lived without worrying about her peeking over my shoulder.

"Fine," I said. "Tell me what you need."

A minute later, I had written down the list of items Eva requested, including her antidepressant medication she'd been without for three days. Then I exited the vehicle with the knowledge of where to find her keycard and trotted across the street, excited to peek around for possible clues that could tell me why Eva may have been abducted.

CHAPTER THIRTY-EIGHT

I WORKED MY WAY INTO THE BUILDING WITH EVA'S kidnapper on my mind.

There wasn't a bellhop or doorman, but it was clear this place wasn't cheap. Heading to the elevators, I walked beneath a crystal chandelier and smiled at the people I passed. There was a man in his thirties with slicked back hair and a woman perched on high heels, her wrists and neck glittering with gold and diamond jewelry.

I knew there was money in Colorado, but I was surprised to have found it here.

At the elevator, I punched the button and glanced back to the entrance. A black Land Rover was parked near the front and I watched the young blonde I just passed climb inside.

The elevator doors chimed behind me and I watched the vehicle take off.

Turning my attention to the cart, I was thankful to find it empty. I didn't want to be seen—only wanted to get in and out as quickly as possible. I hit the button to the seventh floor and waited for the doors to close. A quick ride up and walk down an empty hall brought me to Eva's one-bedroom upscale apartment, asking myself how I ended up here.

I paused to take it all in. It was a clean, well-lit apartment with large windows housing an impressive view of downtown. Eva thought she was taken Sunday night, which meant she hadn't been here for three days. Nothing seemed out of place.

Confident I was safe, I moved further inside, making note of her furniture, how she decorated, and the expensive course books left open on the coffee table in front of a flat-screen TV on the wall. Everywhere I looked was all girl. There were no signs of a man influencing her life, no family life either, only pictures of herself.

I turned around and faced the kitchen, starting to imagine the lonely existence Eva lived. But what I still wanted to know was how she could afford to live here. I had my suspicion she wasn't telling us the complete story, but could I find that story hidden somewhere inside here? I believed I could.

With time ticking past, I kept moving.

I visually inspected her kitchen and found a pair of gold earrings on the counter next to an empty wine glass. Nothing told me why she might have been abducted other than that her life of solitude made her an easy target.

Down the hall, I entered the bathroom and turned on the overhead light. Again, there was expensive jewelry next to the sink and makeup spread out everywhere, but I saw nothing I wouldn't expect to find for a woman her age. No second toothbrush, no men's deodorant, nothing. *Why was Eva taken?*

I collected her toothbrush, grabbed her medication from the cabinet and a few other things she requested and, when my hands were full, I walked to the bedroom in search of a bag.

Tossing the items on the king-sized bed, I raked my fingers over the down comforter and lifted the corner to see the white linen beneath. It was soft and cozy and added to the warmth of home. Then I turned my attention to the closet and began picking through her clothes. Eva had a great sense of style, but I knew how much these things cost. The sheer number of shoes and boots alone must have reached into the thousands of dollars. *Where was Eva getting her money?*

Setting my judgement aside, I laid the clothes on the bed with the pile of toiletries and turned to the dresser. Sliding the top drawer open, I immediately stopped when I came face-to-face with a dildo. Next to it were several sets of sexy lingerie, and suddenly I thought I might have found something of interest. Then I flicked my gaze to the desktop computer and saw the bigger picture I'd been waiting for. Was this what she was doing for work? It certainly seemed so.

Closing the drawer, I moved to her desk. On it was a webcam and next to it expensive lighting—both pointing straight to the bed. It was an oversight that I hadn't already noticed them, and maybe if it weren't for the chaffing on her wrists and ankles, I wouldn't have thought anything of it.

I sat on the edge of her bed, stared at the webcam, and let my thoughts soak up what it was I was seeing. Could Eva really be selling sex through the internet? Anything was possible and looks could be deceiving.

I turned my head to the window and thought how her case was quite different from Megan Hines's. There was a clear age gap between the two women, and everything I currently knew suggested they weren't even related. But where did Jane Doe fit inside this puzzle? Could she be one of the missing persons? That was next on my list of things to do, but the one commonality they all shared was that they were very attractive women.

Needing something to put Eva's stuff in, I turned to the closet and located a canvas tote. I was preparing to leave when I turned my attention back to Eva's computer, nearly forgetting her cellphone. Unable to resist the urge, I wiggled the mouse and was surprised to see the monitor come to life —even more surprised to see it wasn't password protected.

I set the tote at my feet and dropped my bottom into the chair. Clicking around the screen, an instant message popped up in the corner of the screen. I leaned forward and read it. I suddenly wondered if Eva was abducted at all.

CHAPTER THIRTY-NINE

WITH THE TOTE BAG SLUNG OVER MY LEFT SHOULDER, I locked up and walked to the elevator with my thoughts spinning. I couldn't stop thinking about what I'd just read—what this man said to Eva and what Eva wrote back. It wasn't only the language they used that had me blushing, but the description of what she wanted him to do to her.

The elevator was waiting when I arrived. I stepped inside and asked myself if I could be wrong about Eva. Did she know what she was doing? There were so many questions I needed to ask and, in a way, I felt like we'd been duped. But I also didn't want to assume anything yet and make Eva out to be at fault for something I knew little about.

The elevator slowed to a stop on the fourth floor, and the same tall man from the lobby stepped inside. His gaze fell to Eva's bag and I wondered if he recognized it. Showing no interest in me, he turned around and faced the front. I studied his dress and the scent of his cologne. His shoulders were broad and his thighs the size of tree trunks. Did Eva belong here, or was she trying to be someone else? As I thought more about what I read on her computer, it was impossible to not envision a powerful, overly paid CEO on the other side of the message.

Once on the lobby floor, I followed the man to the exit. He turned left and I turned right. The sun glared, and I lifted my hand to my brow to shield my eyes.

Erin and Eva were still waiting in the car, and I headed toward them. A vehicle cut me off as I stepped off the curb, and the passenger stared. I suddenly felt like I was being watched. I looked around and concluded my mind was playing tricks on me.

I trotted across the street, dodging vehicles, thinking how being at Eva's place had left me feeling unusually paranoid. I couldn't explain why that was other than it being a result of past experience telling me I was entering somewhere I didn't belong.

As soon as I was back inside the car, Eva asked for her medication. I gave her the bag and Erin asked if everything was fine.

"It hadn't been broken into, if that's what you're wondering."

While I was away, Erin had switched to the driver's seat. She cranked over the engine and put the car in gear, merging into traffic. I made sure she knew where we were going—the morgue. She confirmed that and I turned to Eva and asked, "Who is Lewis Stark?"

Eva's head snapped up. A look of guilt flashed over her eyes. It was clear she knew what I had discovered.

I said, "I saw everything, Eva."

She turned her face toward the window and swiped a hand over her face.

"Is he the reason you can afford to live in a place like that? Maybe even pay your tuition?"

Erin kept stealing curious glances in my direction, wondering what I had discovered.

"It's not what you're thinking," Eva said.

"What am I thinking?" My tone was much harsher than I intended, but there wasn't time to beat around the bush with Megan still missing and Jenny now on that list. I needed to know everything, and needed to know it fast.

Eva said in a meek voice, "That I'm whoring myself out."

I shared a knowing look with Erin. Erin's eyes rounded and she kept both hands on the wheel as she drove. Eva was right, I did think she was whoring herself out. But it wasn't a baseless assumption. The instant message I saw was evidence to back my claim.

I asked, "Did you meet him online?"

"It's called sugaring." Eva was playing with her cuticles as she explained how her goal was to leave school debt-free. "Men pay me a monthly allowance for my company." She lifted her eyes and gave me a coy look. "I hang off their arms during dates and laugh at their stupid jokes. That's it."

"And sex isn't implied?" I thought back to the webcam and lighting.

"Of course it is."

My shoulders slumped. I barely knew this girl, but I was disappointed with everything she was telling me. How could she? There was a better way to get herself through school, didn't she know that?

Eva continued, "But, like in any relationship, it isn't guaranteed."

We listened without judgement as Eva listed off her reasons for going down this path. I watched her and suddenly understood her motivation. The work—if that's even what it could be called—required the least amount of her time for the highest possible earnings. But what surprised both of us was when Eva said she had fun with it.

"At first I thought I would only be dating creeps," she said, "but instead, I was matched with genuine guys. Guys I liked. And they really cared about me, treated me with respect, and became my friends."

Erin said, "And you failed to mention this to anybody because..."

"Because it's no one's business what I do."

My eyebrows pinched. "Or is it, because its borderline prostitution."

Eva shot me a look. I'd taken it too far—jumped the line of trust I'd worked all day to achieve. Eva pursed her lips and looked away. It wasn't my place to have an opinion. Thankfully, Erin reeled her back in before we lost her completely.

Erin asked, "How many men were you dating?"

Speaking to the window, Eva said, "Two."

"Maybe one of them learned about the other and got jealous?" I said, needing to find a reason she was abducted—some common thread between these other missing girls.

Eva insisted this wasn't the case, but didn't have the evidence to prove it. In her eyes, there was no way either of the men she was dating could have kidnapped her. "I would have known if it was them," Eva said.

"Maybe it wasn't them, but someone they know? Someone they put up to it?" I said. "Because, the way I see it, this gives motive to someone to want you all to themselves."

Erin asked, "Eva, did you deny either of the men any of their requests?"

"If what you're asking is if I ever told them no, then the answer would be yes."

I took a deep breath before asking, "Did you have sex with either of these men?"

Eva's eyelids hooded as she bowed her head and nodded yes.

"Was it Lewis Stark?"

Eva released a shaky breath and said, "Yes. I had sex with Lewis."

CHAPTER FORTY

The medical examiner's office was only a short drive north from Eva's apartment in University. As soon as Erin parked, I requested to speak to her outside—alone.

Eva had gone silent since revealing she'd had an intimate relationship with her client, Lewis Stark. I was afraid of pushing her away, losing her trust, but hoped that giving her some space would allow for her to seriously think about what was at stake and how she could help us catch who might have abducted her—if she really was kidnapped.

With our feet on the ground, we stepped away from the car with Erin whispering, "Well that changes things."

"We have to question him," I said, telling Erin in greater detail about what I saw inside Eva's apartment—including the webcam and lighting.

"Wow. It's worse than I thought."

"Only if I'm right," I reminded her. "I don't want to discredit her story, but if Stark took things too far even with her consent and she later regretted it...well, where's the line? Is she still a victim? If she froze out of fear, is that consent?"

"I'd like to talk with the man she didn't sleep with before

spending our energy going after Stark." Erin pushed her fingers through her hair and we both understood how powerful jealousy could be.

"I'm with you there," I said. "But there is something else. That phone call I took earlier," Erin nodded and indicated she knew what I was referring to, "it was Susan. Her goddaughter's friend was reported missing this morning by her mother."

"How old?"

"Seventeen."

"Name?"

I told her Jenny's name and said I was still waiting to hear back from King. I'd sent him a text as soon as I could, hoping to learn more, but wondered if he'd heard about it himself. Instinctively, I turned my palm and checked my phone. Still, nothing.

"That makes a hat trick," Erin said.

I shook my head no. "I don't think Eva's case is related. Maybe Megan's, but not Eva's."

"Because you think she might have faked her own abduction?"

"That, and because it's nothing like what we know about Megan."

"I can't live with three, Sam. We need to get this story out. It might stop whoever is doing this—at least temporarily. Maybe even give us a chance to catch up and have the police capture this person."

"Or it could put these missing girls in further danger if they're not dead already."

Erin turned to the nondescript redbrick building and I watched her gaze crawl up the windowless walls. "I don't know, Sam, maybe we're wasting our time by being here."

"It has to happen now," I said, looking to the medical examiner's office. "Jane Doe is connected to one of these girls. I don't know how, but she has to be." As soon as I said it, I wondered if Jane Doe was sugaring like Eva.

"All right. Anything I should do while I wait?"

"Keep an eye on Eva," I said. "I shouldn't be long."

Erin locked eyes with me and I turned to the entrance. The police were working faster than usual on these crime scenes, and I needed something more than Eva to point us to the whereabouts of Megan Hines.

I moved up the ramp and entered the building through the green heavy metal doors. The halls were empty and as bright as a hospital corridor. I worked my way as deep as I could before getting stopped by security working the desk.

"I'm here to speak with Chief Medical Examiner, Leslie Griffin," I said.

The woman in uniform picked up a phone from the desk and made the call. Eleven minutes passed before I saw Griffin heading my way. She greeted me by name, and said, "Long time no see, Samantha. I assume you're here because of the missing girl you've been writing about?"

We'd known each other for nearly a decade working the crime beat and had a mutual respect for each other's work. I appreciated her cut-to-the-chase style. It always made things easier when needing to get to the bottom of a case.

"That's why I'm here," I said, stepping out of ear shot from security. "Last night there was a body found in Park Hill. I need to know if it was her."

"If it was, you would have been one of the first to know."

Disappointed, I turned my head and swiped a hand over my hair. Then I asked, "So you retrieved nothing last night from Park Hill?"

"Honey," Griffin tilted her head to the side, "I'm going to need more information to go on than that."

I gave her the best description I had of Jane Doe based on

what Allison told me. Leslie shook her head no and I asked, "How many Jane Does did you get last night?"

Griffin's eyes widened and told me how they had been overrun by the opioid epidemic. Then she followed up with a frown, saying, "Sorry, Sam. There's no record a person by that description ever made it to the morgue."

CHAPTER FORTY-ONE

NAOMI PREPARED TO LEAVE MR. HELTON'S OFFICE BUT WAS stopped by the sight of Principal Wair entering the classroom. Two men wearing suits, badges clipped to their belts, followed close behind and Naomi knew these were the cops Charlie had warned her about.

Principal Wair said, "Naomi, could I speak with you?"

Mr. Helton stepped in front of Naomi and asked, "May I ask what this is about?"

Without taking his eyes off Naomi, Wair said, "It's a private matter."

Naomi hid behind her teacher with her gaze cast to the floor, her heart hammering in her chest. One of the cops introduced himself to Mr. Helton as Detective King. "We'd really like to speak with Naomi alone."

A rush of activity passed through the halls. The noises quieted down and Mr. Helton swiveled to face Naomi. She silently pleaded with him to say no, but she could see he had no choice in the matter.

"You can use my office," Mr. Helton said to the detectives, and Naomi's heart sank.

Detective King stepped forward and motioned for Naomi to take a seat inside. Naomi fell back into the chair and watched Mr. Helton leave the classroom with Principal Wair. The other cop introduced herself to Naomi, speaking in a soft, nonthreatening voice that had Naomi scared to know what she was about to tell her. To Detective King's imposing appearance, Detective Gray was warm and welcoming. Naomi wanted to tell her everything.

"Can you keep the door open?" Naomi asked King.

King paused, thinking about it before latching it shut. "It's best we keep this conversation private."

Naomi swallowed and sheepishly cowered when she thought about the photo Mr. Helton just showed her. She was embarrassed she'd let Jenny talk her into taking it and knew the fallout was yet to hit.

"What's this about?" she asked. "Did I do something wrong?"

"We're here because your friend Jenny Booth is missing." An uncomfortable silence followed. "Do you know where she is?"

Naomi's chest squeezed. Her eyes were glued to her fidgeting fingers and she was nervous to say anything that might get Jenny in trouble.

Gray leaned forward in her seat and rested her elbows on her knees. Looking Naomi in the eye, she said, "We've already spoken to her mother. It's okay. You're not in any trouble. We just want to bring Jenny home. Don't you?"

Naomi nodded.

"What do you know?" King asked.

Naomi flicked her gaze up to him. "There's not much to tell."

King was leaning his shoulder against the wall. He folded his arms and said, "You parted ways after volleyball practice, correct?"

She suddenly regretted lying to Ruth Booth. Naomi had seen Jenny after practice. She knew she had to do right by her friend and come clean. "We went out last night."

Naomi watched the cops exchange a glance. They didn't believe her. And with good reason—her story had changed.

Gray asked, "What were you two doing?"

When Naomi blinked her eyes, she saw Mr. Helton standing at the counter of Burger King. She mentioned volleyball practice with Coach Bennett, and how they went to Burger King for fries and a milkshake after.

"After practice," King stressed. Naomi nodded. "Just you and Jenny?"

"Yes."

"You didn't meet anybody else?"

"No," Naomi said. Then she told them that Jenny just disappeared from the gas station.

"And you didn't think to tell her mother?"

Naomi shrugged. "I thought she'd told me her plans, but I just forgot. She was texting all night with some guy and I thought maybe he picked her up while I was in the bathroom."

"Has she done that before?"

"You never know with Jenny."

Gray turned and gave King a look. King asked, "And that was the last time you saw her?"

"Yes. I've been messaging her ever since."

"And she hasn't responded?"

Naomi cast her gaze to the floor and shook her head no.

"Has Jenny ghosted you before?"

"No. Never. That's why I'm worried something bad has happened."

King asked, "You follow the news, Naomi?"

"No."

"A girl Jenny's age is also missing. Megan Hines. She's also a student at this school."

"I've heard." Naomi's brow furrowed. "Do you think the same thing happened to Jenny?"

"We don't know yet," Gray said. "But the longer a person is missing, the less likely we are to find them alive."

Suddenly Naomi felt ill.

"This guy she was texting with," King pushed off the wall, "do you know his name?"

Naomi felt like Jenny had backed her into a corner. She had no choice but to say, "Jenny never told me his name, but he was older than us and I thought it was only supposed to be a onetime thing."

"Was it?"

Naomi shook her head no, and whispered, "I think she was planning to sleep with him again."

CHAPTER FORTY-TWO

Leslie Griffin left me with more questions than I'd come with. I watched her step through the doors into a private wing of the office and disappear out of sight. My stomach was tight and I asked myself what the hell just happened?

I reached behind my back and retrieved my cellphone from my back pocket. I called Dawson, my editor at the *Times*. Pressing the phone to my ear, I walked down the hallway corridor and found myself a private corner where I could talk without concern of anyone overhearing.

The line rang and my foot tapped lightly against the floor, nervous to learn I may have been right about the mayor. How could a body just disappear? I'd never heard of it happening before. Especially not under Griffin's watch.

When Dawson didn't answer, I killed the call and thought through my next move.

As I stood there debating my options, Archie Smith's theory of an active serial rapist-killer came to mind. Was it possible he knew more about this than I did? And what if we were right; what if the mayor and chief of police were hiding last night's Jane Doe? I only knew what Allison saw and the little of what King told me. As little information as there was, something wasn't adding up. The body from Park Hill should have been here.

"Can I help you find the exit?"

I spun around and found the security woman from the desk giving me an arched look. My mind was churning. I had no evidence to back up any of my wild claims, but I didn't want to leave until I knew what happened to Jane Doe.

"Just making a phone call," I said, pointing to my cell.

Her big round eyes fell to my phone. She continued on her way without another word and I continued piecing together the story unfolding inside my head.

Eva was all I had, and even dealing with her was like walking on eggshells. What if Jane Doe was an escort like Eva? Was that even possible? Could that be why her body seemed to vanish without a trace? I needed to know more about the crime scene, and that meant talking with King. But if I was right about a coverup, then that meant someone with power wanted to make sure their secret remained hidden.

I dialed Dawson again and continued walking.

Maybe if I had let Erin do the talking, she would have gotten a different response from Griffin. Erin didn't have the same target on her back as I did. But would Griffin lie to me? I didn't think so. Something kept popping into my head though, making me question everyone.

I recalled what the mayor's spokesman recently said to me —*Stay in your lane, Mrs. Bell. Death is closer than you think*. I still didn't know what was meant by it. Was it a threat or a hint at something much deeper he wanted me to investigate?

Finally, the line clicked over. Without a greeting, I said, "There is no body. According to the ME, Jane Doe doesn't exist."

"Calm down, Sam," Dawson said. "Is it possible this woman was sent to a different morgue?"

"What other morgue?"

"Arvada, Aurora, Westminster, I don't know."

His comment was insulting. I told him my plate was full and didn't have time to search every morgue in the state. Then I caught him up with Eva, Jenny Booth's disappearance, and told him about my gut feel that Jane Doe could also be an escort.

"Christ, Sam. You weren't kidding."

"Can you help me here?"

"I'll work my sources and see if I can track down your Jane Doe. In the meantime, work Eva's story. It would be nice to have the exclusive on both these stories."

"Thanks, Dawson."

I stiff-armed my way through the exit, needing to know more about these men Eva was dating, what was promised, and what was exchanged. We were going to need all hands on deck if we were going to break through the barriers on this one. Just when I thought about recruiting Archie to help, I saw him arguing with Erin at my car.

CHAPTER FORTY-THREE

I JUMPED OFF THE RAMP AND HIT THE GROUND RUNNING. Erin's face was bright red from yelling, and I knew something bad had happened while I was gone. I looked for Eva as I sprinted to my car, but didn't see her anywhere.

Archie saw me barreling straight toward him and stepped back just before I plowed him over. Stomping on my brakes, I asked what happened.

Erin jabbed her finger in Archie's face. "He took a photo of Eva and won't delete it."

I glanced into the backseat of my car. Eva had her head down, her face buried inside her hands. She didn't seem to notice I was back, or perhaps she was too afraid to look, to reveal the fear and shame glittering in her eyes.

I jumped in front of Archie and blocked his view of her. Our eyes locked and he smirked. Did he think this was some kind of game? It certainly seemed so as I watched the amusement bounce around inside his eyes. It didn't make sense. I thought he would have already gotten his picture of Eva when he followed King to my house, but apparently he hadn't.

Why? Or was this just an excuse to intimidate her into keeping quiet?

"I just needed to know who she was," Archie said, showing me his hands.

"Erase that photo," I demanded.

Archie took a step back. "I can't."

"Why the hell not?" I asked.

"If she's a survivor of the serial rapist-killer the police are trying to cover up, we can expose them for their lies." His eyes crinkled at the corners. "Don't you see, Samantha? We almost have them right where we want them."

Erin waited for me to respond. I hated to even think it, but after what I just learned from Griffin, I knew Archie might be right. Then, in a moment of panic, I thought maybe Archie had followed us to Eva's and now knew where she lived. But then he said, "Last night's Jane Doe never arrived. Isn't that what you just learned yourself?"

Erin asked, "What's he talking about, Sam?"

Archie said, "We came here with the same question. What happened to Jane Doe? No one knows...well, except maybe her." He pointed toward Eva.

I stared at Archie and thought about everything Eva had just shared, what she has been through. Though I was worried what Archie might do with the photo, I wasn't willing to give him the chance he thought he deserved.

Flattening my palms against Archie's chest, I pushed him away from my car. "You crossed a line by taking that picture." Archie stumbled back the harder I pushed. "This isn't how you get your story."

"What will I have to do to convince you that there's a serial rapist-killer working Denver?" Archie asked with his hands in the air.

"You can start by producing a body," I said, opening my car door.

Archie's smile widened as he backpedaled away. "Careful what you wish for, Mrs. Bell. You might just get what you want."

CHAPTER FORTY-FOUR

I STOOD WITH THE CAR DOOR OPEN, MY HEART POUNDING in my chest as we watched Archie leave. I wanted to believe his reason for being here, wanted to trust that it was only coincidence and he wasn't following us with hopes of getting closer to Eva. Either scenario was possible. Until I explained what happened inside with Griffin, I knew Erin wouldn't see it that way.

"What the hell was that about?" Erin asked over the roof of my car.

Archie's car disappeared into traffic and I said, "Get in, I'll explain."

We buckled in and I started the car. Eva was now sitting upright, lips tight as she retreated into herself. I could see her worried look intensifying the longer we stayed out in the open. We needed to get her to Erin's quick.

I backed out and turned the wheels west. Several minutes passed before Erin turned to me and said, "He's following us, Sam."

We were close to Erin's, my eyes on the mirrors the entire

drive, certain Archie hadn't followed. Flicking my gaze to Erin, I said, "He's right, you know? We're after the same story."

"What are you saying? He didn't follow us?"

"I have my doubts."

I glanced in the rearview mirror and caught Eva's gaze. She looked away as soon as our eyes met. Archie knew where we all lived and would soon figure out who Eva was. King had left me with an impossible task. I didn't know how we could protect her, especially if her kidnapper was truly coming back for her like we worried. I never mentioned this to the group because I didn't want to frighten Eva any more than I knew she already was, but I was certain she'd pieced it together.

Instead, I said, "Griffin had no record of Jane Doe ever arriving."

The crease between Erin's eyebrows deepened. "How can that be?"

"I don't know," I said, turning into Erin's neighborhood.

"Let me get this straight. The ME's office has no record of last night's Jane Doe, and we still have two girls whose whereabouts are unknown—Megan and Jenny. Is that what I'm hearing from you?"

Erin hadn't noticed that we'd passed her house when I said, "That's right."

I circled the block, needing to make certain her house was safe to use. With everything looking as it should, and confident it was a safe refuge to hide in, I curbed the car out front.

Erin unbuckled her belt and said, "How can a body just vanish from the morgue?"

"I'm not sure it even made it to Griffin."

"And you think Archie will help you find her?" Erin gave me a skeptical look. "Because that's what I heard you tell him —*to find you a body.*" Erin turned and glanced to her house. She was shaking her head when she continued, "Forgive me if I'm confused, but why does it seem like you actually want to work with Archie after what he just did? Aren't you concerned for Eva's safety, and don't you remember the messages we've both been receiving? The ones that resemble PQK."

I lifted my gaze to the rearview mirror and found Eva staring. Her safety was my top priority, but I still had a responsibility to Megan. But was Archie right? Could Eva be the clue to prove there actually was a serial rapist-killer working the Denver area? With Jenny's disappearance, I was starting to believe he might be right. Eva's experience certainly suggested it. Was Archie the villain or the hero? I couldn't decide.

"What if we share the same goal?"

"What if we don't? He's writing a book, Sam." Erin sharpened her tone. "The only thing he has on his mind is getting himself a fat advance."

I mentioned how I recruited Dawson to also help find out what happened to Jane Doe. With Megan and Jenny also occupying my mind, I knew we couldn't write this story alone. Archie had the experience we needed to turn this investigation up a notch, but Erin was right in reminding me of his obsession with PQK.

Once things died down, Erin got out and conducted a quick sweep of her house just to be sure there weren't any surprises waiting for us inside. While she was away, Eva asked, "Who was that man and why is he so interested in me?"

"He's a reporter, just like me."

"I don't want my picture in the paper."

"I don't either."

"Then what is he planning to do with it?"

"I don't know," I said, pulling the mirror down to fit more

of her face in the frame. Then I asked, "Eva, is there any chance that was the man who took you?"

Eva opened and shut her mouth. I could see she was struggling to decide on an answer. Just as Erin gave us a thumbs up, Eva said, "Maybe."

CHAPTER FORTY-FIVE

As soon as I stepped inside Erin's house, I set my tote at my feet and texted King.

Where are you? Just stopped by the morgue. You won't believe what I was told. Call me.

Erin told Eva to sit on the couch. I was still asking myself if Archie was her kidnapper. Was it possible we were making her an easy target? I didn't want to believe it, but until we could prove otherwise, we had to remain vigilant. We were also targets, working a story we'd been thrown into without warning. Now it was up to us to save her.

"How long will I have to stay?" Eva asked.

"No one is forcing you stay here," Erin snapped, her tone jagged with annoyance.

I gave her a look that said, *Easy. This is what we told her to do.* Erin was losing her patience, and frankly, so was I. Instead of placing the blame on Eva, I started up with the questions.

"Eva, can you tell me more about Lewis Stark, how you met him and when the last time you saw him was?"

Eva was surprised by my question. When she wasn't quick to respond, Erin said, "You better start talking and let us handle your story before someone like Archie writes it for you."

I held up my hand, getting Erin to back off. Eva didn't need further pressure from us, and I preferred to keep her tongue loose by building rapport. But the clock was ticking.

I said, "Eva, she's right. We don't know what he's going to do now that he has your picture, and it won't take him long to find out who you are."

Eva's eyes stung with tears. "Could he really be the man who...took me?" Her voice quavered with fear.

"Chances are he wasn't, but I don't know," I said, pulling out Archie's book on PQK from my tote. I was glad I had brought it with me. My conversation with Erin in the car had me once again thinking about PQK and how the similarities of his crimes related to the cases we were investigating. I wanted Eva to see it, too.

Erin said, "That's why we're asking about the men you were dating. It's important we clear their names before we go slinging around new accusations."

"I don't know what these men do, and I only know where Lewis lives."

I had Eva write down Lewis home address before asking, "Are they married?"

"I never asked because I didn't want to know."

"We know about Stark, but who was the other guy?"

Eva let out a heavy sigh before she said, "Oliver Carr."

I asked Eva to write down both their names to be sure I had the correct spellings. Then I asked, "Did you meet him the same way you did Stark?" Eva nodded. "And how was that?"

"Through a dating website."

"Show us," Erin said, motioning for Eva to follow her into her home office.

Over the next several minutes, Eva logged in and walked

us through the website she used to pick up dates. Erin scrolled through Eva's profile while I looked over her shoulder. Her pictures were professionally done and she looked incredible; this was no typical dating website. Eva was an escort, pimping out her offerings to clients who paid a hefty monthly subscription fee for access.

"And how much does it cost you?" I asked.

Eva said, "Nothing."

I shifted my focus back to the screen. I could see why men reached out to her. She was young and vibrant and had a smile that promised a good time. Over the course of an hour we got a quick education into the life of sugaring. As I listened to what Eva had to say, I kept asking myself if it was possible Jane Doe also found dates through a website like this.

"Can we browse other profiles? Maybe we'll find the other girls on here," I said, wishing I knew what our Jane Doe looked like.

We scrolled, searched, and clicked but were unable to match our missing persons to names listed on the website. There were dozens of women here, a perfect place for a predator to select his prey. Soon we jumped over to the men's side and did the same thing. In their profiles they gave reasons why they were looking for dates, things they were into, the typical questions that helped women decide whether they were a good fit or not. There was nothing creepy about it and security measures were in place for both parties, but still there was room for error.

I leaned against the back wall and thumbed through Archie's book. I wanted to find a connection but, during my quick scan, I found nothing about dating websites. The closest thing was talk about how PQK lured in his victims online by pretending to be someone he wasn't. I mentioned it to Erin just as my cellphone vibrated in my pocket. It was King. I gave the book to Erin and took the call in the hall.

"How is Eva doing?" King asked. "Is she talking?"

I glanced into Erin's office and said in a hushed tone, "Where should I begin?"

"That good, huh?"

I told King about Jane Doe never arriving to the morgue and asked what he knew about Jenny Booth. King mentioned he was leaving South High and said, "It's better we talk about this in person."

I liked that idea. He told me where he was, and I said, "Meet me at my house. We can talk there."

CHAPTER FORTY-SIX

Daniels made a promise to Susan, and he intended to keep it. Their lunch date ended sooner than he would have liked, but he couldn't miss the opportunity she'd presented. Susan shared details he knew were hard to come by, and now he was working to verify their legitimacy.

He'd paid the bill, said his goodbye—promising to do it again sometime soon—and went to work on his phone as he raced out of the restaurant, nearly getting knocked over by some guy not paying attention, and raced across town. He sat in the backseat of his Escalade with his knee bouncing as his driver rushed him to the studio, flutters of anxiety rolling across his wine-filled belly as he got his team in place. He managed to do it in record time and, for Daniels, it wasn't so much about finding the girl as it was being the first to report her missing.

Breaking headlines was gold in an industry whose audience's attention span was short-lived. Moments like these were the reason he got paid the big bucks. As far as he was concerned, Jenny Booth's disappearance was all his.

As soon as he arrived to the office, Daniels moved

through the studio's halls and entered the production control room where his team was on standby. Standing in the back, perched high above his associates, he checked the time ticking down on a digital display clock on the wall above them.

"Two minutes, people," he clapped his hands, "Two minutes."

His muscles were tense. He was silently worried a competing station would beat him to the story. It wouldn't be the first time that had happened, and he kept flicking his gaze between the screens, watching live as Heidi got set up to interview Ruth Booth at her home. It was impossible to say who else knew, but it didn't matter—they had the exclusive which was about to be aired live.

Satisfied with Heidi's quick deployment of resources to bring Ruth to the studio, Daniels couldn't relax. His team had yet to locate Eva Martin, the young woman Susan said escaped her kidnapper's grip. That was the story he really wanted. A mother's plea to bring her daughter home was good, but the chance to relive the terror of what a person experienced was money. He would do anything to find her and have that interview added to his portfolio. He thought he might just know how to get it, too.

The floor manager glanced back at Daniels, and Daniels called him over.

"Any word on the second interview?" he asked.

The manager shook his head. "Our team is ready to go as soon as we can locate her."

"Good," Daniels said. "Make sure they ambush her as soon as she shows."

A call came in on his cell. Daniels sent his manager away and stepped into a dark corner of the room before answering. "Please tell me you found her."

The caller said, "She's not there."

"Are you sure?"

"Sorry to disappoint, but I'm telling you she's not there."

Daniels stopped pacing, rolled his sleeves up. Susan's perfumed scent clung to his clothes and reminded him of yet another conquest he'd set out to win. That one would have to wait. He was sorry for having to end their date so soon, but she understood. He liked understanding women—women who submitted to his powers.

"How can a body just disappear like that?" he asked.

When his question was met by a wall of silence, he let his thoughts fill his ears. Was this the story, or was there something better? *The medical examiner's office loses body at morgue.* The headline was catchy, but there had to be another angle. Daniels thought about the slant, about the people who knew the truth. Someone was going to learn of this, and then what? He glanced to the TV screen, thought about the story he had, and then asked, "Are you sure it just hasn't been misidentified?"

"I was thorough in my research," the caller said. "There is no record it was ever checked in."

Daniels lowered his gaze and pushed his fingers through his hair. The room went silent. When he lifted his gaze, Heidi Mitchell's interview began on the flat screen and Daniels listened as Ruth Booth pleaded for her daughter to come home.

"Jenny, if you're out there listening, please come home. I love you and miss you. Please, honey. Come home."

The gruff voice rustled through the phone line. "Sir, what would you like me to do?"

Daniels stared at Mrs. Booth and thought about the implications of what might happen if he let this go. Eventually the story would get out and someone would claim to know the truth. Could he afford to let that happen? He wasn't confident he could.

Daniels changed the subject and said, "We'll deal with this later. What about that other girl, Eva Martin? Have you been able to locate her? And please don't tell me where she lives, because I already know that."

"Funny you ask. I have located her."

Daniels kept one ear on his phone and the other on Heidi. "You have?"

"She was just here at the morgue, and you're not going to believe who she was with." A quick pause didn't give him a chance to speculate. "Samantha Bell."

Daniels's eyes popped. "Bell? You mean to tell me Bell's going to break this story first?"

"I'm not so sure that's the case."

He needed to stop her. Couldn't allow this to happen. The pieces were falling into place—Susan's information had come straight from Samantha, a rival. He should have kept Susan closer to get ahead of the competition.

He asked, "Well, did you follow them?"

The caller said, "They are keeping her at Erin Tate's house in the Highlands."

The caller gave Daniels the address in the Highlands, and he snapped his fingers to a nearby sound engineer. Requesting a pen, he wrote down the details and said, "Great. Anything else?"

"Actually, yes."

Daniels's expression pinched. "What?"

"Call Heidi and have her ask Ruth if she knew her daughter was sleeping with an older man."

"Are you serious?" Excited by the possibility of a scandal, higher ratings than what he already knew he was going to get, he was concerned there might not be enough time to relay this new request to Heidi. "Do you have a name?"

The caller shared the name with Daniels and said, "She'll

know who it is and when she confirms the name, you can tell her that's who took her daughter."

CHAPTER FORTY-SEVEN

WAS IT POSSIBLE HIS PROTECTED SOURCE ACTUALLY KNEW who took Jenny Booth? Daniels had no reason to doubt him, but could he trust him to keep it confidential? He knew his source was good, but if they kept this new information a secret and the police found out about it, Daniels could be considered an accomplice and possibly charged with obstructing justice. Maybe several other crimes he didn't want to face.

Palming his cellphone, he headed toward the exit.

"Sir, where are you going?"

Daniels pushed through the doors, ignoring the calls for him to return, and exited the control room to debate his options. He was walking on thin ice. Though he knew what he wanted to do, Daniels also didn't want to push his luck beyond what he could easily reel back in if, or when, things went astray.

He lengthened his stride, liking what Heidi was able to achieve in her interview with Ruth. He decided to keep this new information quiet, wanting to milk the story for all it had before headlines inevitably died down. Only then would he reveal the secret to the authorities, telling them he needed to verify his source's information before deciding if it was true or not. It was a story he could convincingly tell if need be. Daniels had years of experience skewing the truth, diverting attention away from himself, and requesting favors when strings needed to be pulled.

Entering his office, he sat behind his desk and reached for the TV clicker. Pointing it at the flat screen on the wall, he replayed Heidi's interview. He listened to Ruth's answers. Each response had a fresh perspective from what he heard before now that a possible suspect had been named in her daughter's disappearance.

He paused the video, picked up his desk phone, and made the call to the medical examiner's officer. The line rang as doubt swirled in his gut. A woman's voice answered and he said, "Public relations office, please."

"Just one second." He was put on hold.

With his elbows on his desk, Daniels's thoughts drifted to Samantha Bell. He was fortunate she worked in print. It could never be as quick as TV—even with the internet. That had him wondering how he could present an offer to Bell and have them work together on this—have her share what she knew about Eva. But that would mean having to give up his source, which he could never do.

The line clicked over and the public relations clerk introduced herself and asked, "How can I help you?"

Daniels asked about the Jane Doe, if they had been able to identify her yet, and if they would be willing to go on record to make a televised statement when the woman interrupted him by saying, "I don't know where you are getting your information from, but you're the third reporter today suggesting we have something we don't."

Daniels pulled back and dropped his elbows to his sides. Feeling slightly lightheaded, he politely ended the call and set the phone back on his desk. Then he picked up Susan's business card when he made the decision to call his source back—this time using his personal cellphone to make the call.

As soon as his source answered, Daniels said, "Don't let Eva out of your sight."

"You got it boss."

As soon as he ended the call, his secretary buzzed his desk. Daniels answered. The secretary said, "Heidi is in the building."

Daniels sprang to his feet and hurried out of his office, traveling down the hallway corridor and bursting into Heidi's office. Slamming the door shut behind him, Heidi turned and faced him, her brow furrowed with a look of concern flashing over her eyes.

"You can't just come in here without knocking," she said.

Daniels closed the enormous gap between them in three giant strides and gazed into her bouncing eyes as he hovered over her. He watched her pulse tick hard in her neck before he lifted a single hand and closed his fingers around the soft tissue, feeling her nerves jump.

He said, "I just received a call from an anonymous source who claims they know who took Jenny."

"What?" Heidi's eyebrows knitted. "How? The story just aired."

Heat from her neck seared the tips of his fingers as Daniels shrugged. Hooking the tip of his finger around the collar of her shirt, he popped the top button free.

"Well, who is it?" she asked.

Daniels titled his head and smirked. Reaching his hand behind him, he retrieved the paper with the suspect's name written on it. Holding the slip of paper in front of her eyes, Heidi swiped for it and missed.

"Not until you give me a little something for my effort," he said.

Heidi cocked out her hip and gave him a look. Crossing her arms, she raised a single eyebrow. When Daniels went in for a kiss, Heidi quickly looked away.

"I can't keep doing this. People are beginning to talk," Heidi said.

"Who? I'd like to know their names."

Heidi couldn't look him in the eye.

A surge of anger ripped through Daniels's body and he took her by the face and turned her head. He could feel her pulse racing. "Owen—"

Fisting her hair, he locked eyes and said, "I gave you a career. I'm about to make you famous. Or is there someone more deserving?"

Heidi hooked her hands on his flexed forearms and forced herself to relax. "You didn't let me finish. I didn't say this can't happen; it just can't happen here." She stood on her tiptoes and pressed her lips against his.

Satisfied, Daniels pushed the slip of paper into her hand. Then he stood back and headed for the door.

Heidi read the name and looked up. "Nicholas Bennett? Who is he?"

Daniels stopped and glanced over his shoulder. "Allegedly, he's the older man Jenny was sleeping with."

CHAPTER FORTY-EIGHT

JENNY STRUGGLED TO OPEN HER EYES. HER GUMMY EYELIDS refused to open, and the florescent light made it too bright to see anyway. Turning her head, she rolled onto her opposite side and faced the wall. Her cheek peeled off the floor as she extended her arms and sat up, wiping the drool from the corner of her mouth with the back of her hand.

Rubbing her eyes awake, Jenny felt drowsy, like she might have been drugged. She wondered how long she'd slept, what time it was, and if it was a new day. As desperately as she wanted to keep track, it was impossible. Time stopped the moment she was kidnapped, and the windowless room erased day and night, blending them together into a seemingly endless moment without the promise of tomorrow.

Sitting against the wall, Jenny pulled her knees to her chest and ignored the hunger pains cramping her sides. She'd been dreaming, but couldn't remember what about. Soon her thoughts rolled to the person who had taken her.

Who was this man holding her captive and threatening her to keep quiet? His scent and build were completely unfamiliar. She couldn't place his identity through his clear

Halloween mask no matter how hard she tried. He gave few clues to who he was, and that bothered Jenny most. She didn't like surprises.

The light flickered overhead and she shifted her attention to the pile of pictures she'd torn from the wall and tossed into the corner, wishing to burn them all. She didn't want to see them, didn't need them to remind her of her situation. She'd kept only one—the picture of her with Naomi.

Her thoughts drifted in and out likes waves lapping against the shore. She wondered if Naomi sent the photo to Dylan. She wanted to be witness to what happened next—if she and Dylan would get together because of it. She wondered what Dylan would send Naomi in return. Soon, her eyes stung with tears pooling in the corners. She feared that sex was what brought her here, like some kind of unspoken punishment for something she'd done but couldn't explain.

Extending her fingertips, she reached for Naomi's picture. Holding it in her hand, she stared into the photo, wanting to be in Mr. Helton's class and sitting next to her best friend. A math test didn't seem so bad now. Mr. Helton's parting words at Burger King rang loud and clear inside Jenny's head.

"Remember, you have more say than you realize."

Jenny knew exactly what he meant. It was the exact motivation she needed to hear to get her to believe in herself. She had a *say* in her future, a *say* in how she would survive this ordeal. Even if she felt impossibly powerless now, it was important she remembered she always had a *say* to fight—and fight she would.

Rolling her neck, she stared at the wall where she'd last heard Megan's whispers. A sense of regret pulled her face down to the floor. When she pressed an ear to the cold wall, a chill lifted the hairs on her neck.

It had been quiet for so long, she wondered if Megan was still there. She could feel the fear buzzing between the studs as she rested her hand on the sheetrock. She wanted badly to call out to Megan, to see if she was all right. But Jenny wasn't sure if her abductor was inside the house or not, and it was too risky to try.

Inspired by Mr. Helton's words to be the one to hold the power, she started with a gentle tap. Slowly, the tap grew louder and soon Jenny surprised herself by saying, "Megan? Are you there?"

Megan didn't answer. She asked again, this time a bit louder, but again she heard nothing.

That worried Jenny. Something bad happened. She'd heard the walls explode and the sounds of muffled screams echo out the last time they talked—the time she thought He was coming for her. Was Megan hurt? Why wasn't she answering? Did He take her somewhere else? Was Jenny all alone now? What was going to happen to *her*?

"Megan. Please. Just tap the wall to let me know you're okay." Jenny's voice cracked in her dry throat. "Did he hurt you?"

"She's gone," a new voice said.

Jenny's breath hitched. Who was that? Another girl? Or was it her captor?

Again, another new voice said, "I heard him leave with her."

"Are we alone?" a third voice answered.

Suddenly, the house came alive and Jenny couldn't believe her ears. Standing, a burst of optimism had her believing that she might actually make it out alive. "We're not alone. We're together," Jenny said.

"How many of us are there?"

Jenny said, "Call out your names. I'll start. Jenny."

"Lucy."

"Nicole."

"Sage."

They waited until the names stopped. Then Jenny said, "There are four of us."

"They took Megan. He heard her plan to escape and took her."

"Who is *He*?"

Everyone had their guesses, but no one knew for sure when their conversation was interrupted by a shrill screech, quickly followed by an earth-shattering scream.

Jumping into the corner, Jenny listened for movement in the house. She couldn't be sure it was Him. Her limbs shook with terror as she waited for the silence to break.

"Shut up!" a new voice Jenny had never heard said. "He's listening, and he'll kill us all if you don't shut up now."

With her heart hammering inside her chest, Jenny wondered how many others there were inside the house who were too scared to talk. More than she wanted to believe.

Sliding down the wall, Jenny tucked herself into a ball and felt her sense of optimism deflate as quickly as it had come. What was she going to do? How could she escape? She didn't have an answer to her questions.

"It doesn't matter." a familiar voice said. "After what he did to me, I'm already dead."

CHAPTER FORTY-NINE

King arrived before I even turned off my car. As soon as I stepped out, I heard Cooper in the window barking his silly head off. The grass clippings clung to my shoes as I stomped over it and met King at his car. He shut the door and, one look in my direction, he knew he had me. It was all it took when I was feeling stressed.

"I missed you," I said, reaching for his hand.

Threading his fingers through mine, King said, "This case is consuming my life."

I led him up the short flight of stairs and dug out my house keys from my purse. I opened the door and Cooper came flying out with his tail wagging. He jumped on King, and King pushed him back down. When he stalled, I threw him a questioning look, wondering what it was that had taken his mind off of me.

"These girls, Sam, they're Mason's age."

His voice was so weak, I knew his heart was shattering. I stepped into his arms and clung onto his waist, wanting him to know he wasn't alone. He held onto me for a solid minute before pulling back. Casting his gaze down, our eyes locked when I tipped my head back.

King said, “Something happened.”

I nodded, knowing he could feel the anxiety buzzing through my body. Taking him inside my house, I shut the door and said, “Eva’s picture was taken.”

“By who?”

My knight was back, ready to fight. I made sure King knew who Archie was before saying, “I’m not sure what he’s planning to do with it—sell it to the tabloids or use it for his own benefit—but I do know he’s after a serial killer I’m certain doesn’t exist.”

“A serial killer in Denver?”

I held his eyes and nodded once.

King frowned and shook his head no. “What makes him think that?”

I told King about Archie’s book about the Prom Queen Killer and said, “I’m afraid he’s more concerned about the fame he’s expecting to receive after his next book is finished than getting his facts right.”

“Now you understand why the department mistrusts members of the media—”

“I get it,” I said, not wanting to lose focus on what really mattered—the girls who were missing and the fact that the police hadn’t yet named a suspect.

King asked where it happened, and I told him.

He turned away and I watched the lines on his forehead deepen with obvious concern.

“Samantha,” he said, “Eva is my only witness to the crime I’m attempting to solve. If this reporter is a problem, I need to know about it now.”

“Eva is safe,” I said, understanding King didn’t want Archie to intimidate his only witness. “She’s at Erin’s place now.”

With his hands on his hips, he asked, "Why were you at the medical examiner's office to begin with? This isn't about your theory that crimes are getting covered up, is it?"

Now we were talking business. I said, "There is no record of Jane Doe ever arriving."

King downplayed the situation. "She probably just hasn't been processed."

"Why wouldn't Griffin have said that if that was the case? Don't you find it the least bit suspicious that Jane Doe's body couldn't be located?" I stared into the eyes I loved, waiting for him to respond. When he didn't, I continued, "I'm not asking you to go to war with the mayor and jeopardize your job, but if someone is attempting to cover-up crimes like I suspect they are, the public deserves to know how. This is an elected official we're talking about, throwing away tax dollars to the exact opposite of what he was hired to do."

King tipped his head back and scrubbed a hand over the lower half of his face. "I'll look into it, but I was there in Park Hill and saw Jane Doe with my own eyes. I can assure you she exists."

"Then how can you explain her having gone missing from the morgue?"

"Mistakes happen when resources aren't allocated properly."

I knew he wasn't defending the mayor, but rather the department that gave him his identity—a badge he wore with honor. "Are you saying the scene was never officially declared?"

King looked annoyed by my questioning. "I'm saying that the department's resources were stretched that night."

I let it go, not wanting to waste our limited time discussing the bureaucracy of the department. Instead, I asked, "But you saw her?"

King nodded, made sure this wasn't on record, and

explained the violence he saw inflicted on Jane Doe. I was horrified by what I was hearing, and hated the fact that we couldn't prove any of this ever happened—at least not until Jane Doe's body was located and identified.

"The body was dumped," he said, "left to rot in an alleyway."

"And you don't know how old she was, who this person is, or if it's any of the missing girls we're looking for?"

"I'm sorry, Sam. I wish I had answers. Believe me, I do. I want to know what's happening as much as you do."

"Was she a prostitute?"

"Maybe. I don't know. LT pulled me off the scene once Eva came to our attention."

My eyebrows stitched. "Pulled off the scene?"

I wondered how much more he wasn't telling me, but suddenly I was again thinking about how it seemed crimes were going unreported. Was someone doing this on purpose? If so, why? Was it to make their résumé seem better than it actually was, or was it to hide a secret? As I stared into King's eyes, I moved Jane Doe up on my list of priorities of questions I needed answered.

"We're getting way off track here," King said. "Eva is talking. What did she say?"

I told him how Eva was sugaring and mentioned the website she'd showed us and that she was dating older men who happily gifted her expensive items—possibly even paying her rent and tuition.

King told the forensics on Eva's rape test came back inconclusive. "There were signs of intercourse but Eva admitted to having sex the day before she was abducted."

An inconclusive report meant there wasn't enough evidence to say whether she'd been raped or not. It wasn't the conclusion I was hoping to hear, but I still had my doubts Eva was abducted at all.

King's cell kept beeping as I asked, "Do you think she made it up?"

He ignored his device and said, "I don't know. But what I do know is that her experience doesn't match what we think might have happened to Megan Hines."

I was careful not to lead him on when I asked, "How many suspects is the department pursuing?"

King wasn't at liberty to discuss the specifics. He'd already crossed the line and shared too much. But I gave him my word and promised to keep this quiet, not wanting my written words to have a direct impact on this case until an arrest had been made.

"Then can you answer this?" I said "Was Eva ever reported missing with the police?"

King whispered, "No."

I touched my temple and thought about her solitary life—thought about the men she admitted to dating and the webcam and lights pointing to her bed. Eva still had the bruises purpling her body like she'd been beat up, but until I spoke with her male suitors, there wasn't enough evidence to confirm her story.

As if reading my mind, King said, "The older men Eva said she was dating, did you get their names?" When I asked why, King said, "Apparently, Jenny was also sleeping with an older man."

That was news to me. I asked for a name, but King couldn't share. He finally glanced to his phone and I slipped further into my thoughts, wondering if there was a connection between victims. If they were connected with a single suspect, he was smart enough to make us question our path. If they were not connected, then we were likely looking for two dirt bags.

I asked, "What else can you tell me about Jenny Booth?"

King took his eyes off his phone, snapped his head up, and looked me in the eye. "I gotta go."

"What it is?" I feared I might have pushed him too far.

King hustled to the door and said, "A body has been found. It might be one of our missing girls."

CHAPTER FIFTY

ALLISON ARRIVED LATE TO SOUTH HIGH, PARKED NEAR THE entrance, and exited her car in a hurry. Making her way to the front of the school, she pushed past the black exhaust billowing from the backs of buses pulling away from the curb. High schoolers hung out the windows, laughing and yelling into air at nothing in particular. Allison pulled her attention away from them and noticed blue ribbons tied to handrails and hanging beneath lamp posts.

Hooking her thumb through the strap of her tote bag, she watched as the ribbons fluttered in the afternoon summer breeze, spaced between student-made signs calling for Megan Hines's safe return.

Shortening her gait, Allison felt her throat close, swearing to herself that these signs and ribbons hadn't been here yesterday—at least not to her recollection. However, she was happy to know not all had forgotten about Megan. There was still hope; and hope, she could live with.

When her cellphone buzzed in her bag, she stopped to dig it out. Her thoughts traveled to last night and the girl found in Park Hill. Allison hadn't heard an update from

Samantha and wondered if the victim's name had been released. More importantly, she said a quick prayer for Megan's safe return.

"Allison?"

Allison closed out her message from work and was surprised to see her friend, Susan, heading her way. "Susan, what are you doing here?"

"I'm here to pick up my goddaughter."

"I didn't know you had a goddaughter."

Susan was explaining who Naomi was when suddenly the doors opened behind them and Naomi exited the school. Gliding over with her backpack hanging off her square shoulders, Naomi casually stopped and stood next to Susan with a glum look on her face. "Naomi, this my friend Allison."

"We know each other," Naomi said.

A surprised look flashed over Susan's eyes, and Allison mentioned her volunteering with the volleyball team, the reason she was here now. "Speaking of which, I'm already late." Allison shifted her eyes to Naomi. "No practice for you today?"

Naomi diverted her eyes. "I can't."

"What? Why? Is everything okay?"

Naomi tucked her chin and said, "It's, uh..."

"Go on," Susan said to Naomi. "I'll meet you at the car."

"I'm sorry; did I say something wrong?" Allison asked.

Susan sighed. Pointing to the blue ribbons, she said, "We just learned Naomi's best friend is now missing, too."

Allison gasped and threw a hand over her mouth. She stared into Susan's eyes, hoping it wasn't true. But when Susan mentioned the missing girl was Jenny, Allison understood why Naomi had been acting the way she was.

Remembering Jenny wearing the baggy shorts only the day before, Allison asked, "How long has it been?"

"Since last night."

"Naomi must be devastated."

"Naomi's mother asked me to pick her up. I can only imagine what she's going through."

Allison faced Susan and asked, "Have you told Sam?"

"I called her earlier—"

They were interrupted by the sounds of a news van's wheels skidding on the pavement behind them when coming to a hard stop. The van door slid open, and the women watched the camera crew get set up to report live. Allison's head was spinning, still not fully grasping the severity of what was happening, or why.

"He actually listened," Susan whispered.

Allison rolled her neck, faced her friend, and said, "Who actually listened?"

Susan blinked away her gaze. "I mentioned Jenny's disappearance to TV executive Owen Daniels." She hugged Allison and said, "I got to go. I'll call you if I need anything."

Allison watched Susan trot her way to the van, where she had a quick interaction with one of the crew members before waving another goodbye to Allison. Then she joined Naomi as Allison stayed out front and watched her friend drive away.

Feeling like she should do something, Allison hurried into the school and was immediately stopped by security. She mentioned she was here for volleyball practice, here to assist Coach Bennett. The new face didn't seem to care about anything other than corralling everyone either in or out of the building.

The security officer motioned for Allison to make a decision. "If you're here to stay, all visitors are required to check in at the front office before proceeding."

Allison headed toward the office. She felt the tension and distrust in the air, and could see the looks of uncertainty on the several faces she passed. Once inside the front office, she asked the secretary what was happening.

"We're closing school early. I can't go into specifics, but extracurricular activities have also been canceled tonight." The secretary knew Allison volunteered with the volleyball team and ensured her Coach Bennett was still in the building if she wanted to speak with him.

With her visitor pass around her neck, Allison left the office and walked the halls, once again thinking about Naomi and Jenny. She wondered what it was about this school that seemed to attract bad behavior. Were these girls more vulnerable than at any other school? Allison didn't know enough to answer that question.

Coach Bennett was at his desk when Allison arrived. She knocked lightly on his door. He lifted his head and waved for her to come inside. Allison stepped inside the room and saw he was watching the news.

"That's Jenny's mom, Ruth," he said, pointing the clicker to the TV. Allison joined him as they watched the interview with Ruth. "No one knows what happened to her."

Allison let her hand fall to his shoulder. He looked her in the eye and forced a smile.

"Practice has been canceled," he said.

"I know." Allison continued looking in his watery eyes, wanting to smooth out the knots she could feel forming in his shoulders. "How are you doing?"

Bennett shook his head and looked away. "Not good."

Just when Allison didn't know what to say, breaking news brought their attention back to the TV. Allison looked up and saw the reporter parked outside the front of the school speaking into the camera.

"We just received word a body has been discovered," the reporter said, "and it's believed to be a student from South High."

CHAPTER FIFTY-ONE

I LEFT BEFORE BEHIND KING, PROMISING TO MAKE MY arrival look like I hadn't followed him to the scene. It was important that King didn't come across as playing favorites or worse, breaking the law by leaking confidential information to the press without authority. It was a constant juggling act, but one we were willing to play in order to stay together.

Several miles down the road, I broke his tail and split right. Though we were both heading to the South Platte River on the north side of town, I took the side streets to slow my travel. Breaking left, I reached for my cellphone and decided to call in reinforcements to make certain this crime was properly documented. The city couldn't afford to have another Jane Doe go missing without a trace, and neither could I—especially if it was one of the missing girls we were all looking for.

Erin answered after the second ring.

"Turn on the news," I said, listening to Erin move through her house. When she asked what was happening, I told her, "A body has been found."

"Is it one of our girls?"

"I don't know. Is anyone reporting on it yet?"

I could hear Erin flicking through the channels, then she dropped a bomb on me that completely knocked me off balance. "You're not going to guess whose picture I found on the escort site."

"Whose?" I said without a thought.

"Archie Smith."

I froze. I couldn't believe what she was saying. "Did he use his own name?"

Erin confirmed he had, then said, "Posed as a suiter."

I stopped at a red light and pressed the palm of my hand into my left eye. Was that the reason he was after Eva? Did he want her as a date? Or was he one step ahead of us all in knowing about an active serial killer? I thought how Eva couldn't say with certainty if Archie was her kidnapper or not. That bothered me, but I couldn't fault her for not knowing.

I asked Erin, "Did they exchange messages?"

"Nothing," Erin said. "And when I asked if he was the one who took her, she couldn't say for sure. I'm not sure Eva recalls exactly what happened. Her story keeps shifting."

I knew as much. Feared this might be the case.

The light flicked to green and I punched the gas. Racing off the line, I didn't like the doubt I heard in Erin's voice. Eva's story needed to be solid if she expected us to make any progress, but I had to accept she might not be the perfect witness.

"Here we go," Erin said. "Looks like 9News is on scene and reporting from the banks of the South Platte."

I tipped forward and glanced up at the sky. A news chopper flew overhead as I approached. "Are they reporting the victim's name?"

"Sam, how did we miss this?"

“What are they saying?” I asked, telling her this must be huge with the news chopper flying overhead.

“They don’t have a name, just reporting that a female body was found buried in a shallow grave. Apparently discovered by a man walking along the bike path.”

Why hadn’t Dawson called? And who was this girl? I prayed it wasn’t one of the missing girls, but something told me it was.

“Sam, you want me to meet you?”

I told her to search Archie’s book about shallow graves and said, “Stay with Eva. We can’t leave her alone with Archie circling our waters.”

“Oh Christ,” Erin sighed.

“What is it?”

“Now they’re saying it’s one of the missing girls.” Erin’s voice cracked as I heard her say a quick prayer. “Sam, what are we going to do?”

CHAPTER FIFTY-TWO

THE NEWS WAS DEVASTATING, BUT WHO WAS IT? JENNY OR Megan? That was what bothered me most. I needed to know what to expect once I arrived.

I reached the scene shortly after ending my call with Erin, and it was as chaotic as I imagined it would be. Parking was nonexistent, and I resorted to parking on the grass. I doubted I would get a ticket—the police were a bit preoccupied—but I didn't care anyway. I just needed to get the story before we lost another one to the mayor's magical eraser.

Swinging my door open, I ran across the asphalt toward the banks of the river and was quickly lassoed in by a young uniformed officer. The cops had the media corralled into a small roped off box far away from where anything could be seen, videoed, or photographed. I reluctantly obeyed his orders.

The news chopper was still circling overhead, the entire cavalry flooding the area. There were local stations as well as their national affiliates. Everyone was getting in on the action. It felt like I was the last to arrive.

Squeezing past my colleagues, I pushed my way to the

front of the line. Between the gaps of large cottonwood trees, I watched the investigators work but was too far away to make out any kind of details to what I was witnessing. From what I could tell, though, this scene was not being treated like last night's Jane Doe.

I glanced to my left and listened to a reporter tell the same story Erin had just told me. To my right was Heidi Mitchell, fixing her hair, preparing to report. Megan Hines's name was being thrown around, and all I could think about was their silence this last week when it seemed everyone had given up on her but me.

Where were they twelve hours ago? I asked myself, absolutely livid at how they chased only ratings. Then everything changed when I spotted my first Federal Bureau of Investigation jacket and knew this wasn't just another crime scene. This was something much bigger.

Had Archie been right all along? Could there actually be an active serial rapist-killer working the Denver area? If so, could that explain what has been happening to these women? Major crimes was the only explanation to explain why the FBI was here. The department had called them in and asked for assistance. But why?

I spun around and searched for Chief of Police Gordon Watts and Lieutenant Kent Baker. I needed to see their faces when they admitted a crime had occurred on their watch. It would be impossible for the mayor to deny this one, I thought. But none of that was the most important question. "Who was the victim?" I whispered.

Details were limited. All we were being told was that the body belonged to one of the missing girls from South High. It remained like that for several hours. Nothing said, nothing done. I couldn't stop speculating on what happened, who it was, until finally the promised press conference began.

We huddled in front of the podium with our phones,

cameras, and microphones pushed in the police chief's face. He was surrounding by his lead investigators and a spokesman from the FBI. King was in the pile near the back, but he didn't risk looking at me.

Over the course of fifteen minutes we were briefed on several details of what happened. We were told the time of discovery, how the victim was found, where the body was retrieved. After, the chief took questions.

Someone asked, "Will you be releasing the name of the victim?"

"The victim is believed to be that of Megan Hines," the chief responded.

An eruption of chatter exploded as reporters shouted their follow-up questions.

"Is Jenny's disappearance related?"

"Do the police have any suspects at this time?"

I listened and kept recording as I was hit with an extreme case of déjà vu. It was like I had been here before. It was like reading passages taken straight out of Archie's book. This crime had all the makings of a copycat killer. I shot my hand up in the air and asked, "Last night there was a victim in Park Hill whose body never made it to the morgue, is her death related to Megan's?"

"Only questions pertaining to this investigation, please," the chief deflected.

I followed up, "Are you admitting that Jane Doe never made it to the medical examiner's office?"

I felt eyes boring into the side of my head and found the mayor's spokesperson who had previously warned me to stay in my lane staring with intense, unfriendly eyes.

The chief said to me, "I don't have specifics on that case."

A colleague next to me asked, "Shall we assume Denver PD is losing the public's confidence since the FBI has been called in to assist?"

"Let's not start on the conspiracies. This is a serious crime we're investigating, and we'd all like to see this end well. Simple as that."

The chief locked eyes with me, as if suggesting I was the one to have started the rumor. The next question, from Heidi Mitchell, surprised us all. "Is it true these girls were involved with older men? Maybe even with a teacher from the high school? Can you comment on the validity of that statement and whether the department has any suspects at this time?"

The chief took a step back and I watched the spokesperson whisper something in his ear. Then I glanced to Heidi, wondering who her source was inside the department. But a *teacher*? Could it really be possible? Or was she on a fishing expedition?

The chief stepped up to the podium and responded, "Our investigators are currently questioning potential witnesses, but there are no suspects at this time. Patrol is currently canvassing the area and we'll update you on a need-to-know basis. That's all for now."

The chief stepped back from the podium and was swallowed up by his people. I felt my phone vibrating in my pocket. The unknown number had me pause, but I answered just the same. I knew immediately who it was.

"What do you want?" I said.

Archie laughed. "It's not what I want, it's what *you* want, Samantha."

The body I asked him for?

"Now do you believe there is a predator quietly working the streets of Denver?"

CHAPTER FIFTY-THREE

FOR HOURS AFTER THE PRESS CONFERENCE, KING WORKED tirelessly to canvass nearby neighborhoods and the surrounding areas with Alvarez. They talked to joggers, cyclists, and anyone else who might have been in the area, including the transient community who had made homes along the banks of the South Platte. Not a single lead was made. Nobody saw a thing. Even King's CIs who owed him favors had nothing to offer. Now, back at the crime scene, it was like the murder never happened.

"Well, partner?" Alvarez gave King a wary look.

King's stance widened as he stared in the direction of the floodlights hanging over the crime scene. "Let's take one more look before Griffin bags up the body."

The men moved toward the light. As they walked, King thought about Eva and Jenny. He was still looking for a connection that could lead him to naming a perpetrator, but he didn't have a solid lead. What could he be missing? There had to be a clue somewhere in this mess. He soon turned his thoughts to Mason, wondering if he could do anything to protect these kids from the monster who seemed to be after them. At this point, he doubted he could.

King's cell buzzed with a text message. Technicians from both the department and FBI circled the big cottonwood trees and combed the riverbank, flagging for evidence. Mosquitoes buzzed in his ears as he read the text from Detective Gray.

Please don't let me be the bearer of bad news again. That was the worst.

King swiped a hand over his chin and knew the empty feeling Detective Gray was experiencing. Gray had left before the press conference to tell Megan Hines's parents of their daughter's death and bring them in to ID her. Now that the news was out, a frenzy of speculation had begun.

The news chopper flew overhead. Alvarez tipped his head back and said, "The media will assume the worst and ride the wave until the next big thing."

King caught sight of Lieutenant Baker and Chief Watts. They glanced in his direction and turned their backs. King said to Alvarez, "Isn't that what they do best?"

Alvarez lowered his gaze and took a step closer to King. "Partner," he jutted his chin toward the chief, "I should warn you that there are whispers the upper brass are out to make your life miserable."

King's brow creased—this was news to him. "What are you talking about?"

Alvarez flicked his gaze over King's shoulders, scanned their surroundings to make sure no one was listening, and said, "I'm talking about your relationship with Sam."

"What about it?" King watched an FBI investigator kneel down and photograph something in the grass.

"I'm hearing that they're losing trust with you."

King didn't need to know who was spreading rumors, just wanted to know why. Though cops were all on the same side when policing the city, each was out for their own careers when it truly mattered. Whether it be medals or publicity they were seeking, King knew who he could trust—or at least he thought he knew. Besides, he didn't have time to worry about rumors when girls Mason's age were being kidnapped and murdered.

Making his hand into a fist, King said, "Sam has never been a problem before, and I assure you she won't be in the future. Her husband was a cop. Remember?" He paused and stared. "A brother in blue. Just like us."

Alvarez's head hung lower as he sighed. "I know."

"But?"

Alvarez flicked his gaze to where the LT and chief were huddled together. "Gavin was a great cop. But that was over ten years ago. Apparently, his currency is no longer accepted."

King leaned in to close the gap between them, feeling the vein in his temple throb with agitation. "My relationship has no direct effect on my police work."

Alvarez raised a single eyebrow. "Your record speaks for itself. I know. But someone inside the department is leaking information to the press, and you're the natural suspect."

King's muscles tensed as he jerked his head away. "Ridiculous."

"I don't believe it, either, but you were there. You heard the questions they were asking Chief during the press conference."

"You throw enough shit at a wall, some of it will stick. They're only guessing at what happened to keep their audiences entertained."

Alvarez raised a hand as he talked. "I'm only telling you this because you're my brother. The last thing I need is for LT to put you on the late show."

"Look around, partner," King spread his arms out wide, "this is the late show. And just so we're clear, Eva requested to be taken to Samantha's. I didn't suggest it, but I'm glad she did. Now we know she might have been an escort."

Alvarez touched his forehead. "Did Sam tell you that?"

King narrowed his gaze and held back the words he wanted to say. The medical examiner caught sight of him and called him over before he could say anything he'd regret.

"Detectives," Griffin said, "you're going to want to see this."

CHAPTER FIFTY-FOUR

GRIFFIN LED THE MEN TO WHERE THE VICTIM LAY. THE dirt had been dusted off the top, but Megan's body remained in the position she had been found—curled into the fetal position, arms falling limp against her thighs. It was the first close-up King had on the vic. Just as it had at the sight of Jane Doe, King's heart shattered once again.

Griffin gloved up and glanced to King. "Marital problems?"

King took his eyes off of the victim and could see Griffin's humor swirling in her brown eyes. He could appreciate her sense of wit in a time of intense pressure. He liked the way she let him know she heard what he and Alvarez were discussing.

King said, "More like a lack of sleep."

"Too bad." Griffin shrugged. "I know a good marriage counselor who might have been able to help."

Alvarez chuckled. "We'll keep that in mind. Now, tell us about the victim."

"This is only my initial analysis before I send out the blood sample and run the post," Griffin took her eyes off

Alvarez and swung her gaze back to King, "but I know the pressure you're under to make an arrest so I'll share my thoughts so you have a foundation to work from."

King kneeled next to the victim. Griffin followed while Alvarez remained standing.

Griffin began by stating the obvious. "White female, sixteen years old." She locked eyes with King. "I place the time of death no more than twenty-four hours, but probably more like ten to twelve."

Staring at the victim, King reminded himself what he was doing twelve hours ago. It was about the time he was dropping Eva off with Samantha before checking out the streets where Bowers said he picked her up.

"There are no signs of decomposition, but I did find ligature marks around her wrists and neck." Griffin lifted the victim's right arm and pointed with her finger. "I'm guessing she died by strangulation."

"Raped?"

"No obvious signs as of now. I'll have a conclusion for you after I run through my exam."

Alvarez stood with a picture of Megan Hines pinched between his fingers. He handed it to King. Even through the dust and dirt and discoloration, there wasn't any doubt they were looking at Megan.

"We'll have her family confirm it's her ASAP." Griffin's expression hardened. "What was the chief thinking, naming the vic at the press conference? She hasn't even been officially IDed. What a headache."

King thought about Alvarez's previous warning when he turned his head and found Alvarez giving him a knowing look. "These ligature marks are similar to the ones we found on Eva."

"Eva?" Griffin asked.

King filled her in, painting a pretty picture of what

happened, making sure to include how Eva escaped her kidnapper's grip. Then King said to his partner, "Maybe that's why Megan was killed—he needed to get rid of witnesses?"

Alvarez shrugged. "Did Eva say there were other girls?"

King needed to check with Samantha. Jane Doe was still the worst King had seen. It wasn't clear, either, how many suspects they were looking for—at least one, but possibly two. If two, were they working together, or feeding off of each other? He needed to get Eva to speak to him—give him more to go on before another murder occurred. But having her agree to meet was going to be more difficult now that his superiors seemed to have a target on Samantha's back.

"Here's what I know," Griffin said. "The media are already speculating this is done at the hands of a serial killer. That's another reason I don't like how details have already been released to the public."

"One murder doesn't make a serial killer," Alvarez said.

King reminded his partner about Jane Doe. "No, but two girls is only one murder away."

Griffin knitted her brows and stared at King as he went on to explain the horrific sight from last night. Alvarez vouched for King and Griffin responded with, "The elusive Jane Doe I keep hearing about."

King asked, "You know her?"

"Everyone has been asking about her. Including Sam."

Without letting on that he already knew the answer, King asked, "Then you identified her?"

Griffin shook her head and smiled. "I'm sorry, Alex, but I currently have at least a dozen Jane Does in the morgue, all of whom are waiting to be identified. But none match the description of the girl you speak of."

How could that be? King knew something wasn't right. "But the sergeant from CSI was there, and EMS picked her up." He swept his gaze to Alvarez. "He must have written a report?"

"If he has, I haven't seen it." Griffin stood and King followed. She said, "Send me the photographs you took. I'd also like to read the report you wrote up. It's possible she's in the morgue and just hasn't been tagged."

CHAPTER FIFTY-FIVE

I HAD BEEN STANDING AROUND FOR THE LAST TWO HOURS and I still couldn't decide if Archie was right. He'd taken my theory that the police were hiding crimes to inflate their statistics and watered the idea until it grew into a monster even I now feared.

Archie was playing games with me. It seemed like he was one step ahead of us all, and I wondered how that was possible. Had he known Megan's body would be found? He certainly convinced me he did. Who told him? Or was he guilty all along and was I right in thinking he was scripting his own true crime book? The thought put chills down my spine.

I glanced back to the crime scene, still lit up by a dozen floodlights, and let my thoughts swirl inside my head. The technicians were still working behind the tall brush and trees, keeping a closed lid on what, if anything, they found.

I was busy writing my own story inside my head, deciding between headlines when my thoughts circled back to figuring out why exactly I was still here instead of going home.

Nothing had happened since the press conference and the throng of reporters had quickly dispersed. Not even King was making an effort to glance in my direction. Was I waiting for him? Maybe Archie was right. Everything about tonight suggested it was bigger than anything this city had seen before, but a serial rapist? Could it be possible? Eva made me believe it was.

I palmed my phone and glanced to the screen.

The vibrations of my heart could be felt in my ears as I debated whether or not to call Megan's parents. Even though I suspected the police had informed them of their daughter's death, I felt obligated to let them know, too. I'd talked to them so many times in the last three weeks, it felt disrespectful to stay away.

But I couldn't find it in me to make the call. It was just too hard. Instead, I stayed put, needing to see Megan's body get bagged up and loaded into the coroner's van before she went missing like Jane Doe.

As I leaned against the hood of my car, I expected Archie to surprise me at any second. Didn't he want to see the crime scene himself? Everyone was here but him. Why? I wanted him to show his face, to prove to me that he wasn't the person behind these crimes. With each minute that passed, the more suspicious I became of him.

"Samantha, what are you still doing here?"

I rolled my neck and found TV journalist Nancy Jordan walking my way. I said, "I thought if I waited long enough, a desperate cop would want to share his secrets with me."

Nancy laughed. "I heard what you said to Heidi earlier."

I didn't react, but Nancy's eyes glimmered with the answers I was seeking. "You know who it is?"

Nancy said, "She's not going to tell you who her source is because it's not hers. It's Daniels's. He's controlling her career and has been for a while."

"And you know this, how?"

Nancy gave a little shoulder shrug. "We had drinks a few

months back. Heidi let her secrets slip and, let's just say, it's your classic case of sleeping your way to the top."

I didn't react—wasn't at all surprised—however, I did ask, "But if she's only doing what Daniels says, then who's *his* source?"

"That, I haven't been able to figure out. I'm curious myself. In my limited research, I can't link anything to a high school teacher sleeping with his students." Nancy raised her eyebrows. "Anyway, you didn't hear it from me."

I motioned like I was zipping my lips shut and Nancy smiled as she wished me good luck.

I watched her walk away, thinking how Nancy and I had worked on a number of stories together—including the sniper case that tore through the Denver community. We weren't the best of friends, and often competed with each other, but she was a colleague who I could trust. But why mention anything about Heidi at all? Was Nancy motivated by jealousy? Heidi did sweep the awards ceremony, receiving many awards Nancy qualified to take herself. There was more to her story than what she shared. There always was when it came to ratings.

My phone buzzed. I recognized the number this time. It was Archie. As soon as I answered, he said, "Quick, Sam. An Amber Alert was just announced. It could be the serial rapist I've been telling you about."

"Where are you?" I asked, looking around, wondering why it seemed as if only Archie knew.

Archie told me where. Then he said, "Catch me if you can."

CHAPTER FIFTY-SIX

KING HELPED LOAD THE VIC INTO THE BACK OF THE coroner's van when Griffin said, "Swing by my office tomorrow. If you really believe this Jane Doe exists, we'll get it sorted out."

King nodded his appreciation and closed the back door. He gave two swift knocks on the side to let the driver know they were finished, and he heard the brakes release just before watching it drive away.

Standing there feeling exhausted, he turned his head and caught sight of Samantha leaning against the hood of her car. Her head was down and she had her phone pressed to her ear. He wanted nothing more than to close out his night wrapped inside her arms, but Alvarez's comments still hung over his head like dirty smog.

Samantha must have felt him staring because she lifted her head and they locked eyes for a brief moment before she got behind the wheel and left the scene.

Not knowing how he was going to approach this new level of scrutiny with the woman he loved, his attention swung to the boots crunching over gravel behind him. Turning to see who was coming, Lieutenant Baker stood by King's side. Without looking, King knew what LT had seen—what it was he was thinking—and it wasn't good.

"Our canvas of the area came up empty," King said. "Griffin thinks the body was dumped as little as twelve hours ago so witnesses may have moved on since." He flicked his gaze to LT. "The sun would have been up. Someone must have seen something."

LT was quiet for a long pause. Then he said, "This whole thing is a fucking mess. Megan's name should have never been given to the press and don't get me started on the FBI coming. I know you and the rest of the team are perfectly capable of handling this case."

"Thanks, LT."

LT turned to face King. "But we still have a missing girl."

"Two, actually," King corrected his superior, reminding him of Jane Doe.

LT gave him a stern look, deciding not to take the bait.

King said, "You *are* aware that Jane Doe never made it to the morgue, aren't you?"

LT turned his attention toward the river. "I was at the press conference. Same as you."

"Griffin confirmed it," King said. When LT didn't respond, King asked, "Did you pull me off that case on purpose? Because Detective Gray didn't need me at the hospital."

"The chief is worried about leaks after tonight's press conference." LT met King's eye. "The media knows too much and has probably already tainted our investigation—possibly even ruined any chances of a conviction once we do manage to catch the S.O.B. behind these murders."

"Are you saying there is only one suspect, because I'm

thinking there might be more than that. There are too many differences."

"As of this moment, we're treating it as if there is only one suspect and I expect you to do the same." LT made it clear this wasn't up for negotiation. "Which is why I need you to focus on this case, here, tonight."

King stared. He heard LT, loud and clear. "You're taking me off the Jenny Booth case? You can't. Not now that Megan has been found dead. These cases are related. What I learn here could save Jenny's life."

"Didn't you just tell me we should be looking for a second suspect?"

King turned his head and swallowed his pride, not wanting to play politics with the person who controlled his career. He was already walking on eggshells by sleeping with a reporter—apparently the same journalist the department had suddenly lost trust in.

"Just so we're clear, it wasn't my call."

King snapped his neck and gave LT a questioning look.

LT warned King, "A loose tongue has destroyed many officers' careers. Don't let yours be next."

King tipped his head back and narrowed his gaze, wondering when LT would learn to keep his mouth shut. Instead, LT continued.

"You hear me? Pillow talk gets men divorced because their wives can't handle the grim realities we see every day. But in your case, pillow talk can make careers."

"You've got my relationship all wrong," King said.

"It's not me. It's the chief who believes your extracurricular activities with Samantha have gone too far." LT inched closer and lowered his voice to a whisper. "You're a good cop, but tonight's press conference was a disaster and there are people with a higher pay grade than mine who aren't happy about it."

"I can't change my life."

"Then redeem yourself by giving them something they can use." LT stepped away and said, "You know how this game is played. It's all about appearances."

CHAPTER FIFTY-SEVEN

Music was streaming from the radio, playing a soft melody in the background as Susan sat behind her desk inside her downtown office. Since her lunch with Owen Daniels, and after dropping Naomi at home, she'd been swept up in work trying to revive a deal that her colleague Carly McKenzie couldn't close.

"Your offer was brilliant. We've just decided to go with another company we feel is better suited for the vision we see," Susan's prospective client had told her.

It was too late to rework a proposal and there was nothing else Susan could do.

After reviewing her accounts and crunching numbers, Susan muttered, "This can't be happening."

She had enough money in the bank to survive the next three months of operation, but if she didn't work something quick, she wouldn't be able to cover her payroll. She looked across the hall and felt the empty pit in her stomach expand when thinking about the responsibility she had to her employees.

She'd thought this gig was in the bag. What happened? In

fact, Susan was so certain this client would agree to her proposal that she declined several other offers while waiting for this one to close. It was a mistake she regretted deeply. She needed a miracle, and quick.

Her cell buzzed. "Hey, I was just thinking about you."

Owen Daniels said, "I have that effect on women."

Susan leaned back in her chair, stared up into the ceiling, and smiled. "What's on your mind?"

"Besides you?"

"Yeah," Susan murmured. "Besides me."

"Not much."

The curl in the corner of Susan's lips deepened. Was Daniels the miracle she needed? She certainly thought he could be. "That might work on other women, but not me."

"Then let me try this." Daniels's voice was light with charm. "I'd like to come inside but the door is locked."

Susan sprang forward, planted her feet into the ground, and peeked her head into the hallway. Gazing toward the front door, a tingling sensation spread across the backs of her shoulders when she caught sight of Daniels flashing a bright smile through the front window.

He said through the phone, "Care to let me in?"

Susan hurried to the front door, twisted the deadbolt, and opened the door. "Hi," she said, feeling a little breathless at his timing.

"Hi."

"Welcome to my second home."

Daniels stepped inside and peeked around. "It's lovely."

Without a thought, Susan reached out and touched his arm. His muscles were as hard as they looked, and the fabric of his three-piece suit as expensive as it felt. He smelled delightful. When he leaned closer, Susan's breath hitched.

His eyes glimmered when he said, "I wanted to reward you."

"Reward me?" Susan's eyes danced with his, curious to know what she'd done to be rewarded.

"Thanks to the information you shared at lunch, we were able to interview Jenny Booth's mother. It aired tonight."

Susan's head floated with elation. After talking to Naomi and dropping her off at home, she hadn't given the teen another thought. She felt ashamed—it was selfish of her to concentrate on work when Naomi's best friend was missing. Her goddaughter clearly needed someone to talk to. It was naïve for Susan to think that one conversation could change anything, but that's all she'd given her. She had responsibilities, too, and her employees counted on her to provide regular work.

"I missed it," Susan said, hustling back to her office to check her phone as if expecting to find a message from Cindy waiting. "Did they find her? Please tell me they found her and that she's all right."

Daniels casually hid his hands inside his pants pockets and gave Susan a look of sympathy. "She's still missing, but when she is found," he stepped forward and raised his eyebrows as he locked eyes with Susan, "*alive*, you will be the hero who brought the world's attention to her whereabouts."

"I just want her to return safely. My goddaughter is devastated over this, and half the school's girls are worrying they will be next."

Daniels's cellphone vibrated somewhere inside his sport coat. Susan watched him check it and ignore it. "You can take it if you need," Susan assured him. "I know how work never rests."

Daniels's expression hardened as he pocketed the device. "We should celebrate."

"An interview is hardly worth celebrating."

"Agreed. But I want to take you to dinner regardless. Where should we go?"

"I haven't said yes."

Daniels smirked, looked around. "You're done with work, aren't you?"

Susan bit the inside of her cheek, debated whether or not this was a good idea. She already felt guilty for not being with Cindy and Naomi. The client she lost today was still looming overhead. Then she remembered Daniels offering her access to his network, and desperation won over empathy.

She asked, "Is this a date, or something else?"

"You can call it whatever you like," he took her hand into his, and added, "but, please, can we not discuss work?"

CHAPTER FIFTY-EIGHT

KING HADN'T MOVED SINCE HIS CONVERSATION ENDED with LT. All he could hear was his superior's parting words, *it's all about appearances.* There was no way he was about to end his relationship with the woman he loved, but he also wasn't ready to hand in his badge, either. The upper brass was clearly looking for a fall guy in this mess, and King knew it was up to him to clear his name. The question was, how? Once he had that figured out, would he be able to do it before time ran out?

Alvarez came out of the shadows and gave him a look from beneath his lowered brow.

King said, "We've been reassigned."

"No. *You've* been reassigned."

King flicked his gaze to his partner. "What are you talking about?"

Alvarez turned and looked to his unmarked cruiser and said, "An Amber Alert just went out."

King's heartrate spiked. This was news to him. King retrieved his cellphone and dialed detective Gray's cell.

Alvarez furrowed his brow and said in a low tone, "You

keep going off the reservation, DPD and the upper brass will make sure you eat your gun."

The line rang in King's ear. He said, "This isn't about Jenny."

"No. Then what is it about?"

"Megan. Jane Doe." King's voice grew louder the harder his heart pumped. "It's about the asshole who is destroying these young women's lives."

Alvarez showed his palms and took a step back. The line clicked over and Gray answered. "I was about to call you," she said.

King asked, "What's happening?"

"It's bad. Something you won't believe unless you see it for yourself."

King was already hurrying to his car by the time Gray told him where to meet. He opened his car door and Alvarez caught his arm. "You better let me drive so you can say I dragged your sorry ass with me."

King didn't put up a fight, instead jumped into the passenger seat and clicked his seatbelt tight over his lap as Alvarez sped away. He raced across town with sirens blaring. King directed him where to go, and Alvarez kept flashing looks of doubt that King caught out of the corner of his eye.

He knew he was deliberately going against LT's orders to stay off the Jenny Booth kidnapping case, but this wasn't about Jenny. Alvarez was right. This was about a city on edge and a possible connection to Megan's killer.

The two-way radio crackled and King turned up the volume. They listened to initial reports coming through, confirming Gray's words; he couldn't believe what he was hearing. How was this possible? On the same day Megan's body was found? Was this perp replacing one with another?

By the time they arrived, there were two patrol cars and Gray's sedan parked out front of a two-story, three-bedroom house on the south side of the city. Gray came rushing out as soon as she saw King arrive. Once he opened his door and stepped foot on the pavement, he could hear a woman yelling for Gray not to leave her. King assumed she was the mother of the missing girl because of how hysterical she was, and understandably so.

King said to Gray, “I heard the reports on our way over. Anything new?”

Gray’s eyes were as wide as a cat’s and her skin flushed. “Seventeen-year-old, Latina, ripped from her mother’s arms as they were walking the streets. A security video was pulled from a nearby convenience store confirming her story, and it showed everything. Two men put the girl in their dark colored passenger van and fled the scene.”

King’s entire body flexed in preparation for war. This was bad, really bad. “What’s the girl’s name?”

“Jessica Hinojos.” Gray’s jaw tightened. “And it gets worse.”

Worse? How could it possibly get worse?

“She’s also a student at South High.”

CHAPTER FIFTY-NINE

OWEN DANIELS CLOSED THE TAB ON A WONDERFULLY luxurious meal and handed it off to the waitress. "Now, if you'll excuse me," he said to Susan who was watching him, "I'm off to the men's room."

Susan smiled, thinking how handsome he was and how satisfying the meal.

Daniels reached for her hand and brushed his thumb over her knuckles in gentle, firm strokes. "Promise to miss me while I'm gone?"

"Only if you promise to not take too long."

Daniels's eyes crinkled as he smiled and kissed the back of her hand. Susan blushed and watched her date weave his way into the back corner of the restaurant. On the opposite side of the room, a pianist tapped the keys next to a violinist. Tonight was perfect. A candlelight dinner from one of the city's top-rated chefs, and a finished bottle of wine—their second of the day. Still, Susan asked herself what exactly she was doing with Daniels. Sure, he was incredibly generous, handsome, and funny, but would she kiss him if he tried?

She opened her purse and applied a new layer of lipstick

as she thought about how unfair life was. How was it possible she could live this life of luxury without a care in the world when another woman was too sick with worry to eat because her daughter was missing and she didn't know where to find her?

As soon as she closed her purse, she flicked her gaze toward the restrooms. Daniels stood in the hallway near the window with his phone pressed to his ear.

Knitting her eyebrows, Susan couldn't help but notice his agitation. The way he carried himself, the way his shoulders appeared tight. Who could he be talking to at this hour? It had to be work. Daniels caught sight of her and smiled before turning his back and disappearing behind the wall.

Susan didn't want to read too far into his actions, but something didn't seem right. She reached for her own phone, thinking about messaging Sam and letting her know she had a way in with Daniels. In the end she decided against it, fearing it might create unnecessary problems for them both.

"Shall we?"

Surprised, Susan turned to find Daniels hovering over her left shoulder. He offered his hand and pulled her to her feet. He smiled, but there was a definite glint in his eye that wasn't there before. Had he used the restroom at all?

She asked, "Everything all right?"

"Nothing to worry about," he assured her. "Just work."

"And we can't talk about that." Susan smiled, attempting to lighten the mood as she threaded her arm through the crook of his.

A small laugh passed over Daniels's lips and they began to walk.

She liked the way she fit next to him—liked how strangers were looking at her with admiration in their eyes. Daniels was at the top and everyone knew it. Outside, they walked beneath a star-studded sky and Susan didn't want the night to end. At the car, Daniels opened Susan's door and said, "I had a wonderful time. Lunch and dinner."

Susan said, "Shall we plan to do breakfast as well?"

She watched Daniels's eyes fill with desire when she realized the implication she'd mistakenly made. Was it a mistake? She wasn't sure—didn't want to think too hard. She just knew she didn't want tonight to end.

Slowly, Daniels tipped forward, lowered his head, and went in for the kiss Susan thought he might try to take. Their lips touched and fireworks exploded behind Susan's eyelids. She kissed him back in an electrifying haze. When he pulled away, he left her feeling breathless and dizzy.

The drive back to Susan's place was mostly quiet, but Daniels remained the gentlemen all the way to her front door. Susan released his hand and unlocked the door with her heart hammering. She turned to Daniels and asked, "Would you like to come inside?"

Daniels paused for a moment of thought, then said with a smile, "I'd love to."

Susan nudged the door open, flicked on the overhead light, and entered her condo. She shed her shawl and heard the door click shut behind her when suddenly her body was swallowed inside Daniels's big arms. Pushing her up against the wall, his lips were on her neck as he hiked up her dress and pulled her underwear down.

Stunned by what was happening, Susan's mind and body went black. *Was he really doing this?* She heard him unzip his pants and she snapped out of her thoughts.

"Stop," she said firmly. "What are you doing?"

Daniels pushed more of his weight against her, wedging her between the wall and himself. He worked himself closer, between her legs.

"Owen. Stop!"

Susan flattened one hand against the wall and raised the

opposite arm, sending a sharp elbow to Daniels's gut. He grunted, and Susan took that moment to twist out of his grasp. She hurried into the living room where she took refuge on the opposite side of her couch. She openly stared, wondering what she'd done to make him think that was okay. Nothing. She hadn't done anything.

Daniels fixed his belt and breathed hard. "I—huh...I'm sorry." He swiped a hand over his head. "I don't know what got into me."

Susan folded her arms, tucked her trembling hands into each of her arm pits, and said, "You need to leave now."

A disbelieving look flashed over Daniels's eyes before he turned to the door and reached for the handle. Before leaving, he said, "Call me when you're ready to commit. I have everything you need waiting for you when you're ready."

CHAPTER SIXTY

I ARRIVED TO ARCHIE'S LOCATION TO FIND AN EMPTY street. I applied the brakes and slowed to a stop. The night was hot, the sky black. It was a little after nine p.m. and an uncomfortable, eerie feeling fell over me.

This was the place where Jessica Hinojos was abducted. A dark street corner brought together by a crumbling sidewalk near a 7-Eleven. It was easy to imagine how it happened, but I still didn't understand why.

A street lamp buzzed overhead and I killed the engine. I checked my phone. Nothing from Archie. I glanced to the convenience store, but he wasn't there either. His absence bothered me more than I wanted to admit, but this was how Archie worked. What could possibly go wrong?

I swung my door open and stepped out. Pushing my bangs out of my eyes, I looked up and down the sleepy street. The air was calm and dry and, though it was a stark difference from where I had just come from, it wasn't the least bit relieving.

What was he trying to prove? Why had I fallen for his trap? Did he want me to feel like a fool? If so, he'd succeeded.

Pulling my hood up over my head, I moved up the street thinking about Jessica. Denver University wasn't far from here, and neither was South High. Who was this person taking these girls? Didn't they know that playing in the same playground would eventually get them caught?

A dog barked and charged the chain-link fence, getting me to jump back. I stared, frozen stiff, into its eyes when the front door to its owner's house opened. The owner met my gaze—stopped and stared. I ducked my head and kept trudging forward.

Soon, I approached the back of the convenience store, edged the side, and came to stop at the corner beneath the security camera I assumed caught Jessica being taken. This wasn't where I was supposed to be—certainly not where Dawson would have assigned me if given the choice—but here I was, standing at the heart of the story. It happened here, not at Jessica's mother's house where I assumed the media circus to now be.

I followed the camera lens to where my car was parked. It was a perfect angle, squeezed between two large oak trees.

Archie brought me here because we thought alike. He wanted me to see this. Walk the grounds, smell the air, put myself in Jessica's shoes. I wasn't sure what I thought about all this—if I liked it—but he did it for a reason, and now I needed to know what that reason was.

Catch me if you can, I heard his words echo between my ears when a tall, well-built man exited the 7-Eleven. He stopped as soon as he saw me, and we both stared.

"You shouldn't be out here alone," he said.

I looked to the only other vehicle around and assumed it was his. There was no one inside the cab. "Neither should you," I said back.

He tipped his head back and I watched as a grin threatened to pull his lips upward. *Did I say something funny?*

"That may be," he said. "These streets aren't safe anymore."

"I've heard."

"But you didn't see it?"

The way he said it made me believe he had. "Did you?"

He was slow to answer. "No."

"Consider yourself lucky."

"I always do." He nodded and said, "You be safe now."

I wished the stranger a goodnight and watched him get into the shining red pickup truck I'd assumed was his. The engine rumbled to a fast start and he backed up and turned right onto the street without using his blinker.

Once again, I was standing alone, tormented by my thoughts. I crossed the parking lot and got behind the wheel of my own car. Through the windshield, I glanced back to the security camera. Jessica was lucky to have it capture anything at all. Just one foot in either direction and we might not have seen her go missing.

I cast my gaze to my lap and watched the video footage of Jessica's abduction on my smartphone for a second time. My gut wrenched again.

How could this have happened? Who were these men? Did this confirm there were two suspects behind this reign of terror they were inflicting upon our city, as I suspected there might be? My thoughts drifted back to Heidi and how she led us all to believe a teacher was behind these attacks. It had me thinking.

Once the video of Jessica's abduction ended, I scrolled through my list of contacts and called Allison. She picked up after the second ring, sounding sad.

Allison said, "I don't know how you do it."

"You've seen the news."

"I can't stop. No matter how horrific it is, I keep watching, praying that it's not real, and that someone will find her."

I inhaled a deep breath, watched a Toyota Prius park in front of the convenience store, and waited for Allison to surprise me by saying something about Heidi's comment making it to the evening news. But she never did. I assumed it had gotten lost sometime between reporting about Megan's murder and the abduction of Jessica. Was that done on purpose? To throw us all for a loop? It certainly felt that way.

I asked, "How well do you know Nicholas Bennett?"

"Why are you asking? Did you see him there? He was supposed to be there."

I asked her to elaborate and Allison shared how Bennett headed to Megan's crime scene as soon as they learned the body found may have been a student of South High.

"I haven't heard from him since," she said, "and I can't imagine he would still be there."

Thinking back, I couldn't recall seeing Bennett anywhere. I would have recognized his face if he was there. "No," I said. "And I was one of the last to leave."

"Oh, jeez." Allison gasped. "Sam, I'm worried about him. These are his girls going missing. Can you imagine? Just when I think I'm starting to like a man, he's closing himself off to me."

"Jessica—was she a student of his?"

Allison was quiet for a long pause. "I don't know."

I felt my expression pinch and debated whether or not to say it. But I had to. "Allison, I don't know how to tell you this, but there is talk that a teacher might be behind these attacks."

"*No.* No, Sam. You're wrong. It's impossible. Nicholas loves those kids. He would never hurt them."

CHAPTER SIXTY-ONE

TO HIM, SHE WAS REAL.

The image of her was lifelike. So crystal clear that he could feel the shine of her black-as-night hair fall between his fingers like water. And her electric smile. Boy, did he love looking at it. It was so innocent and bright; it could light the darkest of rooms with a single flash. And though she was trapped inside the blemish-free pixelated image of his computer, he could practically smell the sweet fragrance of her scent. He thanked her for that. For, without it, he might not have had reason to believe that they were even a possibility.

Ace rubbed his hands together with enough friction to start a fire.

But it was what lay beneath her high cheekbones and heart-shaped face that really got his attention: Her long, slender neck—the one physical feature that constantly brought him to his knees. Hers was marvelous and as he focused in on her throat that gave her voice, he could feel the arteries pump blood to her brain in the tips of his fingers, feel the rigid cartilage of her trachea that fed her lungs—

gave her life—a life they both cherished more than anything else.

Ace's gaze traveled up Naomi's face and lingered in her brown eyes for a beat. He placed himself next to her, sizing his tall frame against her short stature. A warm buzz formed in the tips of his fingers and moved up his arm in waves.

The TV flickered on the wall behind him. He could see the news playing on mute in the reflection of the mirror pinned to the wall just next to his computer monitor. He read the headline script scrolling at the bottom of the screen and reached for the clicker hidden beneath the Prom Queen Killer book opened on his desk. Turning up the volume, he listened.

Amber Alert...Jessica Hinojos...the FBI is working with local authorities to capture whoever is behind these attacks. There are no suspects at this time.

Ace's lips curled at the corners and he hit the mute button. Nothing was more satisfying than watching the cops run around like headless chickens, not knowing how to stop a madman like himself. They were clueless he was behind the attacks, and he appreciated the way the media snagged onto an idea and turned it into something else entirely.

He swept his gaze off the mirror and clicked on the second tab he had opened on his internet browser. Having to re-enter his password, he opened the website and searched for Eva Martin.

Once on her page, he browsed her gallery of images. Then he flicked back to Naomi's.

Yes, he had a type, he laughed. *Didn't every man with a pulse?*

Ace knew Eva was vulnerable. He also knew her kidnapping story was being purposely suppressed by the cops and the few reporters who knew about her. Ace liked that they thought they could hide her secret, and even considered messaging Eva to tell her that he knew what she was hiding.

But was it too soon to request a date? The lure to go after the one who got away was intense, but the risk too high still.

A thumping on the floor below gave him pause.

Ace eased back in his chair, shallowed his breathing, and waited to hear it again.

The soft glow of the computer monitor lit up the white walls that surrounded him. The noise vanished and the house went back to silence. It was just as he liked. No games. No fuss. Only rules to live and die by.

When he closed his eyes, he saw Megan take her last breath before he was forced to set her spirit free. She broke his rule and paid the price. It was a necessary evil, something that had to be done. If he hadn't, the others would begin to rise.

Ace had watched Megan's crime scene unfold from afar. As he did, it was as if he had an out-of-body experience. The news vans, the helicopters circling overhead. The police and the FBI. The fear in everyone's eyes. Thanks to him, he made tonight's entertainment possible.

His eyes sprang open with sudden realization.

He'd reached a new level in his career, one he didn't set out to achieve and was still trying to grasp himself. He'd been at this for over ten years—just like the Prom Queen Killer—but he was having the most fun now. He had to be careful if he didn't want to be caught—if he wanted these games to continue. Which he did.

Slowly, he stood, turned toward the master bath, and began shedding each item of clothing. First his t-shirt came off, then his jeans, and he finished with his underwear and socks, leaving a trail of clothes in his wake.

Ace slipped into the bathtub, felt the cold water engulf him and take his breath away. Sinking deeper, he held his breath underwater until stars flashed behind his eyes. Then he emerged, reached for the razor, and shaved his sculpted body bare before stepping out and walking to the mirror above the sink. There, he opened the contact lens case and placed each of the color lenses in his eyes before hiding his face behind a clear Halloween mask.

Staring into his unrecognizable eyes, he said, "You're the genius that will never get caught. The man who hides in plain sight."

CHAPTER SIXTY-TWO

THE PIERCING SCREAM WAS LOUD ENOUGH TO SHATTER windows.

As soon as Erin heard it, her eyes popped wide open. Awake in a snap, her heart pounded like drums in her ears. She turned her head and looked to her door. Dark shadows danced across the walls, scurried across her floors, but no one was there. The house was quiet and she thought the scream came from her dream.

Lifting her head off the pillow, Erin pushed herself upright and looked to the window. Soft light from the neighbor's house poured in between the curtains. Closing her eyes, she shook off what she *thought* she heard and pulled the bedsheets up over her breasts.

The ceiling fan clacked overhead and the tiny breeze it created sent a powerful chill down her spine. The hairs on her arm stood on end and she ironed them down with her hand as she thought what, other than a scream, she could have possibly heard. Her thoughts then drifted to Eva.

A minute passed without hearing another noise and she convinced herself it was nothing when suddenly she heard

Eva yell at the tops of her lungs, "Help! He's here. He's inside the house!"

Erin tossed the covers and ran across the hall as fast as she could. Pushing Eva's bedroom door open with both hands, it slammed against the wall with a loud thud. Erin flicked on the overhead light. A bright flash caused her to squint, and she braced herself for the worst.

With her hands balled into tiny fists, her muscles flexed, Erin bounced her gaze around the room until her eyes finally landed on Eva.

Eva rocked back and forth on the floor, hugging her knees to her chest. She kept mumbling something Erin couldn't make out through the tears she cried.

"Honey, look at me," Erin said, placing a hand on Eva's kneecap.

Erin wasn't convinced Eva knew she was there. Eva's eyes were closed when Erin squeezed her knee. Eva froze, stopped rocking, and tensed. She opened her swollen watery eyes, tipped her head back onto her shoulders, and asked Erin, "Did you see him? He was here."

Erin asked, "Who was here? Was someone inside your room?"

Eva's eyes bulged, her nostrils flared. New pellets of sweat glittered her brow and matted down her black bangs. Eva said, "Someone was outside my window."

"You saw someone, or you heard someone?"

Eva blinked and a thick tear fell from her eye as she shook her head like she didn't know.

Erin stared into her fearful eyes for a beat before moving to the single closed window on the opposite side of the bed. She approached with caution, sharing quick glances with Eva as she moved. Eva didn't move, only held her breath as if frightened Erin was about to encounter the same terror that sent Eva to the floor.

Once at the window, Erin lifted a finger and was about to peek behind the curtain when Eva sprung forward and said, "Careful. It's not just me he's after."

Erin's eyebrows knitted and she wondered what had happened to the confident and fearless girl she spent the previous day with.

"He'll hurt us both," Eva muttered again.

Erin pulled back the curtain and peeked through the glass. She saw nothing but her own reflection. Now Erin was certain the girl had experienced a nightmare. She checked that the window was locked and sealed shut despite the sweltering heat of August. It was.

Erin said, "I don't see anything."

"He was there." Eva's lips parted as she swept her gaze to the window. "I swear. I heard someone trying to break in. He knows I'm here."

Erin stared at a broken, scared girl and chose her words carefully. "The window is locked, Eva. There is no one outside."

Eva stood and pushed past Erin. Pulling back the curtain, she looked out the window herself. She released the curtain and it swung back into place. "He knows I'm here and is coming for me."

They locked eyes and Erin said, "Only Samantha knows you're here."

Eva wiped her face dry. "You keep saying that, but you don't know."

Erin knew Eva was right. She didn't know for sure. Erin asked, "Would it make you feel better if I stepped outside and took a look around?"

Eva inhaled a sharp breath and nodded her head once.

"Okay. Stay here until I get back."

Erin grabbed a t-shirt from her room and slipped it over her head before pushing her feet into a pair of sandals at the front door. She stepped outside and looked up and down the block, but saw no one. It was the middle of the night. Most people were sleeping. She was certain Eva had had a nightmare, maybe from sleeping in an unfamiliar bed. At least, that was what she hoped.

Erin edged the side of the house, wiped her palms on her shorts, and kept looking over her shoulder, feeling like she was being watched. The grass was tall and she saw no visible tracks. She moved between her and her neighbor's house, listening and watching for anything to prove what Eva heard could be real. The neighbor's house was dark, except for the front porch light that was always left on.

Erin checked the windows on her own house as she passed each of them. They were all locked. When she entered her backyard, she stood outside Eva's window making sure it was locked, too. Again, she saw no signs of tracks or any evidence it had been tampered with.

She relaxed, feeling at ease with the knowledge that her house was locked up and protected. But she still worried about Eva and how scared she looked. Erin made her way to the front of the house and opened the front door, ready to go back to bed. The adrenaline rush was already subsiding. Headlights suddenly came on across the street and lit up the street.

Erin turned and stared into the street.

A red Ford pickup truck pulled away from the curb and sped away.

Erin flew down the short flight of steps and ran into the street, trying to get a plate number, but couldn't. She was too late. It was too fast.

Was that the person Eva thought was outside her window? Erin wasn't convinced. She lived in the city and it never slept. But what bothered her most was that she couldn't recall if her neighbor owned a red pickup or not.

Erin headed back inside, hurried down the hall, and was surprised to find Eva packing her bag.

"What are you doing?" Erin asked.

Without looking, Eva responded, "I can't stay. He knows I'm here."

In the short time Erin was gone—trying to protect this young woman—Eva had pulled herself together and looked like a completely new person. Her hair was combed and tied into a ponytail. She'd shed her pajamas and traded them for a pair of jean shorts and a black tank top.

"There was nothing outside, Eva."

Eva rolled her neck and gave Erin an uncertain look.

"Where are you going to go?" Erin asked. "It's the middle of the night."

Eva shook her head as if not knowing the answer herself. "I have to get home. I need to pay my bills, let Lewis know I'm okay. He's probably been worried sick about me."

Erin stared, surprised she hadn't thought of this before. "Eva, what kind of car does Lewis drive?"

"He's rich." Eva shrugged and continued packing. "He drives several cars. Why?"

"Does he drive a red Ford pickup truck?"

"Yeah." Eva cocked her head. "How did you know?"

CHAPTER SIXTY-THREE

JENNY SMACKED HER LIPS AS SHE LAY FLAT ON THE FLOOR with her arms and legs spread out to her sides like an angel. She chewed on her tongue, which was as dry as a sponge. Starved and dehydrated, she didn't know how much longer without food and water she could go before her spirit, *and* body, broke.

She turned her head and stared at the empty plastic water bottle. It was turned on its side near the far wall, crumbled, looking exactly like she felt. Its cap was separated from the top and lay off to the side, the sign of defeat. No matter how hard she stretched her imagination, nothing but the man who had taken everything away from her could refill the bottle she desperately craved.

"Please," she groaned to an empty room. "I need water."

As if on cue, she heard an upstairs door open and shut.

Staring at the ceiling, she listened to the heavy footsteps creak the floor joists above.

He was home.

Jenny was numb, didn't react. Hopeful but scared, her

mind was listening to the whispers of conversation she'd shared with the other girls imprisoned inside the house.

What he did to me, I'm already dead.

Jenny knew the worst was yet to come. When, and what, would that look like? She didn't know, but assumed it would be as bad as she thought. As she prepared as best she could for what future lay ahead, she stared at the ceiling, wishing harm upon whoever was walking across the floor above.

Water drained through the house plumbing and He moved through the house with ease. Jenny was certain he was alone, but what did that mean? What time of day was it? Would she ever know what happened to Megan? Probably not.

As she lay there with thoughts swirling, her memory of what happened came back to her in waves. Jenny remembered waiting for Naomi outside by the car when her phone rang.

"I told you to stop calling me," she said.

"I have to see you."

"It's over." Jenny glanced over her shoulder and watched a woman fill the gas tank of her car.

"I love you."

Jenny rolled he eyes. "You should be dating girls your own age."

"They don't have what you have."

Jenny walked around Naomi's car, stepped onto the grass. He wouldn't leave her alone, wouldn't accept her decision to not sleep with him again. At first, the idea of sleeping with someone older sounded exciting, and what choice did she have? But the fun stopped the moment he took things too far.

"You hurt me." Jenny's voice cracked.

"It was a mistake."

Jenny dropped her head and began to cry.

"I'm sorry," he said.

Jenny heard his voice first behind her, then through the phone line. Before she had time to turn and look, a hand closed over her mouth and she was pushed into the back of a car with no chance to scream for help.

Or was it a truck?

She blinked. She couldn't decide what the getaway vehicle was when her thoughts were interrupted by Him bursting into her room. Surprised, Jenny's heart skipped a beat as she flopped onto her stomach and crawled on all fours, trying to escape. He caught her ankle and reeled her back as she let out a piercing scream.

Jenny twisted onto her back and kicked at his hands. "Leave me alone. Help!"

The man batted her foot away, blocked her kicks with his forearm, and smothered her with his body. Jenny squirmed beneath him and clawed at the floor, trying to escape. He wasn't wearing much, clothed in just white boxer briefs and a white t-shirt, hiding his face behind that stupid mask that caused Jenny to have nightmares.

"Help! He's going to rape me!" Jenny screamed, tempted to call out the others by name. But she couldn't. Then he would know she'd been talking, and he'd certainly kill her.

A fiery pain jolted her head, shot down her spine. He closed his fist on top of her head and yanked her to her feet by the roots of her hair. Jenny screamed again, fearing for her life. This was it. He was coming for her—coming to rape her, or kill her, or both.

He shoved her forward and Jenny stopped herself by gripping onto the doorframe. "Help!" She stretched her neck and screamed at the top of her lungs, "He's going to kill me!"

Jenny waited for one of the other girls to respond. When no one did, her eyes welled with thick tears. *Where were they? Why weren't they coming to help?*

Clamping his hand around her neck, he slammed her

against the wall and said, "Screaming will only make this worse."

Jenny looked him directly in the eye and yelled, "Help!"

He lurched forward, clamped a hand over her mouth. Jenny bit down, taking a piece of his flesh between her teeth. She watched his eyes wince in obvious pain, but it wasn't enough to get him to release. It only made him angrier.

Pinning her body against his, he dragged her across the basement floor and led her to a closed room where he kicked the door open. As he tossed her inside, Jenny tripped over her feet and caught herself before falling. As soon as she lifted her head and brushed her hair out of her eyes, she realized he'd brought her to Megan's room.

Jenny's gaze bounced between the photographs. He'd done the same with Megan as he did to her, with only one exception—Megan's room had a TV.

"Why are you showing me this?" she asked.

Without speaking, he pointed the clicker at the TV and Jenny watched the screen come to life. Jenny stared at him and he nodded his head for her to watch.

Jenny moved closer to the screen and listened as the news reported Megan's death. She started to cry. "You sick bastard. Why did you kill her?"

He whispered, "That is what happens when you disobey my instruction."

"Is that why I'm here? Because you think I disobeyed your instruction?"

He cocked his head. "Didn't you?"

Jenny wondered how he knew. Had he been home when she talked, or did he have cameras? Would another girl tell him?

"I know about everything that happens inside my house." He moved to her and Jenny was too scared to breathe. Taking her face inside his hand, he stroked her cheek with his thumb. Her bones trembled. “Have you been talking, Jenny? Tell me the truth.”

Jenny was too afraid to answer.

The man gripped her neck and squeezed, cutting off her air supply. Jenny’s eyes widened as she struggled to breathe. “I know you’ve been talking to the others.” His fingers tightened and dug deeper into her flesh as he stretched her neck further until he had her standing on tiptoes. “Shall I kill you, too?”

Jenny squeezed her eyes shut—her body wriggled, desperate for air—and just when she thought she would pass out, he released his hold. She dropped to the floor, gasped, and coughed on all fours. Then, to her surprise, she watched him leave the room.

Did he want her to follow? She didn’t know. Sitting on her heels, she dropped her chin and began to cry. A second later, he was back.

“Here. Eat this.” He pushed a plate near her.

“What is it?” Jenny asked.

“It’s simple but packed full of nutrition. Exactly what your body needs.”

Jenny’s eyes widened a fraction. She’d heard those words before. Turning to the plate, she stared at the perfectly rolled burrito. There was only one person in her life who ever gave her this meal and said those exact words—the coincidence was too great to ignore. But could it really be him?

Slowly, Jenny raised her gaze and stared from behind a curtain of lashes at the large man hovering over her, wondering if it really could be Coach Bennett who was hiding behind the mask.

CHAPTER SIXTY-FOUR

IT WAS THREE FORTY-THREE A.M. WHEN THE PHONE RANG.

I stopped typing, pulled my fingers off the keyboard, and flicked my tired and puffy eyes to my cellphone. Did I want to take this call? Nothing good could come from a phone call at this hour. Could it be Allison following up about Nicholas Bennett taking these girls? Probably not at this hour.

The cellphone was still vibrating when I turned it screen-side up.

Another unknown number.

Could it be Archie?

I set the phone back down. I didn't have it in me to chance a call this late at night.

I couldn't sleep when I'd finally gotten home after swinging by Erin's house to pick up Archie's book and check on Eva. I'd made sure Mason was safe in his bed and then sat down in my living room. I picked up Archie's book on PQK and began to read. It didn't take long to get sucked in. It read like a thriller, and the more I learned about PQK, the more terrifying he became.

Just like the person I assumed the police were looking for

now, PQK picked his victims carefully and disposed of them violently. He was intelligent and hid in plain sight. It was all documented in Archie's book and read as if it was happening in real time. It left me feeling stuck. There was still no sight of Jessica Hinojos, nor of Jane Doe's body. The similarities between what I was reading and what I was living were frighteningly clear.

We just couldn't seem to catch a break. I kept asking myself if these attacks were done at the hands of a copycat—the same copycat that Archie first warned me about at the awards ceremony two nights ago.

My head swam in exhaustion, a throbbing headache moving in from the back of my skull. There was so much on my plate with little to show for my work. The longer I stayed up, the more critical I became of how the DPD was handling the sudden change of events. How could they go from wanting to hide certain crime statics from the public to calling in the FBI to assist with the investigation? I welcomed the move, but it all seemed too sudden.

Cooper stirred at my feet and groaned. I cast my gaze to him and thought about my son, sound asleep in the next room. On autopilot, I clicked my computer mouse and watched the news of Jessica's abduction for what felt like the hundredth time. I paused the footage, zoomed in on the obscure faces of the two men—of the van—and asked myself if this could be the big break we'd been waiting for. I hoped it was. As badly as I wanted to reach out to King for a response, I didn't.

Then it hit me.

I'd forgotten about Mason's permission slip from school. I retrieved it from the kitchen counter and took another look at the fine print. If his school was monitoring student's emails, why not South High too? And, if they were, was there a way to gain access to the missing girls' communications?

There must be, but who would open that door for me? Nicholas Bennett?

My cell started ringing again, and I nearly killed the power to it when I saw Erin's number flash across the screen. As soon as I answered, Erin spoke in a flurry of panic.

"Slow down," I told her.

"Sam, we nearly lost her," Erin said as she told me about her night.

I closed my eyes and imagined Eva packing her small bag as she demanded Erin let her go. Then I asked, "Did you hear about the Amber Alert?"

"This is getting out of hand, Sam. First Megan. Now Jessica. No wonder Eva wants to leave."

"How much does she know?"

"All of it." Erin cursed, as if suddenly realizing something. She said she first thought it was only a nightmare Eva experienced, but when she went outside and saw a cherry red pickup speed away, she began to have doubts.

My thoughts immediately jumped to the man and truck I saw outside the 7-Eleven tonight. I wondered at the odds. I was thinking about Archie when I reminded her, "Archie doesn't drive a pickup truck."

"No, but you'll never guess who does."

My expression pinched when I asked, "Who?"

"Lewis Stark." Erin paused for effect. "And it's him Eva wants to see."

Was Stark a collector of women? Was that what this was about? Where did Eva fit into his life exactly? It was something I planned to find out as soon as I finished paying my respects to Megan Hines's parents. My day was just beginning.

CHAPTER SIXTY-FIVE

FOUR HOURS LATER, I STEPPED INTO THE MEDIA CIRCUS outside Megan's parents' house. I wasn't surprised to find myself jockeying for position, fighting to tell the same story as every other journalist in town. This was the next best thing until the police department gave us an update on their missing persons case—if they ever would.

I moved amongst the crowd, wedged between innocent bystanders, and wasn't surprised to not find Archie anywhere near the scene. Where did that man go? Why did it seem he dropped off the planet as soon as Jessica disappeared?

I hated myself for doing it, but I called Archie and left him a voicemail asking him to call me back. I wasn't sure he would, but at least I was making an effort. *Catch me if you can...*

Everyone from last night was here—local and national affiliates all wanting to get a piece of the action. Since the press conference confirming Megan's death, there still hadn't been an official response given by the mayor and I questioned whether he cared at all. These were his constituents, too, I thought as I looked around.

I found my way to the front of the line and stared at the

Hines' home. Though the curtains were closed and the lights on, this would be the last place I would want to be if I was them. Lucky for me, I had their personal cell number and was about to call when I caught sight of Heidi.

She was packing up with her crew, preparing to leave. I hurried over, wondering where they were going. As I approached, she lifted her head and said, "This is a dud story."

"Who is your source?" I asked.

Heidi laughed. "Still haven't figured it out?"

"I know it's someone inside the department." We shared a knowing look. The irony was that I was the one dating a cop. Yet somehow this was different. "But what I really want to know is who the teacher is you were referring to last night?"

"And give away my story?" Heidi quirked a single eyebrow. "I don't think so."

"Don't you care about these young women?" Heidi ignored me as I followed her to her news van. "Before Megan, another girl was murdered. No one knows who, and apparently her body went missing from the morgue."

Heidi made no indication she cared, nor that she was even listening. She surprised me when she turned and said, "I'll tell you what. You let me meet with that girl you're housing, and I'll tell you the name of the pedophile teacher who I know is preying on his students."

Our eyes locked. I wondered how she knew about Eva. I asked, but she didn't tell. We were at a standstill as neither of us was prepared to share what we knew.

"Exactly," she said. "We both have a secret. Now, if you'll excuse me, my team and I have work to do."

I watched Heidi climb into her van and leave. As soon as I was alone, I thought about calling Erin to tell her to keep a close eye on Eva with everyone seeming to want to get a piece of her when my phone vibrated with a call from Dawson.

"Nice try on getting everyone's attention on Jane Doe," he said, telling me about the walls he hit in trying to locate her, too. "It's like she never existed."

I asked if he received the piece I wrote last night—he did and liked what I wrote on Megan Hines. Then I said, "There might be more to come after I meet with her parents."

He said, "Send them my condolences. Sad the story turned out the way it did."

My throat constricted a little. "I have to go."

"Keep fighting, kid."

Once off the phone with Dawson, I dialed the Mrs. Hines's cell. The line clicked over after the second ring, and I was surprised Karen answered at all. We had gotten close over the last several weeks and I considered her a friend.

"Can we meet?" I asked.

"We're staying at a friend's house." Karen gave me the address and told me to swing by. "I'll watch for your car."

CHAPTER SIXTY-SIX

Twenty minutes later, I climbed the front steps to an unfamiliar house in a neighborhood not much different from the last and softly knocked on the front door.

Sparrows chirped in the nearby trees, the leaves rustling in the gentle breeze. It was a beautiful summer morning despite having to mourn for Megan. I knew the mood inside would be somber.

The drive gave me time to think. I wasn't looking forward to the conversation I was about to have. I wondered how Mr. and Mrs. Hines had managed to escape the media circus. I was glad they had. It wasn't fair of the media to bombard them and turn their grief into another story made for evening news.

The door opened and I introduced myself to the face I didn't recognize. He was tall with sunken, sad eyes. I assumed he was the homeowner—a friend of the family. He stepped to the side. "Rob and Karen are waiting in the living room."

"Thank you."

He closed the door behind me and said, "I'll show you the way."

The house was busy with knickknacks, books, and crafts left out on tables. The walls were as crowded with family photographs and wall hangings. As soon as Karen saw me, she stood and met me halfway. I smiled, stretched my arms out wide, and wrapped her small body inside my arms. She began to cry and I glanced to Rob who couldn't hold my gaze. His eyes were bloodshot from what I assumed to be a full night of crying—mourning the loss of their only child.

"I'm so sorry," I said through a constricted throat, fighting back the sting of tears threatening to burst free.

I was here to let them know they weren't alone. Things hadn't turned out the way we hoped, and it felt silly to mention the obvious during such difficult times.

Karen stepped back, flashed a small smile, and went back to sitting on the couch. Rob started pacing. It went on like this for the next several minutes—awkward pauses and uncomfortable moments of silence with no one knowing what exactly to say.

"The police were here last night as soon as they found Megan," Karen told me. "They still don't know who did this, and then we saw the news."

"Have you talked to any other reporter since learning about Megan?" I asked, thinking about my conversation with Heidi. I also needed to cross Archie off my list of suspects.

Karen said, "No."

From the moment Megan disappeared, her parents had waited to hear from the kidnapper. When no contact was made, their anxiety only grew worse. They remained strong and optimistic throughout it all, but now I could see their spirits had broke. And with good reason.

Rob followed up by saying, "Could a teacher really be behind these kidnappings?"

I stared into Rob's dark eyes and got the impression he was looking for someone to blame. I couldn't fault him for doing so. After my husband Gavin passed, I tried to blame everyone, unable for months to see the truth of bad luck.

"I'm hearing reports of the other victims," I said, "and yes, some are suggesting older men might be involved."

I could see Karen wanted to say something, but she hesitated when she saw the anger in her husband's expression. As I sat on the edge of the couch with my elbows digging into my kneecaps, I looked for an excuse to be alone with Karen, but it never presented itself.

I said, "I know you said Megan didn't date, but could it be possible there was a man in her life?"

"Megan was a good girl," Rob defended his daughter. "Athletic and on her way to an Ivy." He swept his gaze back to me. "This isn't news to you. Megan wasn't interested in dating. She was focused on her grades, on sports."

"Volleyball," I said, remembering our previous conversation.

"Yes," Karen said solemnly. "She was so excited for another chance to repeat last season's success, this time starting varsity."

I cast my gaze to the tips of my fingers, thinking again about Coach Bennett. I had no hard evidence to go on, only that he worked with some of these girls at South High. But my gut told me he was someone I needed to pursue. "Did you know the coach well?" Karen and Rob simply stared at me.

Karen shot an uneasy gaze toward her husband before speaking. "Rob doesn't know the complete story."

Rob's eyebrows pinched and I could hear that he stopped breathing.

"Megan *was* dating," Karen said as she looked to her husband. "She didn't want you to know because she was afraid you'd be angry."

Rob swiped a hand over his mouth and turned his head.

Karen said, "Looks like she was right."

Rob exploded and left the room, a punch to the wall, his parting sound. My insides jumped at the contact. When we heard the back door open and slam shut, I turned to Karen and asked, “Who was this boy? Did you know him? Was he a good kid?”

Karen told me his name and confirmed he was a good kid.

“Then what happened?” I asked.

“She got dumped.” Karen stood and moved to the window. She folded her arms and took a moment to gather her thoughts. Then she continued, “Not long after that, rumors spread about Megan that weren’t true. Soon the boys were calling her a slut, mean names like that. Megan was devastated and confused by it all. She didn’t know how to handle the sudden change or how the school and the boy she thought she loved could turn on her without reason. It wasn’t like she had a lot of experience with boys, and I was afraid this would ruin future endeavors. That’s when everything started to unravel for her.”

I sat there with thoughts jumping of Bennett and King’s mention of Jenny maybe being involved with an older man. Rob’s voice startled me back to the present.

“You should have told me,” Rob said to his wife.

I turned and was surprised to see him back in the room. I hadn’t heard him come back inside. Karen didn’t seem to care. The truth needed to come out. Flicking her gaze back to me, Karen said, “You’re probably wondering what happened next.”

I nodded and she continued.

“Things eventually died down for her, but then one day after school, Megan and her friends were changing for an after-school event in the girls’ locker room when a male teacher walked in on them.”

I asked, “This all happened last school year?”

Karen nodded. “During the spring semester.”

"What did Megan do?"

"At first she made nothing of it. The teacher claimed it was purely an accident."

"And was it?"

Karen shrugged. "Megan didn't think so. She brought it to the administration's attention."

"What happened? Did they discipline the teacher?"

Karen cast her gaze to the diamond ring she was busy spinning around her knuckle. "Megan wouldn't talk about it, and neither would the school when I called. But not long after all this happened, the same rumors as before picked up and apparently didn't stop."

"Christ, Karen." Rob extended his arm and pointed his hand at her. "You're just sharing this to me? Why didn't you tell this to the police last night?"

Karen's expression hardened. "Because we didn't see the news until after the detective left."

They were referring to Heidi's sensational reporting. Though there wasn't any evidence to suggest that what Heidi said was true, I was starting to believe she might be onto something.

Rob planted his hands on his hips, visibly upset.

I asked, "What is the teacher's name?"

The tall man hurried into the room and took Rob's attention away. "Sorry to interrupt, but you're going to want to see this." He flicked on the TV and landed on the local news channel.

As I tuned in to the story, Karen leaned her head close to my shoulder and whispered, "I don't know who the teacher was, never did find out. But there is no doubt something is going on at that school that the administration wants to keep quiet."

CHAPTER SIXTY-SEVEN

THE STAIRS CREAKED AS NICHOLAS BENNETT CLIMBED HIS way to the top. At the landing, he switched the light off and dropped the ceramic plate he was holding to his side when he heard what sounded like tapping coming from inside the walls.

Twisting around, he peered into the dark abyss below with a quizzical brow. The basement walls wept a soft musty odor. When he flicked the light back on, the sound he thought he heard stopped.

Bennett lived in an old house that creaked and whistled its way through life. Over the years, he had framed and finished the basement and was now working on a big kitchen remodel. But none of his equipment was plugged in. With no AC running, there was only one possible explanation for that noise.

He took one step down to investigate when his cellphone began to ring from the kitchen counter.

Grumbling his annoyance, Bennett turned and headed back up the steps, making a mental note to follow up on the tapping, switched off the basement light, closed the door, and retrieved his phone. The TV was still on. He'd been keeping a close eye on the developing story of the missing girls being reported from outside Megan's parents' house.

Bennett glanced to the phone's screen and answered the call from Allison.

"How are you holding up?" she asked.

Bennett kept his eye on the news. He didn't like that they were suggesting a teacher might be behind the attacks. He said, "I'm surviving."

"We have to do something," Allison responded. "I'm falling apart over here."

She waited for him to invite her over. Though she'd given him every opportunity to do so, he hadn't yet. Bennett wasn't the same man he was yesterday. But he didn't have to suffer alone.

Allison said, "I saw the FBI are now involved. Did you see anything last night when you visited the crime scene? I keep watching the news but something tells me they're not giving us all the information."

Bennett's jaw clenched and he turned his attention away from the TV screen. "I didn't make it."

A long silence followed. She final broke it with, "Nicholas, what's happening at South High? This wasn't what I signed up for. Why is someone doing this to these poor girls? The news is saying a teacher might be involved. Did you hear that?"

Bennett flinched. Then the doorbell rang. "I have to go," he said.

"Nicholas!"

Bennett killed the call, stuffed his cell into his back pocket, and opened the front door. He was surprised to find a female student of his looking up at him with glistening doe eyes, as if needing to be saved.

CHAPTER SIXTY-EIGHT

WHAT WAS SHE DOING HERE? DID SHE COME ALONE? Bennett stood frozen at the door, hypnotized by her fragile looking eyes. Naomi Moss dipped her chin and cast her gaze to her painted toes.

"You should be home with your family," he told her.

Naomi's chin hit her chest and she started to cry. Bennett stuck his head out the door and quickly looked to the neighbors to see who might be watching. Once he was sure no one was, he hooked his hand on her shoulder and pulled her inside.

Naomi stumbled forward as Bennett latched the door closed behind her. Her body felt like jelly. It was clear she needed someone to talk to.

"Naomi, what's going on? Is everything all right?"

Her head snapped up. Her expression pinched with a burst of anger. "Haven't you been watching the news? Megan is dead and Jenny is still missing."

Bennett sighed. He reminded himself about Jessica Hinojos, too. "Come on inside." He led her to the kitchen, turned off the TV, and instructed her to take a seat at the table. He asked, "Did you come alone?"

Naomi gave two small nods of her head and looked around, taking in his place for the first time. Bennett hoped he hadn't left anything out that he didn't want her to see.

"I'm in the middle of a remodel."

Naomi didn't comment. Her shoulders hunched as she settled into her seat.

"I'm doing it myself and it's taking longer than I'd like." Bennett kept rambling, filling the silence with anything. "Are you thirsty?"

Naomi's phone dinged with a text. She swiped a thumb over the screen, read the message, and flicked her gaze up to Bennett. Her expression turned cold briefly. There was nothing funny about any of this, so when Naomi burst into a fit a laughter, he frowned, confused by her reaction.

Naomi stifled her laugh and waved a hand through the air.

"I'm sorry, I shouldn't be laughing," she said, giggling.

"That's quite all right."

Soft giggles continued to bubble up from deep inside Naomi's chest before she finally settled down. Then she said, "You always said to come to you if I ever needed your help."

"What can I do for you?"

Naomi's eyes welled with tears. Her emotions were wildly swinging. "I didn't know who else I could talk to. My mom doesn't like Jenny and, besides, even if I could talk to my mom about how scared I am for Jenny, it never feels like she's truly listening to me."

Bennett filled two glasses of water at the sink and placed them on the kitchen table, sliding one to Naomi. He sat across from her and said, "I heard the police came to ask you some questions."

"How did you hear that?"

"Mr. Helton told me."

Bennett let her thoughts form. When she was ready, she said, "I didn't lie. I told them everything I knew."

"No one said you did."

Naomi shared a sideways look with Bennett. After a silent beat, she said, "It wasn't until after they left that I thought about how Jenny said her mother was struggling to pay her bills."

With one hand on his knee, the other on his water glass, Bennett asked, "And what, you think that has something to do with Jenny's disappearance?"

Naomi shrugged a shoulder. "I don't know. Maybe."

"Does Jenny's mom know you're here?"

Naomi rolled her eyes. "God no. She would just assume you were the older man Jenny was sleeping with." They locked eyes and Bennett tried to hide his surprise.

"Jenny had a relationship with someone older?" Bennett's brow furrowed as Naomi nodded. "Did you know who this man was?"

Naomi shook her head no. "You know Jenny. She's a bit crazy, but I think the real reason she was interested in him was to help her mom pay the bills. That's what I can't stop thinking about, what if it *was* him?"

"Because you knew it was wrong?"

"No, because I don't know who *he* was."

Bennett shifted in his chair and glanced to the basement door, mulling over what to do.

A loud thumping could be felt in the soles of their feet when Naomi asked, "What's that noise?" They shared a look. "It sounds like someone walking on your walls," she said.

Bennett leaned forward and said, "You need to tell this to the cops."

"I can't."

Bennett relaxed his shoulders. "Why?"

"Because the police already said if I would have called as

soon as I knew Jenny was missing, she would have been found by now." Jenny's chin quivered. "It will be my fault when she dies."

"Don't say that."

"It's true. Whoever killed Megan will kill her, too."

Bennett stood and walked around the table, offering Naomi his hand. She reached for it and he pulled Naomi to her feet, encasing his arms around her teenage body. She melted into him when he said, "Stay positive, kid. Something tells me Jenny is still alive."

CHAPTER SIXTY-NINE

Naomi flushed the toilet, stood, and zipped up her jean shorts. She didn't actually need to pee, but needed an excuse to collect her emotions that were leaking like a faucet out of her eyes.

Moving to the sink, she washed her hands and pinched life back into her cheeks, making sure her makeup hadn't smeared or run. She felt foolish for crying in front of Coach Bennett, but he seemed confident that Jenny was still alive. She didn't understand how he could be so poised, but it comforted her to hear it. Maybe that was the point—to fill her up with hope.

Turning off the water, she dried her hands on a towel, still not fully understanding why she came here to begin with. Though she trusted Bennett, she knew many students in the school didn't.

Her cellphone buzzed on the counter.

Naomi turned her focus to her phone and froze. She was afraid to answer it.

Since her sexting photo went viral, she had suddenly become the school slut. There was a target on her back with rumors spreading across her social media channels. They were now flooded with her peers calling for her to kill herself, get a boob job, and whatever other mean things they could come up with to make her feel worthless. Maybe that was the reason she came here to talk? In some twisted way, she could relate to his own experience of being the source of far-fetched rumors.

Naomi groaned when her cell buzzed with a second text message. Finally, she gave in and checked to see who it was. It was from Charlie.

I don't want to talk about it anymore, Naomi wrote back.

It's bigger than that, Charlie responded.

What could be bigger than her topless photo? Naomi didn't know.

The news is saying a teacher is behind these attacks. Where are you?

Naomi stared at her device with thumbs hovering over the screen. Should she tell Charlie where she was? No, she couldn't. She wrote, *Out. What teacher?*

Out? Ok. Whatev. Don't tell me. I don't know, but I bet it's Bennett. You know what happened with him and the other girls. The dude is a creep.

Naomi suddenly felt lightheaded. She did know—or at least she thought she knew—what happened between Bennett and the group of older girls last year. Then she remembered what happened the other night when Jenny received the volleyball shorts that were too big. Bennett left the room and followed her, but to where? The girls' locker room?

Her brain hurt. She was thinking too far into these speculations, yet she still found herself opening drawers and cabinets, looking for clues to suggest he was the killer who had taken her friend.

What did she really know about Bennett besides he lived alone? Not much.

In her search through his bathroom, she found unopened tooth brushes, first-aid supplies, washcloths, towels, and a can of air freshener. Nothing suggested he was anything other than who he portrayed himself as. A normal middle-aged man who lived a completely boring life.

Naomi took a step back and inhaled a deep breath. Calming her sudden fit of panic, she didn't understand some of the rumors circling the school that said he was a creep who spent too much time with kids. He was a good coach, a dedicated teacher. She could sympathize with him. Couldn't she?

The doorbell rang and Naomi turned her head toward the door. Her heart jumped into her throat. She didn't want anyone to know she was here. If anyone found out, then rumors would really start to fly.

Slowly, she tiptoed her way to the door and pressed an ear against it. She tried to hear who was at the front door. When she couldn't hear anything, she reached for the door handle and cracked the door open only to be surprised by Bennett.

"Good. You're here," he said.

"Who is at the door?"

"I don't know, but stay here. It's better that we keep your visit to ourselves."

Naomi did as she was told and tucked herself behind the door. She kept an eye on Bennett as he hurried to clean up the kitchen. Why did he suggest keeping her visit a secret? Were the rumors true? She thought Bennett seemed scared, perhaps paranoid, and Naomi wondered who could be at the door. Ruth? Her mom? Susan?

"Who is it?" she whispered.

"Just stay put." He snapped his finger at her.

Naomi kept the door cracked and listened to Bennett

exhale a deep breath as if collecting his thoughts before finally answering the door.

Then Naomi heard a woman's voice say, "Mr. Nicholas Bennett?"

"Please. No cameras," Bennett said.

Naomi's heart raced. *Cameras?* She scooted across the floor and pulled her knees to her chest. She closed her eyes and fought back the tears as she heard the next words.

"Mr. Bennett, you're a teacher at South High, isn't that right?"

"I am. And I'd be happy to talk, but without the cameras."

Seeming to ignore his requests, Naomi heard the woman press harder. "There are allegations you've had inappropriate relations with some of your students."

"That's it. You're done. Please leave."

A small scuffle and protest broke out. Naomi couldn't believe what she was hearing.

"Mr. Bennett, when was the last time a student was inside your home?" The woman paused for a quick beat before continuing. "Is there one inside now?"

Naomi's temperature spiked. She'd been caught, possibly followed. Had she been set up? Or was Bennett the monster people thought he was? The woman's voice sounded familiar, but Naomi couldn't place it. Was it someone from the school? But what about the cameras? Then it hit. She was from a local news station. *Oh my god.*

"Mr. Bennett," the woman asked again, "is there a student with you now?"

Naomi stood, opened the door, and peeked around the corner. She watched as the news lady held up a smartphone Naomi recognized. It was Tommy's. The one Mr. Helton was supposed to have kept and locked away forever. How did she get it?

"Is this yours?" the news lady asked Bennett.

Bennett stared as if looking at a foreign object.

"It was given to me by someone who said it was yours. Can you guess what I found on it? No? Well, let me tell you. There are explicit pictures of a student of yours. Any idea how it got there?"

Naomi knew what picture she was referring to. She slammed the bathroom door open and hurried to the front of the house. Bennett spun around with a look of disappointment flashing over his eyes. He'd been caught in a lie.

"It's not his," Naomi said, feeling the cameras turn to her. "That phone. It's mine."

CHAPTER SEVENTY

I COULDN'T BELIEVE WHAT THE WORLD WAS WITNESSING. Karen and I stared at the TV screen with tight expressions. My insides flinched with each question Heidi Mitchell shot at Bennett, hitting his integrity like a dozen sharp arrows meant to kill.

He was knocked off balance and it made him look guilty. Optics were everything, and I hoped Heidi had this right. The world would now forever see him as the man she made him out to be. Guilty.

This was where she ran off to, I thought. Bennett was the person she'd alluded to at last night's press conference. I didn't know how I hadn't pieced it together before this. If I had, could I have saved him from embarrassment? Bennett still didn't make sense to me. The majority of child abductions were at the hands of parents, close relatives, and rarely done at the hands of nonfamily.

Rob twisted around and gave his wife a look that said, *I told you so.* "I knew something was off with him. He's a loner who spends far too much time with young people. Particularly girls."

I swallowed the lump in my throat, feeling the tension mount. Beneath Heidi's broadcast read, *BREAKING NEWS: Police are still searching for the missing teen, Jessica Hinojos.*

There was no mention of Jenny Booth. Though it bothered me, I didn't allow it to distract my focus. I asked Karen if Bennett could have been the teacher who walked in on her daughter changing. When she rolled her eyes to me, her expression was similar to Bennett's, one of shock and fear swirling between the confusion.

"Of course it was." Rob opened his palm and pointed to the TV. "You think she's just there to make this stuff up? Look at him. He looks like a man who has finally been caught."

Rob was livid. I was surprised he immediately sided with Heidi. Once again, I was thinking about what Nancy Jordan revealed—Daniels controlling Heidi's career, including the source I assumed Heidi was now using against Bennett. Did Heidi know the facts? I wasn't convinced she did. At least not fully.

"I never liked that guy." Rob kept shaking his head back and forth. "Bennett was always with those girls. Day. Night. Weekends. I can't believe the school employed a pedophile."

Out of the corner of my eye, I saw Karen begin to side with her husband. It wasn't my place to stick up for a man I barely knew, so when Allison called my cell in absolute hysterics, I took the call in the hallway. "Slow down, hun. I'm watching the news too."

"He's not the man she's making him out to be. He's a good man. Sam, why are they doing this to him?"

"I don't know," I whispered into my phone.

Allison knew Bennett best. She had a great sense of moral character. I trusted her opinion. It was partly why she spent half of her adult life single—as she put it to me, "The men worth keeping have all been snagged."

When I turned and glanced at the TV, my heart stopped. As soon as I saw Naomi Moss rush toward the cameras from inside Bennett's house, I knew he was doomed.

CHAPTER SEVENTY-ONE

THIRSTY LEANED HIS SHOULDER AGAINST THE WINDOW frame and sipped his Irish coffee as he peered through the glass and into his backyard. With a valium settling into his bloodstream, relaxation was finally coming his way. Though still anxious, he felt the need to keep busy. Or maybe it was the young woman tanning on his lounger that left him feeling unsettled.

He curled his lips over the rim of his mug and gazed up into the bright sunlight, unable to decide what kept him feeling uneasy. There wasn't a single cloud in the baby blue sky and, for some reason, that made him feel exposed.

The girl turned her head and said something he couldn't decipher.

Thirsty stared at his stepdaughter's pretty friend, wishing he could read lips. Her eyes were hidden behind dark tinted glasses, allowing him only to imagine the Caribbean blue eyes that took his breath away. She had a full body, thinly covered by a skimpy bikini meant for women much older than her.

Girls these days. They wanted to grow up so fast.

The sound of high heels approached, and Thirsty heard

them come to an abrupt halt directly behind him. He didn't bother to greet his wife, though he could feel her piercing judgmental gaze bore a hole into the back of his skull. Instead, he continued to drink his coffee and stare at the underage girl's slender neck.

Why couldn't he be as happy as they looked? When did his happiness stop?

"School was canceled," his wife said in an authoritative tone.

Thirsty could see his wife without having to look. Her hip cocked to the side, arms folded as she gave him *the look*. The look of disappointment, like she'd married the wrong man.

"I heard," he said. "One of their classmates is dead, another missing, and this is how they react?"

No one cared. Life was cheap—nothing more than a false illusion created by the sickness of our minds. We were either stuck in or damaged by the past, or chasing an unattainable future that may never come to be. His mind was unsettled, and he thought maybe he needed to up his dosage of medication.

"What would you prefer them to do?" his wife asked.

He raised his mug, took a small sip, and let his head float back up into the clouds. Wedging his hand inside his pants pocket, he retrieved a single Vicodin and popped it into his mouth.

"I don't know," he said. "Show some respect."

The heels clacked across the room and he listened as his wife turned the volume up on the news. Thirsty listened, not caring much about what they said, and began taking pictures of his stepdaughter's friend with his phone.

"Are you serious?" his wife snapped, catching him in the act.

Thirsty dropped his phone by his side, slowly turned, and

walked to the fruit bowl. "What?" He picked up an apple. "The fruit is ripe this time of year."

His wife looked disgusted, maybe slightly worried. She asked, "Have you been taking your medication?"

"It's the reason I can't sleep."

"Are you taking it as the doctor prescribed?"

He glared, then flicked his gaze to the news. Now this is interesting, he thought.

"Maybe we should schedule an appointment or get a second evaluation," his wife said. "I heard you restless and awake last night. What time did you get in?"

Thirsty didn't hear his wife. A bubble closed over his ears as the news stole his attention away. *A teacher. Of course. How brilliant?!*

His wife followed his gaze to the television screen and said, "It makes me sick to know someone is kidnapping and killing these girls."

"There has only been one murder," he reminded his wife as he watched her collect her purse and keys, preparing to leave the house.

"One too many," she said as she headed out the door.

He gave her a small wave goodbye and continued staring at the TV. Thirsty loved how the police hadn't named him as a suspect. The real question was why Owen Daniels deployed Heidi Mitchell to this poor teacher's house when they should be focused solely on finding Eva Martin.

Were these the ratings you wanted, Executive Producer? Of course they aren't. You can do better. And so can I. But, first, you'll just have to find her. Find her for both of us.

Thirsty needed those news bastards to lead him to Eva. And when they did, he'd be ready to retrieve the one who got away.

CHAPTER SEVENTY-TWO

King's vision blurred as he rubbed the dryness out of his eye. He'd worked throughout the night again, and now he was doubting his own effectiveness until he finally spotted something of use.

Pausing the security clip from outside the fill station where Jenny Booth was last seen, he clicked on his computer mouse and zoomed in on the man's face. It was a clear shot, but did it mean anything?

Curling his fingers over his keyboard, King did a quick internet search. A second later, Archie Smith's image populated his screen. He compared his search results with the security footage. It was a clear match. Taken a half-hour before Jenny Booth went missing, the man he was now looking at was the reporter Samantha had warned him about.

King leaned back and his chair squeaked beneath his weight.

Was this coincidence or proof that Archie might be a person of interest like Samantha suggested?

Tapping the ballpoint of his pen against his notepad, King knew he had nothing more than a hunch so far. This suggested nothing about who might have taken Jenny. It wasn't like Archie was the only person to fill his gas tank that day. But something about it had King thinking.

King scrubbed a hand over his face, thoughts churning, remembering Sam telling him that Archie took a photo of Eva. Alvarez talking on the phone at the next desk over brought him back to the present.

"Jessica's mother didn't know who the men could be," Alvarez said, "but is deeply afraid her daughter will die if we don't find her soon."

King didn't know who his partner was talking to. He stayed with his line of thinking and wrote down Archie Smith's name next to Naomi Moss's—they were both at the gas station where Jenny was kidnapped. Around him, computer keys clacked and phones rang. The discovery of Megan Hines shocked the department awake like a defibrillator placed over a dead heart, but it was Jessica's abduction while the police had their backs turned that had everyone scrambling to know just who they were chasing.

Someone smarter than me, King thought. But was that someone Archie Smith? A young journalist turned true crime writer? If so, where was the link?

King set his pen down and went back to clicking around on his computer. He navigated back to the footage taken from Jessica's abduction and wound the clock back a few hours before it happened. He fast forwarded the video, always looking for a sign of Archie. A half-hour passed before he stopped. This time, King didn't find him in any of the footage.

King's thoughts were now stuck on the two men with obscure faces who brazenly took Jessica out of her mother's arms while walking late last night. The police had nothing to identify the men, leaving King feeling absolutely inadequate. This attack was different from the previous abductions. King no longer though it was one suspect they were chasing, rather two parties working simultaneously.

Alvarez ended his call, cradled the receiver, and said, "I hope you're not here to speak to my partner about anything other than murder?"

King turned his head and found Detective Gray responding to Alvarez's comment with a witty response of her own. Then she stepped forward and picked up King's notepad and said, "Jessica has many relatives, some with priors, but they've all checked out."

King pointed to his computer screen. "Recognize him?"

"I'm familiar," Gray said, mentioning Archie's fascinating coverage on the Prom Queen Killer. "But what does he have to do with my case?"

Staring into Gray's eyes, King said, "He was at the same fill station half an hour before Jenny disappeared." Then he explained his two suspects theory, making a bold prediction, "One possible theory is that suspect number one learned and got better with time after his mistake with Eva, while suspect number two," King pointed to the screen, referring to Jessica's abductors, "didn't want to make the same mistakes as suspect number one, therefore recruited assistance to ensure their target didn't escape."

Gray thought for a moment, then said, "And they are, what, using the news to learn from each other?"

King reminded her that they had kept tight-lipped on Eva for these exact reasons. "I wish we had more footage of Jenny, but what really twists my insides is the fact that no one has heard or seen anything from her since she disappeared."

"I don't like how Jessica was taken right about the same time we were uncovering Megan."

Gray glanced down to King's notepad where he had Jenny's friend, Naomi Moss, circled next to Archie's name. "I'd like to speak with her again," she said, referring to

Naomi. "Something tells me there is more to her story than what we heard so far."

"Back of Megan," King met Gray's eye, "The FBI have a profile for our perp."

"Enlighten me."

"You're going to love this," Alvarez said with a hint of sarcasm.

King continued, "He's a collector of women."

"Like we didn't already know." Alvarez chuckled and shook his head.

"Then I'm glad I started looking much further back when reviewing earlier cases." Gray looked to King, a knowing glimmer in her eye. "That's why I'm here. If you're willing to risk the wrath of your lieutenant, I found something I'd like your opinion on."

King was on his feet in a snap. He followed Gray across the station to her desk in the Major Crimes Division. Gray's desk was neat and organized, meticulous in the way she conducted her own police work. Opening a file on her desk, she pulled a sheet out and handed it to King.

"Here is a list of girls who have been missing for ten years," she told him.

King read the names and, as he did, a couple of their stories slowly came back to him.

"Jessica's abduction got me thinking," Gray continued. "All night I reviewed my files and was glad that I kept my notes from all those years ago. I kept thinking we didn't have enough to go on, but when I reviewed these girls' cases, I realized this was the evidence I needed to solve this current one."

King didn't follow.

"Look closer," Gray said. "Are any of those faces your Jane Doe?"

King took his time when reviewing each girl's image. Lucy,

Nicole—but the next face made his heart skip a beat. "Sage Zapatero."

Gray's eyes lit up like this was the reaction she was hoping for.

King glanced back to the photograph. How could this be? If he was in fact looking at Jane Doe, she would have been no more than five years old when she was abducted. It wasn't adding up. This picture was taken ten years ago, and Sage was much older than that at the time, but had a nearly identical face.

King asked, "Are they related?"

"That's what we need to figure out."

King closed the file and tucked it under his arm, hating how this mysterious perp had the entire department looking in one direction while he was apparently out hunting for a new victim. If this girl was in fact somehow related to Jane Doe, he needed to find Jane Doe's body.

"We've got to go," he said.

"Where?"

"The ME's office." King started moving to the exit. "If we can learn who Jane Doe is, maybe we can close the case on Sage."

CHAPTER SEVENTY-THREE

"You have to call him."

Allison said, "And say what?"

My usually calm and collected friend was losing her patience. There was no way she'd seen Naomi on the news in Bennett's house, otherwise she'd be losing her mind. Keeping one eye and ear on the news, my other ear was with my friend. "Tell him anything."

"Anything?" Allison repeated.

My thoughts churned as I considered how it was best Bennett kept his face off camera and his mouth shut before he mistakenly convicted himself—assuming he was innocent. But how could I convey that to my friend without revealing that the world had just witnessed a teenage girl come from inside her teacher's home?

"If you can get him somewhere safe," I said, "maybe he can explain what's going on at that school of his."

"Sam, I'm worried."

You should be, I wanted to say as I focused my attention on the news and was happy to see it cut to commercial. "Save him, Allison. Get him talking."

When I ended our call, I knew what I had seen wasn't good. A part of me worried for Allison's safety, but my advice was given with reason. Allison knew him best, and I trusted her instinct despite what Heidi attempted to portray to the world.

Bennett was an easy target, made vulnerable because of his solitary lifestyle and his work with kids. But could he really be a monster who preyed on children? He didn't seem like our likely suspect. Or was I too blind to and only saw what I wanted to believe?

"I'm going to kill him myself." Rob exploded and rushed past me in the hallway as Karen chased after her husband, telling him to calm down.

My entire body tensed like a rock as I was unable to move. I didn't know what happened, what was said while I was on the phone, but I was growing more afraid of Rob the longer I stayed.

What was Naomi doing inside a male teacher's house, *alone*? I tried to remain calm, file through the evidence inside my head to convince myself Bennett couldn't be the teacher doing this to these girls. It had to be somebody else. But who?

I exhaled a deep sigh. Heidi got her shot for Daniels and the news cycle would repeat itself until she got to Eva.

Eva.

It was time for me to leave.

Karen came back into the room without Rob and quickly apologized for her husband's behavior. I waved it off as no big deal, attributing it to their daughter's murder. Then Karen asked, "What will happen now?"

"I'm not sure," I said, promising to stay in touch.

"What are you going to do?" she asked.

"What I always do," I said. "Chase the story and make sure the truth gets out."

Karen gave a small, reassuring smile when she reached for my hand and squeezed. "Thank you for all you did to help bring attention to Megan. Everyone gave up on her but you."

"She was an incredible girl," I said, attempting to free my hand from Karen's grasp. Her fingers tightened around my knuckles and she tugged me closer so she could whisper something into my ear.

Karen said, "But I need it to stop here."

It felt like I'd crossed an unspoken boundary. Our eyes swayed inside each other's gazes, and I could see the deep pain she was feeling inside her heart.

Had I unnecessarily—and selfishly—dragged out their anguish by thinking I was doing good by continuing to report on their daughter's disappearance?

I nodded my head and whispered my goodbyes. I exited the house with my head spinning as I squinted into the blinding sunlight. I'd come here as a friend and left feeling like our friendship just ended. It was a horrible and sickening feeling, but I couldn't lose my motivation to find who was responsible. Jenny was still somewhere out there, hopefully still hanging onto hope that someone would find her.

I jumped into my Subaru, settled behind the wheel, and raced across town to Erin's place. She was waiting for me when I arrived. As soon as she opened the passenger door I asked, "Where's Eva?"

Erin tossed me an uncertain look, asked if I'd seen the news.

I said I had and felt the fear of Archie bubble up inside me. Had he finally posted Eva's photo? Revealed her location to the world?

Instead, Erin said, "Eva decided she's going home."

"Going home? Or to see Stark? Doesn't she know how vulnerable she is?"

Erin dipped her head further into my car and said, "Eva doesn't think she's safe anywhere."

"Because of the nightmare? It *was* a nightmare, right?"

Erin confirmed her suspicions with a single nod, but then turned her head and glanced back to her house. A look of doubt crossed her face.

I suggested, "If she doesn't feel safe here, we could ask Susan to house her until this is all over."

"Eva won't go." Erin locked eyes with me. "She's done with us, Sam."

It seemed so out of the blue. I wondered who Eva was secretly talking to, if someone suggested that she leave, or if the news sparked some unspoken memory hidden deep inside. As I searched Erin's eyes for answers, I heard the front door to Erin's house open and slam shut.

Eva had a single bag slung over her shoulder, and she stopped as soon as she saw me. Not wanting to lose her, I exited the car and hurried over to her.

"There is nothing you can say to make me want to stay," she said. "I've already made my decision."

"Eva, what is it? What's going on?" Didn't she remember it was *she* who came to us?

Eva's jaw popped in and out as she shifted her weight from one foot to the other, appearing weighed down by her thoughts.

"We need your help," I said. "You can help us catch the monster who took you."

Eva snapped her neck and narrowed her eyes. "How can I help you when you don't even believe I was abducted?"

Everything inside me stopped. That's what this was about. But how did she know?

"That's right. I found Erin's notes." Eva craned her neck when leaning forward. "And here I thought I could trust you."

CHAPTER SEVENTY-FOUR

I watched Eva scurry up the sidewalk. I wanted to follow to make sure she got home safely, but I knew I couldn't. Erin was right. We'd lost her.

My hope was that it was only temporary and we'd be able to recover at some point in the near future. I also had to be real with myself, knowing she might be gone forever.

As difficult as it was to turn my back and walk away, there was nothing we could do now. Eva was an adult who could make her own decisions, even if we didn't agree with what those decisions were.

Spinning around, I headed back to my car where Erin was still standing.

"Should we follow her?" Erin asked. "If we don't, Archie will most certainly find her."

I dipped into the driver's seat, placed one hand on the steering wheel, and felt the pang of regret settle in my stomach. I should have scared Eva into changing her mind. I certainly didn't like the idea of Eva facing someone like Archie alone.

My cell dinged with a message from Dawson.

He wanted to know how my visit went with the Hineses and where we were at with Eva. I knew he'd be angry that I lost his exclusive, but Eva was more than a story to me. I wrote back, *Still working on it.*

How could I protect Eva from the dangers I knew were heading her way? I couldn't. Everyone wanted a piece of her. As I thought about it, I understood why Eva had no choice but to go.

We were part of the problem. I wished I'd never doubted her story. Things were complicated enough, then I had to go and make it harder. But I couldn't erase what I saw in her apartment.

Erin asked, "Who are you messaging now?"

"King," I said.

Eva was his only witness, as far as I knew. I still hoped that she could be the one to help explain what happened to Jenny.

King messaged back. *Was it Archie who scared her away?*

Not entirely, I wrote back.

"It's not all bad news, Sam."

I turned and looked to my friend, who still hadn't apologized for leaving her notes out for Eva to find.

"I learned something about Archie this morning. It's how I think Eva found my notes. Which I'm sorry for, by the way." I waved it away as no big deal and Erin continued, "Anyway, Archie came to Colorado shortly before Megan Hines went missing."

My blood pressure spiked. Was it coincidence? It couldn't be. There were too many of those when it came to Archie. First the similarities in his book, and now this?

I asked, "Any idea where he is?"

Neither one of us knew. I hadn't heard from him since last night's call when he smugly said, *Catch me if you can.* Should I message him again? With Eva on her own, I wasn't sure that was the best idea. Archie would sniff it out, and then what? I'd have something else to regret.

Erin buckled in and said, "Then a good thing I kept Eva's details to her sugaring profile. If Archie messages her there, at least we'll know about it."

I smiled. We hadn't completely lost Eva.

I set the wheels in motion and began to drive. Erin asked where we were heading. I said, "We could either follow the story and head to the high school, report on Bennett with the rest of the crowd. Or we could stick with Eva."

Erin flashed a quizzical look. "I thought you wanted to let her go?"

I grinned.

Erin and I never followed the crowd. Since I had Allison working to get Bennett alone, there was only one thing we should be doing. I asked, "You said Lewis Stark drives a red Ford truck?"

"That's what Eva said."

"Then I think it's time we paid him a visit."

CHAPTER SEVENTY-FIVE

THIRSTY EXITED THE LIQUOR STORE WITH A FIFTH OF vodka in his hand. He didn't care that it was still morning. His wife was getting on his nerves with her pompous stuck up attitude that drove him up the wall.

He climbed in his truck and cranked the engine—a distant gaze glossing his eyes over.

She acted like she was always right, like she never did anything wrong. There was a time he thought he loved her, but not anymore. She made it impossible to be himself. Instead, she wanted him to hide the truth of who he was, and certainly didn't want their friends to discover his illness. With her, it was more important to keep up with appearances than to acknowledge when things were broken. Like their marriage.

"Running around spending Daddy's money," Thirsty grumbled into the bottle.

Didn't she realize how inadequate it made him feel? A husband was supposed to provide, not be mocked in front of the world by the woman who was supposed to love him.

After another healthy gulp, Thirsty made a face and wiped

his mouth with the back of his hand. Backing out, he turned up the street, resting the open bottle between his thighs. He smiled when he felt the numbing warmth begin to mix with his prescription pain pills.

A minute passed before he realized he was driving without a clear destination. He turned on the radio and cranked the volume up after landing on the local news report. The cycle was still stuck on Jessica. Worthless. He only cared about having them track down Eva.

Switching his grip on the steering wheel, Thirsty brought the bottle to his lips. The liquid sloshed its way down his throat and settled in his empty stomach.

"I'm not alone," he said to an empty cab. "There's another monster like me out there."

If only they could meet.

Thirsty turned north and pointed his tires toward downtown. He sensed he was losing and, because of it, everyone was mocking him for being so clumsy in his poor attempt to kidnap the girl he truly loved.

The one that got away.

It wasn't long before he was parked outside the restaurant where the barmaid Isabel worked. The doors would open soon and she could be his redemption. Isabel always did make him feel good about himself. Like she valued his opinion, truly listened to what he had to say. He could see a future with her, the kind he'd always imagined. Except, after one quick glance down his front, he knew he couldn't go in looking like a slob.

Pulling the rearview mirror on his face, he said, "Forget it. There's no saving you."

He put the truck in reverse and his cellphone dinged with a message. A hit of excitement got him curious to know who demanded his attention.

You have an unfinished job waiting for you...

Thirsty didn't bother to read the rest of the message. He knew what it would say. Instead, he found himself swiping through the pictures in his gallery from this morning. His stepdaughter and her friend were so beautiful, he thought. It was times like this that reminded him what peace truly felt like.

Angelic.

Temptation seemed to be everywhere.

The news radio was once again reminding the public how Jessica had been violently taken. Thirsty lifted his gaze and ground his teeth. Everyone was better than him!

Next thing Thirsty knew, he was driving. The alcohol and pills were kicking in. It took him a moment to gain his bearings as he circled the Highlands neighborhood, not exactly sure how or why he'd come, but that's when he spotted her.

Eva.

The woman of his dreams.

She was walking alone. Though he thought he could be hallucinating, one long look convinced him he wasn't. It was his lucky day.

CHAPTER SEVENTY-SIX

Eva's long hair bounced off her shoulders as she briskly walked up the sidewalk. The sun was out, and she didn't like how exposed to the world she felt. She knew she needed to go home even if she thought it wasn't safe.

At the street corner, a funny feeling fell over her. She tucked her elbows and glanced behind her. Cars drove past, drivers not even bothering to look in her direction. She still felt like she was being watched.

"You two better not follow me," she said, fuming about Sam and Erin.

Digging out her phone, she requested an Uber. It was the longest fifteen minutes of her life as she waited for her ride to show. As her toes tapped on the concrete, she kept wondering when she would be spotted. It felt like the entire world knew what happened to her—her kidnapping and near-sexual assault, how her character had been completely humiliated by a man she still couldn't identify.

As the next wave of cars approached, a silver sedan put on its blinker and pulled to the side of the road. Eva's heart beat faster. She couldn't see the driver's face because of the sun's glare. Worse, she couldn't locate the Uber logo. *Was this her driver?*

Exhaling her next breath, she stepped forward and opened the back door. Rolling her gaze to the front, the driver turned and met her eye. They stared for a moment. Though she didn't recognize him, she hesitated to get inside.

The driver said, "You want a lift or what?"

Knowing she needed to do this, she steeled herself for the quick ride ahead and forced herself to slide into the back-passenger seat. As soon as she shut the door, the driver turned his attention forward and drove.

Eva was increasingly aware of her breath as she clutched the straps of her tote in a white knuckled grip. The driver kept stealing glances at her as if sizing her up, and it made Eva only doubt her decision to leave. She thought she would be stronger than this, could keep her poise when having to face the public. But her wounds were fresh and her mind had a long way to go before healing. A part of her thought maybe it never would—that the terror she experienced would live with her forever. But she was so mad at Samantha and Erin's betrayal, she had no choice but to go out on her own and begin carving out a life that only she seemed to understand.

The car stopped at the next light and Eva caught the driver staring in the rearview mirror. She turned away, ignored his stares as she took her mind to some place else.

She asked herself why she thought she could trust Samantha in the first place. It wasn't like she knew her personally. Their podcast was always looking out for women who'd been wronged. But she couldn't blame Sam and Erin. This never would have happened if she hadn't gone for a run that night. When all was said and done, this was no one's fault but her own.

When Eva closed her eyes, all she could see was Erin's doubt last night when Eva knew someone was outside her window. Eva knew what she heard—believed what she saw. The dark silhouette of a man dipping in and out of the shadows as he ran away after getting caught by her.

The car lurched forward and Eva opened her eyes. Her kidnapper would forever hide in the back corner of her mind, taunting her with his masks and whispers of what he wished to do to her. Jessica's name came over the radio and Eva asked, "Can you please turn the radio up?"

The driver turned the dial, and Eva listened to more of the report on Jessica's abduction.

Her kidnapper was still out there, apparently still targeting women, and that made her extremely uneasy. Why would he not come after her again? Did he know she talked to the cops? She needed to go home, pack, and leave before anyone knew where she was.

"You know, you kind of look like the women being kidnapped," the driver said, staring.

Eva's chest squeezed as she gave him a long, hard look. She was only a few blocks from her apartment, but she needed to get out of this car now.

"This is fine," she said, asking to be dropped here.

"You want to get out here?" The driver hesitated.

"Yes."

Eva unbuckled her seatbelt and opened the car door before the wheels came to a complete stop. She hit the ground running and didn't look back. Her heart was pounding and her body started to sweat. Weaving up the block, she rounded the corner on the next street when she spotted a familiar face. What was he doing here? Why did it look like he was looking up at her apartment window?

Eva backpedaled and dipped around the corner and out of

sight before he saw. Her heart beat even faster. If only she knew who'd kidnapped her, then she would know who was dangerous and who wasn't. This man was either here to help or here to destroy, and she couldn't decide which of the two it was.

CHAPTER SEVENTY-SEVEN

DETECTIVE KING PUT HIS UNMARKED POLICE CRUISER IN park and killed the engine. He turned to face Detective Gray. She was on the phone while flipping through Sage's case files, doing her best to track down Sage's family to find out if she had a younger sister.

"Okay, great," Gray said into her phone. "Call me as soon you can confirm it."

The moment Gray was off the phone, King asked, "How did you know Sage looked like Jane Doe?"

Without taking her eyes off her notes, Gray said, "She's his type."

King glanced to the entrance of the medical examiner's office. Indeed, she was the Woman Collector's type. They all were. But if these cases were related, that meant their perp had been working under the radar for nearly a decade. Maybe Archie Smith was right. Maybe there was a serial rapist-killer the department didn't know about. If so, how many women did he currently have, and how many had he killed? King was agitated by the thought.

As if sensing King's unease, Gray said, "The chances of finding Sage alive—"

"I know."

"The case might be officially open, but from what I understand, her family held a private funeral years ago." King turned his head and met Gray's eye. "They needed closure," Gray said.

King opened his door and said, "And so do I."

They entered the medical examiner's office, signed in at the front desk, and was escorted to the back where they entered the morgue. The smell of formaldehyde and death always got to King, but today he ignored the queasiness in his stomach and waved to Griffin through the glass. He assumed she was working on Megan's corpse.

When Griffin indicated she'd be right out, King moved to her desk and began browsing the files on top. She'd been working to locate Jane Doe, but it didn't take King long to realize none of the unnamed victims matched Jane Doe's profile.

"Go ahead, make yourself at home," Griffin said sarcastically as she entered her office, removing her latex gloves.

King straightened and retrieved the picture of Sage from inside his sport coat pocket. "This is what she looks like," he said, holding out the picture for Griffin to see.

"Who's that?" Griffin took a closer look.

Gray explained who Sage was and how they matched her to what King remembered of Jane Doe.

"The plot thickens," Griffin said, eyeing King. "I'm sorry. I pulled an all-nighter and need to see the light of day to cure my sick humor. Anyway, I began looking for your girl, and you're right, she never arrived."

King held up the file he still had pinched between his fingers. "I know."

Gray's cellphone buzzed. She excused herself and took the

call on the opposite side of the room. Griffin moved behind her desk.

"This concerns me greatly," Griffin said. "It's imperative we locate her. I've put a call into the sergeant from CSI but am still waiting to hear back. I'm hoping he can give me details to the EMS team who bagged our body and can figure out where they took her."

King nodded and jutted his chin to the lab. "Is that Megan on the table?"

Griffin nodded and said, "No surprise to either one of us, but I'm ruling her death a homicide. Death by strangulation—"

"And, let me guess, she was sexually assaulted?"

Griffin nodded again. "Unfortunately, I haven't lifted a single strand of evidence off her. My guess is whoever killed her shaves his entire body. Either way, he was extremely meticulous when handling her. It's clear whoever is behind her murder knows what he's doing."

Gray rushed over, her eyes wide. "You'll never guess who just walked into the station."

King knitted his brows and shared a quick glance with Griffin.

"Jessica Hinojos. Our Amber Alert."

CHAPTER SEVENTY-EIGHT

LEWIS STARK WAS GETTING INTO HIS EXPENSIVE SPORTS CAR when we arrived. His four-car garage caught my attention as I curbed my Subaru in front of his house.

"What do you think is parked inside?" I asked Erin.

Erin replied, "Four-to-one: a red pickup truck."

Our shared smile quickly turned to parted lips of surprise as we both noticed the young college-aged girl exit Stark's house. Her hips flared as she bounced her breasts toward Stark.

"This can't be happening. I've got to capture this," Erin said, snapping photos with her phone to be used as evidence if we ever needed it.

The woman looked like Eva. I wouldn't have believed what happened next if I didn't see it with my own eyes. Stark sauntered over to her, took her by the waist, and planted his lips on hers. They tongue kissed and he pressed his pelvis deeper into hers.

"Are you getting all this?" I asked Erin.

Erin said, "Every single ugly second of it."

We were each disgusted by the clear difference in age,

making our first impression of the man neither of us knew quite negative. As Stark pulled away, he slapped her ass and got her to smile.

Stark was a sleaze ball who made my skin crawl. Had he cared about Eva at all? Could he have been the one who abducted Eva? My mind was busy making wild assumptions as I reminded myself to slow down.

We watched the woman get behind the wheel of the sports car, back out of Stark's drive, and speed away.

As soon as she was gone, I opened my door and Stark paused when he saw me wave at him. I called out, "Mr. Lewis Stark?"

Stark gave me a funny look. "Who's asking?"

I shut my car door and rounded the hood, closing the gap between us so I wouldn't have to yell. "My name is Samantha Bell and this is my colleague Erin Tate. We're friends of Eva's."

Starks expression eased. "Is she okay?"

He was quick to pick up on why we were here. Did he know she had been kidnapped? Was he expecting us? It seemed impossible, but I could assume nothing. A part of me kept thinking Eva would arrive any minute, or at least call him like she'd told Erin she was going to.

"When was the last time you talked to her?" I asked, hoping he would say today. When he didn't, I wondered if Eva had anticipated our move.

"You thought she'd be here?"

Erin said, "We did."

Stark's eyes glossed over as he seemed to be staring at nothing in particular. I wondered what it was he was thinking, if I was looking at a dangerous man or not.

"No," Stark snapped out of his head, "I haven't spoken to Eva since last Thursday evening."

"What did you two discuss?"

Stark looked to his neighbors and lowered his voice to a whisper. "I've been worried about her."

My brow furrowed. "Why is that?"

Stark rolled his shoulders back and visibly tensed. "It's complicated and deeply personal."

Was he purposely avoiding having to go into detail, or just naturally obtuse? I couldn't decide. "You two are dating?"

"Were dating," Stark corrected me.

Erin asked, "What happened?"

"I loved every minute I was with Eva. She's a fun-loving girl and she brought great joy into my life. We were wonderful together for a time, but there was another man in her life."

"And did you find this out before or after you two slept together?"

Stark cocked his head and glared at me. "Did something happen to her?" When we didn't respond, Stark lifted his head and said, "I knew that asshole Carr would hurt her."

"Carr?" Erin played coy.

"Oliver Carr." Stark's tone hardened. "The other man. And, just to be clear, I never slept with Eva. Though I would have liked to. It was Carr she was sleeping with."

Erin and I shared a look. This was not the story Eva had shared. We kept our mouths shut to see how this would play out.

"I told her to stay away from him, that he was no good, but she didn't listen." Stark told us stories of abuse at the hand of Carr, saying, "Each time he hurt Eva, she'd show up at my door, ask to stay the night, cry in my arms and be gone the next morning like it never happened. No matter what he did or said, she always went back to him."

"That must have hurt you."

Stark shook his head no. "I'd do anything for her. What you need to understand about Eva is that she doesn't have anyone else in her life to love her. I showed her what love could be and she still chose him. While I disagreed with her decision, I accepted my roll to comfort and protect her."

"And did you *protect* her?"

"You mean, did I ever take the fight to Carr?"

I nodded.

"No. But he brought it to me." Stark flicked his gaze between us as he continued, "As soon as Carr learned about me, he came knocking on my door to lay claim to Eva. He told me to stay away from her, or else. You catch my drift? That's why I moved on. I don't need some psychopath up in my face about some girl we both found on a dating website. If you're here because you think Eva's in danger, I'd bet my house it's Carr who's responsible."

CHAPTER SEVENTY-NINE

Nicholas Bennett's blood was boiling as he peeked through the curtains. He'd somehow managed to get Heidi Mitchell and her cameramen out of his house and off his property, but Bennett could still see them parked and reporting from the street near the end of his drive.

How much did she know about him and where was she getting her information? Something told Bennett his time was up.

"I'm sorry," Naomi's meek voice said from behind.

Bennett closed his eyes, his cheeks searing with anger. He needed to correct this, change the narrative and slow the pace before the tsunami hit. But how could he after what he knew? No matter what he did now, things would only get worse.

His heart beat like a ticking time bomb inside his chest about to explode.

It wasn't only the accusations Heidi threw at him that had Bennett nervous, but now his house had been exposed. The world would know where he lived. That was unsettling. His life of solitude and privacy was ruined forever.

"I didn't know there would be cameras," Naomi continued.

Bennett opened his eyes and stared out over his lawn. He needed to get Naomi out of his house, but how? If she stayed, it didn't look good for him. If she left, who knew what Heidi would do to twist Naomi's words to make him look even worse? Bennett knew it was impossible for him to win.

"I told you to stay put," he said, releasing the curtains and letting them fall back into place.

Bennett moved to the living room and Naomi followed. He turned on the news, flipped the channel until he found Heidi. Together they listened, and Bennett's worries only ballooned.

He turned to Naomi and asked, "Who told you to come here?"

Naomi jerked her head back. "No one."

He didn't believe her. "Then how did she," he pointed out the window toward where he knew Heidi was, "know you'd be here?"

Naomi took a step back. "I don't know."

"You seemed to know everything before. What happened?" Bennett craned his neck and stormed over to Naomi. "Did you suddenly lose your mind?"

Naomi started to cry. He was scaring her. But Bennett knew what it looked like, and it wasn't good for him.

"Dare I ask what the hell was on that phone?" He held up his hand before she could respond. "Forget it. I already have a good idea by the look on both of your faces."

Naomi followed Bennett to the couch. Resting his elbows on his knees, Bennett hung his head and listened to the echoes of Heidi's allegations bounce between his ears.

"The phone wasn't mine," Naomi said, getting Bennett to snap his neck toward her. "I know I said it was, but that was to protect you."

Naomi lifted her hand and was about to place it on Bennett's shoulder when he gave her a look that made her stop. "Lying only makes things worse," he said.

"Coach, it's Tommy's."

Bennett straightened and stared. "Why say it was yours then?"

"Because I'm on it."

As difficult as it was for Naomi to explain to her teacher and coach about the sexting photo of her spreading through the school like a virus, she did. Bennett listened and felt lightheaded. He couldn't believe what he was hearing. It didn't matter how he acquired it, even if it was a confiscated student phone, Heidi was accusing him of being in possession of child pornography.

Bennett swept his gaze to the basement door.

Did Heidi know what was really on the phone, or was she only guessing? And who gave it to her? Was it even the same phone as Tommy's, or did she just pretend it was to get a reaction for the cameras?

Bennett turned to Naomi and asked, "Who was Jenny sleeping with?"

Naomi tucked her chin.

"Was it a teacher?"

Naomi's eyes danced inside his. "I don't know. Maybe."

Shoving his fingers through his hair, Bennett stood and moved to the kitchen, picking up the phone. "I'm calling your mother."

Naomi sprang to her feet and hurried to his side. "You can't. She doesn't know where I am, and she hates Jenny. If she knew I came here—"

Suddenly, the phone started ringing inside Bennett's hand. They exchanged a look of surprise. Bennett answered after the next ring. Allison said, "We need to get you out of there and somewhere safe where you can hide." Bennett didn't know what to say. Allison continued, "I know you didn't do this, and I think I know how we can prove it."

CHAPTER EIGHTY

Gray followed King to his car, leaving the ME's office in a hurry. Griffin promised to call as soon as she learned anything new, and King drove with sirens blaring all the way to the station. They ran inside and found Jessica Hinojos sitting in the interrogation box alone.

"Who brought her in?" Gray asked a detective from her division when reviewing Jessica's file.

"No one," the detective said. "Came in by her lonesome self."

King stared at the young woman hunched over the chrome table, thinking what a sad sight it was. Who was this girl and what was her story?

Gray lifted her head. "Is she talking?"

"Waiting for you."

Gray glanced to King before entering the box. King position himself behind the glass, hoping Gray would be able to get Jessica to tell them enough to locate Jenny Booth. Gray settled in with small talk, befriending the girl, asking if there was anything she needed. "Are you hungry?"

Jessica shook her head no.

"Thirsty?"

Again, Jessica didn't react to Gray's purposeful use of the word. That was a good sign, but it had King wondering if this case was related to Eva Martin's, or even Megan Hines's. Jessica did have the look of the other victims—jet-black hair, tall and beautiful—but was she intelligent and popular, too? King didn't know, but her appearance said it all. She looked broken, a face full of shame and regret. And there was something about her eyes that worried him. Why didn't she seem scared?

"We've been looking for you," Gray said to Jessica. "Your mother is worried sick."

Jessica folded her arms and looked to the mirror.

"Want to tell me what happened?"

King was thinking about Archie and the serial rapist Samantha said he was after when Lieutenant Baker entered the room. King knew he wasn't supposed to be here. He acted like he was despite LT's silence penetrating his thoughts, distracting him from Gray's interview.

"Nothing happened," Jessica said, getting King's attention. "I made it all up."

"Christ," LT said after they listened to Jessica's cry for help. It was a complete hoax.

King said, "Good thing the department devoted more resources to this flake who's only thirsty for attention than the chief did to our missing Jane Doe."

LT stepped closer and whispered into King's shoulder, "I heard what you said last night and I'm as concerned about this missing evidence report as you are." He pulled up his cuff and checked the time on his silver wristwatch. "But I suggest you get your story straight because I'm meeting the DA and deputy chief in an hour."

King looked his lieutenant in the eye. "What about?"

"Why the scene was released before the job was complete."

"You know why," King pleaded, hoping his lieutenant would go to bat for him.

LT held King's gaze for a beat before exiting the room without saying another word. King made a fist and cracked his neck. Could it be the upper brass finally saw the evidence was too overwhelming to deny? Or was something else going on that King couldn't see? It didn't matter. Alvarez was right. DPD wanted him to eat his gun.

The door swung open behind him and Alvarez popped his head inside. "Good. I thought you'd be in here." He paused to catch his breath. "You're not going to believe this, but there is a woman here who believes her husband might have been involved in the murder of Megan Hines."

King stepped out into the hall and asked, "Where is she? What's her name?"

Alvarez told him where she was and gave him a knowing look when he told him her name. "Mrs. Christopher Bowers."

CHAPTER EIGHTY-ONE

WITH HIS BACK TO THE SUN, ACE STARED UP FROM THE sidewalk into what he knew was Eva's apartment window. His body buzzed with a feeling of restlessness. Dancing on his toes, Ace knew his story was coming to a close. He could feel it. And he didn't like how the ending was being written. Even with his tips to the media, he was losing control of the story. He'd worked too long and too hard to keep his secret quiet for it to end like this. He wanted nothing more than to go out with a bang.

Reminding himself what he had waiting at home, he turned and faced the street.

Cradling his injured hand wrapped in gauze, he flexed and stretched his fingers to keep them from cramping. He should have killed Jenny for biting him, but the truth was, he liked her—especially appreciated her strength and courage to fight back. After all, that was the reason for kidnapping her, wasn't it?

A man an inch taller than him skirted past and hurried to the apartment complex entrance, leaving a heady scent of cologne in his wake. Ace made a face and sized him up. He was made of muscle, but not the kind of strength that would hold up in a fight. That was what was wrong with today's men. They slaved in the gym only to keep up appearance, not to prepare for battle.

"People are so superficial," he grumbled.

Turning toward his car parked on the street, he caught a man staring at him from behind the glare of his windshield. Ace paused, but only for a second. Was it an undercover cop? Had he been tailed? Followed here after he dumped Megan's body?

Taking a deep breath to compose himself and hide his paranoia, Ace got into his car and turned the key over. The radio came on, the news still only talking about Jessica. Flicking his gaze to the rearview mirror, Ace stared at the stranger's face and naturally turned his mind to the one woman who he knew hadn't been home for several nights; Eva.

Reaching across the seat, he pulled the Prom Queen Killer book from his pack and turned the radio off. What he needed was some peace and quiet. Hard to do with the constant chatter happening inside his head, but as he flipped through the dog-eared pages, Ace wondered what they would someday call him when this was all over. He had a few names he'd given himself over the years, but none were as good as the Prom Queen Killer.

Lifting his head, he checked his mirrors.

Hiding his true self was the toughest thing he'd had to do. Not abducting young women who trusted him, not having to conceal his identity, nor silence those who dared to challenge his authority. All of that came easily to him. But being a complete fake? That was the hardest of all.

Closing his eyes, Ace breathed out his frustration. With his head resting against the back of the seat, he needed to break free from this umbilical cord that kept him tethered to living the life of someone else.

"You can do this." He exhaled. "Now is your time." He could feel it in his bones.

With his eyes slowly opening, he flipped to the back of the book and retrieved the picture of him with Eva. They were together, side-by-side thanks to a little Photoshop manipulation. He didn't care. In his mind, they were the perfect couple and this picture was real.

The lights of the car behind him came on. Ace watched as the stranger pulled alongside his window and glared as he passed. Ace didn't care. His fantasy of Eva was growing stronger by the minute. There was nothing more he wanted than to prove he was the best by kidnapping the girl everyone had their eyes on.

"I'm coming for you, Eva. Today is our day of holy matrimony."

CHAPTER EIGHTY-TWO

JENNY'S TEETH CHATTERED. SHE COULDN'T STOP SHIVERING. Hugging her knees to her chest, she was curled up in a ball on the floor, fighting off the intense chills burrowing deep into her bones.

The food she ate made things worse. As soon it settled in her stomach, the real problems started. And it wasn't just the cold of Megan's room that was getting to her. She couldn't stop blaming her mother for how she ended up here. If it wasn't for her mother's finances—or lack thereof—Jenny would have never made the bad decision she had.

So it goes, the story of her life.

Megan's room was so much lonelier than her own. Jenny wished she could go back, be surrounded by her own pictures and see Naomi one last time. As that emptiness grew in the pit of her stomach, Jenny couldn't stop thinking how Megan had slept on this same floor before she was eventually killed.

Jenny rocked through another earth-quaking shiver before rolling to her other side.

She hung on to hope only because she'd been fed. That made her believe she'd done something to win her captor over—to convince him she was worth keeping. Why give her the nutrition if he didn't want her to have the strength?

As encouragement swirled between her ears, Jenny stood and tried the door. The handle didn't budge. It was locked. Just like she knew it would be. There was no leaving without his consent, no chance to break free. It had been nearly a half hour since she heard him leave and the house was quiet as death.

"Megan is dead," she called out to the house, getting no response. "You heard him. He killed her, and he'll kill us all too if we don't work together to escape." Jenny waited for any of the other girls to respond. When no one did, she raised her voice even louder, "Didn't you hear what I said? He's going to kill us."

"I just want to see my little sister again."

Jenny recognized the voice. It was Sage.

Sage continued, "She'd be sixteen now, though I doubt she'd remember who I was."

"Sage," Jenny called out, wanting to hold her hand as she could feel Sage beginning to lose hope. "Don't give up. You'll see your sister again. We can do this, but we need to work together."

"It's been ten years. My family's moved on. I'm sure of it." Jenny heard what sounded like Sage's shoulders falling against the wall as she slid down to the floor. Sage said sadly, "He's never going to let us free."

Jenny moved to the wall of photos and began browsing each of them, this time looking closer for clues to who might have taken them. She couldn't believe Sage had been here for ten years. If it was true, Jenny was determined to have her experience be different. That's when she found it. A picture of Megan changing in the locker room.

Jenny inched closer to the wall, her heart beating faster as she remembered the rumors about Bennett circling the school at the end of last year. With her finger on the picture, Jenny said loud enough for all to hear, "I'm here because I slept with an older man."

A minute of silence passed before Nicole said, "Me too."

Then, another girl said, "That's why I think I'm here."

Jenny's chest swelled with hope, which only grew when she noticed a face caught in the reflection of the waxed vinyl flooring of the high school gym locker room. It was a face, and one she recognized.

"No, it can't be," she whispered to herself, taking a step back. Then she said to everyone, "The person who's holding us against our will is a teacher, and one we probably all know."

CHAPTER EIGHTY-THREE

I STOOD NEXT TO MY CAR WITH ONE HAND ON THE HANDLE, waiting for Stark to leave. I didn't know who to trust. Erin said Eva was going to Stark, yet she wasn't here. Either Eva lied or Stark was. But worse was what Stark said about Carr. Would Eva really go back to the man who abused her? Women did it all the time, so why would Eva be any different?

No matter what we decided to do next, I feared we were leaving Eva exposed and vulnerable for at least one of the men to take advantage of her. If Eva knew we were watching her, we'd lose her trust for good.

"What do you want to do?" I asked Erin.

"Nothing until we see what's inside his garage."

We were still looking for the mysterious red truck. As soon as the garage door opened, Erin's chin lifted. I side-stepped to see completely inside. To our surprise, there was no truck at all. Only a black Audi TT alongside two snowmobiles and a Harley Davidson motorcycle.

"This isn't good, Sam." Erin opened her car door. "I think Eva played us."

I buckled myself in and knew we had no choice but to head to Carr's. He was easy to locate. Erin pulled up his address and did what research she could as I drove. It didn't take us long to find his place.

Oliver Carr had a nice upper middle-class home in the Arapahoe Acres neighborhood. We thought Eva might have come here instead of going home. I followed the hedge leading up to the grand entrance of the large house and climbed the short flight of stairs before ringing the doorbell.

We waited in silence for what felt like forever. When Erin was about to hit the bell again, Carr answered the door.

"Can I help you?" he said.

We exchanged formalities, and as soon as we introduced ourselves, Carr knew why we were here. He said, "I've been worried about her."

"And why is that?"

"Are you kidding? Have you not watched the news? The police found a body near the South Platte that looked just like her."

"Can we come in?" I asked.

Carr paused for a moment, then stepped to the side. He was quick to apologize for the mess. "I'm remodeling my basement and, well, it's not going as quickly as I originally hoped."

Carr latched the basement door closed and continued leading us into the living room. He was a man who worked out of his home office. To my surprise, he wasn't the man I was expecting to meet. Instead of being cold and aggressive as Stark described, Carr was warm and welcoming, even charming at times.

I asked, "When was the last time you saw Eva?"

Carr was texting on his cell when he picked his head up and looked me in the eye. "Not since she disappeared."

Did he mean what he said? Did he know she was kidnapped?

"And when was that?" I asked.

Carr was back on his phone and seemed distracted. I wondered who he was talking to. What could be so important to invite us inside only to pretend we weren't here? After he was finished doing whatever he was doing, he motioned for us to follow him into the kitchen. He talked as he walked. "Eva warned me you two might show up."

"She did? When?"

"About an hour ago."

Yet he was worried about her?

Carr turned and met Erin's eye. I watched his gaze travel the length of her as he grinned. It was clear he liked what he saw. I couldn't deny the obvious. A beautiful tall blonde with fair skin was the exact opposite of a black-haired teen with a dark complexion. Erin used his attraction to our advantage.

"Did she say where she was?" Erin asked.

"I'd better not tell." Carr gave half a smile. "I promised her I wouldn't."

I was starting to see the real Carr, the man Stark had described. As ugly as it appeared to be, a part of me was relieved to think maybe Stark hadn't been lying after all. But I didn't like how Carr was making me believe he knew where Eva was.

"Where did you two meet?" I asked. Carr mentioned the sugaring website and I followed up with another question I knew he wouldn't appreciate. "Did the sex ever get rough between you two?"

Carr swept his glimmering eyes off Erin and rolled them over to me where I watched the shine quickly fade. "I never did anything that Eva didn't want." Was that his opinion or hers? His brow knitted when he asked, "Why, did Eva say I hurt her?"

"We've heard, and not from Eva, that things might have gotten rough between you two."

Carr narrowed his eyes. "It was Stark who told you that, wasn't it?"

Erin changed the subject before we lost him. "If you knew Eva was missing, and possibly in trouble, why didn't you call the cops?"

Carr wet his lips and visibly relaxed. "She's not the only girlfriend I have to keep track of."

A woman collector.

"We had a fight." Carr shifted his gaze over to me. "She left here angry."

Motive to kill.

Erin asked, "Care to tell me what the fight was about?"

"Dumb shit."

"I'm sorry," I said, grabbing my stomach, "but is it possible to use your toilet?"

Carr straightened and directed me down the hall, away from the basement I desperately wanted to check out for myself. Something about a remodel made me suspicious. I thanked him and stepped inside, pretending to close the door behind me. Instead, as soon as he was gone, I ducked out and headed down the hall looking for his office. I hoped Erin would distract him long enough for me to see the man he truly was.

I passed a guest room and marveled at his high ceilings. The house was large, but luck brought me into his office after only a short search.

Turning my ear to the front of the house, I listened before entering. Once I knew Erin had his complete attention, I tiptoed my way to his desk and began browsing. I wasn't exactly sure what I was looking for, but Carr certainly knew quite a bit about Eva's disappearance. Was that because he was guilty? His office gave no indication that he was. It was all work, invoices, and to-do lists before I got lucky and found a treasure of secrets in the right drawer of his desk.

Inside were dozens of Polaroid pictures of women exposing themselves to the camera. I couldn't believe they were just laying inside an unlocked drawer, not hidden inside a safe. When I thought about why, and how he got these women to agree to do these photoshoots, blackmail was the only thing that came to mind.

I flipped through the stack as fast as I could, looking for Eva or any other face I recognized. None of these women were the girls I knew were missing. No Megan. No Jessica. No Jenny. They were all new faces, eyes I'd never seen.

Did a teacher murder Megan, or was Carr our guy?

I placed the stack of photos where I'd found them and closed the drawer. I was about to leave when I saw a plain manila folder on the corner of his desk. It was not addressed. No stamp. Nothing. But it was clearly stuffed full. I listened for a moment and heard Erin's voice far down the hall. I opened the manila folder and froze.

"Jackpot," I said, looking at the picture I knew Archie took of Eva outside the medical examiner's office in my car.

I snapped a quick photo of the picture inside the folder with my phone, knowing my time was running out. As soon as I tucked my cellphone away in my back pocket, I heard Carr ask Erin, "Is your friend all right? Maybe you should go check on her?"

"Tell me more about your job," I heard Erin say.

Unprepared for what I found, I exited Carr's office, imagining Erin touching Carr's arm as she stared into his eyes, pretending to care about what he had to say. Hurrying down the hall, I dipped into the bathroom and flushed the toilet, wet my hands under the faucet, and was back inside the kitchen before Carr had a chance to escape Erin's grasp.

Erin turned her head and looked at me. "Ah, there she is.

Feeling better, sweetie?"

"Must have been something I ate," I said with a forced smile.

Carr was giving me a suspicious eye when a call came through his office line. I hoped he would decide to ignore it, but instead he said, "Excuse me, I'm going to have to get that. It's work."

I kept my eye on Carr as he hurried to his study—the same room I was just snooping around—hoping I'd put everything back in place without him knowing I was there. As soon as he was out of sight, I turned to Erin. "We have to leave now."

"What? Why? We're just breaking the ice on this jerk."

"I didn't use the toilet," I whispered. Erin gave me an arched look. "I went to his office and this is what I found."

Erin took my phone into her hand, studied the picture, and I watched her eyes flash with disbelief.

I nodded. We were sharing the same thought.

"You think they're working together?" Erin asked in a hushed voice.

"How else can you explain him having it?"

Erin glanced to my phone again when Carr snuck up from behind. "Everything all right?"

"I'm not feeling well," I said, again pressing my hand flat against my rock-hard stomach. "But if you hear from Eva, please give us a call."

"Certainly," Carr said, taking Erin's business card.

He walked us to the door but, before leaving, Erin turned to him and asked, "I nearly forgot, but do you own a red pickup truck?"

"I do." Carr's jaw set. "Why do you ask?"

"Mind if we see it?"

Carr paused for a beat and lifted his chin. "Sorry, it's currently on loan with a friend."

CHAPTER EIGHTY-FOUR

Mrs. Bowers sat alone two doors away from where Detective Gray was closing out her interview with Jessica. Mrs. Bowers's expression was tight and there wasn't a trace of doubt in her eyes. After Alvarez had learned why it was she was here, he moved her inside the box so she could speak without fear.

King sifted through his thoughts. He hadn't thought about Christopher since his visit to the work site, and now he wondered if he should have kept a closer eye on him.

King asked, "Does Christopher know she's here?"

Alvarez had his hands in his pockets when he shook his head no. "Hasn't mentioned Eva's name at all, either." Alvarez rolled his gaze over to King. "Only Megan's."

King turned his attention back to Mrs. Bowers, thinking about her husband's story of Eva running for her life through the empty streets during the early morning hours when he found her. Had she really been running away from *him*? Mrs. Bowers was here about Megan, but all King could think about was Eva.

Alvarez gave King a look and they entered the interrogation room together. They each took a seat across from Mrs. Bowers and made introductions, reiterating that she wasn't in any kind of trouble.

King looked Mrs. Bowers in the eye and asked, "Can you please tell me again why you're here?"

She flicked her brown eyes to Alvarez before saying, "As I mentioned to Detective Alvarez before, something tells me my husband may have had something to do with that young girl's murder."

"Megan Hines?"

"Yes."

Mrs. Bowers was a concerned wife. Her appearance was first class, her demeanor calm. She radiated a life of privilege and entitlement, but King kept asking himself how someone like her could end up marrying a monster.

"Do you know where your husband is now?"

"He was at the house when I left, but he's a contractor with two jobs in progress." Mrs. Bowers mentioned the neighborhood of her husband's work, Arapahoe Acres, confirming Christopher's story. "A client of his, Oliver Carr, has loaned him a red Ford truck."

Alvarez turned to King and quietly told him that patrol had already run the VIN through the DMV and an APB was sent out, actively searching for both Christopher and the truck.

"I'm worried about him," Mrs. Bowers said. "I'm afraid he's not taking his medication. Chris has been forced to scale back his work because of mental health issues. He's getting help for his manic depression, but I don't think it's doing enough to bring my husband back."

King was taking notes when he asked, "And is he manic now?"

"He's been on a binge for the last week, but this time seems worse than previous episodes."

"Can you explain that for me?"

Mrs. Bowers explained what her husband had been up to. Up through the night, disappearing for long hours without her knowing where he was. His temper was short and his mood was swinging wildly depending on the hour of the day. As King listened, he thought about Christopher's prostitution charges, how he didn't want his wife to know about it. What else didn't she know? Did she know her husband brought in Eva the other night?

When Mrs. Bowers was finished, King asked, "Mrs. Bowers, does the word thirsty mean anything to you?"

Her neck straightened and King saw her eyes flash with recognition. "It's what he calls his manic state."

King gently bit his lip and leaned in as a terrible feeling of being duped draped over him. Mrs. Bowers's next revelation about her husband made King think Christopher Bowers was truly the person behind Eva's abduction, maybe even Megan's murder.

"The reason I came in today is that I found my husband taking photographs with his cellphone of my daughter and her friend sunbathing. Can you imagine? She's only sixteen." Her expression pinched with anger. "He didn't even try to hide it from me."

"And your daughter was home from school today?"

"She's a student at South High. Classes were canceled because of what happened to Megan."

"And you think he had something to do with Megan's murder?"

She nodded. "There was something different in his eye today. He didn't even look tired after being out all night. Since his diagnosis six weeks ago, he does this, and I started putting it together. Each of his prolonged absences coincides developments in Megan's case. He's sick in the head, Detective."

King eased back in his chair, not liking what he was hearing.

"Then I found this on his desk." Mrs. Bowers produced a contractor's house plan. She unrolled the sheet of paper and pointed to the basement floor plan. "He labeled the room '*Play Pen, for girls only*'. It's self-explanatory. I don't think we need to guess what he meant by it."

King pointed to the address labeled in the upper right-hand corner of the house plans and made a mental note of it. His pulse thrashed and pounded in his neck. He'd been to the house already. He now wondered if he'd been standing above where Megan had been kept captive.

The metal door opened behind him and an officer from the squad room peaked his head into the room. "We've got a hit on the truck."

King twisted around and locked eyes with the officer. The officer told him the address and King knew the place. Christopher Bowers was parked outside Eva Martin's apartment complex. Apparently, he didn't get enough of her the first time around.

CHAPTER EIGHTY-FIVE

"I KNOW HE'S NOT A TEACHER, BUT IT HAS TO BE HIM," I said, squeezing my car keys inside my palm. Erin hadn't seen the Polaroids in Carr's desk drawer.

Erin's hand was on her bottom lip, her eyes focused on Carr's house. We hadn't left the neighborhood, and I didn't know if we could now that it was clear he and Archie might be working together to get to Eva.

"She's going back to him," I said. "And there is nothing we can do about it."

Erin's brow furrowed when she turned to me and said, "There's no doubt Carr's a woman collector, but does he like to sleep with younger women, too?"

To me, they all looked like girls. Their true ages were impossible to tell. Jenny was said to be sleeping with an older man; could it have been Oliver Carr? Did we just accidently find the second suspect I assumed was behind these crimes? He and Archie made two, the number I always suspected to be working.

"I don't like this, Sam. I think we need to call the cops."

I had considered splitting up to cover more ground, but I

certainly wasn't ready to call the cops. Instead I said, "And say what? We caught their guy? Everything we currently know is circumstantial at best."

Erin sighed and held her hair up off her neck.

Discovering Eva's picture on Carr's desk furthered my suspicion Archie was scripting his own book. The thought made me sick. Archie still hadn't responded to my requests to call, and I doubted he would now that Carr understood what we were after. There was no doubt in my mind Eva would eventually find herself here. When she did, would we be ready?

"They're going to kill her," Erin muttered.

"We can't let that happen," I said as my phone rang. It was Dawson. I hoped he had some good news when I answered with a question. "Did you find what happened to Jane Doe?"

"Chief Watts is calling a press conference. I need you there."

"Now's not a good time." I told him why.

"Sam, there are early reports that Jessica Hinojos's abduction was a hoax."

I rolled my gaze over to Erin. She leaned across the console and listened in on the call. As much as I wanted to know if what he was saying was true, I knew I couldn't go.

"Dawson, you don't understand. I'm about to crack the case on these kidnappings."

"Sam—"

"I'm sorry. You're going to have to find someone to cover for me," I said, killing the call early, thinking about how Jenny was still out there somewhere waiting for someone to find her. I couldn't abandon her, just like I hadn't abandoned Megan.

Erin whistled a low tune that said I shouldn't have done that.

"He'll get over it," I said, deciding how best we could protect Eva without her ever knowing it.

A part of me still believed Carr might be hiding some undiscovered truth we were close to learning. What that was, I wasn't exactly sure, but something about him rubbed me the wrong way. How could we surveil him, Archie, and Eva with only the two of us?

Erin picked up her phone and began working. After I asked what she was doing, she said, "Going fishing."

I arched an eyebrow.

"If Archie is going after Eva like we suspect, and Eva won't talk to us, we need to make sure we know where he is."

Erin was using Eva's credentials to log into the dating website, requesting to meet with Archie. I wasn't convinced he'd go for it, being that it was the middle of the day, but what other choice did we have?

"Okay," I said, "but what about Carr?"

Erin pointed her painted nail to the mirror and said, "I don't think he's going anywhere fast."

When I flicked my gaze to the rearview mirror, wondering what she was referring to, I was surprised to see a police car turning onto the street. We watched it approach, pass us by, and turn into Carr's driveway. I didn't know how or why this grace from God happened when it did, but I wasn't complaining.

Erin's phone dinged and she smiled. "Would you look at that? Archie is excited for his date with us."

CHAPTER EIGHTY-SIX

EVA CIRCLED THE BLOCK, TRYING TO GIVE HERSELF ENOUGH time for Archie to learn she wasn't home and move on with his day. As she walked, she kept her head down, still believing everyone wanted to see her face and look her in the eye. It was an awful feeling and she couldn't wait to go back to living a more inconspicuous life.

Nearly twenty minutes had passed when she came back around to her apartment building. This time she approached from the adjacent street just in case she had been spotted before. Shortening her gait, she dug the soles of her shoes into the pavement and took a step back when she saw him. Archie was still there, sitting behind the wheel of his small car with phone in hand.

What was he doing? How long would he wait for her?

Eva glanced behind her, then back to Archie, deciding what to do next. She needed to get inside her apartment, if only for a few minutes, to pack up and leave. Then, to her surprise, Archie started his car and pointed the hood into traffic, driving away.

Eva watched him leave. He'd never even looked in her

direction. She could breathe again. Seeing her window of opportunity, Eva made her move and headed for the crosswalk just as a red Ford truck took Archie's spot.

Her heart skipped with hope, but her eyebrows knitted with confusion. The truck looked exactly like Carr's but it couldn't be. Carr never took his truck out with her. Eva hoped to steal a glance at the driver, but he never turned. Her anxiety spread. Was that Carr behind the wheel or someone else? It looked like someone else.

A pang of fear cramped her side as she thought about what Carr might do when he learned she'd been kidnapped by another man. He'd never believe she wasn't touched. With her heart pounding, paranoia and fear got the best of her. Eva froze, uncertain whether to go forward or retreat into hiding.

The traffic lights turned red and the crosswalk flashed white. It was time for her to decide. Just when she took her first step, the man in the truck turned his head and revealed his face.

Eva stopped mid-step. She was certain he wasn't looking at her, but she was definitely looking at him. What was going on? Why was *he* here?

Quickly, Eva spun around before she was spotted. She darted to a nearby tree, hiding behind its thick trunk. With her back against the scaly bark, Eva wondered how the driver knew where she lived. Had she told him? She couldn't recall.

Keeping her body concealed, she peeked around the tree. The little doubt she still had was quickly erased after a second look confirmed it was the man she thought it was.

The driver was now out of the truck, slowly heading toward the entrance to her apartment. He looked around, but never in her direction. It was the man who picked her up the night she was running for her life—the night she thought she was going to die.

It didn't make any sense. Unless—

They were working together. Carr had told him where she lived.

Feeling a trigger coming on, she scrolled through her contacts and called the only person she knew she could trust. After three rings, a man's voice answered.

"Are you home?" Eva said, trying not to sound too desperate.

"Yeah. I'm here. Are you okay? You don't sound too good."

"Listen, I'll tell you all about it, but first I need you to let me in the back."

CHAPTER EIGHTY-SEVEN

SUSAN WOKE FEELING AWFUL. SLEEP HAD BEEN ELUSIVE. After Daniels left last night, she blamed herself for what happened. She was too honest. She'd allowed their relationship to take off too fast. There were so many things she could have done differently, but the one truth she couldn't escape was the unexplainable need she felt to apologize to him.

Daniels had what she needed. He could be her saving grace if she allowed him to be. He'd said it himself on his way out the door. *"Call me when you're ready to commit. I have everything you need waiting for you when you're ready."*

Now, as Susan sat behind her work computer wrestling with fear over the possibility of losing everything she'd worked so hard to build, she believed she was ready to commit. Even if that meant making a deal with the devil.

Gathering her purse and keys, she left the office with a straight face. Her colleagues were busy working as if the business wasn't about to fold. Susan couldn't stomach the thought of letting them down, but the look on Carly's face said it all; she knew she'd failed.

Susan drove across town and, as she neared Daniels's

office, her nerves tightened her stomach. Would he welcome her visit? Be happy to see her? Would she feel comfortable being in a room alone with him? Susan told herself she could do this—that she was strong and had no choice—but the replay in her head of last night wouldn't stop. It was enough to give her pause.

"This isn't about us," she reminded herself. "This is strictly business."

Susan wanted access to Daniels's promised circle of influence. Nothing more. Just a chance to stay in business and do the work she loved.

When she arrived at the studio, she parked out front and was about to turn the car off when the news report playing through the speakers caught her attention. With one hand on the wheel, the other on the keys, Susan listened.

"The Amber Alert has been canceled for Jessica Hinojos. Early reports are saying the teenager is alive and well and the chief of police will be holding a press conference soon."

Susan closed her eyes, breathed out a sigh of relief. It was welcome news, but she still worried about Naomi's friend Jenny. Where was she? If she was still alive, did Jessica know where the police could find her? Susan prayed she could.

Exiting her car, she marched to the entrance and swung open the glass door. Making her way to the front office, she was greeted by an empty reception desk. Susan looked around and decided to find Daniels's office herself. Following the signs only got her so far before she knew she was lost. A young man rounded the corner and Susan asked him for directions.

He looked no older than a freshman in college, but was happy to point her in the direction of where she needed to go. Susan thanked the man and a beat later was knocking on Daniels's door. When no one answered, she looked up and down the empty hallway before peeking her head inside. "Hello?" she called.

No response.

Daniels wasn't here.

Susan entered and was immediately impressed by his office. The expansive mahogany desk, the panoramic view of the Rockies, and all the awards and achievements he'd accumulated throughout his impressive career were on full display. It was everything she dreamed of having herself. A corner office, prominent career, and influential power. But a part of her was happy Daniels wasn't here. Rebuilding his trust would take time, time she didn't have.

Not wanting to wait around for him to show his face, she decided to start small by leaving him a note instead. Finding a pen and paper, she simply wrote, *Let's try this again, Susan.*

She folded the paper into a tent and placed it in front of his computer monitor to make sure it wouldn't be overlooked. That's when Susan noticed Daniels's very detailed interest in the cases of the missing girls. It was clear to her that he'd been following the stories very closely. She read through the notes on his desk, noticing a glaring discrepancy: almost everything was written about Jenny, hardly a mention about Megan, and not even Jessica's name.

Susan pulled at her collar and straightened. She glanced to the door as the temperature in the room seemed to climb. Sifting through more of the pile, she grew more and more confused as names she didn't know began mixing with those of the missing girls.

Who was Josie Zapatero? She didn't know.

Susan made a mental note and continued reading.

Nicholas Bennett... teacher at South High... sleeping with Jenny Booth!!

Could this be true? Susan didn't believe it. Nicholas Bennett was Allison's new man. She was too smart to be interested in someone who preyed on his students. Daniels's next line of notes made Susan even more nervous than before.

Have Heidi sell this story!!!

Susan's hand trembled and the paper she was holding shook.

Sell this story? Did that mean it wasn't true? Why would he want to do that?

"Oh god," she breathed with realization. This was why he didn't want to talk work last night. His work was all lies.

Susan pressed her hand against her forehead and felt her temperature spike. She felt used. Like Daniels was only interested in her to keep close to the story she gave him permission to tell. But why spin it and create sensational fodder? Susan didn't understand.

Daniels's office phone rang and Susan jumped back like someone had entered. Covering her mouth, she listened to it go to voicemail.

"Oliver, it's Hoffman. It's done."

Susan knew the voice and recognized the name. It was the client she'd lost. Her eyes widened as she listened closely, knowing this couldn't be coincidence.

"Now I need the name of that company you promised could deliver better results. Call me."

Tilting her head away, Susan's entire body tensed with betrayal. Did Daniels sabotage her proposal? It certainly seemed that way. But why? Susan hit replay on the machine and listened to it again. She couldn't believe it. Who was this other company Daniels promised? Did he actually have one? How did he even know about her proposal to Hoffman?

As Susan stood, lost in her thoughts, the machine skipped to the next message without Susan realizing it. It was from the night of the award ceremony, the one Susan's company hosted.

The mayor is attending the event and at no point should he find himself in front of the protestors...

Again, Susan recognized the voice, but from where? She began digging into Daniels's life; sifting through papers opening drawers, Daniels clearly had an agenda of his own. Susan wanted to know what it was. Slamming one drawer closed, she opened another and stopped. The answering machine was still playing as she stared at the Polaroids of Heidi Mitchell splayed out on Daniels's desk, naked.

And to think Susan actually dated, and once liked, this guy.

Susan retrieved her cellphone, snapped a few quick pictures for reference, and left the originals on top of the desk for Daniels to find. Then a name came to Susan's mind. She knew who left the voicemail about the protests. She stared at the red light on the answering machine and continued to listen.

...You do that, and I'll make sure to clean up your mess with Josie.

Beep.

The room went quiet.

Susan blinked and knew she had to leave. Fast.

Gathering her things, Susan snatched the note she left for Daniels and stuffed it into her back pocket. She did not need him to know she was here. She headed for the door knowing Daniels was covering something up. Though she didn't know what exactly that was, she was certain it had something to do with Police Chief Gordon Watts.

CHAPTER EIGHTY-EIGHT

My knee bounced off the bench so hard it made the entire booth shake. Erin placed a firm hand on my thigh to stop it. When she caught my eye, I wondered how she could be so relaxed.

"Relax." Erin's grip eased. "He'll show."

I was nervous Archie wouldn't show. Why would he? I didn't understand how he seemed to be with us every second one minute, then nowhere the next. What was he up to? Where had he been since the last time we saw him? He seemed to be leading us on one wild goose chase after another.

I checked the time. We'd already been waiting for a half-hour without any sighting of him.

"I don't know," I said. "I'm starting to have doubts. What if he knows it's us?"

I kept thinking he could have already been to Eva's. Maybe he was meeting with her now and knew it was impossible for her to be in two places at once when we decided to message him and ask him to join us for lunch.

Erin asked, "Do you have a better idea?"

That was just it. I didn't. It seemed like we were out of options. At least we knew the cops were at Carr's house. Then I watched Erin's neck straighten as her gaze traveled over my shoulder and toward the small café's entrance.

"Don't look, but he's here," she said in a low tone.

I slid my elbows across the table and leaned in. "Well, now what?"

We didn't have a plan for when he arrived, and I wondered how Archie would react when he realized he'd been set up. I waited for Erin to respond, to give some kind of indication of what Archie was doing.

"He's looking around the room, and...contact." Erin raised her hand, waved, and smiled.

I glanced over my shoulder. Archie didn't look as angry as I thought he would. Instead, he strode to our table with his signature arrogant smirk that soured my insides. He slid into the booth next to me, shaking his head, flicking his eyes between us.

He said, "Eva's not here, is she?"

Erin shook her head no. "It's just us."

I asked Archie, "Where have you been?"

He eased back, draped an arm over the back of the bench, and quirked an eyebrow. He nodded, as if understanding he'd been duped. "I wondered how long it would take for you to find me on that ludicrous dating site. Did Eva give you her details, or did you steal them to get to me?"

"You're not even going to deny you were on there?" I said, wondering if I was looking into the kidnapper's eyes.

"What's the point?" Archie shrugged. "It wasn't exactly like I was trying to hide it from anyone."

"Why be there then?"

"It wasn't to get laid." He laughed. "Like I could afford to date those women." Archie was cocky as ever in his delivery

—the smooth operator without a worry in the world. "I wanted a piece of Eva, just like you."

Archie's comment rubbed me the wrong way. We didn't set out to exploit Eva's story. We didn't want *a piece* of her. She came to us. Her story fell into our lap, as did her safety. I didn't need Archie to know any of that. I still wanted to trust him, but I wasn't sure I could.

Erin said, "We know you came to Colorado just before Megan disappeared."

I watched Archie's reaction out of the corner of my eye. There was a spark in his pupils as he laughed. "You can't actually be thinking that I'm behind these abductions?"

When we didn't laugh, he knew we were serious. I told him about the cryptic messages we received and how they resembled PQK's communication with the press. Archie seemed amused, so I kept going. I reminded him about his copycat statement at the award ceremony the first night we met, and the coincidences that made him an obvious person of interest. Of course he denied it all, kept his cool, and never once broke, even as Erin and I increased the pressure.

"I went to the 7-Eleven last night," I said. "You weren't anywhere near the place. Why tell me to go there if you knew you weren't going to show?"

Archie locked eyes with me and said, "Tell me, when you were there, walking around, what did you see?"

Had he been watching me? How did he know I was walking around, or was he just assuming I would? I thought of the dark street corner where I parked and walking behind the little building. I looked into his unwavering eyes, asking myself if he knew Jessica's abduction was a hoax or not. I didn't think he did.

Archie dove his hand into his bag before I could answer and slapped a folder onto the table. He opened it up, plucked a single photograph from his extensive pile, and handed it to me.

"That man, did you see him last night?" He jabbed his finger to the center of the image. His look told me he knew I had.

And he'd be right. I did see that man and knew what kind of truck he drove. Was that Carr's truck he was driving? How had I missed this?

My neck craned as I took a closer look at the man's face. Once I was finished with him, I shifted my attention to the other photographs. There, in the pile, Archie had pictures of both Jenny and Naomi at a Burger King. I wondered why and from when. In one frame they were alone. In another, they were talking to an older man whose face looked familiar, but I couldn't recall from where.

"You talked to him last night, didn't you? At 7-Eleven." Archie put the pictures from Burger King away.

"Who is he?" I asked.

Erin laced her fingers and leaned forward, needing to see what Archie was getting at.

"Carr's contractor. The man he hired to remodel his basement."

"We were just visiting Carr," I said, waiting for Archie to react. "He never mentioned anything about a contractor for the remodel. It seemed like he was doing it himself. But he did have the photo you took of Eva."

"He asked to keep it," Archie said by way of explanation.

"What were you doing with him?" I asked. Was he just showing us all these other photos to throw us off his trail? It was ballsy of him to even meet with the amount of evidence piling up against him.

"Interviewing him for my book. When Eva went missing and then turned up, I did some digging and learned about her abusive relationship with Carr. He became a person of interest. Didn't pan out, but he wanted the picture. Besides, it's not me or Carr you're after. It's him." Archie pointed to the man's face from 7-Eleven. "Christopher Bowers. This is who we're after. He kidnapped Eva, pretended to rescue her, may also have kidnapped Jenny, and is now after Eva again."

Had we just unintentionally left Eva out in the open? I swept my gaze to Erin and her face said it all. We may have just made a deadly mistake neither of us was willing to admit —especially not in front of Archie. Instead, Archie said it for us when he packed up and stood.

"Let's just hope he doesn't get to her while I'm here responding to this little stunt you played."

CHAPTER EIGHTY-NINE

With her hand on the doorknob, Susan paused to inhale a deep breath to calm her intense desire to flee. A wave of strength draped over her as she realized what happened last night with Daniels was no mistake. His actions brought her here today so she could learn the truth of what he was up to.

As soon as she opened her eyes, Susan cracked the door and listened. Once she was sure the coast was clear, she ducked out of Daniels's office and hurried to the exit.

As she traveled through the studio hallways, she kept her head down and her focus on taking this new information to Samantha. Sam would know what to do with it and, together, they'd learn the truth behind the secrets Daniels seemed to be hiding.

Exiting through the same door she came in, she was thankful to have gotten out without being recognized. She wouldn't have known what to say to him, and certainly wouldn't have been able to hide the shock buzzing inside her chest after learning the kind of man he truly was.

The bright sun hit her back but wasn't as hot as her cheeks felt. Though she wasn't a spiteful person, Susan felt a deep urge to hit back and punch Daniels where it counted.

Digging out her cellphone from her purse, it immediately started ringing inside her hand. Susan checked the caller ID and hurried to her car. She answered, "I was just about to call, are you with Bennett?"

"That's why I'm calling," Allison said.

Susan pulled her keys, hit the fob to unlock her car, and glanced back toward the studio building one last time before getting into the driver's seat.

"Are you with him?" she asked again.

"No. I'm not with him." Allison summed up what was happening at Bennett's residence. "That's why I'm calling. I need your help. Are you available?"

"Allison, listen to me." Susan started her car. "Bennett is being set up by reporter Heidi Mitchell. None of what you saw is true." Susan explained what she found, how it was all detailed on Daniels's desk. "Heidi is being manipulated to sell this story. I don't know why, but I think Samantha will help us figure it out."

A brief moment of silence followed.

Then Allison cursed. She said, "I never believed it for one second."

Susan mentioned where she was and could sense the urgency in her friend's voice. "Now, what can I do for you?"

Allison requested Susan get Naomi out of Bennett's house. "Can you do that for me?"

Susan's chest swelled as she put the car in reverse. "I'm on my way now."

With her phone on Bluetooth, Allison's voice came through the speakers. "I've talked to Bennett. He knows you're coming."

Susan spun the steering wheel and asked, "Are you sure Naomi is still there?"

"I'm sure. There is no way Bennett would let her leave with Heidi still parked on his front lawn. We just need to get her out of there and reverse the spin on this ridiculous story before it's too late."

CHAPTER NINETY

"Oh God," Cindy Moss gasped. "I knew something like this would happen."

"Cin, calm down. I'm going to get her out of there," Susan said as she pulled into Bennett's neighborhood. "Just hang tight and let me do the worrying."

Susan knew she had to call her friend the moment she got off the phone with Allison. Cindy worked a demanding job, and Susan knew chances were good she hadn't heard the news about Bennett. Susan sped across town and updated her friend on what was happening and how she was planning to solve it.

"Jenny's not in his house, too, is she?" Cindy asked. "Why didn't the school warn me about Bennett's predation on girls? Why was he ever even hired?"

Susan knew better than to feed an unfounded conspiracy. "Don't ask me how, but I'm certain Bennett's being set up."

"Then where is Jenny?"

"I don't know."

"I just never imagined I would have to worry about my daughter being taken advantage of by a teacher."

"Then stop," Susan said, bringing her car to the side of the road. "Go home and we'll meet you there soon."

Susan knew she was in for a fight as soon as she saw Heidi whip her intense gaze in her direction. Susan took a deep breath, checked her makeup in the mirror, and tried not to notice the swelling crowd beginning to congregate on the street as they all waited to hang Bennett for his alleged crimes.

As she opened her car door and stepped out, she wondered if this scene was also purposely designed by Daniels, just like the protestors that interrupted the award ceremony the other night had apparently been. She was angry for allowing herself to be fooled into thinking she needed him. Instead of letting her frustration stop her, Susan used that energy to brace for the impact she saw heading her way.

"Act like everything is normal," she told herself as a couple other reporters turned to look in her direction, clearly hoping to ride on Heidi's coattails.

"I know you," Heidi said, heels clacking as she worked to catch up with Susan.

"Yes you do." Susan kept walking, pushing her way through the knots of people. "I'm picking up my goddaughter."

"Naomi Moss?"

Susan stopped, turned, and glanced to the cameraman hovering over Heidi's right shoulder, recording. She smiled. "Is that a problem?"

Heidi said with a microphone to her mouth, "Are you aware Mr. Bennett is accused of sleeping with his students, and that your goddaughter is inside the house with him now?"

Susan's smile widened. "First, those are some serious allegations. What evidence do you have against Mr. Bennett? And second, isn't that what I just told you?"

Heidi's eyes glimmered like she was about to sink her

teeth into Susan. Susan hoped Allison knew what she was doing because she didn't need her words to later come back and bite her.

Heidi said, "What if I told you Naomi Moss, the girl you say is your goddaughter, conspired with Mr. Bennett to make Jenny Booth disappear so that they could be together?"

Susan leaned in and said, "I'd say that's outrageous."

"Is it?"

Susan smirked. "Let me ask you something, Ms. Mitchell, what were you and Owen Daniels arguing about at the Percy Goodwin State Journalism Award ceremony?"

Heidi cocked her head and stared.

"Outside the venue, during the protests, I saw you two arguing. It wasn't how Daniels organized the protests to steal your spotlight, was it?"

Heidi lowered the mic from her face and her lips made a flat line.

"Or perhaps it was how he keeps this in his back pocket for when he needs you to do something unethical—like what you're accusing my goddaughter of doing." Susan pulled out her phone, scrolled to the revenge porn photos she'd found of Heidi inside Daniels's desk, and pushed the screen in Heidi's face. Susan said sarcastically, "Classy. Were they professionally done?"

"Turn off the camera," Heidi snapped. "Turn them off!"

Susan knew she had her. "What do you think he'll do with them as soon as you stop doing his dirty work?"

"Where did you get those?"

"Does it matter?" Susan flashed a knowing grin. She wasn't proud of taking down Daniels's minion, but Heidi had gotten herself into this mess. "Now that you've seen the evidence, the question is, will you allow him to get away with it? You and I both know this story about Bennett is B.S. What I want to know is why Daniels needs you to sell it so hard?"

The color in Heidi's face paled as she blinked.

"You think about it," Susan said, turning toward Bennett's door. "In the meantime, I'm going to get my goddaughter out of that house without your cameras, or anyone else's, filming our exit."

CHAPTER NINETY-ONE

THIRSTY PUT ON HIS BLINKER AND TURNED LEFT ONTO THE next street. A sense of hope filled his chest when he saw a parking space open up. Easing to a gentle stop, he parallel parked with ease as if he were sober. Once his wheels were peacefully resting against the curb, he turned off the truck, took the keys from the ignition, and shook out the tension he could feel building in his arms.

Eva was on her way home. He was sure of it. The question was, who would get here first?

Minutes ago, he watched her wait nervously on the side of the road for a lift. Watching from afar, Thirsty knew she was on edge. Her eyes darted in every direction and she looked scared. Then, once she climbed into the backseat of an Uber, he followed her south until eventually losing her at a light.

That was four blocks back and a red he should have run. Now he didn't know where she was. Not knowing caused him to suffer unbearable anxiety.

Thirsty sipped from the bottle, hoping it would calm him. He kept his eyes peeled for Eva, taking in the surrounding scene.

The sun was hiding behind a large thunderhead building above, threatening to downpour. The wind swirled around his tires, and Thirsty was sure he had brought the storm with him.

This part of the city always made him feel unwanted, like he didn't belong. It was clean when he wasn't. Rich and vibrant, unlike himself. And, worse, it reminded him of his wife who nagged him to be the person she wished he was.

Turning the rearview mirror on his face, Thirsty stared for a long pause, knowing he was on the edge of depression. His hair was disheveled, a little greasy, and soon the darkness that plagued his existence would snap its cloak around his neck and make him wish he was dead. Time was running out, but he wasn't there yet.

Two women in designer clothes crossed the street and headed his way, their high item purchases swinging in the bags they carried as they pursed their tight Botox lips above pumps that propped them up. Eva might have lived here, but she wasn't like these people, was she?

Thirsty's head pounded.

Perhaps the reason he liked Eva was because she was a younger version of his wife. Not in appearance, but everything else. As difficult as it was for him to admit, he knew it was true. He liked the Barbies and high-maintenance women who smelled nice and thought the world owed them everything.

"If you can't beat them, join 'em." Thirsty chuckled into his bottle.

Twisting the cap closed, he hid it away in the glove box and stepped out of the truck. Pulling his sunglasses over his eyes, the world went dark. He stumbled his way up the sidewalk and stopped to peer into the window he believed to be Eva's.

"Are you home, sweetie?" Thirsty grinned. "Daddy's here to save you."

The entrance to the building was locked. He cursed and yanked on the door harder when his cell buzzed in his back pocket. Stepping to the side, he raised his glasses off the bridge of his nose and read the text.

Where are you? I have a mess on my hands. Call me.

"Fucking Carr," Thirsty grumbled as he sauntered back to his truck.

Rich man Oliver Carr was part of the problem, too, Thirsty thought as he reached for the door handle. But before climbing in his truck, Thirsty turned his head and caught sight of a woman about Eva's height walking briskly with her head down.

Pulling his shades down on the bridge of his nose, Thirsty squinted and took a closer look.

The woman's dark hair bounced with each flare of her hip.

It was Eva.

The one that got away.

Releasing the handle, Thirsty turned, tucked his chin, and jogged after Eva, who never saw him coming.

CHAPTER NINETY-TWO

I HAD THE GAS PEDAL FLOORED AS I YANKED ON THE steering wheel and propelled my car forward through congested traffic. I kept glancing at the clock, knowing I wasn't going fast enough.

"Don't you think she knows?" Erin screamed at Archie from the front seat.

I couldn't afford to take my eyes off the road. Not for one second. But I could feel Archie clenching on to the backs of both our seats. He leaned forward from the backseat, his head nearly level with ours.

They were still arguing about where to go without consulting with me, the driver. I knew there were only two places Eva could go—her apartment or Oliver Carr's house. Since the police had Carr covered, I raced to her apartment complex as fast as I could.

The car shifted gears and the RPMs relaxed. But only for a bit.

Eva's apartment complex seemed worlds away at the pace we were moving. Traffic was getting the best of us, but what worried me most was not knowing what Eva would do once she got there. Would she stay? For how long? Where would she go next?

"Take this exit," Archie said, his long arm extending over my dash as he pointed through the windshield.

Erin twisted around and snarled. "Would you just let her drive?"

I kept my wheels straight, choosing my own path. I knew the city better than he did, and I still had plenty of questions for him, questions we didn't have time to ask back at the café where we left his car. I directed my comment to Archie, and said, "Instead of you two arguing about which route will get us there quicker, why don't you tell us how you came to be in Colorado?"

Archie told us how he didn't plan on telling this story. After his smashing hit true crime novel on the Prom Queen Killer, his publishers wanted more. Somewhere along the way, he caught wind of how Denver's mayor was possibly downplaying the city's crime statistics and decided to chase that story and see where it led him. Then Megan Hines disappeared and it opened up an opportunity he couldn't refuse.

"She was beautiful," he said. "I knew the world would love her."

Erin and I listened without interrupting. As soon as he was finished detailing his journey to Colorado, I asked, "If you were after Megan, how did you discover Christopher Bowers took Eva?"

There was a long lead up, and I wondered if Archie would get to telling us how he figured it out before we arrived to Eva's. Instead of just getting to the facts, Archie profiled Bowers for us. I eased into my thoughts as he explained Bowers's mental health issues, his work as a contractor, and how, after three years of marriage, Bowers learned he'd entered a life he wished he hadn't.

"His wife is controlling, believe me. I've seen it first hand

and just watching them together makes me want a divorce." Archie shook his head and continued, "Anyway, she pushed him to be someone he wasn't. He escaped his life by working long hours, or at least that's what he told his wife."

"So, if he wasn't working, what was he doing?"

"Pretending not to be the monster he was." Archie raised both eyebrows and nodded. "The hospital has records of it, and so do the police. I'm not going to waste my breath explaining why I don't have the official reports, but let's just say Bowers has been after Eva since she got away."

"Why take the risk?" I asked, wondering why someone would pretend to save the very person they kidnapped.

"The thrill of getting caught." Archie smiled. "He likes to put himself in the middle of his own crimes. It's why you saw him at 7-Eleven."

I shook my head. "It can't be him. Jessica's kidnapping was a hoax."

Archie gave me a look of disapproval. Then he said, "That can't be true. It's what he does. He drives around the city all night, hunting for vulnerable women. At night he's a different person and has grand illusions of being someone he isn't."

"Did you catch him in the act?" Erin asked.

Archie never did.

I was thinking of Bowers's manic depression when I said, "You might be right about him wanting to get back what got away, but I think he's a copycat to whoever murdered Megan and abducted Jenny."

"Copycat to who, though?" Erin asked.

The Prom Queen Killer was my first thought, but then I said, "It wouldn't be Carr, would it? I mean, he did lend Bowers his truck."

"Carr hired Bowers to remodel his basement. It's probably where Bowers first met Eva," Archie said as he dug around looking for something inside his bag. "A copycat makes sense."

"Why is that?" I asked.

"Emulating the real killer would excite him and he would certainly want a piece of the fame for himself."

"But who is the real killer?" Erin asked. "If his only goal is Eva, who has Jenny? Who killed Megan? And what about Jane Doe? Where does she fit in?"

A thought struck and I asked, "That man you photographed talking to Jenny and Naomi at Burger King, who is he?"

Archie retrieved the folder and opened it up on his lap. As he sifted through photos, I angled the mirror down and saw him flip through to the same photos he'd showed me before. "He's a teacher. Name's Scott Helton. No one to worry about. His record is clean. I've checked."

"Shit." I punched the gas and the car lurched forward as the engine whined.

Archie flew back into his seat and cursed as his papers spilled to the floor. "What the bloody hell is going on?"

"Heidi might have been half-right," I said to Erin. "Right theory about a teacher, wrong teacher."

Erin nodded. She pushed her fingers through her hair and said, as if reading my mind, "But we've got to get to Eva before Bowers gets."

CHAPTER NINETY-THREE

Eva knew freedom was just on the other side of the building. She was so close, yet it felt so far. A funny feeling fluttered up her spine and spread across her shoulders that made her believe something wasn't right. She swept her gaze up and looked around at the world in front of her. Then she turned up the block, heading in the opposite direction from her apartment.

As she hurried up the sidewalk, she felt the rush of city traffic sweep the air behind her. The burden she carried weighed her down, but it didn't stop her. She had to be smart enough to outmaneuver the men she knew were out to get her.

Without slowing her pace, she glanced over her left shoulder, looking for the man whose name she couldn't remember. She was now certain he was working with Carr, and the thought sent a paralyzing wave of paranoia down her back.

Eva's vision tunneled and she kept marching forward, following the white light with hopes of finding freedom behind her apartment building.

Everything was beginning to make sense. She should have

seen it coming, but couldn't because she was too close to what was happening. But Carr's jealously of Stark and his constant need to control every aspect of her life was the reason all of this happened to her. Eva was certain of it, and now she deeply regretted lying to Erin and Samantha about who she was actually going to see.

She gulped back gallons of air, but it still felt like she was drowning. Her pulse was ticking hard in her neck below a clenched jaw, and she had a compulsive need to keep looking back, feeling as if she was being followed.

Her cellphone dinged. Her neighbor was waiting at the back door as promised.

Rounding the corner, she needed to hurry. Eva was scared for what might happen if she didn't get to the door in time. The last thing she needed was him to catch her outside without a Plan B.

As she approached the intersection, she lowered her head and swept her gaze toward where she last saw Carr's truck parked. Behind a curtain of lashes, she lengthened her stride when suddenly she heard her name being called.

"Eva!"

Her heart fluttered inside her chest as she took off running. She knew it was him. He was back.

"Stop. I want to talk to you!"

Eva ran past the entrance to her apartment building, gripped the corner and propelled herself around the side when the sounds of sirens filled the summer air. She continued running without stopping. She wasn't sure if the footsteps she was hearing were her own or his.

Coming around the back, her friend was standing at the door. As soon as he saw her coming, he quickly unlocked and opened the door. Eva skidded inside and closed the door behind her. With her sweaty hands on the glass, her eyes darted back and forth as she looked for the man who was chasing her.

"Eva, what in the world is going on?"

Eva fought to catch her breath. She looked everywhere for him, but he wasn't there, and now she looked like a fool in front of her friend. As soon as she stepped away from the window, the man wrapped his arm around her waist and leaned in to kiss her cheek.

He said, "It's good to see you."

CHAPTER NINETY-FOUR

As soon as we arrived to Eva's apartment building, Archie said, "Bastard took my exact spot."

We rolled past what appeared to be Carr's red truck parked not far from Eva's front door. I was thankful my bet had paid off. I didn't want to have to go chasing Eva down. At least we could assume Bowers was somewhere in the vicinity.

But our job wasn't finished yet. We needed to find Eva, get her to trust us again, and get her somewhere safe until we could figure out exactly what was going on.

I parked a half block east from the truck and the three of us stepped out at the same time. Without speaking, I headed for the entrance. Erin and Archie followed close behind. As soon we got to the door, a woman exited the building and graciously let us inside.

It was impeccable timing. I thanked her and acted like I belonged. The elevator was waiting for us and we took it to the seventh floor. The hallway was as quiet as I remembered it being the first time I was here. As I marched toward Eva's door, I rehearsed what I was going to say to convince her to let us to come inside.

I knocked gently before calling out to her. "Eva. It's me. Samantha. Can you open up?"

Erin was bouncing on her toes as Archie stared at the door handle.

"Eva." I knocked again. "Please, we need to talk."

When she didn't answer, Erin tried calling her cell. As I listened to it ring in Erin's ear, my thoughts turned back to the conversation we had in the car. We were here to save Eva from Bowers, but Helton appeared to be involved somehow, too. I wanted to know more about him. Was he was the teacher Megan Hines wanted to report last spring? He seemed to have all the qualities of Archie's serial rapist, and worse, he might have been one of the last people to have seen Jenny before she disappeared. I wondered if he was on King's radar.

I locked eyes with Erin. She shook her head.

Where are you, Eva?

"We need to spread out," I said, trying the door, not surprised to find it locked.

I worried about this manic depressant Archie described with multiple personalities that had already fooled Eva once and could probably do it again.

"We know Bowers is somewhere nearby because his truck is parked out front," I said, "and we can only assume Eva will try to come home at some point if she hasn't already."

"I'll walk around the block," Archie said.

"I'll stay out front and keep calling," Erin offered.

I moved toward Eva's neighbor's door and stared at the brass knocker that had the word *Ace* engraved in the middle. I thought about knocking when the sounds of police sirens caught our attentions.

Archie ran to the window at the end of the hall as the sirens grew louder. Erin and I met him there and we all saw an unmarked police cruiser and a squad car speed past below.

Something was happening on the streets and my gut told me it had everything to do with Eva.

CHAPTER NINETY-FIVE

King drove with a white-knuckled grip. His sirens wailed above his head as the sea of traffic parted in front of him. So much was going through his head as Alvarez silently hung on in the seat next to him with radio receiver in hand.

King flicked his gaze to the rearview mirror and thought about Detective Gray tailing him in the squad car as he listened to the cop radio chattering with the latest updates.

He knew where Eva lived, had looked up her address before she requested to have him take her to Samantha's when she was in the hospital. Now he wondered if Bowers was the reason Eva didn't want to go home that night. Thinking back, she had to know Bowers wasn't safe, so why didn't she say something?

Thirsty, thirsty, thirsty. It was all King could hear, rattling around inside his head.

Reaching his hand into his jacket pocket, he tossed Alvarez his cellphone. "Call Samantha. Ask her if she's with Eva."

Alvarez looked at the phone on his lap as if it was radioactive.

"I need her to be with Samantha." King flicked his gaze to his partner, willing him to make a move. "We all do." Sam had told him early this morning that Eva left Erin's, but she could have come back. Could have realized she was safer with someone than alone.

"Sorry, partner. I don't want to get involved." Alvarez picked up the cellphone and slid it back into King's pocket.

King ground his teeth, hating the current animosity between the department and the local journalists. The city seemed to be unraveling at the hands of the mayor, though King felt personally responsible.

The radio squawked to life as the voice announced, "Suspect under the influence. Refusing to cooperate."

The tires squealed against the pavement as King turned left and flew beneath a traffic light. As soon as his wheels straightened, he spotted the cherry red Ford pickup truck parked out front with the squad car behind. Planning to block it in from the front, suddenly the truck pulled out in front of the patrol car and sped away.

"Here we go," Alvarez said, calling in the chase.

King propelled the cruiser forward and was on the truck's tail in a matter of seconds. The driver made no intention of stopping and, when King saw his chance, he whipped the steering wheel hard left, hit the gas, and managed to get out in front of the truck, forcing it to the curb where it came to an abrupt stop.

Gray's squad car blocked it in at the back, and King and Alvarez got out with their guns drawn, calling for Bowers to show his hands.

CHAPTER NINETY-SIX

Eva couldn't decide if she wanted to stand or sit. Helton had welcomed her into his apartment and, though clean and orderly, Eva couldn't relax.

"Please, Eva, sit and unwind. You're making me nervous," Scott Helton said.

Eva turned away from the window and glanced down her front. Her arms were tightly wound around her torso and a small tremor moved up her spine.

"What's gotten into you? I've never seen you like this before."

Eva dragged her feet across the floor and dropped like lead onto the couch, apologizing.

"Honey, there is nothing to be sorry for." Helton walked in from the kitchen and offered Eva a cold soda. She shook her head no, and he placed it on the coffee table in front of her in case she changed her mind. "Did he hurt you again?"

Everything inside Eva's body stopped as she looked up at Helton from beneath her brow. He knew everything. Helton had heard her arguments with Carr through the walls, seen what he had done to her dozens of times before, and had probably listened as she wept herself to sleep on those nights Carr abused her either physically or emotionally, sometimes both.

"Sweetie, you don't need to tell me what I already know." Helton reached for her hand, but she pulled away and hid it under her arm.

Eva turned her head and looked away, fighting back the sting of tears welling behind both her eyes. She hated herself for not recognizing the truck to be Carr's the night she climbed inside and was whisked away to the hospital only to be further humiliated by having to do a rape test. But what was the driver's name? Why wouldn't he just leave her alone?

"I'm worried about you," Helton said. "I've seen the news."

"And you're wondering when I'm going to learn my lesson?"

Helton sighed. "Eva, darling, I'm not saying Carr is guilty of those crimes, but he's certainly shown he's capable. I don't want that to be you. That's all."

Eva laced her fingers on her lap and stared at her unopened soda can. Sweeping her gaze to the left, a deck of cards was stacked next to Owen Daniels's business card. Turning her head, she locked eyes with Helton and asked, "Why do you care?"

"I've seen what can happen to someone when they don't get out before it's too late." Helton's expression softened as he stood. "I have something for you."

Eva watched Helton disappear into the back and return with a gift.

"Happy birthday," he said.

Eva accepted the gift and noticed for the first time Helton's injured hand wrapped in gauze.

"I wanted to give it to you sooner," he said. "But you weren't home."

"What happened to your hand?" she asked.

"Cooking accident," Helton said, holding up his wrapped hand.

The sounds of knocking vibrated the walls, making them both pause and turn their attention to the front door. They heard it again, and Eva knew it was coming from her place. Next, her cellphone vibrated in her pocket. She stood and Helton caught her arm.

"Let me," he said.

Eva snapped her elbow and hurried to the door. Peering with one eye through the peephole, she couldn't see anything but knew it had to be him.

"Eva, it could be him," Helton said behind her.

Suddenly, Archie passed in front of the door and Eva's eyes bulged.

"Shit," she said, dropping down on her heels. It seemed everyone was after her with nowhere to go. Having to hide from one person was hard enough, but escaping from two was near impossible.

Helton surprised her by placing his hands on her shoulders.

"Get the fuck off me," she screamed.

Helton stepped back, showing his palms.

Eva's body quivered and she began to cry. "I was kidnapped. That's why I wasn't around. And now I don't know who to trust."

"You can trust me, Eva," Helton said softly as he took one step forward. "Say it. I trust you..."

Tears leaked from her eyes as the sounds of sirens grew louder by the second. Eva locked eyes with Helton and, when she saw a glimmer of empathy light up his eye, she murmured, "I trust you."

CHAPTER NINETY-SEVEN

SUSAN TURNED HER BACK ON HEIDI AND SMILED. STANDING straight as an arrow, she rang Bennett's doorbell, finding confidence in Allison's plan. She was aware Heidi was staring, along with another dozen sets of eyes, wondering if Bennett would open his door.

When no one answered, Susan turned and glanced toward the street. Heidi turned her head, pretended to not be staring, and went back to work loading up her van, packing up as if the story here was finished. Susan flicked her gaze to the other reporters and was happy to see them following Heidi's lead. Mumbling a few choice words beneath her breath, she discreetly reached for the doorknob.

Locked. Darn.

The plan only worked if she was let inside, and Allison assured her Bennett knew she was coming. What else did he know and could Susan be sure she could get Naomi out of the house without any further scrutiny?

She leaned into the door and quietly called for Naomi. "It's Susan. Please let me inside."

Susan listened to footsteps lightly pad their way to the

door, then, a second later, the lock clicked over and the door cracked open. A voice from behind the door told her to come inside.

Susan entered the house and the door quickly shut and latched behind her. Bennett barely looked at her when wagging his head, motioning her to follow him to the living room. Susan followed, moving through the dark house, and smiled when seeing Naomi sitting with her knees pulled to her chest on the sofa chair near the TV.

Naomi jumped to her feet and ran over to her. When Susan wrapped her up in a tight squeeze, the world around her disappeared and she knew everything would be all right.

"Thank god you're here," Naomi said.

Susan tucked her chin and took Naomi by the shoulders. "Are you okay?"

"I'm fine."

"You were supposed to stay home and wait for your mother."

"I know. I'm sorry. I just needed someone to talk to. I didn't know this would happen."

"No one could have predicted this."

Susan glanced to Bennett and watched as he lowered himself onto the couch. He rubbed his temples as if warding off an excruciating headache. His eyes were puffy and stressed; he looked like a man heading toward an awful fate.

"My mom is going to kill me," Naomi said in a tone that only a teen could muster. Susan realized Naomi had no idea what the world was going to make of her now that Heidi brought her reputation into question.

Susan brought her eyes to Naomi's and said, "Your mother can't wait to have you home."

"Then she hasn't seen the photo that reporter is going to share."

"Don't worry about that. I took care of it."

"You did?"

That got Bennett's attention, too. He lifted his head and stared with bright, hopeful eyes.

Susan asked him, "Does the name Owen Daniels mean anything to you?"

"No. Who is he?"

Susan told him.

Bennett said, "Go figure. But why are they doing this to us?"

"I wish I knew."

Bennett's cellphone kept ringing. He said, "It's Principal Wair. I can't answer it. I know I'm going to get suspended unless I can somehow prove these allegations are wrong."

"There might be a way."

Bennett's body tipped forward.

"Allison hasn't told you her plan, has she?"

"Not entirely."

"Well, it's one we can all believe in. In the meantime, I'm not convinced it's so much about you as it is about someone wanting to create a diversion to what's really happened to Megan and Jenny."

"Tell her what you told me," Bennett said, snapping his fingers at Naomi.

Naomi stepped forward. "I think Jenny might be with our teacher, Scott Helton."

When Susan asked her why she thought that, Naomi mentioned Jenny's obsession with him, how she was always talking about his sex life and she was dreaming about him.

"We saw him the night she disappeared. It couldn't have been a coincidence. All Jenny could talk about was how much she wanted to sleep with him."

Susan now understood why Allison wanted to hack into Jenny's student email account. When she heard a van door slam shut and an engine rumble to a start, she hurried to the window, peeked behind the curtain, and glanced to the street. The crowd was dispersing.

Flicking her gaze to Bennett, she said, "We don't have a lot of time, but I'm going to get both of you out of here before the real crowds with pitch forks arrive."

CHAPTER NINETY-EIGHT

As I watched King put Bowers into the back of a squad car after failing his roadside sobriety test, I kept thinking about what Archie said on our ride here. Something about it didn't sit right with me. I tried to understand how the police knew about Bowers, but not a single officer would say.

King slammed the car door shut and kept his distance. He was giving me the cold shoulder, and I wondered if my critique of the mayor had finally come down on him. It wasn't my intention, but it wasn't like our relationship was a secret, either. As much as I wanted to talk to him, hold his hand and make sure we were all right, I kept my eyes on the prize.

Patrol had diverted traffic to the next street over, and I kept waiting for Heidi Mitchell to show. There were two news vans on the scene already, but I assumed she was stuck on the idea of breaking Bennett's story wide open.

"Show's over," I heard an officer say. "Time to go home, people."

I stared at Bowers, thinking the show was far from being over. He was slumped in the backseat with his head hanging low. He looked disheveled, had the appearance of a complete amateur. Archie had to be right about him. He couldn't be the true Woman Collector. Only a copycat. The real perp was someone these women trusted, and it wasn't Bowers.

"There is something sweet about watching the police make an arrest," Erin said as I glanced up to Eva's apartment window.

"She lied to us about Stark." I lowered my gaze and stared into my friend's curious eyes. "Why?"

"I wouldn't be here if I knew," Erin said. "But with Bowers in custody, I think she's safe."

"At least from him," I said, tipping my head back and peering once again into Eva's apartment window, wondering if she was up there looking down at us.

I hoped Erin was right, but what was Eva hiding if her abduction was real? I couldn't let that go; the secrets. I didn't care if Eva lied or what her intention was. I just needed to know the truth so I could go to sleep at night knowing I'd done everything I could to protect a woman I cared for.

"Remember, Sam, this is what she wanted."

I knew Erin was right. But we didn't just give up. Not on ourselves, and not on anyone else. So why were my thoughts turning to Jenny and Naomi and the spectacle that played out at Mr. Bennett's house earlier?

When I heard hands clapping, I turned on a heel and watched a few officers reach their arms inside the window of a black SUV with tinted windows, shaking the hand of Police Chief Gordon Watts. Everyone was celebrating like they caught their guy. It felt over.

"How could they be celebrating with Jenny still missing?" Erin asked.

"They must know something we don't," I said.

No official charges against Bowers had been announced. I knew he'd get taken in and questioned and possibly thrown into the tank to sober up if he was lucky. But our answer came when Erin spotted King cornering Archie one hundred yards to our left.

"He's not going to arrest him, is he?"

I shared a quick glance with Erin before we ran to Archie's defense. King looked angry, and Archie was barking back at whatever King was saying. It had to be about Archie's book and how I thought he might be behind these crimes. Now, as I ran, I regretted sharing my wild assumption with King.

When King raised a fist in front of Archie's face, I yelled, "Alex, no. Stop!"

"Stay back, Sam!" King snapped his elbow and pointed his finger at me.

His tone surprised me. I stopped, stared, and was completely confused by his harsh gavel of a voice. Now I knew something between us wasn't right.

"I was wrong about him," I said. "Archie thought Bowers was the serial rapist."

King wasn't listening. He kept yelling at Archie, asking him where he was the night Megan was murdered. I tried not to take it personally, but the look King was giving me was different from anything I'd seen before.

Then King stopped, turned to me, and said, "Your boy Archie was at the same fill station where Jenny was last seen."

"And so was Christopher Bowers," I said, thinking about how that teacher Helton was, too.

King cocked his head and gave me a questioning look. "Careful, Sam. You're running with the wrong crowd by associating yourself with a potential accomplice."

Emotions were spilling over and King was taking it out on me. I tried not to take it personally, but the pebble in my throat was quickly expanding into the size of a rock. For the first time in our relationship, I felt like our personal lives had entered our professional and it was going to be what ended us.

"Archie was there because he was following Bowers," I said, feeling the need to defend myself for believing Archie. "He was right in thinking Bowers could be the person behind these crimes." I listed off the traits Archie explained to us earlier.

"Good," King said. "Then it's over. We have our guy."

Except I didn't think they did—at least not both of them. Before anything else could be said, our disagreement was broken up by Alvarez. He gave me a hard look and placed a hand on King's shoulder, angling my man's attention away from the three journalists who were ready to pounce on any ounce of truth.

My stomach clenched when I overheard him remind King he shouldn't be talking to me.

"Forget about it," I said, turning toward my car.

Archie and Erin followed, knowing we still had work to complete. "Sam, did we do something to get King in trouble?"

It certainly seemed that way. I reached to open my door but stopped short when I noticed what appeared to be another cryptic message left on the front seat. Picking my head up, I swept my gaze in King's direction and then found myself staring into Archie's golden eyes. This time I knew it couldn't be from him. So where did it come from?

Just when I thought this investigation couldn't get more interesting, I now had this to worry about.

CHAPTER NINETY-NINE

We drove not more than a block away from where Bowers was arrested before pulling onto a quiet side street and tearing open the manila folder we all couldn't wait to get our eyes on.

My heart was beating as loud as Erin's as I peeked inside. She leaned a bit closer and I rolled my eyes to hers.

"What?" she asked. "More cut out letters?"

Archie tipped forward from the middle of the backseat and stuck his head between us. His interest was piqued. We were all prepared to decipher another code when I stuck my hand inside and pulled out a complete police report.

The air went still and everyone stared.

Holding it up in front of my face, I wondered how this report found its way onto the front seat of my car. Who gave it to me? When? We'd been so distracted by Bowers's arrest, was it possible it came before that?

My eyes scurried over the text and my thoughts struggled to keep up. There were so many loose ends I was attempting to tie together, I had to take a deep breath just to slow down. The further I worked my way down the report, the more sure I was that only one person had the power to get this to me.

Erin took the envelope from my thigh and turned it upside down. A pink Post-It note floated to her lap, and I turned to see what I had missed. She pinched it between her fingers and read it out loud.

"Put this to print and don't tell anyone where it came from." The crease between her eyebrows deepened as she leaned over and asked, "Is that what I think it is?"

My heart was beating faster than before. Everything inside my mind was screaming for me to pick up my phone and call King.

"It appears to be the Jane Doe police report," I said in a tone much calmer than I felt.

"King must have put it there when we weren't looking?" Erin suggested.

I wasn't so sure. And neither was Archie.

Erin asked, "If not King, then who gave it to us?"

The mayor's spokesman's words kept echoing between my ears.

Stay in your lane, Mrs. Bell. Death is closer than you think.

Though I never saw him anywhere near the scene, it didn't mean that he couldn't have had someone else put it there for him. But if it was him, was this a threat or a hint? A threat I understood, but if it was a hint, I had to dig a little deeper into understanding the meaning behind his words.

When I closed my eyes, my lips fluttered in thought.

If you change lanes, you'll get further away from the truth?

It was a stretch, but possible.

But if I was right, did he also give us the cryptic messages? I didn't think so. This report was clear and to the point. There wasn't any room for interpretation. Little was hidden in the report, whereas the messages from before were entirely up to us to put together.

"Any names we recognize?" Erin asked. I kept thinking about the police's premature celebration outside Eva's apartment.

"Nothing yet," I said, continuing to read, hoping to find Scott Helton's name somewhere between the lines. But then my eyes stopped on a name I didn't recognize. I backed up and read the previous section again. Then I turned the page, angled the report to Erin, and pointed to a single name.

"Josie Zapatero?" Erin's eyes met with mine. "Who's that?

"That's our Jane Doe."

CHAPTER ONE HUNDRED

COOPER WAS BARKING MADLY IN THE WINDOW WHEN I arrived home. Erin and I unbuckled and stepped out while Archie stayed at the car, knowing my dog was directing his anger at him.

Moving toward my house, I looked over my shoulder and said, "C'mon Archie, I swear he'll only take a finger."

Erin laughed as we climbed the short flight of stairs and stepped through the front door. Cooper ran to me, nudged his head against my thigh, and rolled onto his back, begging me to rub his belly. I greeted my dog and kneeled at his side, turning my head to Archie who didn't have the confidence to follow me inside.

"Go on, Coop. Go greet our new friend, Archie."

Cooper rolled onto his feet and jumped on Archie. Archie stumbled back, surprised by the weight of him, and laughed when Cooper caught the tip of Archie's chin with his slobbery tongue.

"Mom," Mason called from the kitchen. "Allison is hacking into South High's email system. I'm trying to tell her she'll never coach with the school again if she gets caught."

When I caught sight of Allison, she rolled her eyes at Mason's comment. "How many times do I have to tell you, I won't get caught."

I gave my son a hug and asked Allison how it was going. The moral gray area we were in was beyond the wrong and right of Mason's understanding.

"Almost through. Their security is pretty good, considering," Allison said, her fingers clacking away at the keys as she mentioned how Susan managed to get both Naomi and Bennett out of the house without any news cameras harassing them.

"How did she manage that?" I asked.

"You wouldn't believe me if I told you."

Allison seemed relaxed and I couldn't wait to hear how Susan had managed that, along with getting Bennett past the rabid Heidi Mitchell. It had to be something big—as big as my idea to get Allison to agree to hack Jenny's student email account.

"That's great," I said, "because I'm going to need to enlist everyone's help to track down Jenny's whereabouts."

Erin took a seat at the kitchen table and I introduced Archie to my family. Together we sat, flipped open our laptop computers, and began poring over the police report, making notes and highlighting details that we knew were important. We all were curious to know who Josie was and why no one seemed to be able to locate her body.

Cooper barked and the front door swung open. Susan called out, announcing her arrival, and I hurried to the front of the house with Allison close behind. Susan had brought Naomi with her and I smiled at all three of them. Bennett latched the door closed once everyone was through. They all looked a little beaten up, but as soon as I locked eyes with my friend, the corners of hers crinkled into a reassuring smile.

I reached out for Susan's hand and pulled her into a hug.

Then I hugged Naomi and welcomed her to my house, doing the same with Bennett when I heard Susan apologize to Allison for what happened to him.

"This was all my fault," Susan said. "I told Daniels about Jenny and Eva, hoping he could bring attention to their story and end this."

"You didn't know," Allison responded.

Then the entire house came to a stop when Susan said, "There's good news though. Naomi thinks she might know who Jenny is with."

"Is that true, Naomi?" I asked.

Naomi looked me in the eye and nodded. "It's our teacher, Scott Helton."

Erin reached for my arm. I shared a knowing look with both her and Archie. Our investigation came full circle, funneling its way into my house. Helton had to be the serial rapist the police were looking for. Archie caught him on camera at Burger King the night Jenny went missing. We knew he had direct ties to both Megan and Jenny. I wondered if he was also behind Heidi's attack on Bennett to throw everyone off his trail. Where Josie Zapatero fit in, I wasn't sure yet. But there was too much evidence against him tying him to the other girls. We had to at least check him out.

Susan was reading my expression when she helped Naomi explain the connection so there weren't any doubts. Naomi said, "Mr. Helton was at the same Burger King as us the night Jenny disappeared." Archie nodded, and I pictured the photo he'd showed Erin and me.

I thought back to my visit with Rob and Karen Hines, wondering if Helton was the teacher who silenced Megan after walking in on the girls changing in the locker room last spring. Naomi sealed my suspicion when she said Helton was the one who confiscated the phone that had a revealing picture of her on it—the phone supposedly given to Heidi.

I turned to Bennett. "And Heidi Mitchell thought it was yours?"

Bennett nodded his head once. "After I heard Naomi's story, I can only assume it was Helton who tipped Ms. Mitchell off."

Allison moved to Bennett and slid her arm around his waist. He draped his big arm over the backs of her shoulders before Allison let go and headed to work on her computer. She seemed motivated by the news and, frankly, so was I.

I went to work on the police report, searching for a connection between Josie and Helton. Erin was on her computer looking for a link, too, when I turned and asked Naomi, "Was there a Josie Zapatero at your school?"

"Josie Zapatero?" Susan had a quizzical look on her face. "I know that name."

I lifted my head and said, "You do?"

"Her name was written down in Owen Daniels's office. And I heard it on his voicemail." Susan repeated what she heard, giving the most basic explanation of why she was there to begin with. "*The mayor is attending the event and at no point should he find himself in front of the protestors... You do that and I'll make sure to clean up your mess with Josie.*"

A shot of adrenaline pumped through my heart. First Helton and now Daniels? Were they working together? Were these crimes even related? I didn't know what to think, but it seemed possible Daniels was guilty of at least one murder—Josie's.

I asked Susan, "Do you know who left the message?"

"I'm certain it was Police Chief Gordon Watts's voice."

"Holy shit," Erin said. She stared at me and I knew we were thinking the same thing. The city really was hiding crimes, just as I'd been suspecting.

It was our first solid piece of evidence the mayor was actively falsifying crime statistics, but did Daniels murder

Josie and have the chief clean it up? It would certainly explain why her body suddenly went missing. The timing of the protests couldn't be coincidental, but planned to act as a diversion for Josie's murder.

I picked up the police report and thought about the sticky note attached. This was the story we were supposed to tell. A cover up to hide a crime committed by Daniels's accomplice inside the police department.

I lifted my head and flicked my gaze to Bennett. I felt bad for him. His innocence was ruined by Daniels, who brought an innocent man down to keep the murder of Josie Zapatero out of the media. But what was in it for the chief?

I asked Bennett, "Do you know where Helton lives?"

"He lives in an apartment in University." Bennett gave the name of the complex and the entire table stood in a panic. It was Eva's building. I asked if he knew the exact apartment number and my heart stopped.

I'd seen the brass knocker with the word Ace engraved in the middle. We were there. If Helton was home at the time, he heard us knocking on Eva's door. He knew we were closing in. Did Eva know he was dangerous? I doubted she did.

"Jesus," Erin said. "You don't think she's with him, do you?"

I didn't know. She hadn't talked about any friends, but she must have known her neighbor. I snapped my fingers and told Erin to call Eva. She dialed and Eva never picked up. I tried Carr, then Stark on my own phone, and Eva wasn't with either of them. Then I called King, hoping he hadn't left the area. He didn't answer, but I left a voicemail.

"King. Listen. Eva has a neighbor, Scott Helton. He's a teacher at South High, and I have very good reason to think he might be the person who abducted Jenny Booth. You don't have to call me back, but please check it out."

Cooper lifted his head and growled just as Allison announced, "I got it."

I hurried to stand over Allison's shoulder. Together we searched through Jenny's school email account. I heard Erin explain to Bennett and Naomi what we were doing. Bennett didn't protest. He just wanted his name cleared and his reputation restored. We seemed to be getting nowhere fast until Allison clicked back into Jenny's inbox. Then I pointed to the screen and said, "Open that one."

The email opened and we read it. "That's it. Helton has tenants and a room opened up for Jenny."

Cooper growled again and Archie looked worried that he might attack. I told my dog to knock it off and kept reading, trying to decide what the hell kind of relationship Jenny had with Helton.

"Tenants?" Bennett said.

I looked him in the eye. "That's what it said. You know what he means?"

"She's not at Helton's apartment, but at his rental."

"Rental?" I parroted.

Bennett told us how Helton was always talking about an old investment property he picked up that required him to be on site a lot. He was remodeling it. This was news to us, but if we were right about Helton having Jenny, something told me that tenant was code for captive women.

"C'mon, let's go check it out," I said, hurrying to the door. "If Eva's not with him, I'm certain Jenny is."

Reaching for my keys, I opened the front door and understood what Cooper had been growling about. The muzzle of a gun was pointed directly between my eyes.

CHAPTER ONE HUNDRED ONE

Eva wrapped her arms around herself, the tips of her fingers digging deep into her ribcage as she waited for Helton to return. It had been at least ten minutes since he left, and she wondered what was taking him so long.

Feeling her worries begin to surface, she stopped pacing and turned to stare at Helton's framed pictures perched on the end table. He had nice blue eyes that sparkled like tiny diamonds. It was the first thing Eva noticed when meeting him several months ago. Helton also had a bright, trusting smile. He was a man full of confidence who excelled at everything he did.

Why didn't he ever ask me out?

Secretly, Eva wondered if he was gay, but most likely it was simply because Helton knew she was too caught up with Carr to be bothered by the drama that came with it.

Turning on a heel, Eva moved to the coffee table. Glancing to the deck of cards, all four Aces were turned right-side up. Though she wondered what it was about—his strange obsession with everything Ace—she reached for Owen Daniels's business card.

It didn't take her long to figure out who Daniels was. With South High closed and multiple students missing, Eva could only assume that someone at the news station wanted to interview Helton about his colleague, Nicholas Bennett, who was accused of sleeping with his students.

Tying her hair up, Eva rubbed her arms until her hairs relaxed.

She felt a sense of urgency to get out of here and to some place far away. And fast. She knew time was against her. The longer Helton took, the more likely someone would be back to knock on her door.

Traveling the same path she carved out in the carpet from endlessly pacing, she moved to the window, peeked past the curtain to the street below, and was eased when seeing everything getting back to normal after witnessing the man who had been following her get arrested.

Eva knew better than to jump to conclusions.

She wasn't safe until she was gone, out of the city.

Archie was still somewhere out there. Because of it, her anxiety swelled with wanting to know why she had suddenly become every man's interest.

The sounds of keys at the front door had her spinning around.

She waited, and when Helton entered, he locked eyes with her. "I moved the car near the back door."

"Did you see anyone?"

"No one you mentioned." Helton sighed. "If we're going to leave, we must do it now. I don't think we'll get another chance."

Eva nodded, but her feet didn't move. Helton read her hesitation and closed the gap between them, clamping his strong hands around her arms and smoothing down the gooseflesh populating Eva's soft skin.

He whispered, "I believe in you. You can do this."

Eva's gaze fell to the floor, but her head continued bobbing up and down. "Are you sure I shouldn't bring anything with me?"

"It will be quicker if we don't take bags." Helton hooked Eva's chin with his finger and brought her eyes up to his. "I have everything you need at the house, and I can always come back and get more if you absolutely need it."

Eva stared into his coffee bean colored eyes. "How long do you think I'll have to stay?"

"Not long. Just until things die down."

Eva turned her head and glanced to the pictures of Helton on the end table, thinking about his blue eyes glistening like the ocean.

"Wear this," Helton handed her a hooded sweatshirt, "and put the hood over your head."

Eva pushed her arms through the sleeves and pulled the shell over her head.

Helton smiled. "Now, let's go before anyone notices we're gone."

CHAPTER ONE HUNDRED TWO

King rubbed his lower back with his right hand, attempting to smooth out the dull pain filling his side. He couldn't take his eyes off Christopher Bowers.

He'd been here for no more than fifteen minutes, asking himself if this bipolar lunatic was his ticket to clearing his own name or just the asshole who had kidnapped Eva. He was hoping for both.

Bowers sat with his hands cuffed and on his lap. His head swung wildly back and forth above a knee bouncing so high it knocked the table. If King didn't know any better, he would have thought Bowers had headphones stuffed inside his ears while rocking out to music only he could hear.

"How will I get your attention?" King whispered to an empty room.

Bowers was certainly drunk, probably high, and his arrest could have gone to hell quick. Instead, King counted his blessings for not having to fire his weapon during the arrest.

But something still didn't sit right with King.

He questioned if Bowers was Megan's murderer. Mrs. Bowers was certain of it. They'd found enough evidence inside the truck Bowers was driving to suggest he was involved in something. The missing link was how someone like Mrs. Bowers could go for someone like Christopher.

How could she not know he was a kidnapping murderer before today? They seemed worlds apart. King's first meeting of Bowers at the hospital seemed like forever ago. King had a hard time believing he was looking at the same man. King had believed he had rescued Eva that night. Had he? They'd gone after him because they thought he killed Megan, but was there more to his laundry list of crimes? Was Eva his victim? Could his wife be lying about who her husband truly was?

King rubbed his fingers together and brought them to the tip of his nose. He could still smell Bowers's sharp body odor mixed with the scent of enough alcohol to breathe fire. Bowers had let himself go and King wondered if this was the reason for his wife to turn on him.

His phone buzzed with an incoming call. King didn't bother looking, letting it go to voicemail.

"You'll disappear with them if you're not careful." Bowers kept repeating the same mantra he'd been touting since King brought him in.

"Is this the drugs and alcohol talking?" Detective Gray slid up alongside King and folded her arms as they both looked on. King hadn't heard her enter the room, but was glad she was here.

"We found a nearly empty fifth on his front seat," King said.

"I got the call back," Gray said, turning her neck to gaze up into King's eyes. "Sage's younger sister's name was Josie Zapatero."

"You found her parents?"

"Would have certainly made things easier if I did. Unfortunately, her father died of a work-related injury seven years ago and I was told their mother moved back to Mexico."

"Then what the hell was a fifteen-year-old Josie still doing here in the States?"

Gray shrugged. "Wish I knew. I'll let the ME know that we have a name, if still no body."

When Gray made a move toward the door, King said, "At least stay for the show."

"As much as I would like to see you break this lunatic down," Gray smiled over her shoulder and reached for the doorknob, "I'll take a raincheck on today's matinée."

CHAPTER ONE HUNDRED THREE

BOWERS WAS STILL ROCKING AND MUMBLING UNDER HIS breath when King stepped inside the interrogation room with today's newspaper tucked beneath one arm, a case file held in his opposite hand. He was anxious to know what Bowers was doing outside Eva's apartment.

King dropped down and sat in the metal chair opposite Bowers. He opened the newspaper and turned it so Bowers could see today's headline. King waited for a reaction.

"Murdered," King said. "Put in a shallow grave. She was only sixteen."

Bowers stopped moving.

When Bowers didn't react to the news about Megan's murder like King had hoped he would, he asked, "Any idea who might have done it?"

Bowers kept still.

"Some people think it was you." King then opened his case file and slowly spread the pictures of both Megan and Jenny out so Bowers could see. "Recognize these girls?"

Bowers blinked and looked away.

King inhaled a breath of hope when he said, "I know you

do. And what do these two girls have in common? They share a similar look to Josie Zapatero."

King raised his brow and waited for a reaction. Bowers's body was unusually still and he couldn't look King in the eye. Did he know Josie, too? King wasn't certain he did. Bowers reeked of guilt, just for what, it wasn't yet clear.

"We brought you in because your wife is afraid you murdered her." King gently laid his finger next to Megan's image.

Bowers snapped his neck and growled, "I didn't murder no one."

King mentioned the evidence they discovered in his truck.

"Rope and duct tape, are you serious? I'm a contractor by trade. What are you going to tell me next? That this girl was killed by a strike from a framer's hammer?"

"You know what else your wife said? She said she caught you taking pictures of your stepdaughter and her friend with your phone this morning." King then revealed that he knew about the specific room he'd labeled *Play Pen* at the house he was working on. "There is a team at your worksite now, and something tells me they are going to find the room where you kept Eva Martin captive. Bold move to hold her at a worksite."

Bowers brought his cuffed hands to the table and pulled the newspaper closer to his chest. King watched his finger begin tearing single words off the page until they formed a single sentence.

He'll kill the girl if you don't help.

"Who, Christopher? Who is it we're supposed to help?"

Bowers continued tearing the paper into tiny pieces as he mumbled, "You have the wrong man. I'm not the person who you want."

"Who do I want?"

"There is someone better than me doing this."

"Who, Christopher?"

"An educator." Bowers glanced up at King from under his brow. "I saw it with my own eyes. He took her."

"Took who, Christopher? Took one of these girls?" King pointed to the photographs.

"He took Jenny after she told him she didn't want to sleep with him again." When King asked how Bowers knew, he said, "I was at Burger King. I saw because I wanted Naomi and Jenny for myself. But he got to them first."

King's blood pressure spiked. "Where did this happen?"

Bowers told him. "And if you don't believe me, ask her friend. She'll tell you. She talked to him, too."

"Talked to who? Who are you referring to, Christopher? I need a name."

"My mentor." Bowers cocked his head to the side and grinned. "The man who wants to be the next Prom Queen Killer. Mr. Scott Helton."

CHAPTER ONE HUNDRED FOUR

It wasn't the first time I had a gun pulled on me, but never had I had one this close to my face. My life didn't flash before my eyes and time didn't speed up or slow down. Instead, my heart sent blood to the tips of my fingers that desperately wanted to reach out and touch his tense shoulders while I looked him in the eye and told him that he was loved.

Rob Hines was a man who was hurting. I saw it before, and I was witnessing it now. Those same grief-swollen eyes were dulled by confused anger, and I hoped he hadn't been drinking. Uncontrolled grief made our minds cloudy enough, and I needed him to be present when I began talking him down.

"Rob, put the gun down," I said in a mild but firm tone as I reached behind me and latched the front door closed.

I knew why he was here. His parting words kept ringing in my ears. *I'm going to kill him myself.* It wasn't me he was after. He wanted to serve the cold dish of revenge to Bennett.

His eyes clouded with tears and the crease between his eyebrows deepened into a narrow valley. Straightening his arm, he pressed the gun's cold metal to my forehead, causing my breath to hitch with surprise.

"I can't," he said through gritted teeth. "You know I can't."

I remained calm—didn't dare move. My palms were facing out when I thought how Susan unknowingly led him here when she'd left Bennett's house. Even as my mind prepared my body to receive the bullet he was about to shoot into my skull, I wasn't mad or scared. I'd made my peace with God long ago. But I didn't need my son to see this.

Mulling over my next words, I remembered how hard Rob had taken the news of his daughter's secrets. One wrong word could be the end of me. I was walking a tightrope and took my chances when saying, "Think about your wife. She needs you now more than ever. Don't leave her today, Rob."

A tear squeezed out of his left eye. His trigger finger threatened to send the hammer flying.

"Leave Karen out of this," he barked.

"Okay, easy Rob. I'm here to help," I said with Karen's words—*this ends here*—echoing in my mind. I wished she had told her husband to do the same. I knew better than to think she knew where he was and what it was he was trying to do.

"Then you can start by getting out of my way."

I kept my eye on his steady hand, remembering the pride in a father's eyes when discussing Megan's many successes. I admired the love he had for his daughter and the way he defended her reputation, even in death. Soon my thoughts traveled to my son and how, if in a similar situation as Rob, I would want to do the same. But Rob was mistaken. Heidi had fooled him—had fooled us all. It was up to me to convince him Bennett wasn't the man Rob thought he was.

"I'm sorry, Rob. I can't let you make that mistake."

"Get out my way, Samantha, or I'll shoot you, too."

Keeping my hands raised in the air, I stepped forward, feeling the muzzle press harder into my head.

"He killed my daughter."

"It's not him."

"Someone has to pay."

I felt the pressure pull back and I saw Rob losing strength. "Trust me, Rob. Your daughter didn't die in vain. Justice will be served. I just can't let you do it like this."

"It's not fair." His voice cracked for the first time and I kept inching my way forward.

I knew then that I had to end this now before someone actually got hurt.

"You heard what Karen said he did to Megan."

Rob was now crying. He had to be thinking of all the things his daughter could have been, could have seen, could have done if only her life hadn't been cut short.. Suddenly, the door opened behind me. I calmly turned around and told Erin to go back inside. She threw me a look that said I was crazy.

"Everything is okay. Right, Rob?"

Rob's body crumbled to the ground as he sobbed. I kneeled next to him with one hand on his back. His entire body shook as I managed to take his gun away without him ever realizing it. It was over. Nicholas would live to see another day.

CHAPTER ONE HUNDRED FIVE

KING WAS ABOUT TO EXIT THE ROOM WHEN HE TURNED AND glanced at Bowers one last time before leaving him to his thoughts. He caught Bowers giving him the eye and King hoped his intel was accurate. King didn't have time for another wild goose chase.

As soon as King stepped out, Alvarez was waiting for him.

"Did you catch that?" King asked.

Alvarez nodded. "Scott Helton."

They walked. "You know him?"

Alvarez shook his head no. "But I confirmed it with Mrs. Bowers. Helton is a teacher at South High, their daughter's school. He could be telling the truth."

They edged the wall, skirting passed a desk, as they meandered through the precinct. Something told King that Bowers wasn't lying. Perhaps it was the envy he saw swirling inside his eyes, like Helton had what Bowers wanted. How he knew Helton was the one? That was anybody's guess. King needed to see how Josie fit inside this crazy puzzle.

King caught Alvarez up on Jane Doe. "We need to track down Helton and hear what he has to say about all this. But first I think we need to see if he's in any way connected to Josie."

King rounded the corner and came to an abrupt stop when he saw the chief, lieutenant, and someone who looked like he could be a detective from IAD standing at the far end of the room. Alvarez lowered his brow and knew what it was King was thinking. The clock was ticking. Soon they would be coming after him for a mistake he didn't make.

Chief rolled his gaze to King before turning his back and continuing on their march into Lieutenant Baker's office.

"Assholes," Alvarez said.

The pain in King's spine was back. He knew he was part of a fishing expedition spearheaded by politicians who knew nothing about actual police work. They were only after votes, and nothing was easier than to blame the boots on the ground for their failed policy.

"C'mon," King said, focusing on what he could control. "Unlike them, we have meaningful work to do."

CHAPTER ONE HUNDRED SIX

TEN MINUTES LATER, KING LEANED BACK IN HIS CHAIR AND glanced to the clock on the wall. Detective Gray was looking into Sage Zapatero, and Alvarez was working the phone next to him. The minutes were escaping them and King had to decide on his next move.

They hadn't been able to link Josie to either Bowers or Helton. As the chaos circled around him, all King could think about was that Naomi never mentioned seeing Helton that night at Burger King. Why would she do that? King could only assume it was because she knew the truth behind Jenny's relationship with their teacher.

Then there was the message from Samantha.

As soon as King heard Alvarez set the phone back in its cradle, he stood over the partition and handed his partner his cellphone.

"No one was home at the Hines's residence," Alvarez said, giving King's phone a funny look. "What's this?" he asked.

"Listen."

Alvarez threw him a look and pressed the phone to his ear. King watched his eyes widen a fraction.

King said, “Helton tried to block us from speaking to Naomi, remember that?”

“I do.” Alvarez flicked his gaze to the door, then said, “I also remember Naomi thinking Jenny was planning to sleep with the older man she was seeing again.”

Helton had to be their guy. When Gray came rushing into their office with news about Sage, excitement grew. Gray said, “Sage was his student.”

This was it. The proof in the pudding. King could feel it in his bones. It was time to confront Helton and ask him some very tough questions about his relationship with Jenny Booth and where he was the day Megan was murdered.

“But I also have bad news,” Gray said.

King stopped and stared.

“Griffin spoke to the EMS van who bagged Josie. Her body has been cremated. They mixed up their cargo and Josie was dropped at the funeral home instead of the morgue.” Gray frowned. “It’s too late. We’ll never know the specifics of her death.”

CHAPTER ONE HUNDRED SEVEN

"OKAY," HELTON SAID, GLANCING TO THE BACKSEAT, "IT'S safe for you to get up now."

Eva was lying across the bench of the backseat in Helton's car, staring up into the clouds, praying for peace and solitude to find their way back into her life when she felt the car roll to a stop.

Helton insisted she keep her head down as he drove, that the hood over her head wasn't enough to keep the outside from coming in. It didn't take much to convince her that he was right. Eva remembered the way Archie had tracked her down at Samantha's, and then found her again outside the medical examiner's office. The last thing she wanted was to live a life on the run, having to constantly look over her shoulder. This was her last escape before going into hiding.

Eva sat up and looked around. Helton met her eyes and smiled, but Eva couldn't return the gesture without feeling like a fake. It was his brown eyes she knew were blue that had her thinking he was up to something, but she didn't know what. Before he could read her thoughts, she flicked her gaze to the ace of diamonds dangling from the rearview mirror.

There it was again, another sign of his greatness. Helton was a man who excelled at everything he did, so how could he lead her astray?

"Where are we?" she asked.

"My rental house."

Eva could see the tops of the mountain peaks to the west, but didn't recognize any distinguishable features on the skyline to the northeast. She had a general idea of where she was, but something made her think she'd been here before.

"No, I mean what neighborhood is this?"

Helton smiled, opened his door, and stepped out with his shoulder bag slung over his neck. He moved to Eva's door and held it open for her. "C'mon. We'll talk inside where it's safer."

Eva adjusted her hood and kept her head down as she followed Helton into the two-story ranch house. Helton switched on a couple overhead lights and said, "I'm currently between renters."

Eva was slow to enter, wanting to take in her surroundings before fully committing to stay. She felt the hairs on the back of her neck stand on end and, though there was nothing to be afraid of, she couldn't shake the thoughts of familiarity. Perhaps it was the layout of the rooms, or how the house smelled like pine. It was furnished and looked lived in, but didn't look like any house Eva had ever rented.

Helton dropped his bag on a chair at the table and said, "You must be hungry. Can I make you something? I make a killer burrito."

Eva shook her head and asked to use the bathroom. Helton's smile dropped from his face and pointed the way. "Right down the hall," he said.

Eva locked herself in the windowless bathroom and sat on the toilet. Burying her face inside her hands, she began to cry.

She was scared for what the future would bring and knew with absolute certainty that this school semester was shot.

Once her tears dried, she flushed and was at the sink opening cabinets when she discovered Helton's contact lens case. Curious, Eva twisted the cap open and was surprised to see the lenses were colored brown.

Why hide his beautiful blue eyes? she thought when she heard a door slam.

Eva peeked her head out. When she heard nothing, she rushed to the front of the house to find Helton gone. She called out. Her heart was racing. Helton didn't answer. Turning her head, she glanced down and found herself staring at the Prom Queen Killer book stuffed inside Helton's bag. She'd seen it at Samantha's house, knew why Samantha had been curious to know what was inside, but why did Helton have it?

Reaching inside the bag, she took the book into her hands. It looked well studied—dog-eared and crinkled. Eva heard a noise and quickly dropped the book back into the bag and stepped away from the table.

Helton came around the corner holding linens.

Eva slowed her breathing, but nothing could calm her thundering heart. The look he was giving her was darker and more intense than before. She stared into Helton's brown eyes and didn't hear what he had said. "I'm sorry, what?"

"Your room. It's ready for you."

Eva blinked, blew out a breath, and followed Helton past the kitchen to the back of the house. Helton handed her the linens and opened the door. Eva couldn't stop looking into his eyes as she skirted past him and entered the bedroom he'd saved for her. Once inside, she couldn't believe what she saw.

"What is this?" she asked upon seeing her own images tacked up and filling the walls.

“It’s your room.” Helton blocked the doorway with his body. “The one I made for you.”

She wondered when and how he had taken these photos. They were of her personal life, but she couldn’t recall ever seeing him take them. A chill had her shivering. He’d been stalking her. It was the pearl white wedding dress hanging from the mirror that had her really concerned about his plans.

“This was a bad idea,” Eva said, dropping the linens on the bed when suddenly she was tackled by a masked man who seemed to come out of nowhere.

CHAPTER ONE HUNDRED EIGHT

Rob climbed inside his truck and hunched over the steering wheel. I gently closed his door and backed away as I listened to the engine turn over. Not once did Rob glance back. I could only hope that he would do what he promised—go home to be with his wife and forget that this ever happened.

Erin came off the front porch and met me at the sidewalk. I asked if Karen answered her call. "She thanks you for letting her know where her husband was. She said he's having a difficult time with all this."

"No kidding," I said.

"I didn't mention how he had a gun to your head, or that he wanted to kill Bennett."

"All she needs to know is that her husband is on his way home," I said, not fully trusting that was what he was doing. But at least I was still in possession of his Glock 17 handgun.

As soon as I closed my eyes, my head floated into the clouds. I was still high on adrenaline as the reality of just how close I'd come to being the next victim in this saga.

I didn't know what I should do with his gun. He never

asked for it back, and probably never realized I took it. But I couldn't give it back. At least not until his temper cooled. There was no predicting what he would do next, and I hoped it was the only firearm he owned.

Susan exited the house next and peeked around. When I said it was safe for her to come out, it was clear that everyone inside knew what had happened.

I was swarmed by a dozen arms, all wanting to feel for themselves that I hadn't been hurt. "Thank God you're okay," I kept hearing everyone say.

"You certainly have a way with words," Allison joked and had us all laughing.

I had my arms wrapped around Mason when I glanced to Bennett. He was quiet and standing off to the side, but I could see his gratitude for what I'd done sparkling inside his eyes. Allison was most gracious of all, and it was clear that this ordeal was bringing them closer together.

"Now, where were we?" I said.

"Helton." Erin reminded me.

I took a deep breath and said, "Right."

My car keys were still in my pocket and I hoped the stunt Rob pulled hadn't delayed us too long to get to Helton before it was too late. Eva still wasn't answering our calls, and I worried something had already happened to her.

Erin made for my car, but I stopped her. "Go with Susan and meet me there."

"Split up? You can't be serious?"

I was. I couldn't trust Rob wouldn't change his mind and decide to follow me. At least if we took two different routes, he would be forced to make a decision on who to follow, leaving at least one car to get to Helton instead of no one.

"We'll stay with Naomi and Mason," Allison offered.

It was a good idea. All our bases were covered.

"I'll take 6th to Sheridan. You get off at Federal and make your way from there," I said, opening my car door. Without anyone seeing, I took the Glock out from my belt and placed it on my lap.

Erin and Susan jumped in Susan's car and we split, each going in opposite directions with the intention of rendezvousing outside Helton's house in a few minutes.

I drove quick but kept my speed within reason. I couldn't afford to get stopped, and it wasn't just because I was in possession of a firearm that wasn't registered in my name.

With headlights in my mirrors, I thought about what Susan uncovered at Daniels's office. It seemed the mayor may have recruited Daniels to control the airwaves in his favor. And now Chief Watts seemed to be involved with Daniels, too. I hoped I was wrong, but feared that I wasn't.

I was first to arrive to Helton's house in Lakewood. After killing the engine and glancing in my mirrors, I checked the Glock to see if it was loaded. A bullet was in the chamber and the safety was on. Not a single shot had been fired, but I was happy to have it for my own protection. If we were right about Helton, I knew what he was capable of, and I felt safer with it than without.

I was on edge. My mind was sharp, but my nerves were jumpy. I knew it was because of Rob. I opened up my cell-phone and sent King a quick text telling him where I was in case this meeting went south.

A light flicked on in the house and I could see movement inside.

There was no sign of Susan and Erin, and I couldn't wait for them to arrive.

My mind told me to go now, that something bad was about to happen.

With Glock in hand, I exited my car and headed into the shadows, praying this would end well for everyone involved.

CHAPTER ONE HUNDRED NINE

THE SIRENS WAILED ABOVE KING'S HEAD AS HE YANKED ON the steering wheel with both hands. The roads were clogged and vehicles were slow to part. He threaded his way forward, losing what little patience he had.

Alvarez drummed on the dash and kept glancing in the mirror to make sure they hadn't lost Gray who was following close behind. "C'mon. Move people."

King knew they'd messed up by thinking Bowers was it. They should have stayed in University, checked on Eva. But he'd followed orders. Now he couldn't help but think that if something were to happen to Eva, he'd get the blame. Just as he was being blamed for Josie.

He couldn't believe she'd been taken to a funeral home. Everything was off that night, including the orders coming from the top.

A text came through and a car horn honked. The tires squealed when King took his eyes off the road and pulled his phone from his pocket. Alvarez was quick to grab the wheel.

"He's not at his apartment," King said, taking the wheel back into his hands.

"What do you mean, he's not there?"

King hit the brakes, yanked hard on the steering wheel, and spun the car around. Alvarez leaned into the turn and called out as King nearly crashed into oncoming traffic. Punching the gas, they flew in the opposite direction.

"You sure you know what you're doing?" Alvarez asked.

"Samantha has him at a house in Lakewood."

"Samantha? Shit."

King flipped his gaze to his partner and tossed him a knowing look.

Without saying a word, Alvarez got on the radio with dispatch requesting a squad car check out Helton's apartment in University, then letting Lakewood police know their investigation was spilling over into their jurisdiction.

Alvarez said, "I hope she has this right because it's your job on the line. Not mine."

There was less traffic going north and King was able to pick up the pace. He kicked himself for letting Sam go after Helton alone. He only hoped she knew what she was doing. He lowered his head, shifted gears, and pushed the engine to its limits.

King smiled. "Ride together, die together."

CHAPTER ONE HUNDRED TEN

I REACHED BEHIND MY BACK AND GRIPPED THE GUN WITH my right hand. It was secured in my belt, the cold metal pressing into my side. I was worried I'd be surprised and wanted to be ready to react if that happened.

I crept toward the front of the house, keeping my eyes focused on the window. Blinds had been drawn and I lost my visual inside. A dog barked in the distance and an airplane flew overhead.

Once at the house, I pressed my back against the siding and tried the door. My body buzzed on heightened alert as I realized it was unlocked. Slowly, I pressed the handle down until I heard the latch release. Then I cracked the door open before working my way inside.

I was greeted by Eva's scent, but the house was quiet, lights on. Latching the door shut behind me, I paused, taking my time to study the layout of the house.

There was a short flight of steps directly in front of me, one side going up, the other going down. Going up led to the living room with TV and couches and, off that, was the kitchen. I flipped a mental coin and decided to go up.

The house was much nicer than I imagined. Once at the top of the steps, I noticed it was well-kept and up-to-date on both furniture and appliances. But this was no rental. Helton lived here.

Keeping my ears peeled for any sounds, I padded lightly to the kitchen table where I found Archie's book. It was clear Helton had been studying it, perhaps even drawing inspiration from it, too.

A noise came from the back and I jumped into action. Holding my breath, I reached for the gun and closed my fingers around the handle. The noise disappeared, but the feeling that I wasn't alone stayed with me.

I moved into the kitchen and came to the back of the house. A light was on in the basement and I descended the stairs to see what I could find. The bottom opened up into a series of doors, each one of them closed and locked. A foul odor like sewage filled the air I breathed and that's when I heard it. The floor directly above my head started drumming like a marching band practicing its routine.

I sprinted back up the stairs, gripping my gun out in front of me like King had trained me to do. I searched everywhere, sweeping each room whose door I kicked in, always expecting to find Eva in the next. Then I heard it again. This time it was Eva's voice coming from the room next to mine.

As soon as I kicked the door in, I couldn't believe what I had found. It was Helton, and he was on top of Eva wearing a clear mask, stuffing her body into what appeared to be a wedding dress.

CHAPTER ONE HUNDRED ELEVEN

I POINTED THE MUZZLE AT HELTON'S HEAD AND TOOK AIM. "Get off of her now!"

Helton had Eva pinned to the floor. She was half-naked, the top part of the dress over her head and around her neck. The moment she saw me, she screamed. "Help! Get this lunatic off me!"

Helton immediately sprung his wrist and clamped his hand around Eva's neck when he turned to look at me. "Excuse us, but you're interrupting my day of holy matrimony."

I narrowed my eyes and held my hand steady. "Get off her, Scott, or I'll shoot."

He held my eyes with his and laughed a sadistic howl. I watched his fingers dig deeper into Eva's throat. I could see in her eyes that she was having trouble breathing.

"Go ahead. Shoot me." Helton raised his mask and grinned. "But just know that if you do, they're all dead."

Eva started kicking her feet and I hesitated to pull the trigger. I wasn't sure I could call his bluff. "Like how you killed Megan?"

Helton eased his grip, but only a fraction.

I kept distracting him with more questions.

"Why would someone as smart as you want to work with an amateur like Christopher Bowers?"

Jealousy flashed in his eyes and he pulled his hand away from Eva's neck but kept her pinned to the floor with both his knees. "That asshole, Bowers, gives people like me a bad name. He took her," Helton glanced to Eva, "and I had to save her from him. Save her from all the other assholes she let into her life. He's nothing like me."

"You mean like a pedophile who preys on his students?"

"I didn't want it. They came to me. Just like Eva did today." He took Eva by the face and said, "Isn't that right, sweetie?" Then he snapped his neck back to me. "Bowers ruined everything. So did Megan. It all went to shit because of him."

"Is that why you framed Bennett? Because you knew the police would find out it was you?"

"Naomi gave me an opportunity and I took it." He shook his head like a dog and had his hand back on Eva's neck. "It's so easy to manipulate the media when you have someone like Daniels who's a ratings whore."

I kept the gun on Helton as I thought about the mysterious ways the world worked. The irony of one killer contacting another didn't escape me, and I doubted Helton knew Daniels killed Josie like we suspected.

Eva stopped kicking as she started losing consciousness.

The moment Helton looked away, I lunged forward and swung my hand back like a hammer with the intention of striking Helton's head. He must have sensed me coming, because he ducked and rolled off to the side, managing to sweep my feet out from under me with one kick of his leg.

I hit the ground hard. The gun dropped from my hand and stars flashed in front of my eyes as my head hit the floor.

Before I could catch my next breath, Helton was on top of me, pinching my windpipe shut just as he had with Eva.

I punched his forearms, hit him in his ribs, but he only squeezed harder.

When I heard Eva coughing, I fought even harder.

Helton took one hand off me and was searching for the gun. I kicked and bucked, but he was too heavy. Nothing seemed to break his hold. He was too strong. And just as the lights in my head began to fade, I heard a single pop.

CHAPTER ONE HUNDRED TWELVE

"THERE." ERIN POINTED TO SAMANTHA'S CAR.

Susan pulled in behind it and parked. There had been an accident on Federal Boulevard, and it had taken them longer than they anticipated. They were here now, but didn't know where Samantha was.

"She's not here," Erin said, looking around.

Susan swiped a hand over her head and asked, "She wouldn't be inside, would she?"

Erin gave her a knowing look. They both knew if Samantha saw something she didn't like, she wouldn't wait for them. They turned to the house and approached the front door with caution. There were lights on inside and it had the appearance of someone being home, but it was too quiet. Susan brought her hands to her eyes and attempted to peer through the window past the drawn blinds.

"I don't see anything," she said.

Sirens wailed in the distance.

Susan asked, "Do you think they're coming here?"

"Let's cross our fingers they are," Erin said just as they heard the screaming sirens stop.

Then an engine roared down the street and the women watched as a cruiser came to an abrupt stop in front of the house. The emergency lights were still flashing in the grill, and they were blinded by a beam of light coming from the car.

"Put your hands on your head."

Susan and Erin laced their fingers behind their heads. Erin recognized the voice. It was King.

"Alex. It's me. Erin. We think Samantha is inside."

Boots rushed toward them, and neither of the women flinched at the guns the detectives were holding. King apologized for not recognizing who they were when suddenly they heard a gunshot come from inside the house.

CHAPTER ONE HUNDRED THIRTEEN

I COULDN'T OPEN MY EYES.

My body trembled beneath the weight of Helton. His blood was all over me and I wondered if he was dead. Turning my head, I managed to free my right hand. I wiped the blood from my face and away from my eyes. As soon I opened my eyelids, I saw Eva.

She wasn't more than ten feet away, sitting on her heels, still pointing the gun at Helton with a wide expression filling her eyes.

I slid out from under Helton's body and told Eva to put down the gun. She was in shock, couldn't hear my voice. I checked for a pulse on Helton. It was faint and on its way out. He'd be dead soon without help.

"You're safe now," I said, touching Eva's arm.

Eva blinked and turned her eyes on me. The dull look on her face vanished and was replaced by a trembling bottom lip. When her gaze fell to the gun, I watched her fingers snap open. The gun dropped to the floor with a heavy thud. I immediately wrapped my arms around her, embracing her in a comforting hug, reminding her she saved my life.

"Help! Help us!"

The house erupted with screams and calls for help. It seemed to be coming from the floor and through the walls. I thought about my journey to the basement and the locked doors I'd seen. Jenny had to be down there. But there were more voices than just hers.

"We need help!"

Eva's body was limp in my arms. She couldn't stop crying. I continued to hold her, knowing Susan and Erin were on their way.

"Can you stand?" I asked Eva.

She lifted her head off my shoulder and nodded.

"There is help on the way," I said, looping my arm around Eva's waist.

Together, we supported each other as we stood. She was wobbly on her feet but had enough strength to walk on her own. That was when I heard the front door snap open and heavy boots run through the house. It was a familiar sound, and something told me my message to King went through.

"They're here for us," I said, needing Eva to believe her nightmare was over. When I saw King's face come around the corner, I knew it was over for me, too.

CHAPTER ONE HUNDRED FOURTEEN

I WAS SITTING IN THE BACK OF THE AMBULANCE GETTING cleaned up and evaluated when I stopped the paramedic to watch four young women get escorted out of Helton's house. They were wrapped in blankets and looked like they hadn't seen the light of day for a very long time. Not surprisingly, one of them was Jenny.

They were the voices calling for help.

Against the paramedic's wishes, I climbed down from the back of the van, needing to get a closer look. I wondered who the other three women were and how long Helton had kept them locked away from the outside world.

I floated between the officers and detectives and overheard that Josie Zapatero wasn't here. I didn't know if all his captives made it out alive, but the only body I saw get carted away was Helton's.

Jenny glanced in my direction and I smiled. When she didn't smile back, I naturally took a step toward her. There was so much I wanted to say, so much to ask, but mostly I just wanted her to know that she hadn't been forgotten.

A hand caught my arm and I turned my neck to find King.

His eyes crinkled at the corners and I fell into his chest.

He held me like he always did, and it felt good to have him back. But I still had to tease him for being so hard on me earlier.

Tipping my head back, I said, "Are you sure you want to associate yourself with the press?"

"You're a victim today, and I'm here to protect and serve."

We both laughed. Then I said, "Your Jane Doe's name is Josie Zapatero."

He nodded once, like he knew the name but was surprised that I did. He hadn't leaked the police report. What he didn't know was what Susan heard on Daniels's voicemail. I told him, and said in a hushed voice, "It seems like Daniels might know something about how she died, and Chief Watts might also be involved."

King gripped each of my shoulders and gave them a reassuring squeeze as he lifted his gaze and nodded. Susan came running over to us holding out her phone.

"Sam, take a look at this. Heidi Mitchell went rogue. Look at what she just put on live TV."

I took her phone into my hands and together King and I watched a replay of Heidi's reporting on Owen Daniels.

"We're at the scene where Josie Zapatero was found murdered only days ago. Tonight, we're learning her body has been mistakenly cremated before an official autopsy could be conducted. The case is currently under investigation, but a source close to the police department has assured me that they are searching for this man, executive producer to our own news team, Owen Daniels."

I locked eyes with Erin. "Crazy, right?"

I couldn't believe it. Neither could King. I said, "Anything I can do to help?"

King chuckled. "You can start by getting yourself home."

CHAPTER ONE HUNDRED FIFTEEN

Six weeks later...

I had lost track of time and was doing anything to keep from checking my social media.

Work had been nonstop since Bowers's arrest and Helton's death, but it was the combined reporting by Heidi and myself that had the city spinning off its axis. I was determined to ride this wave until the end, despite the threats we had each received.

After Heidi brought Josie's story to the world, the *Colorado Times* published the leaked police report on my behalf. The source remained elusive, but I was able to confirm its authenticity. I also learned that I'd seen the report before King, so I knew he didn't share it with me. That was enough to get Daniels to turn himself in shortly after, but not without arranging an army of defense lawyers to protect him from the hammer he knew was coming his way.

Though his case file was sealed, it was believed that Daniels had paid for sex with Josie and only after did he discover she was underage. It was enough to scare him into murdering the only witness who knew about his crime.

But it didn't end there.

Amazingly, Daniels then took his attempted coverup a step further by involving Chief Watts who had, before Josie's murder, recruited Daniels to assist in suppressing as much of the city's crime reports as he could. Their plan had worked. Until Daniels murdered Josie. They nearly got away with it, too, and if it weren't for that phone call from Allison to let me know about Josie Zapatero's murder scene, they might have.

The coverup went deep. While we knew about the voicemail from Watts to Daniels, it was since erased, severing their connection. Daniels wasn't speaking and the mayor's hands appeared clean, too—continuing to hold press conferences with promises of transparency and implementing action to root out corruption inside the department he oversaw. His argument was convincing. Even I was starting to think he hadn't been involved. All we could do was continue applying the pressure on the Denver Police Officer Association to call for the chief of police's resignation and hope, at some point, evidence proving his involvement would come our way.

I eased back in my chair and closed my eyes, listening to the surrounding chatter.

The newsroom was as lively as I remembered it my first year on the job, a time when threats of layoffs and budget cuts weren't a constant point of stress for me or my colleagues. It was a good feeling to be reporting on news important to us all, even if we knew the good times wouldn't last.

When I opened my eyes, I grinned at the sight of my blog, *Real Crime News,* flashing on my computer screen like a little beacon of hope. Articles I'd written over the past week covered my desk, and it had me thinking about the cryptic messages Bowers had given both Erin and me. He'd used a play out of the Prom Queen Killer book, trying to get us to connect Helton to the crimes before we figured out what he was up to. It hadn't worked out the way he'd hoped. In the end, Bowers confessed to Eva's kidnapping and took a plea deal, accepting lesser charges for false imprisonment and aggravated assault rather than that of kidnapping which would have, if convicted, put him behind bars for up to twenty years. I could live with the result, but what he really needed was proper treatment for his mental illness.

As for Scott Helton, the police tore his house apart and discovered he'd been working under the radar for nearly ten years, secretly holding these women captive in his basement. What he did to them was unspeakable, and they all had a long road to recovery ahead of them. The biggest irony of all was that Sage Zapatero was Josie's older sister. It was only coincidence Josie died the same week Sage was found, but it still tore me up inside.

When my cellphone buzzed, I saw Erin was calling. I answered with a question, "Did she let you leave without a fight?"

"She's now officially a resident of Fort Collins."

I smiled and thought about Eva. Erin and Allison had been working tirelessly to get Eva moved out of her apartment in University and headed north to a new college town where she hoped to transfer and start college again in the spring. I liked the idea. Eva didn't have to go far to feel like she could begin a new life. Away from Helton. Away from Carr. She'd been so scared of Carr during our investigation that she'd lied to us about him, afraid of any fallout that would bring his wrath down on her. Fort Collins was only an hour's drive. Eva promised we could visit her any time. Which we planned to do often.

She was never charged with Helton's death, which the DA ruled as self-defense. I was witness to that, and some nights I still lay awake in bed thinking what could have happened if

Eva never pulled that trigger. There was no doubt in my mind I'd be dead if not for her bravery. I was forever indebted, and would make sure I paid my dues.

"That's great," I said. "I assume you got Susan's text about drinks?"

"You going to bring King?"

Susan wanted to bring everyone together after closing the Hoffman deal she nearly lost to Daniels. It was a happy time for us all, and I was planning to pick up King shortly to join the celebration. I thought to ask, "Is that a problem?"

"Not at all. I hear Allison is also bringing Bennett."

There was a hint of jealously in Erin's voice. It was the first time since I'd met her that I wished she had somebody to call her own—if not for love, at least for her own protection.

"Then I'll see you soon," I said.

"Yeah. See you soon."

Once I was off the phone, I closed out my internet browser, not wanting to read the latest threat on my life from some internet cowboy stating how they wished Helton raped and killed me instead of Megan. It was unnerving to read, and I tried not to think too much into it. I knew it was affecting both Erin and Heidi who were also dealing with the same harassment.

Stepping out of my cubicle, Dawson caught me by the door.

"You did good work, Samantha."

"Thank you."

His smile faded from his lips and I could see concern swirling in his eyes. "I know the mayor has assured the public he wants full transparency of the police department, but you have a target on your back unlike anything we've seen before."

I shrugged. "It's nothing I can't handle, Ryan."

One side of his lips curled. "I know."

I never did go to the therapy sessions that were offered, and I'd said little about how the threats on my life had escalated since Daniels's arrest. Dawson knew it all when I gripped his arm and squeezed.

I said, "Then I'll see you tomorrow."

Dawson stood there with his hands stuffed into his pockets and watched as I headed down the steps and pushed my way through the exit. Dawson was a good man and he'd seen me go through this before. This time felt different, though.

As I approached my car, I dug out my keys and listened as a high-pitched whine zipped over my head. I followed the sound with my eyes to see what it was and, when I heard it again, the sound had settled directly behind me.

Slowly, I turned and stared at the drone hovering directly at eye level just out of arms reach. With its blades whirling, I squinted into the tiny camera lens which was locked on me and thought about the violent threats I'd been receiving.

I was being recorded and pursued in the most invasive way. Before I could swing my tote and knock the device out of the air, the tiny aircraft lifted its way back into the evening sky and disappeared behind the newsroom building. It seemed as if I'd found myself a dangerous new type of stalker—one that played by a different set of rules, and one who wouldn't leave me alone.

A WORD FROM JEREMY

Thank you for reading MAD AS BELL. **If you like the stories I'm writing, don't forget to rate, review, and follow. It really helps my books get in front of new readers.**

AFTERWORD

One of the things I love best about writing these mystery thrillers is the opportunity to connect with my readers. It means the world to me that you read my book, but hearing from you is second to none. Your words inspire me to keep creating memorable stories you can't wait to tell your friends about. No matter how you choose to reach out - whether through email, on Facebook, or through a review - I thank you for taking the time to help spread the word about my books. I couldn't do this without YOU. So, please, keep sending me notes of encouragement and words of wisdom and, in return, I'll continue giving you the best stories I can tell. Thank you for giving me an opportunity of a lifetime.

Never miss a new release. Sign up for Jeremy Waldron's New Releases Newsletter at JeremyWaldron.com

ABOUT THE AUTHOR

Waldron lives in Vermont with his wife and two children.

Receive updates, exclusive content, and new book release announcements by signing up to his newsletter at: www.JeremyWaldron.com

Follow him @jeremywaldronauthor

facebook.com/jeremywaldronauthor

bookbub.com/profile/83284054